MACKENZIE *fire*

ALSO BY ELLE CASEY

New Adult Romance

Shine Not Burn (2-book series)

By Degrees

Don't Make Me Beautiful

Rebel (3-book series)

Adult Contemporary Romance

Full Measure (written as Kat Lee)

Just One Night (6-part romantic serial)

Lost and Found

YA Paranormal Romance

Duality (2-book series)

YA Urban Fantasy

War of the Fae (4-book series)

Clash of the Otherworlds (3-book series, follows *War of the Fae*)

My Vampire Summer

Aces High (co-author with Jason Brant)

YA Dystopian

Apocalypsis (4-book series)

YA Action Adventure

Wrecked (2-book series)

YA Romantic Suspense/Thriller

All The Glory

MACKENZIE *fire*

The Sequel to Shine Not Burn

ELLE CASEY

This is a work of fiction. Names, characters, organizations, places, events, and incidents are either products of the author's imagination or are used fictitiously.

Published by Montlake Romance Publishing, Seattle

www.apub.com

ISBN-13: 978-1503945234
ISBN-10: 1503945235

Cover design by Sarah Hansen

Printed in the United States of America

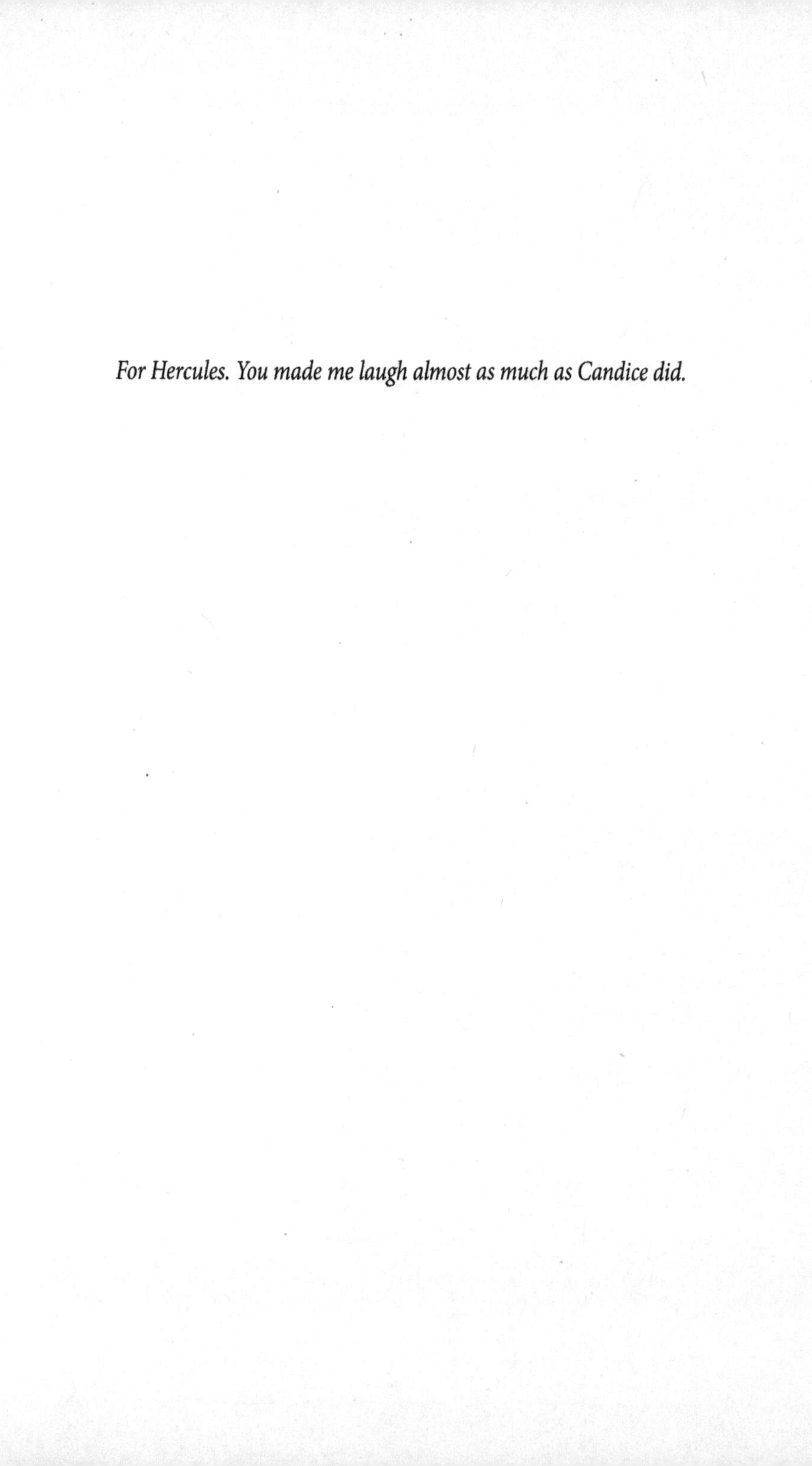

For Hercules. You made me laugh almost as much as Candice did.

CHAPTER ONE

The air in Boise, Idaho, is so cold, when I inhale, it freezes my nostril hairs. I wiggle my nose around and literally feel crackling going on in there. That is just so wrong. I'm from Florida. Nostrils never *ever* crackle in the tropics.

The air outside looks blue. I attribute that to the coldness. Cold equals blue, warm equals orange. That's why the sky in Florida always looks orange. It's a meteorological fact; you can look it up. I'm thinking on the equator, everything is probably more red.

The misty clouds really high up in the grey sky look like they're in the mood to drop some snow on my head, and that's going to be a problem because I spent a ton of time making sure my hair would be perfect. The ash-blonde color with natural-looking highlights on top and lowlights underneath is a hard setup to get perfect, but I've done it. Of course. And the purposely careless look to the wavy style takes me over an hour to get just right with the help of copious amounts of product and a flat iron. A hat would totally ruin the effect. Hair is my business, and I am always advertising.

I scan the arrival pickup area and ask myself for about the tenth time since the plane touched down why I'm here, but then I see my roly-poly best friend waddling down the sidewalk outside the airport, and I remember; I wouldn't want to be anywhere else in the entire world than right here on the frozen tundra that is the Northwest, awaiting the birth of my first godchild.

"Candice!" Andie shouts happily, picking up the pace. "You're here!" She looks like she's going to tip over, first to one side and then the other. Her feet are angled out like a duck's. The snow on the sidewalk squeaks and crunches with the rhythm of her footfalls.

I run over to meet her and her cowboy escort who's trailing behind, the dingle-ball pom-poms on the top of my boots banging around my ankles and calves. I found these babies online, and I could not wait to wear them. I never get to wear fur-lined pom-pom boots in Florida, but here, I'm turning out all the northern exposure fashion. I can't let that degree from UF go completely to waste.

I'm almost to my BFF's embrace when I hit a patch of ice.

"Whooop!"

My arms fly out in an attempt to create some wind resistance and slow my descent. I'm not sure it works this time, although the theory is sound. The sky turns upside down and switches places with the ground. I can't see anything but those wispy clouds, and then my butt lands hard on the sidewalk. The cold wetness immediately starts to seep into my Diesel jeans.

Ass? Meet ice. Very cold, very hard, ice.

"Holy crapola," I grunt out as I try to sit up, "that sidewalk is like concrete or something." My body is a little too stunned to obey my commands just yet, and my gloves are sticking to the ground. I now know how a turtle feels when it gets flipped over. *Poor turtles.*

A cowboy hat blocks out the grey sky, and an emotionless face is there above mine. "That was graceful," he says.

I frown at him, ignoring the pretty green eyes and chiseled good looks of this Oregon born and bred cowboy. "Of course it was. I've been practicing."

He holds out a gloved hand, which I take under protest. Andie's brother-in-law, Ian, is on my list. My doo-doo list. Andie has kept me apprised of his sorry butt via email, text, and telephone calls for the last year, so I have plenty of reason to not like him. Apparently, his attitude after his brother's wedding hasn't improved a whole lot from when Andie met him for the first time. We've analyzed the situation ad nauseum and have come to the conclusion that he's still blaming Andie's husband, or maybe even Andie, for his messed-up life.

"Are you okay? Oh my god, that was a bad one." Andie is fluttering her hands around me, patting me all over once I'm standing.

"There's nothing broken but my ass, and that already had a crack in it. I'm fine." I hold her hands out to her sides so I can see her midsection and distract her from her crazy mother hen program. It's really weird to see her acting so different. I'm willing to bet Party Girl is never in the hizouse anymore.

"How are you doing?" I ask. "Ready to pop?" Her white, goose-down coat is puffed out so much she looks like the Michelin Man or maybe the Stay Puft Marshmallow Man. I can't actually see her belly at all, but it must be huge, the way it's turning my formerly tiny lawyer friend into a giant human snowball.

"You have no idea." She pulls me into an awkward hug. She has to bend over to keep her belly from hitting me, and I have to fold in half to meet her since she's shorter than me. "I've missed you soooo much!" She sounds almost weepy.

I roll my eyes over to Ian, who's pretending to be bored out of his skull. "Yeah, I know. Nothing to do but stare at cowboys all day. Poor girl." She has a small legal practice in the town where she lives, but she does all her work at home. I've learned there are the three MacKenzie men, some friend of the family named Boog, and then a few other ranch hands who are there every day working. "You must really be missing city life. You've sacrificed a lot."

Ian doesn't look at me, but his face twitches.

Good. Let him suck on that lemon drop for a while. He's going to get a piece of my mind later for being a butthead to my best friend after she gave up her whole life to come out to the middle of nowhere and be a rancher's wife. I narrow my eyes at him, willing him to look over at me and bask in my silent threat.

He ignores me, jingling a set of car keys over and over.

"Come on," Andie says. "Let's get back to the truck. It's too damn cold out here."

Ian's already moving to get my luggage, but I run on tiptoe past him, making sure to hit the salted parts of the sidewalk so I don't have to test my wind-resistance-fall-breaking theory again.

My boobs are bouncing in my lacey bra, and I can't help but smile when no less than three guys look over to admire the view. I'm not ashamed to say that I appreciate the attention, which is part of the reason I chose this probably less than warm enough coat. It's way better for emphasizing curves than goose down. I refuse to be a Pillsbury dough girl on this trip or any other, for that matter.

"I can get it," I say, beating Ian to my bag.

"Nah, I got it," he says, bending over.

I slap his hand away. "Back off, John Wayne. Don't touch."

He stands up straight and frowns at me, his shoulders going back and giving me great perspective for how wide they are. *Holy mother of all things muscular.* He could probably carry two of my bags on those things.

"You're gonna carry that all by yourself?" he asks. "What are you . . . some kind of women's libber?"

I look at my bag. It is pretty big. And heavy. But he'll probably throw it around and then think he's mister big man for helping me. I don't want to give him the satisfaction. He has a lot to learn about women, and I'm just the one to educate him. If I get nothing else accomplished while I'm here in no-woman's land, I'm going to make sure my best friend has an easier time living with this dude-ranch dude. *R-E-S-P-E-C-T, find out what it means to me. Oh, yeah.*

"I got it on the plane, didn't I?" I grab my bag and drag it by the handle, muttering to him or maybe just myself since he's probably not even listening. "Women's libber? Who says that anymore?"

Wrangling my bag into a straight line becomes my biggest challenge since arriving in this arctic hell. The sound of the wheels collecting snow, salt, and slush beneath them makes me want to give myself a mental kick for not allowing Ian to carry it. Less than a minute later, and I'm not sure who's learning what lesson.

Andie comes up next to me, and I let go of my bag with one hand so we can link arms. Unfortunately, walking side by side like this forces me to pick up her waddling gait. My bag and I have quite the rhythm going now: waddle, waddle, slussshhhhh . . . waddle, waddle, slussshhh . . . So much for my tight jacket getting me attention. Now I'm just getting stares of pity.

Ian chuckles as he walks behind us.

I refuse to admit I made a mistake. He doesn't deserve the satisfaction. Besides, my pride won't allow it. I blow my long bangs up out of my face so I can see.

"So, what did the doctor say at your appointment today?" I ask, trying to get my mind off my poor choice in luggage transport.

Waddle, waddle, slussshhh . . .

"I'm almost ready to go. Any day now."

"Should you even be out here waddling around?" I ask, eyeing the patches of dangerous ice all over the place. Their pavement salting technique leaves a lot to be desired. The guy who did it had to be drunk.

"Excuse me, but I don't *waddle*. I *glide*. And probably not. But I dare anyone to try and stop me from coming to pick up my best friend at the airport."

Ian hisses out some air, but we both ignore him.

Waddle, waddle, slussshhh . . .

"Where's Mack?" I ask, looking ahead, almost expecting to see him pulling up in a truck. He's not exactly possessive, but he's definitely in big-time love with Andie. She says he can't stand to be away from her for longer than a few hours at work, especially now that she's visibly pregnant.

"He had to help his father with some babies being born. Calves are dropping everywhere at all hours of the day and night."

"In the snow? That's awful."

"I know. Cows have my total respect these days. I'm not having my baby anywhere but in a puffy warm bed inside a heated room with my husband's gorgeous face hanging over me."

Ian picks up the pace and goes around us into the parking lot, stopping down the lane of cars at the back of a pickup truck. It's a monster of a thing, the tailgate sticking out several feet farther than the other cars.

"Do we have an actual birthday date set?" I ask, wiggling out of her grip and dragging the bag up to the back of the truck's bed. I'm trying to figure out whether it will fit in the back seat or have to go in the bed of the truck when Ian grabs the handle.

"No," Andie responds. "Doc says I have to just do it the old-fashioned way. The baby decides when he's coming, not us."

"Ooh, fun." I watch, cringing at how Ian so easily launches my bag into the back, heedless of its designer tag. *So much for using the back seat.* I shake my head as he casually tosses a tarp over it. He expects me to complain—I know he does—but I'm not going to give him the satisfaction, even though the bag cost me more hours cutting and coloring hair than I care to think about.

"Need help getting in?" Ian asks, lifting an eyebrow at me. This is a challenge; I know it is.

"Please . . . ," I respond, rolling my eyes, "I'm not handicapped."

"I wasn't talking to you," he deadpans. Then he looks over at Andie, waiting for her response.

"Oh." My face is on fire. I guess it wasn't a challenge. How did I read that so wrong? Men are usually my specialty. I am fluent in man-talk, man-expression, and man-think.

"Candice can help me, can't you, Candice?" Andie waddles over to the passenger door. This truck actually has four doors, not just two. I have no idea how it's even fitting into this parking space.

"Sure, no prob." Opening the front passenger door, I gesture for her to go in before me. "Alley-oop, my little roly-poly friend."

She points her finger right up in my face. "Do *not* call me roly-poly." Then she turns around, grabs the door with one hand and the side of the seat with the other, and tries to step up into the truck.

There's a grunt.

A considerable amount of straining.

And possibly about an inch or two of actual liftoff.

Then Andie's back on the ground on two feet, her face flushed and her expression annoyed. "Are you going to help me or what?" She glares at me over her shoulder.

I brace myself behind her with my hands on her waist, squatting down to lift this heavy load with my legs and not my back. "Okay, try again."

As she starts to move up, I push.

Nothing happens. She's like a ton of bricks. The song "Brick House" starts playing in my head. "She's a brick . . . *berp berp beeerp berp* . . . house . . . she's mighty, mighty . . ."

"Come on!" she yells, her one foot up on the running board and the other a frog's hair off the ground.

I bend down farther and put my shoulder under her butt. "One, two, three, *go*!" I heave her up with all my might.

Her whole body lifts off the ground in a big surge of movement, and her head bonks the top of the doorway.

"Ow! Not so high, Candice!"

I'm losing my grip on her butt, and my foot is slipping. "Go in! Go in!" I'm grunting right along with her, and now I'm sweating too. *Dammit!* I hate sweating; it totally ruins my makeup.

Suddenly her weight is gone and I'm falling forward. I do a face-plant into the side of the passenger seat, my head bounces off from the impact, and then my feet slip out from under me. My hair whips sideways and gets caught in my lipgloss as gravity takes hold and drags me downward.

I land on my knees and then roll over onto my back to keep from breaking anything. I read that you have to go with the movement of a fall to keep the shock from being absorbed by the body. It's Newton's law or something. I'm all about the rolling, rolling, rolling now. Like a stunt girl, but not one of those butch ones.

Grey skies.

A cowboy hat.

A barely concealed smile on Ian's stupid face.

"Need some help?" he asks.

I start pinwheeling my hands above me, slapping at him. "No! Go away, John Wayne!"

He disappears from view, but I can hear his annoying chuckle as his snow-and-salt-crunching feet go around the back of the truck. It's possible I hear him mutter, "High maintenance" too.

I lie there for a few seconds, contemplating my world. I haven't even made it across the border into Oregon, and my hair is already ruined, and my underpants are wet through. *This is not a good sign.*

I struggle to sit up, wincing as more water seeps into my panties. The only way I can stand is to splay my feet out under me like a duck, and I'm not even pregnant.

I finally make it into the back seat of the truck and spend the next five minutes trying to get my hair back to amazing. It refuses to cooperate. There might not be any snow in the air, but that doesn't stop the invisible humidity from making me look like a wet dog. I'm doomed to arrive in Baker City looking like a homeless woman Andie and Ian picked up off the street corner. Even my pom-poms are ruined, stained with street goop and soggy wet.

Andie's gabbing on and on about cows and horses and all kinds of other nonsense, but all I can think about is the bad voodoo going on here. These are all terrible signs, right? Two falls to the ice within five minutes? Ruined hair? Dingy pom-poms?

What else could possibly go wrong?

CHAPTER TWO

By the time we arrive in front of Ian's family homestead, I am beyond recognition. My hair? Flat, wet, and just plain ruined. My makeup? Smudged and missing in spots, probably. My jeans? Soggy. My eyes? Bloodshot. I'm sure they're bloodshot because they're burning right now. My hand mirror is in my bag in the back of the truck, and I didn't want to be obvious and lean into the front seat to use the rearview mirror, so I've had to suffer for over two hours, wondering what I look like. My imagination has turned me into Sasquatch with a bad dye job.

The MacKenzies have already met me once at Andie's wedding, and I was absolutely fabulous then, thank goodness. It was summer, and I had a great tan, my hair was highlighted blonde, and my tummy was as tight as it's ever been. My appearance today is going to be a serious letdown for everyone involved. I always pack on a few pounds during winter, so there's that . . . and apparently, my hair products were not made for cold, snowy conditions found in the Arctic Circle. It feels like I have glue in my hair.

"Come on—let's get inside. Ian, will you grab Candice's bag for me?" Andie's sliding down off the front seat and onto the snow-covered ground below her. Now who's the stuntwoman?

"Yeah, I got it." Ian disappears behind the truck, probably to go abuse my luggage some more.

I cringe at my girlfriend, worrying she'll bite the dust when she makes contact with all that frozen water. But it appears as if my worry is unfounded. She has obviously done this a lot. She lands safely with just a tiny crunch of snow and turns around to wait for me.

Attempting the same dismount, I'm not nearly as sure-footed or successful. Thank goodness I was holding onto the door with one hand and the seatbelt with the other, using my kung-fu grip; otherwise, I would have taken another tumble, only this time in Oregon and not Idaho. I backpedal for a few seconds before my feet decide it's time to grip the ground for me.

What. The. Hell. I've never been so clumsy in my entire life.

What is it with these top-left states anyway? Why can't they be more like Florida or Georgia, states in the bottom right of the map? I never *ever* fall in the bottom-right states. I'm graceful and elegant there, like a swan or a flamingo. Here, I feel like a water buffalo or something. And that makes sense, since they have buffalo here and water with all this snow. I'll bet water buffalos originally come from Oregon, which is how they got their name. I'm going to have to google that when I get a chance, but until I verify, I'm going to go with it as fact. It totally makes sense.

"Careful," Andie cautions. "The ground is really wet. And hard." She holds out a hand to steady me.

"Yeah, I know." I roll my eyes at her as I gain my feet again. No way am I going to take her offer of help. I'll end up taking her roly-poly self down with me and causing her to go into labor, and I am not into seeing baby goo. I leave that kind of nonsense to the doctors. "I have the proof of how hard this ground is on my ass, thank you very much. I'll be bruised for the whole week."

"Well, that's great. It means you'll have a whole two weeks of not being bruised before you have to go back." She grins. She really is cute when she does that, but I'm not falling for it.

"I can't stay for three weeks, I told you that. Two weeks only. That's all the time I have." I feel a little guilty about it since I hardly ever see her anymore, but not as much as I did on the airplane. The snow and the ice have tempered my enthusiasm for this place considerably. Screw pom-pom boots. The fashion isn't worth the butt-cheek frostbite I'm suffering right now. Nothing better fall off—that's all I'm saying.

"Oh, she's here!" exclaims a voice from inside. The porch door flies open and an older woman with poorly dyed brown hair swept up in a bun comes running out. She's wearing heavy house slippers with jeans and a man's flannel shirt over a turtleneck. I can't help but smile at her lovely face and sadly coordinated fashion.

"Hi, Maeve! So nice to be here!" I shall now commence the lying. I'm happy to be with these people, yes, but not in this frigid place.

"Come, come, come . . . get in the house. It's terribly cold out today. Unseasonably so, isn't it Andie?"

Andie snorts behind me as she clomps up the stairs. "Oh, yeah. Normally, it's super balmy."

"You're so bad," Maeve scolds her daughter-in-law as she ushers me into the house. The door bangs shut behind us with the force of Ian's brawn.

The warmth envelops me in its arms, and I breathe out a sigh of relief. My nostril hairs are instantly thawed. I inhale and wiggle my nose just to be sure there are no remaining icicles in there. Having one of those drop out would be more than a little embarrassing. *Nope. No crunching.*

My smile is genuine. "Thank you so much for having me, Maeve. I really appreciate it. I don't want to be a bother, though, so I'm happy to stay in town."

"Nonsense! You're staying here with Angus and me. We wouldn't hear of you staying so far away."

The three of us girls walk into the kitchen and take seats around the dining table. They have a perfectly nice living room, but as far as I've seen, it never gets used. The wood stove is in the kitchen, and that's where everyone congregates, even in the summer.

"Where do you want her bag?" Ian asks from the doorway.

I try not to look at him, but it's impossible not to. His presence is totally commanding. I've heard that expression before, but until being around him, I never really appreciated what it meant. He's like the boss of my eyeballs or something.

Do not look at his package, Candice. Do not look at his package. My eyes move of their own accord. *Oh dammit, you looked at his package! And . . . oh my . . . Oh my, my, my . . . There's a giant bulge! Hooray for giant bulges and the jeans that let me see them!*

"Put her in Mack's room," Maeve says, getting up from the table. She has no clue that I just eye-groped her son, thank goodness.

"But that's . . ." He clamps his mouth shut and says nothing more.

"That's what, dear?" his mother asks, getting out mugs and turning on the coffee pot.

"He was going to whine that it's too close to his bedroom," says Andie in a teasing tone.

"Nooo, Ian wouldn't say that," says Maeve, laughing it off. "He's a big boy." She looks up at her son. "You're not afraid of a girl being across the hall from you, are you Ian?"

He shakes his head as he turns to leave. "Don't be ridiculous." He and his glorious package are gone, and my luggage goes with them. And oh my goodness, does he not have the finest ass there ever was? Yes, sir, he does. That's one thing I remembered from my last trip out here. No man has ever filled out a pair of jeans like Ian MacKenzie. Too bad that ass is connected to a big dope of a guy.

Still, he doesn't need to be a nice guy to be a good roll in the hay. I smile at the idea that's forming in my brain. *Note to self: Ask Andie if they have hay anywhere around here.*

"What's that all about?" I ask, jerking myself away from the sexy thoughts in an effort to control my raging hormones. Normally, I'm not all that into buttage, but Ian has some weird power over me that makes me stupid. Must be the pheromones. I'm totally not rolling in the hay with him. I don't care how big that bulge is.

"Oh, he's just fussy is all," says Maeve. She sounds a little sad.

"Fussy? I call it asshole-y," says Andie.

"Now, now." Maeve brings over empty mugs and sugar. "Don't let his moods get to you." She pats Andie on the cheek gently before returning to the coffee pot. Apparently, being pregnant gives Andie a free pass to be bold-faced honest about Maeve's son. It's actually pretty impressive. I'm not sure who to admire more for it, Andie or Maeve.

I kind of melt a little inside seeing Maeve be so sweet to my friend. Andie's real mom is a real piece of work. My BFF deserves to have a loving mommy in her life.

"Kind of hard when he's all up in my butt all the time." Andie says it under her breath, but it's clear she's not trying to keep her opinion from her mother-in-law.

"He just needs more time," Maeve says.

"What he needs is a swift kick in the patootie if you ask me," says Andie. "He's had plenty of time to get over his broken heart. Now he's just wallowing."

Maeve stands at the coffee maker, watching the dark liquid drip out from the grinds. "Everyone has his own time frame for grieving. His is just longer than the average person's."

"Grieving?" I ask, looking from Maeve to Andie. "Did someone die and I didn't hear about it?" I wonder if it's that Booger guy Andie's talked about before. He's a friend of the family and apparently has been for most of Ian's and Mack's lives. She hasn't mentioned him in a while, though.

"No, nobody died," Andie says, obviously not impressed with her brother-in-law's grieving process. "He got dumped at the altar or he dumped someone at the altar, and he still hasn't gotten over it. It was, like, years ago." She rolls her eyes.

"It was three years ago, and granted that's quite some time, but he's still genuinely hurt. He's sensitive." Maeve turns to look at us. "You can't know what it's like to have someone be dishonorable toward you until it happens to you personally. No one knows how they'll react when trust falls apart, so we shouldn't judge."

Andie casts her eyes down to the tabletop. "I'm not really judging. I'm just mad at him for being sad all the time. He deserves to be happy."

"Agreed," says Maeve, taking the half-full pot off the burner and bringing it over to our mugs. "And he will be. Someday soon, I hope. We all hope." She pours out some steaming liquid into a mug for me, and I waste no time dumping four teaspoons of sugar into it and a bunch of milk, followed by a healthy dose of vigorous stirring with my tiny spoon. It takes a little while, but soon I have some almost foam floating on the top of my drink.

"What's that all about?" Andie asks, sipping at her black coffee with a grin while she looks pointedly at my mug.

"Backwoods cappuccino. You should try it. It's delish." I take a sip and pretend I'm telling the truth again. *Bleck. This stuff is awful.* I keep smiling through the pain. I'm going to be so awesome at lying by the time I leave here, I should probably start playing poker so I can clean up at the Hard Rock Casino when I get back.

"Whatever gets the blood pumping, right?" Maeve is sitting down opposite me and smiling into her cup too, after exchanging glances with Andie.

I nod like I know what she's talking about. Maybe there's a joke going on here, but I don't want to act paranoid and demand to know what it is. It's probably one of those country-bumpkin things I wouldn't understand, being a bona fide dyed-in-the-wool city girl.

What I can't figure out is how it is that Andie's melded so well into this lifestyle. It's like she's been here her whole life, and I know very well she hasn't. She's just like me. Her favorite thing to do on a Thursday is to go for manis and pedis at the Blissful Spa downtown at lunchtime, followed by an all-nighter at the law firm, doing massively boring research. This whole great-outdoors, freezing-nostril-hairs, pulling-cow-babies-out-of-bovine-VJs, wearing-unflattering-puffy-jackets thing? No. That's not Andie.

Maybe I should spend some time out here trying to convince her to come back to civilization. She did tell me that Mack would follow her wherever she goes. I chew on my lip as I try to decide whether to plan this out or not. I'm probably going to have to fake an injury or something to make it work. Like an aneurism, maybe. But that's no biggie. I could limp around with crossed eyes for a few days. I'm really coordinated when I'm not on ice.

"I see your hamster running," Andie says, putting her mug on the table. She tilts her chin down and looks up at me, just staring. She's totally got the scolding mother thing down pat.

I don't know what the hell she means about hamsters, though. "What?" I look behind me, misgivings taking over my thought process. *Does Maeve keep hamsters in the kitchen? Is that even sanitary? Why would she do that? Oh my god . . . Does she eat them?* I'm picturing horrific hamster kabobs when I face Andie again. "Oh my god, I am totally not eating a hamster while I'm here. I'm serious, Andie." I look over at Maeve. "I know you eat cow balls and all that, but I'm not going there. Not even if Andie threatens to withhold crowning me godmother." I shake my head and clamp my lips together so she can see how hopeless it will be trying to convince me otherwise.

Andie's laughing so hard she can barely get the words out. "What are you talking about?"

"You're the one who brought up hamsters. What are *you* talking about?" I'm missing out on the joke once again. I hate when that happens.

"I said I can *see your hamster*. The one running on the treadmill in your head, powering your brain. He's about to pass out from asphyxiation brought on by acute overstimulation, Candice. Stop scheming and planning."

How dare she figure out what I'm thinking! So rude! My most innocent expression comes in to save the day. Up go the eyebrows and eyelids, making my eyeballs as wide as possible. "What on earth are you talking about? I'm not scheming. I never scheme."

"What am I missing?" Maeve asks, looking first at Andie and then me.

Andie points at me. "Look at that expression on her face. Memorize it. Whenever you see it, run. Grab the fire extinguisher. That's her scheming look. Bad things happen when the hamster runs out of breath."

I frown, playing it off. I cannot believe she's reading me like that. And there ain't no hamster running this super computer either. More like a panther or a leopard. I'm going to have to google spying techniques so I can hide my intentions better. At this rate, they'll know my deepest secrets by Tuesday.

"She's crazy," I say, my tone casual. She's the nutty one, not me. "I never scheme. I'm a rational, adult woman who just lives her life and lets other people live theirs." I snort for emphasis. "As if."

"So now we know she was planning on interfering in someone's life." Andie nods knowingly at Maeve. "I can read her like a book."

"That's impressive," Maeve says, still smiling. "Who's life will it be, I wonder?"

I put my mug down and hold up my hand. "Okay, okay, joke's over. Ha-ha, very funny." I place my palm flat on the table and lean in a little. I look like an anchorwoman getting ready to report the most amazing, juiciest news of the year. "Can we please get back to the subject of this baby thing? Because I'm a little stressed, if you must know the truth."

There. That'll do it. Andie has baby fever, and I know once I get her tractor beam locked on this subject, it'll take nothing short of C-4 plastic explosives to get her off. Talk about scheming. She has no idea. I can control her *mind* without her even realizing it. I'm dangerous like that. She should fear me more than she does.

Andie leans over her mug with both hands wrapped around it. She grins like a fool. "Yes, let's do that. Let's talk about babies."

See? Told ya.

Maeve stands. "I'd love to, but I have some warm chicken buns that need to be relieved of their offerings. I'll catch up on the baby talk later." She walks out onto the back porch, pulling the door closed behind her before I can respond.

I look over at Andie. "Please don't tell me she's going to touch chicken poop."

Andie's face is totally impassive. "Nope."

"Phew. That's a relief." I lift my mug to my lips. The coffee is awful, but at least it's warm, and Maeve just let in a big woof of cold air. The goose bumps on my legs are making stubble grow out instantaneously.

"She is going to touch their eggs, though."

I pause before drinking, slowly lowering my mug to the table. Suddenly backwoods cappuccino doesn't sound as appetizing as it once did. "Then she *is* going to touch their poop."

She laughs, sounding confused. "How so?" She takes a sip of her drink as she waits to be educated by me.

I cringe. "*Ew*, Andie. Because the eggs come from their butts, of course."

Andie laughs so hard she spits coffee out at me. Then she bends over, riding the chair sidesaddle since her belly is so big she can't fit going forward. "You've got to be kidding me." She wipes tears away. "Oh, man, Candice, I sure have missed you."

I frown at her obvious ignorance of all things chicken. "I missed you too. But why are you laughing over simple scientific facts? Google is your friend, you know, Andie. You really shouldn't neglect your googling."

CHAPTER THREE

Mack's room is sparse, which doesn't surprise me one bit. He's a no-nonsense kind of guy. Putting my clothes away only takes a short time, and twenty minutes in the bathroom puts my hair and face to rights. Now I can present myself to the rest of Baker City and not look like a granola hippy fresh off a cow pie commune. A spritz of my favorite perfume makes me feel almost human again.

"Phew. Easy does it," says Ian as he walks past the bathroom, waving his hand in front of his nose. I can see his stupid face reflected in the mirror.

"I'll have you know that this perfume costs over a hundred dollars an ounce, and it's from France." I put the silver cap back on it and look at the small, round bottle, wondering if I should doubt myself. *Pfft. Right.* What does he know? He's a total bumpkin. His idea of a delicious scent is probably fermented pig turds.

His voice fades as he moves down the hall. "I'll have *you* know that you'd've been better off spending your money on plain old soap."

My jaw drops open as he disappears into his room. How dare he insult my signature scent! I spent years waiting for the perfect one to come my way, and I happen to know for a fact that men love it. I have them following me around like puppies back home with just one whiff. This stuff is pure sex appeal captured in a tiny bottle.

I put it down and step out of the bathroom. "Yeah, right," I say, following him, stopping when I reach his doorway. "I'll bet the women you usually go out with wear the stuff they buy in the grocery store. That stuff gives new meaning to the words *eau de toilette*, you know." I lift my chin and sniff, confident in the knowledge that I am way more sophisticated than any girl he's ever been with.

"Yeah," he says without even glancing my way, as he pulls a baseball hat out of his dresser drawer and puts it on his head. "It's called soap." He moves the hat up and down. "You should try it sometime."

"Not your color," I say, ignoring his insult. I won't even dignify that comment with a response. I use soap. Very nice soap, in fact. It's got lavender essential oils, also from France.

He frowns and pulls the blue ball cap off his head, staring at it. "What's wrong with the color?"

I roll my eyes and stride into the room, yanking the hat out of his hands. We're both standing in front of the mirror over his dresser, looking at his reflection. His hair is slightly skewed, and his expression is disbelief mixed with shock. I love this look of confusion on him, since he always seems supremely confident, but I'd never tell him that.

I hold the cap up next to his head with one hand and point to his cheek with the other. "You are a *summer* person, not a winter person. That means you should stick with warm colors." I shake the hat for emphasis. "This is a cool color. It clashes with your complexion." I put it back in his drawer and dig around to find another one. He has an impressive collection. I pull the best one out, slap it onto his head, and look in the mirror with him. "See?" I take the old one back out of the drawer and hold it up next to his head so he can see the difference. "Way better, right?"

He twists his mouth up and grabs the hat out of my hand. Taking the other one off and tossing it over his shoulder, he slaps the old one back on. "Nah. This one's better."

"Do you argue just for the sake of arguing?" My hands are on my hips.

"Do you always butt your nose into other people's business without being invited?" He slams his drawer shut.

"I have a degree in fashion, for your information. And since you're Andie's brother-in-law, I have a moral obligation to keep you from walking out of this house looking like a half-wit."

He stops at his doorway on the way out, looking down at me from under the brim of his hat, his glowing green eyes staring right at me for the first time. Normally, he looks at me kind of sideways, and now I know why. Power like he has should be used sparingly, if for no other reason than for the sake of my blood pressure. I'm too young to have a stroke.

"I thought you cut hair," he says.

I can't help the small thrill that runs through me at the idea that he remembered what I do for a living. I would have sworn he didn't know or care. "I do. *And* I give fashion advice, even when it's pretty much a hopeless case and people don't appreciate it. You should listen to me, you know. I know what I'm talking about."

"I'll keep that in mind," he says. He might be smiling too, but it's hard to tell since he's already gone.

"Where are you off to?" I ask, rushing to the door in time to see his back disappearing down the stairs. I'm a little breathless, but it's not from exercise. My, oh my, he can be really cute when he wants to be.

"Nowhere you'd like to be," he says.

For some reason, letting Ian get the last word is not acceptable to me. My first reaction with him is to argue every point. Why that is, I don't know, but there's no use denying it. I'm normally not the argumentative type, but something about his attitude makes me want to duke it out with him. Besides, how does he know where I'd like to be? Maybe I'd like to be *exactly* where he's going.

I run into my room and pull on my super-cute cowgirl boots. I totally splurged on these babies. They're embroidered all over in several colors, and the leather is a dark purple with a natural finish, making it look a little mottled. They're vintage cowgirl awesome, and I am totally ready to take this town by storm when I have these on.

"Wait up!" I yell as I run from my room. "I'm coming with you!" My feet clomp a lot louder than I'm used to as the heels of my boots bang against the floors. Normally, I'm practically a ballerina the way I flit and float everywhere.

"No, you're not!" he yells back, slamming the front door on his way out.

I snag my short leather coat off the hook by the door as I run past, making it to the porch in time to see him climb up into his truck. He must have run across the yard or something. What a jerk.

"Wait!" I yell, holding out my hand like I'm hailing a taxi. I go down the porch steps at lightning speed and am ready to take off like the sprinter I used to be in high school.

Only problem is, I'm not exactly wearing my running shoes. I soon learn the hard way that awesome vintage cowgirl boots do not have a hell of a lot of traction. Or any at all, actually.

One second I'm pedaling in reverse getting nowhere while my arms are pinwheeling out at my sides, and the next I'm on my back, staring up at the grey sky. My head hurts something awful. I'm pretty sure I hit it on a boulder.

The engine to the truck goes on, rumbles and revs, and then a few seconds later it stops making sounds completely. I'm not sure if Ian's still here or if he took off so fast, he's already halfway up the mountain. I'm afraid to lift my head and check. I could possibly be paralyzed.

Will anyone miss me inside the house in time to rescue me from death by freezing or maiming by frostbite? I'm not sure. Time to pull on my vast resources of personal power, so I can save myself from dying or becoming toe-less way too young.

Inventory time. I wiggle my tootsies to see if I'm good from the waist down. *Yep.* Toes are moving. Ass is . . . wet. Again. *Dammit.* I twitch my fingers. *Yep.* Those work too. But damn, they're cold. I'm not going to be nearly as adorable with all my fingertips gone. Tightening my hands into fists seems like a very smart idea.

I'm working on moving my shoulders up and down when Ian's face is suddenly hovering over me. "You're getting pretty good at that falling-on-your-ass thing." He holds out a hand.

I punch it away since my hands don't want to open anymore. Sitting up, my concerns for paralysis are quickly replaced by annoyance. "I told you . . . I've been practicing . . . on purpose."

"Seems like there are easier ways to get on your back than slipping on the ice."

Is he suggesting I turn into a slut? He is totally going to pay for that. I roll over and get up on my knees and then my feet. My boots slip around immediately, causing me to reach out and grab Ian's jacket at the shoulder to steady myself.

"Are you calling me a ho?" I ask. Turning slightly to get my feet under me more firmly is a mistake. My feet slip out completely and I have to grip Ian with both hands to keep from going down again.

Unfortunately, he wasn't expecting my extra weight on his shoulders, so he's knocked off balance. His feet shuffle around on the ice and snow for purchase, but it's hopeless.

He lands on his back, and I land on top of him, my forehead banging into his chin.

"Ow, mother fudger!" I moan. "Holy crap, you have a hard chin." Reaching up to rub my head, my finger goes into one of his nostrils by mistake.

"Jesus, get your finger out of my nose, would ya?" He lies there, lifeless, with his eyes closed, as I pull my hand back and rest it on the snow next to his head.

"Ow, God, I hurt my back," he grunts out. His arms then fall to his sides.

My eyes widen in alarm. "Ian? Ian, are you okay?"

He doesn't answer.

I tap his cheek, first gently and then harder. "Ian! Are you okay?!" I'm yelling in his face because I'm in a panic. I'm just about ready to call out the troops when one of his eyes opens.

"Are you going to lay on me all day or what?"

My face flames red. "Ha. You wish." I move around, trying to get off him, but it's not as easy as it sounds. He's big, and the ground all around him is too slick for me to get a grip on, even with my hands.

"If you don't quit moving around like that, we're both going to be sorry. Come on, get off."

I speak through clenched teeth. "Shut up, idiot—I'm trying to get off."

He chuckles. "I can tell."

I suddenly realize the double meaning of our words, and embarrassment makes my cheeks go hot red. Without thinking, I grab a handful of snow and slap it right onto his face. That'll cool him off, the butthead.

"Hey!" he sputters, his hands coming off the ground to swipe at his face. He blinks several times hard and then scowls at me. "What was that for?" He's half angry and half laughing. I think he's as confused as I am.

"That's for perving out on me when I'm just trying to get *up*." I push on his chest and manage to roll off him and onto my back again. I'm once more staring up at the Oregon sky. I'm really beginning to hate that thing. Stupid top-left state.

And then my mouth is full of snow.

I'm busy getting over my shock and spitting out the cold, melting mass as Ian whoops it up, lying partly on his side now, with his upper body twisted toward me.

"Ha-*ha*! How's that taste, City?!" He's smiling from ear to ear, and his eyes are aglow.

I throw my arms out to my sides, grab two handfuls of snow, and twist onto my side. "You tell me, *Country*!" I shove both barrels right up his nose.

He starts sneezing, and I take the opportunity his incapacitation provides to get away. I roll and roll and roll. It's my only chance since my feet are useless in this snow with these boots on.

Once I'm a few feet away, I struggle up onto my knees and start crawling. My knees are sliding like crazy on the ice, so I only get about two inches for every six strokes of my legs. I kick my speed up a notch to put more distance between us. Probably my feet are just a purple blur right now to any onlookers, I'm going so fast and furious.

I make it almost to the porch before Ian grabs my ankle. Fear and maybe a little bit of excitement coming from the thrill of the chase surges into me, like I'm the victim in a horror movie being pursued by a hot killer. I can't help but shriek.

"Where do you think you're going?" he growls.

"Aaaack! Get off!" I try to kick him, but all that does is offer up both feet for capture. My body slides easily across the icy surface of the yard. Before I know it, he has me trapped under him, with the two of us chest to chest.

He immediately begins grabbing handfuls of snow and slapping them down onto my face, my head, my neck . . . anywhere there's an exposed surface.

"Take that, City! Eat that snow! That's right, girl! Yum, yum! Tasty, tasty Oregon snow! Hope there ain't any of the yellow stuff in there!"

A door bangs open, and a holler comes from somewhere on the porch. "Ian Michael Angus MacKenzie, what on *earth* are you doing?!"

Ian's hand freezes in mid snow-shoving.

I spit out the mouthful of snow I have and blink through the water that's melted onto my lids. Ian's expression is classic. *Busted.* Tilting my head back, I can see Maeve standing at the top of the stairs. I smile past my frozen lips.

"Uhhh, hey, Ma," he says nervously. "What're you doing out here?"

She puts her hands on her hips, her open, sleeveless down jacket flying up on both sides like moth wings. "Apparently I'm bearing witness to an assault and battery on our house guest by a savage moron whose rear end is about to become reacquainted with the business end of my kitchen spatula!"

I start giggling and singsonging at the same time. "You're in trouble, you're in trouble . . ."

He grabs one more handful of snow and stuffs it in my face. "It was worth it," he whispers in my ear before standing up. He gets onto his feet with a grace I didn't think possible with all this slippery stuff around. He heads toward his truck while he answers.

"I'm outta here, Ma. Gotta get some feed. You can beat my ass later."

"You bet your sweet hippy I will too. Savage beast of a boy." She doesn't sound all that mad anymore. More like she's just made a promise she intends to keep.

I'm afraid to attempt getting up, so I stay on my back, using the pause in the drama to clear my face of all the snow and water. My hands are pretty much frozen solid at this point.

"Oh dear, oh dear, oh dear," Maeve mutters as she walks gingerly down the stairs. "I cannot believe what I just witnessed. He's gone completely off the range. He used to be such a gentle soul."

I burst out laughing at that load of poo, and when she looks at me, confused, with her bun all lopsided and her superwoman vest cape flying out behind her, I can't help it; the hysteria takes over. I'm ready to pee my pants by the time Andie comes out to see what's going on.

"What's she doing on the ground?" she asks.

Maeve stands there with her hand on her chest, shaking her head slowly at me. "I'm not exactly sure. Call Boog for me on the radio, so we can get her up."

"No, no, I'm good," I say, embarrassed about the idea of some big hairy beast of a man coming to my rescue. I've only seen him once, but that was enough. He reminds me of a deranged Wookiee.

I crawl over to the stairs and use the railing to get up. Once under the protection of the porch roof and on the salted ground, I can stand. I take a deep breath in and out, happy to be alive and invigorated beyond reason. It's like I just ran a 5k or something.

"What are you wearing?" asks Andie, staring down at my feet.

I tilt one up so she can admire the embroidery. It's only a little stained from the water. "Vintage cowgirl awesome. You like?"

She smiles. "Yes, I like. But the bottoms are way too slick for ice and snow. Come on inside. I've got some other boots you can use while you're here."

"But I like these," I whine as I follow her in. Not only are they gorgeous, but they make Ian fall and roll all over the snow with me. These babies were worth every stinkin' penny.

"I don't want you to die while you're here, so wear these." Andie reaches into a closet and pulls out the butt-ugliest boots I have ever seen in my entire life. It would be bad enough that they look like they're made for someone with a serious case of cankles, but they're camouflage too. The word *heinous* doesn't even begin to describe them.

"You cannot be serious." I gesture toward them and then my body. "What is it about me that says, 'Dress me like a Duck Dynasty chick'?"

Her gaze slowly moves over my body, starting at my soggy wet knees, sliding over my water-stained leather jacket, and ending up at my hair. She grimaces. "Um . . . yeah. May want to take a look in the mirror, sweetie pie."

My eyes widen and I dash into the hallway bathroom.

The image that stands before me is my worst nightmare come true. "Oh . . . my . . . GOD!" I cannot believe what I'm looking at. This cannot be real. Is this a trick mirror from a funhouse?

My mascara has somehow made its way down to my upper lip. It's like I'm sporting a Hitler mustache or mini-snatch on my face or something. My hair is matted to my head, and the highlights that before looked like perfect sun-kissed glory now look like someone painted my head with mud. "Oh my Tiny Baby Jesus." I lean in for a closer look and then quickly lean waaaay back. No one should have to see a close-up of this disaster.

Andie steps into the doorway so I can see her reflection in the mirror. "Welcome to the country, city girl."

I jut my chin out and swipe the mascara off my cheeks with a tissue from the box on the counter. For some reason, I find it really annoying that my best friend has melded into this life so well while I'm having a hard time even looking human after just five steps in the snow. "I can hang. I'm adaptable." I hate that she's done so well here, and I literally can't even stand on my own two feet once I walk out the door. I always thought I was tougher than this.

She pats me on the shoulder. "Sure you are, sweetie. Sure you are. I'm going to go make you a hot cup of tea."

She disappears, leaving me to stare at my sorry self in the mirror. I move my mouth this way and that, making sure to get all the mascara and other makeup off my face with the washcloth I find under the sink.

My mind wanders as I clean myself up. Am I deficient or can I pull this together? I frown at the very idea of being incapable. Of course I can. I can totally do this country thing and do it with style. Other people do it, and they can't be half as awesome as I am. I just need to figure out a few things first. Like how to walk on ice and snow without landing on my ass. And how to deal with Ian and my growing hormonal problem where he's concerned.

I'd say he's like an older brother with the way he makes me want to harass and tease him, but no girl should ever feel the way I do about Ian toward a brother. *Ick.* No, Ian is way too cute and way too sexy for him to be anyone's older brother.

The question is, what do I want to do with all these feelings? *Hmmm* . . . a little sexy time while I'm out in the middle of nowhere might not be too awful . . . Could I do that with Ian? Do I *want* to do that with Ian? I'm thinking maybe I do. Just the idea makes my blood pump faster, and my neck gets all blotchy.

I definitely need to learn how to walk properly out here. That way, next time he tries to drive off, I can keep up with him and make him take me along.

I smile at the plan that's forming in my mind, without questioning my motives for a second. I'm just here to have some fun, and there's no reason in the world that I shouldn't fill my time with some goofing around while I wait for that sweet little baby to be born. I can hang on the ranch. I can be a cowgirl. Ian doesn't think I can, but I'll show him. He has no idea what he's in for. City girl, my butt.

I smile at my reflection and wink. This trip is going to be so much more entertaining than I imagined it could be.

CHAPTER FOUR

A steaming mug of tea is doing a good job of thawing my body, inside and out. I cup the sides of it to bring my fingers back to life. Andie sits across from me, drinking some herbal concoction that's supposed to relax her uterus or something. I'm not exactly sure I want to see a relaxed uterus anywhere around me, but I don't say anything to Andie. I've seen pregnant girls go nuts before and it ain't pretty. And besides, if you can't relax your uterus around your best friend, who can you do it with? I sigh, praying I won't see anything weird. I don't have the strongest stomach in the world.

"So what's Ian's deal?" I ask, totally cool-like. Andie will never suspect my motives are to find his weak spots. Ian MacKenzie? Oh, yeah. Challenge accepted. You are so going down, mister.

"What do you mean?" She takes a sip of her drink.

"You know . . . why's he so cranky all the time? What's he do here? Is he seeing anyone?"

"Do you want me to answer the last question first?" Andie asks, barely holding back a smile.

I shrug, like I'm not picking up her hint. "Whatever. Doesn't matter to me." Because I'm super cool, and you have no idea what I'm up to, Andie, so don't even try it!

"Well, let's see . . . he's not seeing anyone as far as I know. I really don't know a whole lot about his current social life other than he goes out to the local bar a lot and drinks more than anyone would like. He never brings girls back here, but he also doesn't always come home every night, so you can do the math on that one."

"Interesting. Anyone you know that he's been with?"

"Not really. Just his ex-fiancée, Ginny. And I don't think he's been with her since the breakup."

"Ex-fiancée? I remember you saying something about her before. How'd she become an ex again?"

Andie leans over her cup a little. If I'm not mistaken, she looks a little guilty. "When Mack went to Las Vegas, the night I met him, he was there to celebrate Ian's engagement. It was his bachelor party."

"Oh, yeah, I remember that. You ruined the party for everyone."

"Hey!" She throws a plastic napkin ring at me.

I duck and stick my tongue out at her. "Missed me."

She glares at me for a second but then continues. "Anyway, when he got back, rumors were flying about the whole thing being a bust because one of the guys disappeared all night with some girl, and Ginny thought it was Ian, so she did something stupid, and Ian found out about it and that was the end of that."

"Whoa. Back up. What did Ginny do exactly?"

Andie looks around, checking to see if anyone's listening. Lowering her voice, she answers. "She made a move on Mack."

"Whaaaat?" I look around too and lean in closer. "She made a move on your man? Ian's *brother*? What kind of skanky ho makes a move on a guy's brother?"

"The kind that's named Ginny, I guess. I've only seen her around town a couple times. I don't know her at all." Andie leans back in her chair. "They were together for a really long time."

"Hmmm . . . so Ian's probably really bitter on women, huh?"

"Not too bitter, since I guess he's sleeping with some. But he's bitter on love, I can tell you that."

And since I'm not interested in love, that doesn't bother me one bit. "So it's been, like, years now, right? Since the breakup, I mean?"

"Yes."

"So why's he still being a prick?"

Andie sighs as she stares into her cup. "An excellent question. Do you want my version of why?"

"Of course."

"I think he wants to be in a city somewhere."

I snort. "No way."

"Yes way." Andie looks up again. "He's an architect. I guess he was headed to Portland to start a new job when the whole marriage thing fell apart. He stayed here for whatever reason, but he's not happy about it."

"Why doesn't he just leave if he's not happy?"

"You'll have to ask him that. I don't dare rock that boat."

"What do you mean?"

Andie gets up with difficulty and waddles over to the sink to wash her mug out. "He's very touchy about anything having to do with that stuff, and to keep things copacetic between him and Mack, I stay out of it."

"Wow. That's very adult of you." And so not like how I would handle it. I'd be all up in their business if I lived here.

She turns around and grins over her shoulder. "I've learned a few things since I moved out here."

"I think your mother-in-law is rubbing off on you." I pause before clarifying. "I mean that as a compliment, by the way."

"And that's how I'm taking it too." Andie comes over and sits back down with a grunt. "She's my adopted mom. I love her to pieces."

"What's up with your real mom? You haven't said much about her." I finish off my tea as I wait for her answer. Andie's mom is kind of an asshole, but she came to the wedding, so I have to assume the asshole is trying. I haven't asked Andie about her much over the past year because I've wanted to avoid unhappy issues.

Andie shrugs. "She's in Seattle. I don't see her much. We talk maybe once a month. It's the best I can do with her right now."

"That's better than nothing, I guess."

"Yeah. Maybe."

"Do you have to work today?" I tap my fingers on the table, searching for something to talk about when this conversation is done. This place is way too quiet for comfort.

"Nope. I cleared the decks for the birth. I'm pretty much just checking messages a couple times a day, but otherwise, I'm free. Are you bored yet?"

"Who, me? No, don't be silly. This place is beyond stimulating."

She laughs. "Come on." Standing is a struggle, but she manages. "Let's go into town."

I get up and walk with her to the front entrance. "What's in town?"

"Civilization," she says with a smile. Then she points to the boots she tried to get me to wear and suddenly goes serious. "Put those on and don't give me any crap about it either."

I stare at the hateful things and whine. "But they're soooo ugly!"

"Tough. We can buy you new boots at the store."

That cheers me considerably. "Okay. You've sold me." Leaving my cowgirl awesome boots by the door, I slide my feet into the surprisingly comfortable but still way too fugly clodhoppers Andie provided.

As soon as I step out onto the icy snow, I can appreciate that old adage that looks aren't everything. "Oooo, squishyyy," I say, smiling when the sound of the crunching snow does not also mean I'm on my ass staring at the sky for a change. These puppies are eating up the ground. I feel like a man on the moon, bouncing up almost in slow-mo with every step.

Andie talks while she waddles to the car. Her feet crunch the snow with every short stride. "Trust me, I learned pretty quick around here to adjust my mindset about a few things, footwear being one of them."

I scoff. "Maybe in winter, but not summer."

"Wrong. Summer too. There are snakes out here, so sandals around the ranch are a bad idea."

Snakes? I run to catch up to her and stop only when I'm attached to her side. "Snakes?" I look over my shoulder to make sure none of them are trying to sneak up on me.

Andie tries to slap me away, but I'm not dissuaded from self-preservation that easily. I cling harder.

"Not in the winter, goof. They hibernate in the winter or go dormant or something." She finally succeeds in pushing me off when we reach the driveway area.

"Or try to find somewhere warm to curl up," I squeak, jumping up onto the running board of the truck she's pointing her key ring at. Its lights flicker and the horn beeps once as the locks open.

"Just relax. You don't need to worry about snakes right now. Mountain lions, yes. Snakes, no."

My jaw drops open as I watch her walk around the front of the truck. My voice comes out high and squeaky. "You can't be serious! Mountain lions? Really?"

"Hurry up and get in," she says as she opens her door. "There's a lion over there behind those rocks, and I don't want him to eat my best friend."

My heart convulses in my chest, and I squeal involuntarily as I try to get the door open while also trying not to knock myself off the truck's running board.

"Lion! Lion!" I whisper loudly, without even realizing I'm doing it until the words are out. I fail miserably in my attempts to get in the car, and land in the snow on my knees. There's not enough time for any of it to melt and get me wet, though, because I can move surprisingly fast when the idea of being eaten alive is motivating me.

Slamming the door behind me, I can finally breathe again, although I sound like a frigging freight train. "Wow. That was close." I swallow once to try and calm myself. It feels like my heart is in my throat. "Should we call the cops or the animal control people or something?"

Andie is trying to pull herself up into the truck, but she can't because she's laughing too hard. For a second I feel guilty that I didn't help her pregnant butt in first, what with the lion and everything, but then I get suspicious. She's not acting like she's running for her life. Shouldn't adrenaline be giving her the oomph she needs to get more than a half-inch off the ground?

"Were you just messing with me?" I look out the back window, trying to see that mound she was talking about. There's nothing there but some patches of snow. "There aren't lions here, are there?"

If I had a snowball, I'd throw it right in her face. I don't care if she's pregnant. I'm pretty sure I just lost a year off my life, or a month at least, with that scare.

She's inside and buckled before she answers, her cheeks bright red with happiness as she lets out a long sigh. "No, I swear, there really are mountain lions here. And coyotes and bears and wolves and all kinds of other scary shit. But there wasn't one back there. I was just kidding about that one."

I point my finger in her face. "That pregnancy excuse will only take you so far. I can still smack you. Just remember that."

She swats my hand away and starts the truck. "Just keep your eyes open when you're outside, that's all I ask. I'm sure you'll never see one, but just in case . . ."

I picture myself coming upon a lion wandering around the ranch and make my decision. "Do they sell guns here?"

She snorts. "Is the Pope Catholic?"

"How about winter running shoes?"

"No. You're getting boots."

"Fine." I cross my arms, trying to picture how I'm going to arm myself for outdoor Ian stalking activities while also protecting myself from these man-eating beasts. A gun is probably a good idea. Plus some sort of shoe I can sprint over the snow in.

"What are you scheming up over there?" Andie asks, shooting me glances as we bounce over the rough road that leads to the highway.

"Nothing. No scheming. Just thinking about buying a gun."

She laughs. "You're not buying a gun. Don't be ridiculous."

I say nothing because she's not the boss of me, and I am too going to buy a gun. A girl's got to protect herself, right?

CHAPTER FIVE

What are the chances that driving into town I'll spy a gun store and be able to pull off a sneaky trip inside without Andie knowing?

Very good. Very, *very* good, in fact, because apparently pregnant ladies need to pee a lot, and they like to shop for baby clothes, and in Oregon, baby clothing shops are sometimes located right down the street from gun stores. She totally bought my lies when I said I wanted to browse around the nearby wig shop while she was in the supermarket using their potty. We agreed to meet in the kid clothing place just down the street after.

I walk into the gun store and stop just inside, staring at all the firearms on display. There are what I assume to be hunting rifles all over the walls and a glass case near the register with handguns in it. A few aisles have other hunting-type paraphernalia in them.

I walk over and stare down into the glass case. No one is here that I can see, but voices float over to me from down an aisle near the back of the store. The conversation filters through, and I listen in shamelessly.

"I've got a thirty-ought-six already. What I'd really like to try is the Mathews Creed short bow. Got any of those?"

"Yeah, I got one. The 2014, if you want to give it a shot. No pun intended." The man giggles and I'm reminded of *Dukes of Hazzard* re-runs I watch when I'm in need of a quick redneck sizzle. I do love me some Bo and Luke in those tight jeans of theirs.

Is that Roscoe back there? I stand on tiptoes to try and see over the junk, but it's too far back and too dimly lit to make anyone out.

"Yeah, let's do it."

Footsteps have me turning back to the glass case. I don't want them catching me listening in on their conversation, so I frown at the hunting knives under the glass instead.

"I got it in the back. Just give me a sec and I'll open up the range for ya."

They're almost to me when I hear the customer's voice more clearly. My blood pressure spikes.

"What are you doing here, City? You following me?"

I turn around and act surprised. "What? Oh, hello, Ian. Fancy meeting you here."

"This is getting a little creepy, don't you think?" he asks. "You stalking me now?"

"Please. Get a life." I roll my eyes, playing off the fact that my neck is blotching up as he speaks.

The man who was helping Ian glances at me as he walks by. His belly is very round and well insulated under a thick flannel shirt. "Can I help you, miss?"

"Yes," I say, smiling with all the charm I have in my body, "you can. I'd like to buy a gun."

He smiles back, fully facing me now, a little dazed looking. "Well, aren't you as cute as a bug's ear."

"Henry, you feeling okay?" Ian asks.

Henry's smile disappears in a flash. "Hush up now, Ian, I'm having a conversation with the little lady here."

I smile again, completely ignoring Ian. "Aren't you sweet? Henry is it?"

"Yes, ma'am, I'm Henry. Henry Dawkins at your service. Did you have a particular gun in mind?" He moves behind the counter.

"Hey! I was here first!" Ian protests. "What about that bow?"

Ian is behind me, but I won't give him the satisfaction of turning around. I resist the urge to elbow him in the gut.

Henry frowns at him. "Just keep your pants on, Ian. Ladies first."

I look over my shoulder now that my triumph is complete. "Yeah, Ian. Ladies first."

His lips thin and then his gaze drops to my feet. "Nice boots."

I put my hands on my waist and stick out a hip, twisting left and right a little to show off my footwear. "You like? I call this country chic."

Henry leans over to see what I have and looks hopeful. "You like Sorel boots, ma'am? Cuz I got a new shipment in of all the latest styles, prettier than the ones you got on now."

"Aw, come on, Henry, don't show her your boots! I'll be here all day waiting!"

"So wait," he says, coming around the corner to lead me over to another part of the store.

I follow along with a huge grin, knowing this is making Ian nuts. I'm going to buy some boots just to tick him off.

"See, right here," Henry says, stopping in front of a small display that looks like an afterthought in the corner of the store. "I got purple if you like colors or you could just go with a more leather look."

I check out his selection, surprised to see it doesn't suck. I was going to buy a pair just to piss Ian off, but now I'm going to buy a pair because they're going to look fabulous with my new jeans. "Do you have these in an eight?" I ask, holding up a pair with the cutest fur rim on the top. These babies'll go all the way up to my knees, ensuring my legs will never be wet again in this godforsaken place.

"I sure do. Just have a seat right there and I'll get 'em for ya so you can try 'em on."

I sit down on a little wood stool and take one of Andie's fugly boots off. Ian walks around the corner as I'm pulling up my sock.

"You know, I have things to do here." He crosses his arms over his chest.

"I'm not stopping you." I turn my attention to my cuticles. I can't look at him. He's too cute when he's all fired up, and I need to stay strong.

"Yes, you are. You got Henry all worked up and now he's never going to get my bow while you're in here."

"What do you need a bow for anyway?" I ask, looking up at him. "Going to run around town playing Robin Hood?"

"No. For your information, I'm going to shoot with it."

"Shoot what?" I start to frown as I realize what we're talking about. He'd better not say animals.

"What do you think, city girl?"

"Targets?" I know it's not the right answer the minute it comes out of my mouth. That makes me sad.

"Wrong again." He walks away and leaves me there.

I stand up and follow him, my one booted foot clomping, the other two inches shorter without the clodhopper on. "Shooting animals is murder."

"Not around here it's not," he says, still walking. "Here it's called feeding the family."

"You have a whole ranch full of beef. You don't need to shoot anything."

"I like to shoot things."

I stop following him at that. His sexiness just went right out the window for me. Instead of continuing the conversation, I return to my seat and wait for Henry.

Ian's back in less than a minute. "What's the matter? All upset now because some fuzzy animals are going to die?"

"Go away, Ian. You're not funny." Supremely disappointed, I refuse to look at him. Instead, I busy myself with the laces of my other fugly boot.

"It's a fact of life out here, City, better get used to it. People have to eat."

He makes me so mad, it's impossible to keep ignoring him. "I don't have to get used to killing animals, *Ian*. You can eat what you find in the grocery store."

He laughs. "Do you even listen to yourself when you talk? Where do you think that meat comes from?"

"Not from the wild!" I say a lot louder than I probably should have.

He actually has the nerve to keep laughing. "Oh, yeah. That's right. Because animals raised on farms and ranches are somehow different."

I open my mouth to agree, but then stop. He's twisting around what I mean to say and making it sound stupid. "I'm not going to play this game with you anymore, Ian. I'm done. Go away."

"What're you talking about? What game?" He's not laughing anymore.

I sigh heavily before looking at him, blinking a few times. "Listen . . . I get that we had some chemistry before, and I thought running around with you while I was here might be fun, but you can just cancel that plan because I don't find murderers attractive in the least. You can be on your way now." I wave him off with my fingers. "Go on. Scat. Go shoot a bunny or Bambi or something. I've got nothing left to say to you."

He stands there and sputters for a few seconds before he finds his voice. "You are something else, you know that?"

I lift my chin. "So I've been told."

Henry walks up with a large box in his hands, saving me from having to listen to Ian anymore.

"Here you go, ma'am. Size eight, just like you asked for. They're water resistant too."

"Thank you so much, Henry," I say, oozing charm. Opening the box, I find the boots I liked inside. The first one fits like a glove, and I can't help but smile at how cute it is on me. "Absolutely perfect." I put on the second Sorel. It's gorgeous.

Twisting around and jumping up and down a few times tells me they're just as comfy as they are cute. Double score. Usually I have to sacrifice one for the other, but not today. Baker City doesn't suck quite so much right now, even though there are murderers living here.

"Come on up to the register and I'll show you the guns. You can try out any that you like."

I gather up the fuglies and put them in the box, wearing my new lovelies right past Ian. He's become some sort of statue, just standing there, scowling at me and Henry. I'm ignoring him completely.

"What do you mean I can try them out?" I put the boot box down on the floor by the cash register so I can see the handguns under the glass. "Like, just pull the trigger here in the store?" I look around but don't see any bullet holes in the walls or anything. Maybe he has blanks I can use.

"We have an indoor range," he says, smiling proudly. "It ain't big, but it does the trick."

"Cool! I've never shot a gun before."

His smile slips just a little. "Oh, isn't that . . . nice. And why are you buying the gun, may I ask?"

"Not to shoot anything," I say. I try unsuccessfully to suppress the shudder that moves through me.

"Okaaaay . . ."

He's apparently still waiting for an explanation, so I continue. "There are some lions out where I'm staying, so I just wanted some protection. You know . . . in case a lion tries to eat me or my friend. I'll use the gun to scare it away."

"Lions?"

Ian is behind me now, snickering.

I roll my eyes. "Never mind. Just show me the guns. Which one is good for protection?"

Henry looks down into the case. "From lions? Well . . . I suppose any of these could work if you hit the lion between the eyes. Do you think you're a good shot?" He looks up at me, hopeful, possibly a little stressed too.

I nod enthusiastically. "I'm sure I will be. I'm a hair dresser."

Henry stares at me. Now he has the statue problem that Ian had. Unfortunately, Ian doesn't have it anymore himself. He's standing at my side and pointing to something in the case.

"Show her that one."

"The nine millimeter? Don't you think that's a little much for her?" Henry asks. His happiness is all gone. Now he just looks worried.

I frown at him. "Of course it's not too much for me. I hold blow-dryers and flat irons all day long. Have you ever done a two-hour blow-out? Because I have. Without breaks." I snort. "Trust me, I can handle it."

"Okay," Henry says under his breath, "if you say so."

A couple minutes later, I'm standing at the end of a long hall, holding up the heaviest piece of metal I've ever had in my hand, and staring at a target. FYI, blow-dryers are way lighter than handguns.

Ian is standing next to me, pointing at the paper that has black rings on it, and generally being annoying. "Just point and shoot. Pull the trigger. And be careful of the kick." His voice comes to me muffled due to the fact that I'm wearing ear protection.

I totally feel like an FBI agent right now, with my legs spread and my arms out straight, gripping the gun. I'll bet my butt looks awesome. "The kick?" I look over my shoulder at him. My arms are already getting tired from holding the gun up.

"It's going to kick back with the force of the shot. Just be prepared for it."

"Okay." I squint at the target, holding the gun like I've seen FBI guys do it in the movies. I am so badass.

"That's too high," Ian says.

God, he's so irritating! "How do you know?" I have one eye closed and the other squinting so I can see down the barrel of the gun to the far wall.

"I've been shooting since I was six, and unless your plan is to hit the light fixture over there, I'd lower it a little."

I snort, but follow his advice. Before he gives me any more of it, though, I pull back on the trigger. I'll show him who knows how to shoot a gun.

Even with ear protection, the *BOOM* is amazingly loud. And I know I was supposed to be prepared for the kick, but mentally preparing for something you've never experienced is way more difficult than you'd expect. The sound effects do not help.

The gun goes flying out of my hand and lands on the ground with a giant bang. It sounds like another shot, it's so loud. Good thing I had my ear protection on.

Ian shouts behind me and then starts jumping all over the place.

"What is your problem?" I ask, sliding the earmuffs off. "I just dropped it—it's not a big deal. It's not broken." At least I don't think it is.

"You shot me! You fucking *shot* me!" He's screaming so loud, Henry comes in from the store.

My heart stops beating as I try to figure out if he's just messing with me. Shouldn't there be blood if I shot him?

"What happened?!" Henry yells, looking at the gun on the floor and then Ian.

"Oh, he's being ridiculous," I say, praying I'm right. Did I really shoot him? I don't see any blood. There's nothing but him acting like a human pogo stick. *Boing! Boing! Boing!* He's pretty cranky too. I don't think he's faking that part.

"She shot me!" Ian says, pointing at me. He stops jumping around and stands on two feet, now gesturing to his lower leg. "See?!"

There's a hole in the material near his ankle. When he lifts his pant leg, there's a dark red mark on his skin, but no blood.

"Looks like you got grazed," says Henry. He looks up at me. "How'd you manage that?" Then he looks out at the target. "Nice shot by the way."

I look over my shoulder and see that I've nailed the target almost exactly in the center. I can't help but grin like a fool. "Check me out."

Ian's voice goes up an octave. "You're standing there all proud of yourself after you *shot* me?"

I look back at him, feeling loads better that there's no blood and that I haven't just killed my best friend's brother-in-law. I'm a little dizzy with the relief, actually. But I don't want him to know that.

"Hey, it was an accident, okay? I'm sorry I grazed you with a bullet. Geez." I roll my eyes. "What a baby."

He stands there staring at me with his jaw open. Then he laughs, but he doesn't sound very happy. "You're nuts, you know that? You're dangerous. You need to just stay the hell away from me."

"Oh, believe me, I plan to." I ignore the sting of rejection. He's a Bambi killer anyway. What do I care if he wants me to stay away?

"No, I'm serious. Stay far away. I'm too young to die."

"Oh, please, stop being so dramatic. Besides, I already told you that you're not my type and I have no interest, so just stay out of my way."

"Hoo-hoo-hooo," Henry chuckles, "y'all got some issues. When's the wedding?"

"Shut up, Henry," Ian growls. "You're not funny. And you know what? You can keep your bow too. I gotta go home and ice my leg." Ian storms out of the practice room with an exaggerated limp, and I assume he leaves the store since I can't hear him whining anymore.

"So, you like the gun?" Henry asks, a hint of a smile still on his face.

"Heck yeah, I like the gun. I hit a target *and* Ian MacKenzie with it already. I'd say it's a keeper."

Henry laughs until he's beet red in the face. His belly jiggles around like a bowl of Jell-O. It's both gross and fascinating at the same time. I can't stop staring.

"I'll just go start the paperwork. Feel free to shoot some more rounds if you like. Just watch the kickback next time."

"Yeah, good advice." I pick the gun up off the ground. This time when I point it at the target it doesn't feel as heavy or as foreign.

"That's right, lions," I say mostly to myself as I raise it up and stare down the barrel. "Come at me now."

I empty the clip, scoring more hits in the center ring, and then go back into the store to do the background check stuff. I am so going to be a badass with this baby on my hip and my new purple boots. Ian MacKenzie better just stay out of my way.

CHAPTER SIX

I'm just leaving the store when I find Andie walking down the sidewalk headed right for me. *Busted.*

Dammit. I have to think up a good lie quick. The heavy gun and a box of bullets are in my purse, and if she even touches my bag she'll know they're in there.

"What in the heck are you doing?" she asks.

I'm all innocence. I could totally work for the CIA as a super spy, the way I can hide my emotions. "Who, me? Nothing." I hold out a leg for her to admire. "Just scored me some gorgeous Sorel boots. Check me out." The big box that holds her fugly boots bangs against my hip, and the cheap plastic bag crinkles. I'm surprised it hasn't broken through already, leaving my packaging to get soggy in the slush that covers the sidewalk.

"I got a text from Mack. He said you *shot* his brother." She looks up at the storefront we're standing in front of. "You didn't really shoot him, did you?"

I frown, acting like she's crazy. "Don't look so worried. Of course I didn't shoot him. I merely grazed him. Big difference." Hooking my arm through hers, I lead her down the sidewalk. The smell of greasy fried something is calling to me, and I need to distract her from this line of questioning. I feel guilty enough as it is; I don't need to add causing pregnant lady stress on top of it. "Come on. Someone is spelling my name out in strips of bacon right now."

Andie puts on the brakes, and when she does it with all that weight behind her, it's very effective. I almost go down, even with the awesome tread on my new boots. I struggle to right myself. I really hate ice. It's impossible to look graceful or cool on the stuff.

"No, I'm not going into that diner."

I disengage myself from her to keep from falling again, glad that I've distracted her from the shooting incident, but now curious about her diner-o-phobia. I fully intend to stay upright as I get to the bottom of this issue, so I keep my legs spread kind of far apart just in case the ice has other ideas. It's probably a good thing I don't have my gun on my hip yet; I'd look like I was ready for a shootout at the O.K. Corral.

"Why?" I look over my shoulder at the greasy spoon. "It seems harmless enough."

"That's where Hannah works. She and I are not on good terms." Andie takes a few steps backward. I admire her ability to reverse on ice without even batting an eye. Puffy Girl's got skills.

I don't follow her, feeling safer with just keeping my feet planted on somewhat solid ground. Trying to negotiate the icy sidewalk, avoiding the subject of Ian, and also talking about town gossip all at the same time could be a problem for me right now.

"Hannah?" I ask. "As in, Hannah Banana?"

Andie smiles, but without much humor. "You remember her, I guess."

"Who could forget? Daisy Duke from the wrong side of the tracks—and a bad dye job. I thought you guys had moved on." Hannah had a thing for Mack if I remember correctly. But since Mack never liked her back, I thought it wasn't a big deal.

"Yeah. We moved on by avoiding each other."

My eyes roam the street, and the image of the town map that's burned into my brain pops up. I'm a human Google Earth like that. Once I see a map, it's permanently in there. "That can't be easy in such a small place." I feel bad for my friend. Maybe she feels trapped out there on that ranch. Maybe that's why she works from home most of the time. It can't possibly be because she likes the smell of cow poo.

She takes me by the hand and tries to pull me in the opposite direction, but I resist. The traction on my boots is amazing when there's salt on the ground. I'm totally in the mood to do a high-kick right now just because my new footwear makes me so happy, but I don't. I could accidentally hit my pregnant friend and with the gun incident earlier, it makes me wonder whose side Lady Luck is on today. I'll do that kick later when I'm back at the MacKenzie house. There's plenty of space in my bedroom for a little Rockettes action. I try to do some high kicks every day just to keep my legs looking good.

"Come on, don't be stubborn," she says.

"Stubborn? Me?" I really don't know what she's talking about. I'm all about compromising and giving in to other people's desires. A stylist has to know when to keep her mouth shut and just let the frosted tips and mullets happen. Sometimes a bad experience is a much better teacher than pure advice.

She laughs. "As if that's news to you. Come on." She waves her hand over and over like she's trying to tempt a child.

I stick out my lower lip. She cannot resist me now. "No. I'm hungry." Truth is, I'm really not that hungry. I just want to see that Hannah Banana chick and let her know, without Andie catching me, that she can't keep making Andie feel uncomfortable. This is my BFF's home now. She should feel free to go anywhere she wants. She's going to have a baby soon, and that baby is eventually going to want to eat a pancake.

She tries to use reason on me. "We just ate."

"That was hours ago," I argue. "It's almost lunch time."

Andie looks at her watch. "It's ten in the morning, Candice."

"See? It's past noon on the East Coast and I'm jet-lagging like a bitch. Come on." I take her hand and pull her along. "I heard all about the pancakes they have there. And you know I love bacon."

"Their pancakes suck. It's their waffles that are good. Or so I hear."

"Yeah, that's what I meant. Waffles. I heard that too."

I manage to get her almost to the door before she balks again. "Seriously, this is a bad idea. If you're hungry, we can go to the grocery store and buy a whole package of bacon. You can eat the entire thing yourself."

I grab the door that's covered in credit card stickers and an old rodeo flier, pulling it open and letting out a blast of deliciously warm and bacony air. "Nothing beats the food from a greasy spoon. You know that." I gesture with my bag. "In you go, Tubby Tubblenstein."

Her mouth drops open. "Oh my god, you did not just call me that."

Oops. Did I say that out loud? Quick! Think of something!

"No, it was Ian who did. I'm just repeating his words." That's a total lie, but I can just imagine how much crap she's going to give him for it and then how outraged he'll be when he finds himself falsely accused. I start giggling just seeing it in my head. It's really not a bad nickname, come to think of it. She is pretty tubby. I love it when my brain just spontaneously takes over like that. It always surprises me.

"He's going to pay for that," she says, her expression going dark.

"Yeah. He should." I follow her inside, feeling like I just smoked a drug or something with how much joy I'm experiencing. Ian's going to get yelled at, I have purple boots on, and there's a delicious waffle about to get in my belly. So *this* is what happiness feels like.

The air is thick with grease, steam, and the smell of people who should have probably used a little extra soap before stepping outside the house. I flap my arms a few times, trying to get my perfume to fog up around my face. My bag flops around, banging into me and the door.

"What are you doing?" Andie whispers loudly. "Trying to call attention to yourself on purpose or what? I told you, Hannah and I . . ."

My perfume kicks in, and all that's left of the strangers around me is the slight scent of cumin. *Do they serve tacos here?*

"Well, well, well, look who decided to drop by and grace us with her presence," says an exaggerated Southern fried voice from behind the counter.

How is it that a girl who's spent her entire life in the top-left corner of the country is talking like a girl from the bottom-right or the bottom-middle part, like Texas or whatever? I don't know. I might be able to figure it out with more time, since linguistics is a special interest of mine, but right now I'm too distracted to try.

I can't focus on anything but the horrible bleach job that's been done to the poor girl's hair. Her cuticles are totally fried, making her hair look like a stack of straw on her head, and the color is what those of us in the industry call chicken-fat yellow. Sooo not attractive.

"Hello, Hannah," Andie says, all demure, like she isn't pissed that this girl just said something that sounded rude to me. "How have you been?"

We move farther into the room. Andie's headed to a booth in the corner.

Hannah comes from behind the counter to follow me. I'm tempted to walk backward so she can't get a butter knife between my shoulder blades, but I don't. Why? Because Hannah Banana doesn't scare me. She's named after a fruit, for chrissakes. How can she possibly be dangerous? If her nickname was Hannah the Horrible or Hannahbelle Lecter, maybe. But banana? Nah. No way. Besides. I've got a gun and a buttload of bullets. Oh yeah. They call me The Duke. No . . . The Duchess.

I turn around as I stop at a booth and catch Hannah all smiles. She does have nice teeth, I'll give her that. It doesn't hide the bad hair, but it does distract my attention from it a little.

"Oh, I been good," she says. "Real good. Been spending some time with Ian, you know."

My mouth pinches up without me even realizing it. I quickly smooth it out when I catch Andie staring at me. She's next to the booth, ready to sit.

I take the spot across from her, a Formica table rimmed in aluminum between us. The vinyl-covered seat collapses under my butt with a wheeze of protesting air, but not at all under my thighs at the edge. I feel a lack of circulation coming on already. I better not get a leg vein over this or I'm going to be pissed. No waffle is worth a leg vein.

"Really? With Ian? That's nice." Andie squats down to sit, but then stops when her belly keeps her from fitting into the booth. She's got about four inches of too much baby to ever think of making it in.

"Oh, lordy, you are getting huge, girl. I mean, like, *hugely* huge." Hannah looks back over at the kitchen area. "Joe, you seen this?"

The man cooking doesn't even look up, but that doesn't stop Hannah. "Maybe you should move to a table. You could fit in a regular chair, probably. I think. You could probably sit sideways or something. My god, you must have terrible stretch marks."

My eyes widen. Them's fightin' words if I've ever heard any. My trigger finger twitches a little.

Andie's nostrils flare, but she keeps her cool. "No, I'll be fine." She grunts as she pushes against the edge of the table. "Just need to move the table a bit."

"It's stuck there, and you ain't gonna be able to move it." Hannah steps back.

"Sure we can. Just needs a little shove." Andie grunts once more as she tries again to make more space.

I can see being able to fit into this stupid booth is important to her. Sadness overwhelms me as I see my best friend feeling self-conscious about her weight and this dingbat banana waitress lording her thinness over her. I feel terrible that I called Andie Tubby Tubblenstein.

The emotion fills me with super-human powers of strength and determination. I literally can feel it surging through my veins. Gripping the table on my side, I pull with all my might.

The table lets out a mighty crack, a screech, and something like a dog bark before separating from the floor. It's nearly diagonal between the two benches now and I'm almost ready to sweat.

I look down at the floor to check out the damage, assuming from the noise we made that screws will be sticking up out of the linoleum. Instead, I find a pile of dark gray goop that used to hold the table's one leg in place, and I'm pretty sure it's not glue. There's fuzz sticking up out of it too. *Ew.*

Andie sits down with a huff of air, her face pink and coated with a sheen of sweat. "See? No big deal."

I grin as big as I know how. "Yep. No big deal at all." Looking up at Hannah, I lift one of my eyebrows for emphasis. "You might want to get something to clean up that disgusting goop on the floor, though. I think it's been there for a while. Don't you guys ever clean around here?"

Hannah gives me a bitchy look. "Of course we clean the floor. We clean it every day." Her hands go to her hips.

I look down at the gray spot on the floor and shrug as I give Andie my famous bug-eye. "If you say so." And then I giggle.

Andie smiles, and the two of us stare at each other while we send private brain-wave messages back and forth. She's loving me, grateful that I got the Banana girl off her back and also very happy that she can still fit in a booth. I'm happy that I could help make that happen for her. Maybe she'll forget for the time being that I shot her husband's brother.

"Do you want anything, or did you just come in here to do a health inspection?" Hannah taps her foot on the floor.

I look up at her and smile sweetly. I can afford to be magnanimous because I won this round. "I'll have one of those waffles I've heard so much about and a cup of coffee." I shift my gaze. "Andie?"

She's back to being serious. "I'll have some herbal tea."

"Sorry, we're all out." Hannah gives Andie a tight smile. She doesn't look very sad about it.

"Okay, how about some decaf?"

"Nope. We're all out of that too."

Glancing over to the spot behind the counter where the coffee machine rests, I can see very clearly that there are two pots there and one of them has an orange top. *Hannah, you lying b-word.*

I stand without thinking about my next move. Once again, my amazing brain takes over and saves the day. "Hey, Joe!" I wave like a maniac in his direction.

Along with the cook, everyone sitting at the counter turns to look at me. Joe the cook is clearly confused. He's probably not used to strangers calling him out from the middle of the restaurant, but desperate times call for desperate measures. Pregnant ladies should not be denied their herbal tea. I mean, what if Andie's uterus starts to relax too much? We can't have that happening around bacon and waffles. These people would be scarred for life. I know I would be.

"You got any herbal tea in the back?" I yell.

He shrugs and then says, "Yeah. Guess so."

I sit down and scrunch my nose up all cute at Hannah. "Guess you got some in the back you forgot about."

Hannah spins around and leaves us without another word. Not one single strand of her brittle hair-nest moves. I almost feel sorry for her. Almost.

Andie rests her chin on her hand with a sigh. "Just what exactly are you trying to accomplish here?"

I take the paper napkin from under the silverware and use it to buff the water spots off my knife. "Just trying the waffles."

She folds her arms on the table in front of her. "You know I have to live here, right?"

"Of course I do." I line my silverware up and put my messy napkin in my lap, smoothing it as best I can. I can't meet her eyes right now. She'll be able to detect the fact that her uterus makes me nervous.

"If you could *not* make enemies of half the people in town, that would be awesome."

I look up and stare at her because I'm shocked she feels this way about me. Now I've forgotten all about her silly womb. After all I've done for her so far, this is what she has to say to me? I'm starting to worry about Mack's influence. Maybe it's not as good as I thought.

"Enemies?" I say. "What are you talking about?" Maybe pregnancy makes her talk nonsense. I know having too many beers does.

She shifts her gaze over to Hannah, who's busy banging cups around behind the counter. Then she looks back at me and lifts a brow.

"Who? *Her?* Banana girl? Pffft. She's just a silly old kitty peeing on walls. She just needs to know that you expect her to use the litter box, that's all."

Andie frowns. "I don't follow."

I sigh. It's a pain always having to explain things to her. She never gets my metaphors. We function on a totally different level sometimes. "You know how sometimes you get a cat, and instead of using the litter box, it pees on the wall or the side of the bed or in your laundry basket?"

"Uh . . . no."

"Okay, well it happens. It's the cat trying to tell you that it's not happy. You're not doing things the way it wants. And cat pee stinks." I wait a moment for my wisdom to sink in.

"Yes, I guess it does."

"So you just have to whack that kitty." I mime smacking a cat on the buns. "Pop! Show it who's boss."

"Whack the kitty?"

"Yes. Whack the kitty." I nod. She's finally getting it. *Phew.* I thought this was going to be one of those times I have to walk her through it step by step. Those times give me headaches.

"Do you whack kitties?" she asks.

"Of course not. What do you take me for, an animal abuser?" I instantly picture Ian with a bow in his hand. "Oh, and by the way . . . speaking of animal abusers, did you know your brother-in-law kills animals?" I nod but don't wait for her response. "Yeah. It's true. I thought he was cute before, but once I found *that* out, I decided he's not cute at all. He's ugly. Maybe not on the outside, but on the inside, yes. I'm glad he's bouncing The Banana. They deserve each other."

Andie sighs like she just let out all her stress in one breath and smiles. "You have no idea how much I've missed you."

I smile back. "Of course I realize it. You're stuck in this one-horse town surrounded by bumpkins. How could you not miss my metropolitan charm and intellectual banter?"

She starts laughing so hard, she chokes. I have to get up out of my seat to pat her on the back. It makes me wonder how far the hospital is from here, just in case.

"Here. Maybe this will help," Hannah says from behind me. She's holding a cup in a saucer. She doesn't sound very concerned.

"What is it?" I ask, taking it from her.

"Tea, duh," she says, making a stupid face. "Herbal. Just like she ordered." She leaves without waiting for me to respond, which is probably good. Andie did ask me not to make her an enemy.

"Here," I set the tea down in front of my friend, "take a sip before you turn your lungs inside out."

She sips and then speaks with a croaky-frog voice. "Is that even possible?"

I sit back down. "Of course it is. What goes down must come up, right? That's just simple physics."

"Down? Lungs go down?"

"How else do you think they got where they are?" I shake my head. She really has no medical knowledge at all. I suppose it doesn't matter since she's not working in a hospital, but you'd think she'd at least wonder about this stuff. I know I do.

I explain, just in case she really does want to know. "Yeah. When you're a zygote, everything's on the outside. Then as you turn into an embryo, it all goes inside. Boys get testicles, we got ovaries, but it's all basically the same equipment. Lungs in, lungs out. Physics."

She frowns over her cup as she sips her tea. Then she shakes her head and swallows. "You seriously scare me sometimes."

"I know, right? How do I keep all this knowledge in one brain? It's just one of those medical miracles. I scare *myself* sometimes. I'm going to donate my brain to science. Maybe they can unlock some secrets of the universe from in there."

"More like unlocking Pandora's box," Andie mutters.

"Do you use that music app? I do. It's pretty good."

She shakes her head but stops herself from responding when Hannah shows up again, food in hand and a white mug of coffee for me.

The plate with a single waffle and a blob of whipped butter on top distracts me from my next thought. Hannah leaves without a word, which is fine by me.

"So what were you doing in the gun store?" Andie asks.

I busy myself with drowning my food in syrup. The smell of pecans and maple has me going light-headed with pleasure. I'm a sucker for breakfast foods I shouldn't eat.

I answer without looking at her. I have to act casual, like I was just hanging out, shopping for awful flannel shirts or whatever. "Just buying some boots. See?" I hold out my leg so she can re-admire my footwear.

"You weren't buying a gun were you?"

I stab a chunk of waffle. "I shot one in there. They have an indoor range. Have you ever seen it?" I shove the big bite into my mouth, hoping I've adequately distracted her from the fact that I haven't actually answered her question. I don't want to lie, but I also don't want her trying to talk me into returning my nine millimeter. I've already named her Millie, and I like the weight of her in my bag. I could probably take someone out just hitting them with it instead of actually pulling the trigger.

"No. But why *you* saw it is my question."

"Welp . . ."—I wipe off my mouth and cut my next bite—"I was in there, looking at boots, and Ian was there too, talking about a bow and acting like he's all Robin Hood and stuff . . . and the guy asked me if I wanted to shoot a gun in his range. So I did." I shrug and eat some more waffle.

"And you shot Ian?"

I wave my fork around, talking with my mouth full. "No, he pretty much shot himself."

"Did he have a gun?"

I swallow so I don't choke. My waffle is kind of dry and maybe a little too salty. "No, I did. But he was standing behind me giving me a bunch of crap, and he'd just revealed the evil truth of him being a killer, so one thing led to another, and then he got grazed."

"I'm completely lost. How did he shoot himself?"

"Karma."

"Karma?"

"Yes. Karma. All those animals he shot? Karma loves that shit. My gun dropped, a bullet came flying out, and it hit him in the ankle. So actually it was Karma who shot him. Karma's a bitch. He should know better than to mess with her."

She leans in close and talks in a loud whisper. "You actually shot him?! I thought it was a joke!"

I put my fork down and stare at her. Does pregnancy make people hard of hearing? I'm going to have to google that. "No. He got *grazed* by a bullet that *Karma* aimed at him. I didn't even have my hand on the gun, so how could *I* have shot him?" I shake my head, disappointed in my friend. She's supposed to be a lawyer. This should be easy for her.

I pick up my fork and push another bite onto its tines. "He's fine. He said he was going home to ice it. It's just a bruise. There wasn't even a drop of blood. He was acting like a big baby if you ask me."

She takes a sip of her tea. "Life is never boring with you around, Candice, that's for sure."

I smile awkwardly, my mouth full of waffle. "You know it."

She laughs.

"Where are we going next?" I ask, taking a sip of my coffee. It's cold. I glance over at Hannah and catch her smiling. *That bitch.* She probably put ice in it. I look down into the cup to see if there's anything else floating around in there. There'd better not be a loogie at the bottom.

I miss the expression on Andie's face, but not the tone of her voice. "Maybe the hospital?"

"Huh?" I look at her and see her skin going pale. Her eyebrows are coming down from her hairline.

"The hospital?" I ask, fearing her answer.

"Yeeeaaah . . ."

She doesn't seem very sure. Now I'm suspicious. "Why?"

"Because either I just seriously peed my pants or there's amniotic fluid on the floor by our feet."

And just like that, I lose my appetite for waffles and bacon.

CHAPTER SEVEN

I drop my fork and place both hands flat on the table, staring deeply into Andie's eyes. "Do *not* panic."

"I'm not panicked." She gives me a worried smile.

This is no time for joking, so I don't smile back. "I'm serious. If your uterus falls out, I don't know if I'm prepared to deal with that. I've never googled that before."

She shakes her head. "My uterus isn't going anywhere. But I do need you to go get the truck."

I look over at Hannah and lift my arm, snapping my fingers rapidly. "Yo, Hannah!" I look under the table to see what we're dealing with. There's a very small puddle of what looks like pee there. "Bring a mop over, would ya?"

Hannah looks at me like I've suddenly sprouted two heads, so I go back to ignoring her in favor of Andie. "Can you get up?"

"I don't know. I think so. But I'll need your help."

Getting out of the booth, I try to remember what that guy in the gun store said about the waterproofing on my new boots. When they say "waterproof," do they mean uterus water too? Guess I'm about to find out.

I lean down so Andie can use my shoulder to stand. She pulls a bunch of my hair out by accident.

"Holy mother of all . . . watch the hair, Tubby!"

"Don't call me that!" she says, half out of breath. Finally standing, she moans and holds the bottom of her stomach.

I look down just in time to see more water pouring down her leg. "Oh . . . my god . . . that's nasty."

"Candice, shut up. Just get the truck."

"Okay, I will. Come on. You walk over to the door, and I'll run across the street."

"What's going on over here?" Hannah says, sounding annoyed.

"Baby coming," I say, waving her out of the way. "Clean up on aisle three."

She looks at the floor and than at Andie. "Oh my god, that's . . . should I call an ambulance?"

I consider it, but then shake my head. "Nope. I'll get her there faster. It's not far."

"How do you know?" Andie grunts out, shuffling as she holds her belly.

"I google-mapped it," I say, almost to the door. It's then that I realize I don't have the key to the truck. I turn around and hold out my hands, ready to catch. "Throw me the car key."

Andie fishes around in her bag and tosses me a hunk of metal so big it bruises my hand when I grab it.

"What the hell?" I look at no less than twenty keys dangling from a conglomeration of four key chains.

"It's the blue one," she says, annoyed for some reason. "The blue one!"

"Okay, already, lighten up." I'm saying that to both of us. I'm about to blow a gasket over this whole situation. Why'd she have to go into labor before I finished my waffle? As I throw the door open, I yell, "Call your husband! Tell him to meet us there!"

I run like the wind to the truck. The ice only kicks my butt twice, but I jump up and keep on going like nothing happened because I'm tough like that when in a crisis. I slide to a stop two blocks down from the diner at the tailgate of the truck, out of breath.

Dammit! This cannot be happening! The mighty metal beast is jammed between two other vehicles, both of them so beat up they look like they've been used in derbies. It's so cramped in there, I can't get any of the damn doors open enough to get inside.

No one's standing around to move their stupid cars, so I do the only thing left to me. I climb up into the bed of the truck and push on the sliding glass window that's behind the back seat. Thank goodness it's not locked.

I'm glad I stopped eating bread two weeks before I came to Baker City. Otherwise, I never would have fit through that tiny hole. I'm halfway in when I realize that my super-cute cowgirl belt buckle is hung up on the frame of the car. I kick my legs and grab the front seat to pull myself in, straining with everything I have. It's possible I look like I'm trying to swim through the truck.

"What in the Sam Hill are you doing now?" says a voice from somewhere outside.

I look up and see Ian staring at me through the front windshield. He's standing on the sidewalk in front of a store that sells everything for ninety-nine cents.

"Shut up and help me!" My voice comes out sounding a little unbalanced. I feel a lot unbalanced right now, so I guess that's appropriate.

"How about a please?" he says, smirking.

"How about your sister-in-law is in labor and her uterus is about to fall out? How about that?!"

His face goes blank. "You serious?"

"Get me in this damn truck, you dumbass! I need to get her to the hospital!"

He disappears for a couple seconds, and then I feel his arms on my waist. Instead of pushing me in, though, he's pulling on me. I kick like mad to get him off me. If I could slap him, I would, but my arms are inside the cab. "Get off, you idiot! I need to get in, not out!"

"Fine!" he yells, jamming his hands into my butt and pushing with all his might.

My buckle snaps and my pelvis and upper thighs scrape hard against the window frame, but at least I'm inside. I fold in half so the rest of me can get in, ending up on the floor of the tiny back seat. My back cracks in protest. I am going to be so sore tomorrow. He's going to pay for that.

Ian's head is sticking in through the window, and he's looking down at me. "You know they have these things called doors on trucks. Way easier to use than the windows."

I scramble over the back seat and take the driver's spot. The keys fall to the floor as Ian chuckles at his own joke, the big dummy. I don't bother answering, my brain focused on only one thing: *Get Andie to the hospital.*

The engine turns over with a roar, and I throw the truck into reverse. The gas pedal is much more powerful than I was expecting. One push and I'm halfway out of the space.

I hear a big boom and a yell. Ian's legs fly up into view in the mirror.

"Hey! What the hell!" He shouts. A second later, his head is barely visible in the rearview mirror as he sits up from his fall.

Ignoring his issues, I reverse the rest of the way out and then slam that puppy into drive.

Bet you didn't know a giant truck can peel out; I know I didn't. But this one sure does. Must be those studded tires it has or something. One second I'm diagonal in front of a strip mall, and the next I'm zooming down the street, headed away from the diner. *Shit.*

"What the hell are you doing?!" Ian yells. Glancing up in the mirror, I realize he's still in the bed of the truck. He's holding onto something above the cab and standing spread-legged like he's surfing or something. Oh well, not my problem.

I wait for the traffic to clear and flip a big old U-ey right in the middle of the road. The back tires slide, but we end up in perfect position to pull up outside the diner. I see faces lined up at the glass as I slide to a stop.

"All aboard!" I yell, lowering the window on the passenger side.

Ian jumps to the ground and puts his face in the open window. "Are you completely insane?! You almost killed me . . . *again*!"

I wave him off, focused on the front door of the diner. "Quit crying and get Andie. I don't have time for your damage right now."

The door opens and the bells on the handle jangle, catching Ian's attention. He turns around and freezes.

"Andie? You okay?" he asks.

"I need to get to the hospital." An older man is holding her by the elbow, walking her out carefully. "Hannah called Mack for me. He's going to get there as soon as he can. But I need to go now. I can't wait."

I cringe as more liquid runs down her leg. Her boots have got to be half full of that stuff by now. Talk about squishy.

Ian jumps into action. "Easy, easy . . . easy now." He practically carries her to the car and then picks her up.

"No! Wait! I don't want to stain the seat!" she cries.

"Oh, for crying out loud . . ." Ian puts her down and we all look at each other.

"Fine." I whip off my leather jacket and lay it on the seat. "You owe me a jacket." I stare out the front window, trying to get my heart rate under a thousand beats per minute. This is nuts. I just sacrificed my five-hundred-dollar leather bomber, and my best friend is about to drop a baby on the floorboards. I'm pretty sure I didn't sign up for this. Or maybe I did, but I didn't mean to.

"Thanks," she says, kind of breathlessly.

Ian picks her up and places her gently on the seat as I glance over at them again.

"Meet you there?" he says.

Andie nods.

As soon as her door shuts, I take off.

"Where are you going?!" I hear someone yelling.

Stupid Ian. He's standing out in the middle of the road, waving his arms behind us. I can see him in the rearview mirror acting like a fool.

"Do you know the right way?" Andie asks. She's leaning her elbow heavily on the armrest, trying to get comfortable. I don't think it's working.

"Of course I know the right way. Map's up here," I say, tapping my temple.

CHAPTER EIGHT

For some reason, we're the last ones to show up at the emergency room door. Ian, Mack, and Mack's mother are all standing outside in the slowly falling snowflakes that started ten minutes into my drive. It must have been the traffic that made it take so long. I still don't know the shortcuts around town. Thank goodness, the baby didn't decide to come out while we were driving around. My jacket has already seen enough punishment.

"Oh, thank God," Andie says. And then she moans and bends over her stomach, holding it with both arms.

The first one to her door is Mack. He's usually a pretty cool guy, but today I can tell he is stressed to the max. His face is all lines and hard angles. He pulls the door open and lifts his wife out like a baby. It makes my heart go all mushy just watching it. He's super strong. She's almost the size of a small elephant with her coat on.

"I can walk," Andie says, holding an arm out to the side like a canoe outrigger. She's struggling to get down.

"The hell you can," he responds.

A nurse arrives with a wheelchair, and he puts her in it like she's made of glass.

"You can't park here," says Ian, his face in my window. "You want me to bring it around?"

I chew my lip. Part of me hates letting him do anything nice for me, but the desire to see my friend into her room wins out. "Yes. Do that." I make sure the truck is in "Park" before I get out.

After I've opened the door, Ian stands in the way, holding out his hand to help me down. We both look at it at the same time. He seems bewildered that he's even offered, and I feel kind of shocked myself. Before I can take him up on his manners, though, he pulls his hand back and stuffs it in his back pocket.

"Wouldn't want your women's lib card to get pulled or anything," he says.

I grab my purse and make sure to land on his toe when I slide down out of the high seat and onto the ground.

His eyes go wide and he grunts.

"Oh, I'm sorry. I landed on your ugly poo-covered cowboy boot. Did that hurt?"

"How much do you weigh, anyway?" He tries to back up far enough to escape my revenge, but the door stops him.

I have no idea what makes me do it, but I tweak his nipple right through his jacket, giving it a good twist. "Don't call me fat, you uncivilized bumpkin."

His jaw drops open, and he barks out a single laugh before rubbing his chest with the palm of his hand. "Owww . . . son of a . . . you just gave me a purple nurple." It's clear he can't quite wrap his head around that one.

Good. I find I like keeping him on his toes.

"Where I come from they're called titty twisters. Remember that next time you feel like commenting on my weight."

I walk around the front of the truck with my head held high, making my way into the hospital. I'm at the entrance to the emergency room when his voice comes sailing out of the passenger window. "Revenge is a real bitch, you know that?!"

I don't even look back. "Bring it, Country!"

"Oh, you know I will, City!"

My whole body heats up just imagining what he could possibly mean by that.

CHAPTER NINE

I have to wait in a little side room with Maeve for about thirty minutes before the nurses let us in to see Andie. She's hooked up to an IV drip and some machine that's making a lot of noise, a rhythmic *whup, whup, whup.*

I go over to her free side, and Maeve stands next to Mack, who's on the other side of Andie's bed. He holds her hand, and Maeve rests her fingers lightly on Andie's leg.

"How are you feeling?" I ask.

"Better, now that I'm here." Andie's hair is spread out over the pillow in a tangle, and she already looks tired.

I fish around in my purse until I find my brush. Moving to the head of her bed, I drop my bag to the ground and start fixing the mess. There will be plenty of pictures taken soon, and I don't want her hating me for not taking care of this problem beforehand.

"How many centimeters are you dilated?" Maeve asks.

"Three? Four? We're not sure yet." Andie sighs and stares at the door.

"Was that your water or pee?" I ask, trying to distract her from whatever is bothering her. "In the diner, I mean."

Mack smiles when Andie rolls her eyes and answers. "It was my water, Candice. Geez."

"Hey, how would I know?" I shrug as I brush out a knot in her hair. It's clear I'm going to have to give her a cut while I'm here. Whoever did her layers needs some serious retraining. "I've never seen someone's uterus blow before."

"Blow?" Andie closes her eyes. "God, that's disgusting."

"Tell me about it. I'll never eat waffles again." I finish with her hair and put my brush back in my bag. "Can I get you anything? Coffee? Tea? Massage by a man wearing a thong, maybe?"

"Some tea would be nice." Andie smiles up at me.

"No tea," says a mean-looking nurse who busts into the room without so much as a knock. "No liquids, no food."

"Why?" I ask, offended for my friend. It's on the tip of my tongue to call this woman Nurse Ratched.

"Just in case she needs a C section. She can have a few ice chips when we get closer to the actual birth, but for right now, the IV will take care of her liquids."

I frown. *Ice chips?* This seems like a special kind of torture. We are on the border of the Arctic Circle, after all.

"Go ahead and get yourself a coffee," Andie says.

When I see the nurse snapping on some gloves and lubing them up as she moves over to Andie's crotch, I nod, quickly forgetting the whole drink issue. We'll let the IV take care of her liquids or whatever. "Yeah. Good idea. I'll go get a coffee."

On my way out, I look at Mack and Maeve while carefully avoiding looking at Andie's crotchal area. "Anyone else?"

They both shake their heads, all their attention focused on Andie. I'm so busy watching them, I don't notice Ian standing in the doorway until I bump into him just outside the room.

"What are you doing?" I ask, annoyed, trying to right myself without looking like a complete fool. Tossing my hair over my shoulder, I pretend to be searching for something inside my purse. I hate that I can't look him in the eye right now, but there's no sense in denying it.

"You're the one who attacked me."

I raise an eyebrow and readjust the strap of my purse over my shoulder, abandoning my search and my reticence over looking him in the eye. "Attacked? Come on now, don't you think that's a bit of an exaggeration?"

"Lemme see . . ." He rolls his eyeballs to the ceiling as he thinks, counting off on his fingers as he goes. "First, you shoot me. With a bullet. Then you toss me around in the back of a truck while you drive like a maniac through town. After that you give me a purple nurple . . ."

"Titty twister," I correct.

"Whatever . . . and then you stomp on my toe." He looks at me and stops with the annoying counting. "And now, here you are body-slamming me in the hospital."

I shake my head in mock disappointment. "So sad."

"What's so sad?"

He's standing way too close for comfort, but I'm not going to be the one to back away and give ground. Let *him* do it.

"So sad that you're so precious. I thought country boys were tougher than that."

"Precious? I'm not precious."

I stick my bottom lip out really far. "Awww, poor baby . . . how's your nipple? Do you need some ice for it? Maybe a bandage? Good thing you're in the hospital. Maybe you should go to the ER."

"My mom's gonna kill me," he says, out of the blue.

I frown, confused. "Why?"

"Because-a this."

He reaches up and actually tweaks my nipple. Then he smiles. Big. Real big. I can see his wisdom teeth he's so damn happy.

I can't move. I'm frozen in shock. "You . . . you just . . ."

"That's right, City. I just got you back. Tit for tat." He starts laughing. "Literally."

My eyes narrow as I consider my options. "You are so going down right now."

He sees the look in my eye and stops laughing immediately. "Hey now . . . this is a hospital, young lady. You need to behave yourself in here." He's waffling between laughing and being scared.

I take a step toward him, and he moves back two paces. His hands go up in a defensive gesture. "I'm serious." He points at me. "Act like a lady."

That was the wrong thing to say. "When you treat me like one, I'll act like one." I leap into action, my boots giving a special spring to my step.

He tries to run backward but gives up and spins around, tripping over himself to get away. He pushes off the wall to keep from falling.

We wind through hallways with me in pursuit, only slowing when someone is nearby. I chase him all the way to the cafeteria, where he finally slows to a walk. I pull up next to him and pinch his butt hard. He pushes the door open and we both walk through at the same time.

"Youch!" He scoots his pelvis forward, trying to move his buns out of my reach. "Easy now, City," he says in a low tone meant only for me. "I have witnesses." He straightens up and tries to look cool.

"Better watch your back," I say just as quietly. I separate from him and go over to the coffee area. I'm totally out of breath, but I try to hide it by breathing out of my nose. My nostrils are flaring, trying to get enough oxygen into my system. I can't tell if my heart is racing from the running or the chemistry that's flared up between us again. He actually touched my nipple! How dare he! I'm still tingling from it and not because it hurt. It definitely didn't hurt.

I feel something warm on my back and leg. It's Ian standing way too close. His breath washes over my neck. "Better watch *your* back," he says.

I laugh, too cool for school. "Wow, that was original." Taking a coffee cup, I reach up with my other hand to press down on the button that will fill me up with caffeine. I'm not sure I need it at this point, but at least it serves as a distraction.

"Not original enough for ya? Okay, how about this one . . . better watch your *neck*."

I frown as I put some sugar into my cup and stir it. "What . . . are you a vampire now?"

I sense his intention before I feel it. "Maybe." His mouth is suddenly on my skin, the spot between my shoulder and my neck. His lips have clamped on and he's sucking.

I spin around, completely taken by surprise. We end up face to face when his mouth is forced to detach from me.

"What are you *doing*?" Trying to act cool is taking every bit of talent I have in that area. My hand holding the coffee cup is trembling.

He smiles, all lazy-like and smooth. I hate that he's way cooler than I am. "Just getting a little revenge."

My neck keeps tingling. It's like his lips are still there. "You better not have left a hickey."

He glances at my skin and smiles. "Or else what?"

I debate in my mind what I should say next. That I'll give him a worse one? No. He's a Bambi killer. I don't want to trade hickeys with him. Even though it felt really nice and I love the way he smells.

"Or else you'll just have to wait and see." I go back to administering to my coffee. "Keep your murderous lips off me in the meantime."

"Murderous lips? Wow, you must have really liked that hickey I just gave you to say it about killed you."

I roll my eyes. "You wish." I feel like I'm back in high school. What is it about this man that makes me feel and act sixteen again? I haven't run indoors like that since I was late for Mr. Wilkie's chemistry final.

He follows me over to a table and takes the seat across from me.

I take a sip of my hot drink and try to ignore him, looking everywhere but in his direction, but he keeps staring at me. He's leaning back in the chair like he doesn't have a care in the world. My prayer that the thing will slide out from under him goes unanswered.

I sigh heavily and give up on avoiding him. "Why are you here?"

He looks around. "In the hospital? Same as you, I s'pose. Waiting for a baby to come out."

"No, I mean why are you here with me in the cafeteria?"

He smiles again, his gaze dropping to my chest for a second before going back up to my face. "I'm not here *with* you. I'm just in the same place as you are. It's a coincidence."

"Whatever." I focus on my drink and anything else in the room but him. The walls in here are the ugliest color of green I've ever seen. Psychologically, it has to be bad for people. You can make a person go insane just by painting his walls a certain color. Hospitals should be more aware of that stuff. They should hire me as a color consultant.

Without warning, he slides his chair around so he's next to me, effectively interrupting my thoughts and my distress over the lack of interior design in this place. His arm goes up over the back of my seat and he leans in.

"Well, that was a big change of heart." I look at him like he's nuts, which he is.

He's not smiling anymore, and he looks worried. Maybe it's that green paint having its effect on him, but it came on kind of suddenly.

He leans in closer, and I struggle a little to get some distance between us. The heat from his body is soaking into me. "What are you . . . ?"

"Shhhhh!" he whispers, clamping onto my shoulders even more. "Just go with it."

"Go with wh . . . ?" Before I can get the last part of my sentence out, he presses his lips onto mine.

At first I'm so shocked, I freeze up. Then I feel how soft the skin of his lips is and how good his face smells, and I relax. I have no idea what we're doing, but I'm not going to be the one to stop it.

As he senses me give in, he presses into me more firmly, his lips moving to make the kiss more intimate. We're both enjoying it now, believe it or not. I'm loving the way his mouth moves on mine. This is the kind of heat I usually save for the bedroom, but right now I could care less who's watching. Lightning bolts of desire are ripping through me. I lean in closer, wanting to press my breasts against him, anything to ease the ache. When the tip of his tongue comes out to touch mine, I gasp with surprise. It's the happy kind.

"Hello, Ian. What're you doing here?"

I hate it when he pulls away to answer the question of the girl standing in front of us. Total cold shower, but I think I like this green paint after all.

He clears his throat and swipes at his mouth before he answers. "Oh, hey. Uh, Andie's in labor. Just waiting for the baby to come." He tightens his arm around my back and pulls me closer. I'm pretty sure we couldn't look more awkward. I'm as stiff as a board, realizing that his sudden passion had a different motivation behind it than the paint or my cleavage.

The girl's eyes shift over to rest on me. "And who's this?"

Ian leans in and kisses me loudly on the cheek. "This is Candice. She's my new girl."

My heart stops beating for a few seconds, and my jaw drops open. The only thing that revives me is Ian shaking me several times with his arm. "Babe, this is Ginny. Ginny, this is Candice."

Ginny holds out her hand over the table. "Nice to meet you. Are you from around here?"

I shake her cool, dry hand, hoping she doesn't notice mine is clammy. I open my mouth to answer, but the only problem is, my voice doesn't really seem to want to work.

"Uhhh . . ."

"She's from back East," Ian supplies. "Big-city girl. You know how I love the big city."

"Back East, huh? How did you two meet, then?" Ginny cocks her hip, giving every indication that she plans to get to the bottom of this situation before she leaves.

She doesn't seem angry, just curious, which is weird because I'm pretty sure this is the chick Ian was supposed to marry. How many Ginnys can there be in one small town?

Poo. I guess that's why I'm the new girlfriend. Poor guy can't stand the fact that she might find him still single after all this time. I don't know what I was thinking letting my head go all fuzzy where he's concerned. Of course he doesn't want to jump me in the hospital cafeteria. That green paint is truly hideous.

The gears in my head start cranking away. Now that I know I'm not about to get all hot and heavy with Ian, I have two options here. I could totally call him out and humiliate him in front of this girl . . . whoa, talk about revenge. Or I could go along with it and then have him owe me a big, fat favor after.

I can't help the Cheshire Cat grin that comes over me when I consider Ian owing me a debt of gratitude. This is way too awesome to pass up. Option B it is.

I turn my head, grab his face with my two hands, and plant a huge wet kiss on his lips, angling my mouth so I can tangle my tongue up with his. He is my sex slave, and I command him to French-kiss me!

After a couple seconds of that and my heart going bananas, I stop, pull back with a loud smacking of lips, and look at Ginny as

I sigh with immense happiness. I am not faking that emotion either. I get to make out with this master kisser *and* have him owe me a favor after? Hell yeah. Double points. Life is good. No, life is *great.*

"It was meant to be," I say. "We met at a wedding. Do you know how many people fall in love when they're at other people's weddings?" I sigh again, like I can't get enough of my man as I sink into his side. "What can I say? I'm the luckiest girl in the world." My left hand slides over to rest on his thigh. I move it up and down and then closer toward his crotch. "Ian is the *best.*" I giggle to add a little extra pizzazz to my act, and squeeze his leg.

He grabs my hand and pulls it into his lap to keep it from getting any closer to his package. I'm a little relieved, to be honest. Sometimes I can get carried away in the moment. I'm pretty awesome at method acting. I can totally get into the character and forget who I really am. Besides, I admit to being pretty damn curious about what he's packing.

"That's nice," she says in a neutral tone.

I can't tell whether this chick is upset or doesn't give a hoot. She's good. Real good.

"So," she continues, "are you going to the party at Boog's this weekend?"

"Nah, I don't think so," Ian says. He digs his fingers into my shoulder. I think he's telling me to keep my mouth shut.

"You should come," Ginny says to me. "All of Ian's friends will be there. Have you met them yet?"

"No, I haven't." I sit up enough so I can look at my honey and show off my boobs. I'm not disappointed when he glances down at them. "We've pretty much been spending all of our time inside, if you know what I mean." I smile slyly. Ian suddenly looks sick. His skin almost matches the color on the walls.

"Well, then, it's about time you got out, isn't it?" Ginny starts to walk away. "See you Saturday. It was nice meeting you, Candice."

"You too, Ginny," I say, never breaking eye contact with my new beau.

"Are you trying to kill me?" he asks quietly.

I lean over quickly and kiss him on his open mouth before pulling away. "I told you that you were going down. That was a friendly warning. You better start listening or you're going to be sorry."

He looks up at the ceiling and slides down in his seat. "I'm already sorry." His arm slides off my back and flops down by his side, and he releases my hand in his lap.

"Don't be such a poop." I squeeze him high up on his thigh, making sure my pinkie finger slides against something it isn't supposed to.

He jumps out of his seat so fast, he nearly knocks his chair over, causing people to glance over at the ruckus he makes. He stares down at me in bewilderment.

I look up in total innocence while holding out my hand and batting my eyelashes. "Help me up, would you? I find myself in need of a man's assistance."

He grits his teeth together hard enough to make his jaw bounce out, but he holds out his hand and takes mine as I stand. "You better watch it, girl, before you bite off more than you can chew." He's almost growling at this point.

Letting go of him, I walk away with my purse over my shoulder, like I haven't a care in the world. "Never happened before, not gonna happen now." I let my words flow over my shoulder, not bothering to turn and sneak a peek at him. *Chew on that, country boy.*

Leaving him in the cafeteria, I'm ready now to watch my best friend have her little baby. I do my best to ignore my racing heart, my spiked blood pressure, and my lonely lady parts.

CHAPTER TEN

Nurse Ratched won't let me in the room. She's ordered me to go wait in the little room down the hall with Mack's parents, but I'll be damned if I'm going to listen to her and abandon my friend. Andie needs me close by. What if she yells my name, and I'm not there to hear it? What if she needs hot water and towels, and Nurse Ratched is out on a smoke break?

"What're you doing out here?" Ian asks, coming up behind me.

I have my ear pressed to the door. "Shhh! I'm listening for screams."

"Why don't you just go inside?"

I stand up and turn to face him, since he's determined to ruin this moment for me. "That bitch nurse won't let me in there, that's why."

"Oh. Well, why don't you go down to the waiting room with everyone else?"

"Because I'm not everyone else. I'm Auntie Candice, and Andie needs me here." I go back to pressing my ear against the door. "Actually, she needs me in *there*, but Nurse Ratched is exercising her tiny speck of power and keeping me out."

I stiffen as I hear Andie moan. I think it was a moan. Either that or a very long burp.

"What was that?" Ian asks in a hushed tone.

"That's my friend needing me." My pulse is going nuts. I can't stand still any longer. "I'm going in there." My hand slides down to the handle.

Ian grabs my arm. "Better not."

Jerking my arm away, I face him again. "What is your problem, Ian? I need to be with her!"

"No, actually, you should probably stay out here."

For once he actually looks serious. It kind of deflates my emotional bubble a little. "Give me one good reason why."

"Because. Childbirth is a special moment between husband and wife. Having a whole crowd of family in there might not be what they want, and you should do what they want, not what *you* want."

My heart hurts at his words. I cross my arms over my chest without conscious thought. "I'm not a crowd. I'm just me. One person. And I know Andie would want me in there."

He laughs. "You are not just one person, Candice. You're a whole tornado of a person. And if Andie wants you, I'm sure they'll come get you. Maybe sometimes she just wants Mack and no one else, and there's nothing wrong with that. It doesn't mean she loves you any less."

I narrow my eyes at him, suppressing the spark of happiness that comes when he actually speaks my name. I hate to admit it, but he might have a point. I've never been married, but if I ever am, I want it to be like he describes. But instead of telling him that, I focus on the most interesting part of his little lecture. The part where he describes me as a tornado.

"I can't tell if you're complimenting me or criticizing me when you call me a force of nature."

Before he can respond, the door opens behind me, and someone bumps into my back.

"Hey!" I exclaim, turning around so I can see my abuser. "Watch it."

"I told you to go wait in the waiting room," says the mean nurse. "You're in the way here."

I open my mouth to let her have it, but my voice is cut off when Ian wraps his arm around my waist, pulls me to his side, and plants his lips on my cheek, letting out a loud smooching sound.

I cringe away from him, not because I don't like it, but because it's so unexpected. Who is this person, and why does he look so happy?

"I'll get rid of her for ya," he says, when he finally stops.

"Good. We'll come get you when she's ready. It could be hours, though, so don't expect anything soon."

I'm standing there like an observer, watching a television show or something. Words have failed me. I'm a tornado being kissed by a person with dual personalities.

"Come on, darlin', let's go read some magazines." Ian is guiding me down the hallway.

"But I don't want to read any magazines."

"Okay, then you can watch me read magazines."

"I don't want to watch you read magazines. And I don't want you to kiss me anymore either."

"Could-a fooled me." He's smiling, obviously very proud of himself.

I shove him in the ribs with my elbow, detaching him from my waist. "You're such a jerk." It's like he knows he sends my heart racing with every touch, with every stupid joke. I hate that he has me in such a mess. This was supposed to be a fun fling at first, and then it was supposed to be nothing at all. I don't kiss hunters. So why do his lips keep pressing against me? And why haven't I slapped him for it yet?

"Here." Ian grabs a book off the table as we walk into the waiting room. "Some light reading for ya."

I look down at the heavy volume in my hand. "The King James Bible. Oh goody." Looking around the room, I realize it's too quiet. All the chairs are empty, and the television in the corner is off. "Where are your parents?"

"Who knows? Maybe getting coffee or something."

Sitting down in a not very comfortable plastic chair, I crack the well-worn book open to a random page. Might as well brush up on my psalms or whatever.

"You should read it," he says. "You could learn a lot from it." He leans back in a chair a couple down from mine, picking up a tattered magazine and resting it on his leg.

"Oh yeah?" I read out loud from the page in front of me. *"No one whose testicles are crushed or whose male organ is cut off shall enter the assembly of the Lord."* I look over at Ian. "Awww, no eunuchs allowed in Heaven. Bummer." Dropping my gaze to his crotch, I add, "Maybe you should start wearing a cup, just in case."

He puts his hand over his jewels and turns his legs away from me, his expression going worried. "Just in case what?"

I shrug. "Just in case you get your testicles kicked by a crazy bull or whatever. Wouldn't want you to miss out on Heaven just because you have crushed nuts."

He leans over and snatches the book out of my hands. "That's enough Bible reading for you, lady." He tosses it down on the table out of my reach.

I laugh. "Hey! I was enjoying that. I was just about to learn the rules about bastards."

"Bastards?" He frowns, looking over at the book.

He probably thinks I'm making this up, but I'm not. It was right there in black and white. "Yeah, and ten generations after the bastard too. They can't get into Heaven either, apparently. Bummer for them."

He shakes his head at me like he can't believe what I'm saying. I don't see what the big deal is. I just read it from the book that he gave me. Honestly, I've never read any Bible from cover to cover. Guess it was just my luck I found the testicle passage. I'm thinking I should read it more often if it's going to be that entertaining. I've tried before, but I always fall asleep at the part where it starts talking about Adam and all his grandsons. He had a lot of them.

"You go to church back East?" he asks.

I shake my head, wondering how weird this conversation is about to get. "Nope."

"Me neither."

I nod. This is *so* not interesting to me. Changing the subject seems like a great idea. "So . . . party this weekend at Boog's, eh?"

"I'm not going. *You're* not going. No one's going."

"Of course we are. Ginny wants me to meet all your friends."

"Too bad."

I smile evilly. "Too bad for you, you mean. You owe me."

He gives me a pained expression. "You can't be serious."

"Of course I can." I sit up straight and smile. "I'm really looking forward to it, actually." Checking my nails. "And since I saved your butt with your ex, you have to bring me."

He bends over and covers his face with his hands while he leans his elbows on his knees. I can't tell if he's really sad, really angry, or just really tired. Maybe he's all three.

"So what's the deal with you and her?" I ask, sensing weakness to be capitalized on. "You were going to get married, right?"

Ian looks up, letting his hands drop away. He looks around the room, maybe checking to see if we're alone, which we still are. It makes me wonder where all of Andie's friends are. Surely she has some around this town, so where are they?

"I don't want to talk about it."

"In general or specifically with me?" This is waaay more interesting than crushed testicles and bastards being turned away at the pearly gates. No way am I'm letting him off the hook that easy.

"Both. Neither."

Time to go for the throat. That'll get this party started. "I heard she cheated on you with Mack."

He lets out a loud stream of air and leans back in his chair. "You heard wrong."

"I don't think so. I heard she made the major move on him when you came back from Vegas." I nod for emphasis, like I'm all hooked into the town grapevine.

He's staring off into the distance as he responds. "It wasn't a major move. It was a minor move that went nowhere."

"Seems like it went somewhere to me. It ended your marriage."

"There was no marriage." He looks at me. "No wedding, no marriage."

"Okay, so it ended everything."

He smiles, but it's not the happy kind of smile. "You can say that again."

"Okay, so it ended everything."

Closing his eyes, he shakes his head slowly. "You are something, you know that?"

"Something awesome. Yeah, I know." I move over to the chair next to him, but he doesn't budge. I take that as an invitation to pry deeper. Crossing my legs, I let my top foot bounce a little, casually showing off my cute boots to distract him from realizing he's giving me the goods. "So, how long did you date? . . . Before the breakup I mean?"

"Years. Since junior high. Too long."

"Too long?"

"Yeah. Too long. We got too comfortable with each other. Started overlooking things, I guess." He shrugs and looks away.

"Like what kind of things?"

He pauses and turns to stare at me for a few seconds. "You sure are nosy."

I wiggle my foot to distract him from resisting me. Wiggle, wiggle . . . wiggle, wiggle . . . He looks down at my fur lining and frowns.

"Nosy? More like bored." I swat him lightly on the arm with the back of my hand. "Come on. We're going to be waiting for hours and hours. Might as well tell me all your innermost secrets and get it over with. I won't rest until I've plumbed the depths of Ian."

He laughs, looking back up at me. "Do you have any idea how wrong that sounds?"

I wave his silliness away. "Oh poo. Admit it. You're impressed with my poetic expressions."

He laughs. "If that's poetry, I'm Deputy Dog."

"What's that? Your nickname?"

He closes his eyes and leans his head back on the wall. "I'm taking a nap. Don't bother me."

I stare at the magazines on the low table in front of us. There's one featuring NASCAR, one about Corvettes, and one covered in motorcycles. Who stocks this place with reading material, anyway? Jeff Gordon? Talk about lame. No way can I abandon my line of questioning when this is all I have to look forward to.

"So, what did you mean when you said you started overlooking things? Or was it her that started overlooking things?"

He doesn't respond, so I keep prompting.

"What did she overlook? Was it your personal hygiene problems? Your lack of social graces? Your terrible taste in hat wear?"

He remains still, as if he can't even hear me, and for a moment I think I'm going to have to get pushy to get my answers, but then he surprises me.

"No, it wasn't any of that. And it was both of us, I guess, not just her or me."

"What are some things *you* overlooked?" I ask. I'm on the edge of my seat, knowing I'm about to get some juicy stuff.

"I don't know."

"Sure you do. Tell me. I swear I'll keep your secrets."

He opens one eye and stares at me with it. "You expect me to believe that?"

"Of course. My brain is a steel trap. Nothing gets out until I release it, and I don't release things unless I have permission."

"You? You're the grand repository of secrets?" He closes his eye, and then he kind of snorts. I think it was a snort. Or maybe he has allergies.

"Exactly. That's my brain. So tell me."

He sighs loudly and lets his head wobble from left to right a few times before he starts talking again.

"Well, I guess I overlooked the fact that she wasn't entirely happy with having me as a husband."

"That's kind of a big one."

He opens his eyes and stares at the ceiling. "You're telling me."

"What else?" I prompt. I've got him on a roll now.

"She overlooked the fact that I didn't like Hawaii." He sounds particularly bitter about that one, especially when he scowls at the ceiling.

I try to figure out how Hawaii could be connected, but I give up pretty quickly. I don't want him falling asleep on me while I try to decode his messages. "Um . . . confusing?"

He talks and sighs at the same time. "She wanted to go to Hawaii for a honeymoon. I had no interest in that, but it didn't matter. We did whatever Ginny wanted to do, always. She was the leader of the show."

"There always has to be a leader, you know," I say, knowing I could never be content to follow some guy around like a lap dog. That's why I'm never going to Abu Dhabi. If I had to walk five paces behind some guy all day, I'd for sure be giving him flat tires all the time on purpose. That would probably end in divorce or a public flogging or a stoning or something. Nah. I'm definitely not cut out for that following mindlessly stuff. Plus I'd have to wear one of those all over body robes and cover up my gorgeous hair and adorable outfits. Talk about a waste of effort.

"Yeah, I get that," Ian says, sitting up in his chair a little but still slouching, "but it doesn't always have to be the same person being out front, you know?" He looks at me. "It *shouldn't* always be the same person. Once in a while you gotta let the other person call the shots, have the final say. Otherwise . . ."—he shrugs—"they get lost."

"What do you mean, 'they get lost'?"

Now he's gesturing with his hands as he speaks. It's like he has an invisible audience out in the waiting room in front of us, but it's still just me in here. I can't believe how animated he's become.

"See, being the decision maker puts you out front and the other person behind, right? And some people are okay with being back there in the shadows, but most people aren't. They need some time to shine too. But you put someone who doesn't want to be in the shadows there too much, they start to lose a part of themselves." His face twists into something bitter. "I lost myself somewhere along the way with Ginny, and I don't know that I'll ever get him back."

"Wow. That sounds massively depressing."

He laughs once as he stares at the ground. "Tell me about it." He rubs his hands together, as if he's trying to get a cramp out of his muscles that will never go away.

I can't believe a big, strong, smart guy like him is so messed up over something so not a big deal. People break up all the time. Since when does it mean someone died?

I'm so disappointed in his pee-poor attitude. Why has everyone let him go on like this for so long? I can't stop my judgment from flying out of my mouth. "It also sounds like a bunch of bull crap to me."

His head twists sharply to the left so he can glare at me.

"How long has it been?" I ask, already knowing the answer. "Three years or so? I mean, come on . . . six months is the longest anyone would need to get over that. It's not like anyone died or anything."

His jaw, which was slowly falling open as I spoke, slaps shut. Then he says, "Are you kidding me?"

"No, why would I do that? Obviously you two weren't meant to be together. Your breakup was a good thing. Seriously. You've been hosting this pity party for waaaay too long, Ian. Time to cowboy up and stop feeling sorry for yourself."

He leans way back away from me. "You know what? You can just shut up right now. You have no idea what you're talking about."

"No, I'm serious."

"I can see that, but it doesn't mean you shouldn't shut up about it." He stands, heading for the door.

"Running away when things get difficult?" I ask, challenging him.

"More like getting away from a damn harpy who doesn't know when to mind her own business."

When he's almost to the exit, I sigh loudly so he'll hear. "Good thing Ginny got rid of you when she did, I guess. No one wants a big crybaby for a husband anyway."

He spins around and faces me. "Did you just call me a crybaby?"

I give him my very best innocent look and bat my eyelashes a few times for extra effect. "Yes, I did. What do you call a guy who has the good fortune of getting out of a big mistake before it's an even bigger mistake and then makes everyone miserable about it for three years? A hero? I don't think so. More like a whiny baby."

His nostrils flare and his jaw tenses. It's possible he's considering putting a hole through the wall with his fist.

I hold up my hands. "Hey, don't shoot the messenger."

He puts his hands on his hips. "That's not what that expression means," he says, his teeth pressed together.

"Sure it is. I'm giving you the message that it's time for you to stop feeling sorry for yourself. You're getting all cranky after hearing my message, and I'm just sayin' . . . don't be hatin' on me because I'm just telling you the things people are saying all over town about you."

He takes a step toward me, his anger falling away to something else. Worry maybe? Fear? Curiosity?

"Are you serious?" he asks. "Who's saying that about me?"

I snort. "Please. Who's *not* saying it would be an easier question to answer." I actually have no idea if anyone is saying anything about Ian, but does that stop me? No. He's so much cuter when he's not feeling sorry for himself. Maybe he's been acting like a butthead for three years because no one's kicked him in the pants yet. He sure needs a kick in the pants—that much is obvious.

Surprisingly, he comes back and sits down next to me. "You need to tell me who's been flapping their lips about me and Ginny."

"No, I don't." I smile and point to my head. "Steel trap, remember?"

"Screw your steel trap." He stares at me intensely.

I grin because I cannot help it. He's positively adorable when he's mad. "Do you have any idea how wrong that sounds?"

"How wrong what sounds?"

"That you want to screw my steel trap."

He leans back, a ghost of a smile playing on his lips as his body goes slack. "I didn't say that."

I shrug and check my nails again. "If that's what you want to tell people. I'll back you up."

"You'll back me up." He says it like a statement. I can tell he's looking at me, but I don't return his gaze. The atmosphere has suddenly gone . . . warm.

"That's what I said." I cross my legs and play with the furry top of my awesome boot, still not looking at him.

"I think you would," he says, sounding like he's actually admiring me.

I look over at him to see if he's messing with me. My heart does what can only be termed a pitter-patter. "You think I would, what?"

"Back me up. Have my back. If I needed you to, I mean."

I picture Ian needing a helping hand, and there's just no question which side of the line I'd be on. He's Andie's brother now. "Hell yeah, I would. You're practically family." I shrug and go back to fiddling with my boot. "Family gets automatic, unquestioned backup at any time. That's my rule."

He says nothing for a little while and then comes out with "I like your rule."

I look at him and wink. "I know you do." I have no idea what that means. I just have this desire to flirt with him that apparently knows no bounds. I'm not even making sense anymore. This situation is so confusing. Floor and ceiling, feel free to change positions, because at this point I'm not going to know the difference.

He laughs as he rolls his eyes. "Girl, you are something else."

The mood in the room has gone from silly to sad, to tense, to explosive and back to happy and relaxed, with almost no effort on my part. It's like a circus, but without clowns or animals or gymnasts or any of that other stuff. The only explanation is Ian. It's all his fault. He sure is a moody butthead. Why that makes him even more attractive to me than he was before, I have no idea, but there's no denying it does. I guess even though I'm nearing thirty and should know better, I still find bad boys enough of a challenge that I can't walk away. And Ian is most definitely a bad boy.

I stare at him, taking in his lean, muscular form, his chiseled-from-stone good looks, his wind-burned cheeks, his gorgeous green eyes, and his stupid blue hat that does not match his complexion at all, knowing he would give me a serious run for my money if I were interested in that kind of thing with him. How this man is not yet married is some kind of miracle. The girls in Baker City have got to be stupid. Or maybe they don't like hunters either.

The thought sparks an idea in my steel trap of a mind. Maybe if I ask him really nicely, he'll stop shooting animals. Then he could find a new woman and be happy again. Andie's brother-in-law should be happy. Then she'll be happy, and Mack will be happy, and the whole damn world will be happy. I could leave for Florida knowing I've left the world here a better place. I sigh with bliss, thinking this must be what Mother Theresa felt like.

"What would it take to convince you to stop hunting animals?" I ask, my plan already in motion.

He stares at me for a long time before he finally answers. "A lot more than you can afford to give, believe me."

I just smile at him, knowing my battle is almost half won already. This man has no idea what he's in for.

CHAPTER ELEVEN

Nurse Ratched puts her head in the waiting room. "You can come to Andie's room now if you want."

I leap up out of my chair, leaving Ian in my dust.

"Is she pushing yet? Is the baby almost here?" I scoot past the evil woman without waiting for a response.

She doesn't answer me, but I catch her rolling her eyes at my back when I look over my shoulder, so I know she heard me. Bitch.

I'm pretty sure I'm going to have to report her to the administration when this is all over, but for now I have to focus on Andie. Maybe they'll let me cut the umbilical cord if Mack's too squeamish to do it.

I push open Andie's door and burst through the opening, determined not to miss a single second of the event. Maeve is going to be so sad she wasn't here for it. I can't believe she left the hospital when the baby was almost here.

Andie's in bed, sitting up, holding a bundle of blankets in her arms.

I stop short and stare at her and Mack. He's leaning over her, looking into the blankets, smiling, as goofy as I've ever seen him.

Andie's smiling too, but she looks exhausted. Maeve is sitting quietly in the corner in an armchair. My brain starts short-circuiting.

"Did I miss something?" I ask, walking over slowly. I'm trying not to sound hurt. Why is Maeve here and I wasn't?

"Nope. You're here just in time." Andie moves the edge of the blanket over to the side. "Candice, I want you to meet your goddaughter, Sarah Jayne MacKenzie." She looks down at the pink coconut-looking head in the blankets. "Sarah, this is Candice."

And just like that, I'm not quite as hurt anymore. Godmother? Note to self: *Read Bible tomorrow, but skip the part about Adam's sons.*

I'm close enough now that I can see Sarah's little scrunched-up face. "Wow. She looks like she just did a couple rounds with Mohammed Ali."

Mack chuckles, his eyes never leaving her face.

"She was pretty squished in there, I guess," explains Andie. "Isn't she beautiful?"

I decide lying is the best plan of action in this situation. "She is the most beautiful baby that ever came out of a vagina, that's for sure." I look up at my friend and try to force a full smile out past the remaining hurt I'm suffering over being left out. "You did really well, Mommy. How does it feel to know you brought a human being into the world?"

"It feels like a miracle." She looks over at Mack and starts to cry. "I'm the luckiest girl in the entire world."

Mack leans in and gives her a very sexy kiss. "You make me really happy, you know that Mrs. MacKenzie?"

"Yes, I do know that, Mr. MacKenzie."

"Can I hold her?" I ask, a little nervous about the whole idea, but not letting it stop me. I have to get this baby imprinted on me ASAP so she knows I'm her second-in-line-momma. And before Kelly, Andie's second-best friend, gets here. Sarah J. is going to love *me* best—I'm going to make sure of that.

"Sure. Just watch her head. You have to support it."

"I know, I know. Hand over the goods." I reach out and take the baby gently from her mom. Sarah is so light it feels like I'm just holding blankets. I move the edges away to be sure she's still in there.

The delicate golden fuzz on her face makes me kind of melt inside. "Well, hello, pookie poo, Wookiee woo, mookie moo."

The door opens, but I don't bother looking up to see who it is.

"Do you know who I am?" I ask the baby, waiting for some sign of recognition that I'm here. Her eyes are closed and her mouth is making some sucking motions, but I keep on talking. Maybe hearing it subliminally would be better anyway. "I'm your number-two momma and future BFF. Yeah, that's right. You're the luckiest girl in the world. I'm going to read to you, I'm going to do your hair, I'll teach you all the things you need to know about men, and I'll make sure you get into a good college. And when you want to run away from mommy and daddy, you'll come to my house, and we'll do our nails together and talk about how unfair they are."

There's a sound next to me and I look up. Ian's standing there, looking over my shoulder at the baby.

"She's little," he says.

"Six pounds even," says Mack. "Eighteen inches long."

I smile because he sounds like he's bragging about the length of his dick or something. Mack usually isn't so animated.

"Wow. Ain't nothin' but a little bit," says Ian. He pokes his finger into her cheek. "Whaddya think, L'il Bit? You big enough for a nickname yet?"

I turn so he can't touch her anymore. "Keep your dirty fingers off her face."

"I'm pretty sure she hasn't even had a bath yet. Her face is dirtier than my hands are."

"Her name is Sarah Jayne, not *her*."

Ian smiles. "That's a real pretty name, Andie. Suits her perfectly."

It warms my heart to see Andie's response to Ian's kindnesses. He really is a good guy underneath all that awfulness, I guess.

I walk over and give the baby to Mack. "I'm afraid I'm going to drop her," I say as an excuse. Actually, I know I would never do that, but staring down into her pretty pink face and watching her little lips and that nose while Ian stands behind me and says all those nice things makes me sad for some reason. Today is the first day of my life that I've felt old. And alone. I'm really not prepared to deal with those kinds of emotions.

"Well, I need to get going," I say, trying to act all breezy casual about it. I think I need a good cry, and I can't do that in front of anyone.

"Go? Where are you going?" Andie seems worried.

"Oh, I have some shopping to do. Things to get done at the house. I'll come back later or tomorrow morning."

Andie looks at Mack. "Will you stay?"

He smiles and strokes her hair. "I'm not going anywhere. I'll be here until you're ready to leave."

They stare into each other's eyes, and Andie starts to cry again.

"Yeah, well, if anyone cares, I'll be heading back to the ranch too," says Ian, lifting his hand to say good-bye.

No one says anything.

"Call me if you need anything from the house," he says.

Mack waves but says nothing, never breaking eye contact with his wife.

"I'll be back in a few hours," Maeve says to Ian. "Keep a dish warm for me and Angus. He's out with the herd on the south field."

"Will do," Ian says.

Ian and I leave the room, and both of us let out long sighs. His sounds refreshed. Mine is more depressed.

He looks at me and I look at him.

"What now?" he asks.

I hold out my thumb and smile weakly. "Can I get a ride?"

CHAPTER TWELVE

The ride home is almost completely silent. It would have been the perfect time to grill Ian about Ginny and life since Ginny, but I'm too deep into my own pity party at this particular moment to care.

"What's your problem, anyway?" Ian asks, as he pulls onto the dirt road leading to the ranch. It's more like an ice-chunk road now, but I can see bits of gravel and brown smears through the snow that tell me normally this is a place full of dust, rocks, holes, and snakes.

"I don't have a problem." I look out the side window. My chest is achy. Maybe I'm coming down with the flu.

"You got all sad in the hospital room. You should be happy for your friend."

I glare at him. "I *am* happy for my friend. Why would you say that?"

"Because. You looked mad when we were there, and you beat it out of there pretty quick. Like you didn't want to stay." He pauses, shaking his head. "I don't get it. First you bang your head on the door trying to get in and then all you want is out."

"That's not what happened." I look out the window again. I'm afraid if he catches my eye, he'll guess what I'm thinking, that he'll see he read the situation exactly right, and it doesn't say anything nice about me as a person.

"So what happened, then? Tell me."

I glance over to see if he's serious. He sounds like he actually cares. Normally, I wouldn't share my thoughts on this subject with anyone but Kelly, but right now I can't keep it all in for some reason. I need a priest or something to confess to, but Ian is the only thing I have at hand. He'll just have to do.

"I was just . . . I don't know. Feeling old or something."

He laughs. "Looking at a baby makes you feel old?"

"No. Well, yes, kind of."

"You want to be a baby again?"

"No, don't be ridiculous."

"What is it, then?"

I can't believe I have to spell this out for him. "I guess you could say it's my biological clock or something. Reminding me I'm getting old and running out of time."

He snorts. "Yeah, right. What're you . . . twenty-five? You've got a lot of hours left on your clock, believe me."

I can't help but smile just a tiny bit. "I'm almost thirty, actually, and I know rationally I'm not old, but seeing my best friend all settled and with a baby makes me feel like I'm getting left behind."

I can't believe I just said that out loud. Talk about pitiful. I grit my teeth together to keep anything else from spilling out. Ian is so going to mock me hard over this. Here I was, just an hour ago, giving him shit about feeling sorry for himself about something silly. Now who's the whiny baby? Yeah. It's me.

He pats me on the leg. "Aw, you don't need to worry about that. Everyone is on her own time schedule. You don't need to be on hers, and she doesn't need to be on yours. You just need to be patient."

I bite my lip to keep from saying anything else. Ian being nice and understanding is not what I was expecting. Sarcasm and teasing

I can handle. Kindness I cannot. I'm liable to start crying like Andie any second.

"Here we are, home sweet home," Ian says.

Just that phrase makes my heart hurt all over again. Man, I'm in bad shape. Why is he being so damn nice?

He drives over to the left to make room for a truck leaving the property. We stop when they're side by side.

"Where you headed?" he asks his father after rolling down my window.

"To see the baby and pick Maeve up," Angus replies. "Why don't you see to dinner, and we'll join you later?"

"Sure thing," Ian says, rolling the window back up. I'm grateful, since it's snowing again and several flakes were trying to get in and ruin my hair.

"He wants us to cook dinner?" I ask.

"Yup." Ian pauses before driving into his space. "Can you cook?"

I panic. Then I snort. "Are eunuchs de-*nied* at the pearly gates?"

"So I heard."

"Well then, you have your answer." It's a total lie to say that I cook. I mean, it's not just a fib or a slight exaggeration, but a straight-up, bold-faced *lie*. But Ian doesn't know that.

I wonder how long it would take me to learn if I googled it?

CHAPTER THIRTEEN

I have my answer thirty minutes later: not long. This cooking thing is a breeze, apparently. Spaghetti and meat sauce, coming right up.

"You sure you know what you're doing?" Ian asks as I open up different cupboards trying to locate the pans that the online article said I'd need.

"Of course. Do you have any ground beef anywhere?"

"This is a cattle ranch—what do you think?"

I look over my shoulder to find him smiling at me. "Where would I find it?"

"Freezer." He sits down at the table in the kitchen and turns his chair so he can watch me.

"Garlic and onions?" I ask, trying to keep my nervousness from showing in my voice.

He points to a wooden box on the counter. "In there."

"Okay." I find a big old sharp knife in a drawer that looks like the one in the picture I saw, and put the papery vegetables on the cutting board that's always out. "So I'm going to cut these up first."

"You might want to peel those outer layers off first," he says as I struggle to figure out where to start.

"Of course I will. I was just figuring out the best angle. There's always a best angle for these things."

"Uh-huh. If you say so."

I work for what seems like way too long, peeling off the fine layers of skin that surround the onion and the garlic thingies. When they're finally bare, I cut them into squares. My eyes begin to sting so bad I can barely see. I think my nose might be swelling too.

"Holy crap, this garlic is strong."

"Sure it's not the onion?" he asks. His tone suggests he knows the answer.

"It's both. *Gah.* I can't see." I turn around. Ian's face is a mere blur through my half-open eyes.

"Ma's got goggles in the drawer if you want to use 'em." He points across the kitchen.

"No, that's alright." I have no idea why he wants me to wear goggles. Do people wear goggles in the kitchen? I've never seen that on TV, and the article didn't mention it. "I'm almost done."

I give up on chopping any more vegetables and just sweep them into a pan with some oil. Some of the onion is still pretty big, but oh well. They immediately start sizzling. By the time I can see properly again, they're turning brown.

"Sauce?" I ask, sniffing hard. My nose is running like crazy after the onion incident.

"What do you mean, 'sauce'?"

"Where's the spaghetti sauce?"

Ian shrugs. "I don't know if we have any."

My heart skips a few beats. *No sauce?* There was no contingency plan in this recipe for a kitchen without sauce. The "Quick-n-Easy Fifteen-Minute Spaghetti" might not be so quick and easy without that main ingredient. *Oops.*

He gets up and walks into the pantry. A few seconds later, he comes out with a can. "Here's some tomatoes. Could they work?"

"Of course," I say, having no idea if this is sauce or not, but it has tomatoes on the picture and sauce is just tomatoes, right? I put on my brave face. "Open them for me, would you, please?"

"Sure." He opens the can and hands it to me.

I stare at it. The sauce inside doesn't look anything like the pictures on Google. I dump it into the pan with the onions and garlic anyway, because I don't have any choice.

"Shouldn't you start the noodles?" Ian asks. He's hovering just behind me.

"In a minute. I need some . . ." I search my memory for the herbs mentioned in the article. "Basil, oregano, thyme, and uh . . . parsley."

Ian opens a cabinet right next to me, standing so close I can feel the heat from his body. "Take your pick."

I ignore the chemistry building between us and find the bottles I need. I have no idea how much to use, so I put in a few shakes of each.

"Want me to do the pasta?" he asks.

I put my hands on my hips and turn around to face him. He's way too close, but I don't back away. "You seem very worried about the noodles, Ian. If it's that big a deal, go ahead."

I'm actually glad he wants to take over because I'm clueless about how to cook that stuff. Never in my life has that mattered, because I prefer eating out or buying already made meals from this place down the street from my apartment, run by cooking school students, but today it feels like a big hole in my life education. How am I going to impress this man if I can't cook him a plate of spaghetti? And why do I even care about impressing him?

I watch very closely as he goes through the process of putting pasta on to boil. Seems simple enough. I could have done it, probably.

"How do you tell if it's done?" I ask. "I mean, I know how *I* tell, but what's your system?"

"Throw it on the fridge."

My eyes widen. "Throw it on the fridge? Are you serious?" Is that what everyone does? Have I been eating noodles that have been stuck to a wall or that have fallen on the floor my whole life and just never known it? Wow. I really should have tried to learn to cook when I was a teenager. I probably would have been anti-pasta my entire adult life if I had.

"Yep. You'll see." He winks.

I have to act casual; otherwise, he'll know I'm clueless. "Can't wait," I say, going back to my stirring.

"You gonna add the meat anytime soon?" Ian asks.

"Yeah, sure. Get some for me, would you?"

There's some rustling around behind me, and then Ian's there, holding out a hunk of red meat. It's frozen solid.

"What am I supposed to do with that?" I ask before I can stop myself.

He shrugs. "Whatever you normally do? I don't know."

My mind goes blank. What did that damn recipe say? I cannot remember. This is a major step, but I don't have a single memory of its mention.

I take the meat from him and dump it right in the middle of the sauce. "Thanks."

"You aren't going to brown it first?"

"No, this way is better." Hell, I might not know how to brown meat, but I certainly know how to defrost stuff. Most of my meals have to be defrosted first before I eat them, and when my microwave broke one time, I just put everything in the one pan I have and heated it on the stove. This will work. Heat equals melted ice. Simple science.

"Okay. If you say so. Need anything else?"

I shake my head. "Nope. You can just sit down and relax while I do all the work."

"How about if I set the table?" He moves over to another cupboard.

"Sure." Why a man setting the table makes me go all silly inside, I do not know, but it does. I'm nearly thirty years old, and every meal I've had with a guy has been at a restaurant. This feels really intimate and nice. This baby thing has really messed with my head, apparently.

I push the lump of meat around, accidentally spilling sauce over the edge of the pan. It catches on fire a little and starts to stink up the kitchen. I quickly wave the smoke away until it stops coming up.

"Smells good," says Ian from across the room.

Turning around to see if he's kidding, I see that he's not looking at me, too busy setting the table for two. I lose my train of thought when I see what he's done. There are candles in between the two plates. Were those there before, or did he put them there? It strikes me as very romantic.

I turn back to the stove so he doesn't see my expression. I'm so confused right now. This dinner by candlelight probably means absolutely nothing to him, right? I mean, we need light and that lamp above the table is kind of dim. But what if it does mean something more than just illumination to him? What if he's making it romantic on purpose? But then again, what if he's playing a prank on me, letting me *think* that's what he's doing so that I'll say something stupid?

The way our relationship has gone so far, I could never trust him to be serious. And there's nothing more embarrassing than thinking someone is into you when they're just messing around with your head. No way am I going to fall for that. He's still mad at me for almost shooting him. He's definitely planning some sort of revenge. These candles could be part of that.

"Are the noodles done yet?" Ian asks.

"That's up to you," I say. "Better start throwing them around." I can't wait to see this.

He stands next to me, using a spoon from a container on the counter to fish a couple pieces out. "I don't think they're ready, but let's see." Pulling one of the noodles off the spoon, he grins at me. Then, without warning, he throws it against the refrigerator.

I stare at the pasta as it slides down the front of the appliance and then plops onto the floor.

"Nope. Not ready." He eats the other piece on the spoon. "Too hard."

I resist the urge to make a comment. Instead, I push on the slightly thawed hunk of meat, trying not to be worried about the pools of brownish-red *something* that are collecting around the sides of the pan.

"Probably should've given you the ground sirloin," Ian says, looking over my shoulder into the pan.

"Why do you say that?"

"It's better, that's all." He moves over to the table. He picks up a nearby folded newspaper and says, "That chuck has a lot of fat."

My heart seizes up. Who's Chuck? Is he a person in the news or something to do with our dinner? I decide that silence is my best bet for a response.

I stir the sauce, trying to mix in the brown stuff. Maybe it'll make the sauce taste better, but I doubt it since it looks pretty unappetizing. It must be meat juice, but why isn't it mixing into the tomatoes? It just moves around making me chase after it with the spoon.

"So how long have you been cooking?" Ian asks.

"All my life, pretty much." Damn, that slipped out before I could stop it. I hate when lies get bigger on their own like that.

"What's your favorite thing to cook?"

"Ummm . . . dinner."

He laughs. "I mean your favorite dish."

"Oh . . . uhhh . . . pie, probably. Lemon pie."

"Really?"

I look over at him. He seems very interested all of a sudden, no longer reading the news about Chuck.

He puts down his paper. "Lemon meringue?"

"Of course? Is there any other?" I flash him a fake smile over my shoulder before turning back to face the stove and cringing. Is there a shovel in here? Because I think I just dug my grave a little deeper.

"Oh, man, that's my favorite. How'd you know?"

"I didn't." Why did I have to say lemon?! I could have said chocolate or apple or . . . shit, whatever other pies there are that I can't remember right now.

"You'll have to make me one of those before you go."

"Okay. I can do that." Hello, Google? I need a little help. Or a lot of help.

"You make your own crust?"

"Of course. Who doesn't?" Oh, God. What am I *doing*?! Now I have to learn how to make crust too?

"Mmmm, I can already taste it. I wish we had some lemons right now. I'd get down on my knees and beg you to make me a lemon meringue pie."

My eyes go wide. Could it be possible that the key to Ian's heart is a simple lemon pie? I feel like I have true power in my hands right now with this knowledge. The question is, do I share this power with a worthy woman who will make Ian a happy man, or do I use this power myself for selfish purposes? I try to picture Ginny making him that pie, and it makes me want to punch her in the face. I think this means I'm going to be making a pie soon.

"Noodles are probably ready," he says. "You want me to drain 'em?"

His concern for the pasta wakes me up from my pie-making, girl-fight fantasy. "Yes, please. Sauce is almost done too." The last hunks of meat are still clinging together, but it won't be long before they're separate. The stupid brown puddles are getting bigger, but maybe I can just scoop the sauce from around them and avoid them altogether. I'm afraid to taste the sauce and see if it's fit for consumption.

What if it's horrible? I don't know why, but I'm more afraid of admitting I can't cook a single thing than having him taste something awful. Maybe because it doesn't smell half bad. Maybe there's hope.

Ian's busy next to me and then at the sink. A few minutes later, he has two plates of noodles held out in front of him. "Ready, Chef."

"Ready?" I'm afraid there's a critical step to spaghetti making that I'm not aware of.

"For the sauce. Is it done?"

"Oh! The sauce! Yes, it's done." I grab a large spoon and take my time, scooping out tomato chunks, meat, and all the sauce I can find that doesn't have the brown goop in it. It's only enough for the two plates of noodles he's presented me with.

I look down into my saucepan at the mess of onion scraps and brown goo. "I didn't make enough for your parents."

"Eh, don't worry about it. I'll order them some pizzas."

I cringe inwardly, realizing that we could have done the same thing and spared both of us this experience. *Please don't let this dinner suck!*

He leaves me at the stove and sits down at the table. "You like wine or beer with your spaghetti?"

"Wine, if you have it." I'm kind of surprised to find that they drink wine out here. I had them pegged as Budweiser people.

"Yup." He gets a bottle from a small collection on the counter. "Andie bought some when she was in Seattle. My mom likes this one a lot. Says it goes good with red meat." He pours a glass for me and then opens a Sam Adams beer for himself. He's standing behind his chair waiting for me.

The picture in front of me makes me want to cry. Pasta. Candlelight. The most gorgeous hunk of man I'd ever want to see. And a stupid blue baseball hat perched on his head, making his hair curl around the edges of it. He's a working man, someone who uses his hands and body to do things around a ranch with horses and cows and stuff. I'd give just about anything to see him naked once.

He sees me looking at his head and quickly reaches up to take his hat off. He stuffs the brim in his back pocket and ruffles up his hair, trying to smooth away the pressed-in spots. "Sorry about that. No hats at the table. House rules."

I can't help but smile. He can be so charming and adorable when he wants to be. Or when he's not trying to be, is more like it. It's his natural state. The one he fakes is the jerky Ian. It boggles my mind that he would spend so much energy doing that when he could be so amazing with no effort. It makes me wonder if Ginny knew the real Ian or the fake one.

I take the seat he's holding out for me. "Thanks."

"My pleasure." He sits down too and picks up his fork, dropping a napkin into his lap a second before he takes a big helping of noodles and spins it into a nest shape.

I stare at him, waiting to see if he's actually going to eat it.

The forkful is halfway to his mouth when he freezes. "What?"

I shake my head and take my fork. "Oh, nothing. Sorry. I was spacing out there for a second." Watching out of the corner of my eye, I see him take a bite.

The noodles slowly spin up onto my fork, but I'm still waiting for his reaction before I try any.

"Mmmm . . ." He nods, his eyes moving around the room. "Mmmm . . . ummm-hmmm . . . mmmm." He swallows.

"Well? Is it any good?"

"Delicious." He takes a long gulp of beer and smiles. "You can cook for me anytime."

My entire body catches fire. I drop my fork, lean over, grab him by the sides of his head, and kiss him right on the lips. Just one kiss. Real quick. I couldn't help myself. I quickly go back to my fork and spaghetti.

"What was that for?" he asks, bewildered.

"For complimenting the cook." I grin and stab my fork into the pasta.

He laughs and takes another sip of beer. "Can't wait to taste your pie."

My hand freezes.

My fork drops out of my hand and clatters onto the plate.

My ears are positively on fire.

I look up at him and watch as he goes from smiling to panicked to embarrassed.

"Oh, shit," he says in a low voice. "I can't believe I just said that."

I'm laughing. I can't help it. It's too crazy stupid not to laugh at it.

"Shut up," he says, still smiling awkwardly.

"You can't wait . . ." I point at him, laughing too hard to finish.

"Yeah, I heard myself." He's nodding slowly, like he'll take the punishment he deserves.

"You can't wait . . ." I'm laughing harder, still pointing.

"Yeah, yeah. Ha-ha, very funny."

"To taste my pie . . . " My stomach hurts so much right now. I have to hold onto the edge of the table to support myself.

He pushes on my knee under the table with his hand. "Get over yourself—you know what I meant."

The feel of his hand on my leg sobers me up pretty quickly, but not enough to let his gaffe slide completely. I pick up my fork and get some pasta on there before I give him my response.

"Well, Ian, I am also looking forward to the day that you taste my pie. I'm pretty sure you're going to love it."

CHAPTER FOURTEEN

After I eat half my noodles, I have to stop. I'm too nervous to finish it all, even though it doesn't exactly suck. I'm no Top Chef of course, but at least I pulled that one off without too much of a hitch.

I'm pretty sure Ian suspects nothing. Google is my best friend today, and Andie my second best. Or maybe Sarah should be my best friend now that I'm her number-two mommy. That would make Google second and Andie number three. No, wait. That doesn't feel right. When has Andie ever been number three?

"Want to watch some TV?" Ian asks as he puts the last dish in the dishwasher. The sound of his voice pulls me off the track my brain was running on. I have to shake my head a little to get it back into reality. My last thought on the subject is that reordering priorities at my age is . . . difficult.

"Uhhh . . . . TV? Sure. What's on?" I'm glad he's suggested something to kill time. It's only seven o'clock and way too early for me to go to bed, even with the time-difference jet lag I have going on.

"*Castle.* My favorite. I've got it on the DVR."

"Really? I didn't figure you for a *Castle* guy."

He walks down the hall into the main living room, with me right behind. "Oh yeah. Me and *Castle* go way back."

We settle onto a couch, him on one end and me on the other, an entire cushion's distance between us. There's a knitted blanket over the back that I gather up to put on top of me since the room is kind of chilly.

"You cold? Want a fire?" He glances over at the fireplace on the far wall.

"That thing actually works?" I snuggle under the colorful throw blanket and peek out over the edge at him. My feet curl up under me, hoping my butt will thaw them out.

"Yeah." He laughs. "Why wouldn't it?"

"I don't know." My garlic breath is rank, and it's billowing up around my nose, making it hard to breathe. I have to pull my face away from the blanket to get some fresh oxygen so I can finish my thought. "All the ones I've seen back home are just ornamental."

He walks over to the mantel and squats down, busying himself with stacking things inside the gaping, ash-covered hole in the wall. "This one works just fine. It's not good for much more than this room, but that's alright. We have central heating too."

Once the flames have started, Ian leaves the room. He's back in less than a minute with another glass of wine and a beer. He sets them on the coffee table in front of us before picking up the remote and sitting back down on the couch. This time, he's a little closer to the center than he was before. I wonder if it's on purpose. It makes me happy to think that it might be.

The show starts. I can't help but glance over at Ian from time to time to see his facial expressions. He is so damn handsome. It's too distracting for me to pay any attention to the actual story line.

"What do you like about this show so much?" I ask, wanting to know more about what makes Ian tick.

He shrugs, still staring at the screen. "I don't know. I guess I like that he's living in the city, working on his own stuff, keeping life interesting by doing different things, living a little dangerously with a sexy, take-no-crap woman by his side. And I like his sense of humor. Nathan Fillion's a great actor."

I look at the guy he's talking about, the character Richard Castle, currently giving his cop partner a hard time. Man, is he cute. He could give me a hard time any day of the week and twice on Sunday. "He's hot, I know that."

"Hotter than me?" Ian tips his head in my direction and wiggles his eyebrows at me.

I kick him lightly in the hip. "Maybe if you'd take that stupid hat off he might not be."

Ian takes his ball cap by the brim, lifts it off his head, and flings it across the room toward the fireplace. It hits the mantel and falls to the ground, landing on a pile of loosely stacked firewood.

"What are you doing?" I ask, laughing at the same time. I can't believe he just did that. It's like he actually cares what I think about his looks. That can't be right. He specifically put that hat on today because I told him it was awful.

"Gonna burn that sucker once and for all, get you off my back about it."

I kick him again, but this time he's ready for me. His eyes sparkle as he catches my foot and drags it over into his lap.

Suddenly, the mood shifts. We both turn back toward the TV, acting like this isn't what it feels like. My heart is going a million miles an hour. Am I in high school or what? Because that's what this feels like . . . one of those first-kiss, do-you-like-me?-Check-yes-or-no, will-he-try-to-get-to-first-base kind of things.

"Damn, girl, your feet are colder than ice." He rubs them briskly with his giant hands.

It makes me wonder what it would feel like to have them on other parts of my body. *Rawr.*

I play it off like it's nothing. "Well, it's practically the Arctic Circle up here in Baker City. What do you expect? I'm a Florida girl, not a polar bear."

"You've never lived anywhere north of there?" His attention breaks away from the television as he continues rubbing my foot. It's not doing much for my toes, but it sure is heating up other parts of my body.

Easy, Candice. Breathe in, breathe out. You can do this.

"Nope. Never." When his face goes blank, I add, "Not that I wouldn't, I just never have."

He nods and goes back to staring at the TV.

Why did I just say that? It sounded like I was hinting he should ask me to move out here or something. What is my problem? Since when am I such a doofus around a good-looking guy? Jesus, I'm a mess. No wonder Andie married his brother after knowing him for an hour. These MacKenzie guys are dangerous with their sexy man-voodoo.

I reach over and grab my glass of wine, stretching my other foot out in the process.

Ian takes that one and pulls it into his lap too.

Trying to hold on to my last shred of cool, I take a small sip of my drink. But when his thumb presses into the middle of my foot and slides up and then back, and I feel a tingling right up there in my lady parts, I gulp the rest of the glass down in two swallows.

He looks over at me and smiles. "You have a wine mustache."

So much for cool, I guess.

I wipe it off with the back of my hand, trying to keep the burp of air I swallowed as delicate as possible when it escapes me.

"What's the matter?" he asks, rubbing deep into the sole of my foot.

Sweat droplets are popping out on the top of my lip and between my breasts. The special spot between my legs is getting all twitchy. Antsy. Like it needs him *there* instead of at my feet. I wonder how big he is under those jeans of his.

Holy *shit.* Maybe it's the wine or the fireplace or something, but I'm almost to the point where I'm going to need to change my panties. I look all around the room, wondering if I've been drugged.

Nope. The TV is still there showing images of Richard Castle, the pictures on the walls aren't talking to me—not yet anyway—and the chairs aren't dancing with the side tables. But even without any pharmaceutical help, if he keeps this up, something very inappropriate is going to happen on this couch and nobody's even close to touching my VJ. How is that even possible?

What the . . . ?

"What the hell are you doing?" I ask, suddenly suspicious as I catch his sly expression.

A slow smile begins to spread across his face. "What? Me?" He looks down into his lap. "Just rubbing your feet." He looks at me again, and that smile is still there. Then he lifts an eyebrow. "Feel good?"

He could not possibly look sexier or more devious than he does right now.

I try to pull my feet back, but he grabs me by the ankles and hangs on. "They're still cold. Let me rub them up a little for ya. Get you niiiice and warm."

He's not scaring me, but I don't like this feeling of not being able to control my libido when he's so close. "Stop. Stop it." I sit up and push his hands away from my feet, slapping at him a little when that doesn't work.

He uses his elbow to fend me off, still holding me and keeping me prisoner.

Then the front door opens and we hear voices. "Just chill out," he whispers, winking at me, and then he looks up as his parents reach the entrance to the living room and stop to stare at us. "Oh hey, Ma. Dad. Pizza's on the way."

"Smells like you already had some," Angus says, lifting his nose toward the kitchen.

"Hi there," I say, twisting around to see them better, grateful for the interruption. My blood pressure is quickly going back to nondangerous levels. "We made spaghetti, but there wasn't much of it left. Ian called in some pizzas for you."

"Okay, sweetie. Thank you." Maeve takes her husband by the arm and leads him down the hall like she's in a hurry. Angus is looking at us over his shoulder. He's not quite in the kitchen before the sound of his voice floats back into the room.

"I thought he hated feet."

"Shhhh. Just sit down and I'll make you some soup."

The door dividing the kitchen off from the hallway, which has stayed open since I got here, closes, leaving Ian and me alone again.

I narrow my eyes at him. "If you hate feet, what are you doing rubbing mine?"

He goes back to looking at the television, but I can tell he isn't seeing anything on the screen. He's smiling too damn much.

"I guess I think yours are too cute to let freeze."

I catch him off guard with my sudden ninja moves by yanking my feet away in a blur of speed. Tucking them under me and wrapping the blanket around and under them, I scowl at him. A certain Google search I've performed in the past is coming to mind, and I slowly realize what this is all about. I should have known better than to think he was just being nice to my poor little old cold feet.

"Or maybe you've read too many articles about reflexology, and you think you can trick me into an orgasmic foot rub."

His head jerks sideways to look at me. He laughs a little and then stops. "You know about that?"

I snort and roll my eyes. "Please. I'm practically an Internet MD. Nice try." I'm still sweating from the almost orgasm he just gave me with a stupid foot rub. Damn that Ian MacKenzie! He's *so* going to pay for that one.

While I'm mad that he tried to manipulate me like that, I have to admire his creativity and general slyness. I've never met a guy more like me in my life than Ian MacKenzie. This could be dangerous.

He chuckles low in his throat. "Can't blame a guy for trying."

"Oh, hell yes, I can," I say softly. I want to kick him, this time really hard, but I'm afraid he'll try to capture my foot again and I'll let him.

We watch the rest of the show in silence, but my brain is a beehive of activity. What does it mean that he tried an orgasmic sneak attack on me? Was it the ultimate revenge for the ankle grazing he got at the shooting range or an actual desire to get me all hot and bothered?

Oh, this man has got to be the most maddening human being I've ever dealt with. I can't tell if he's really the awesome guy he's acting like or if this whole act is just a diabolical plan to get me back for the non–shooting incident.

I'm going to have to be on my guard for the next few days until I can figure this out. Thank goodness, I took two weeks off work. That should be enough time to determine his motives, have a little fun, and then end things on a high note, all while soaking up some of that BFF and Sarah-baby love.

My confidence restored now that I have a plan of action, I smile inside, thinking about how awesome Baker City is turning out to be. Ian MacKenzie is so going down, and he's not even going to see it coming until it's too late.

CHAPTER FIFTEEN

After abandoning the couch for Mack's bedroom and much-needed sleep, I spend hours tossing and turning. Sometime around one in the morning, I take out Millie, my new gun, and practice loading bullets into the clip and taking them out. After an hour, I'm pretty much qualified for the FBI.

I try to fall asleep again at 2:00 a.m. and finally go unconscious sometime after three in the morning. Then some ridiculous rooster starts crowing at five and forces me to get up after only two hours. I'm pretty sure I didn't get any REM sleep either.

Mental note: Buy earplugs in town today. Maybe I'll have to go introduce Millie to Mister Rooster so we can come to an understanding. *Say hello to my little friend.* I'll let him know that he can crow anytime after eight, but any time before that is just plain rude.

Ian's door is shut, but I can't tell if he's inside or out in the snow, doing chores. It seems like that's all they do around here. I'm tempted to knock, and if he's in there, ask him what his plan is for the day, but I don't. A hot shower is calling my name, and since the coffee kind of sucks here, it's all I have to wake me up from my exhausting two-hour nap. Besides, I don't want him thinking the first thing I want to do when I get up is see his face, even if it is.

As the hot water starts to steam up around me, my thoughts clarify. My first order of business is visiting Andie and Sarah. Then I'm going to buy some earplugs and some hair products more suited to this snow stuff. Then I'm going to . . .

Huh.

I frown.

There's nothing in my brain but a void. My thoughts stop there because I have no idea what else I'm going to do here. It's not like this is a hot spot of metropolitan life. There are no art museums, malls, or amusement parks, even. My entire day's plan is only going to take two hours. What am I supposed to do with the other twelve or so?

I shampoo my hair as I consider my options. I could probably follow Maeve around. Learn to can stuff. Maybe make some pickles or something. I could go look at some cows.

Yeah. That sounds like tons of fun.

Lie.

Or I could go find Ian and do whatever he's doing.

I smile as I picture it happening. The look on his face—irritation probably—and his smart-ass comments, him insisting I leave him alone . . . yes, this is a great plan. Way better than making pickles.

I hurry through conditioning my hair so I can be dressed and ready to go by the time he's up. Maybe I can even get him to take me into town for lunch. Then we'll see if he's really dating that Banana Hannah girl. We can go right into the diner together and see how she reacts. That way, I'll know everything I need to know before our big party at Boog's.

I have to make sure he doesn't try to get out of that little soirée. I'm really looking forward to meeting all these people who should have been in the waiting room while Sarah was being born. There's something going on here in this town, and I'm going to get to the bottom of it. I don't like the idea of my best friend being isolated without any friends to hang out with. A girl can go crazy without time to gab and gossip.

Luckily, I do hair, so I get to do it on the job all day long. Being a lawyer makes that almost impossible for Andie. She breaks laws when she gabs. How lame is that, I'd like to know. Why she ever decided to be a lawyer is beyond me. She's super smart and good at it, but damn, attorneys are no fun. She and I almost broke up over it. I'm so glad she met Mack and changed back to her old self.

I'm almost done drying my hair when there's a knock at the door. I don't have any makeup on, but that doesn't stop me. I crack it open and smile, expecting to see Ian there, insisting I let him use the facilities. I'm slightly disappointed when I find it's Maeve, but try not to let it show in my expression.

"Morning, sweetie. Ready for some breakfast?" She smiles, moving her whole head of hair up a little in the process.

I smell toast and it makes my stomach growl. "Sure. In about ten minutes—is that okay?"

"Sure thing. Everything's out on the table; just serve yourself." She turns to leave.

I open the door more fully and put my whole head out. "Is Ian still sleeping?"

She hesitates at the top of the stairs. "Oh, no, he's long gone."

I can feel my face fall. "Long gone? As in how long? How gone?"

"He's up for chores at four. I suppose he might be back for breakfast around eight, though."

"Eight?" What in the hell am I going to do for two hours? "Okay. See you downstairs." I start to go back into the bathroom, but Maeve's voice stops me.

"You want me to take you somewhere?"

I stick my face out again. "Oh, no, that's okay. I'll catch up with Ian later. I have things I can do." Like watch my nail polish dry or something equally stimulating.

"I can call him, if you like. If you need him for anything."

My face goes a little red. Did I sound that desperate to see him? God, I can't let his mother know I want to get in his pants. *Ack!* "No, no, don't bother. I'm fine—really, I am. I just need to finish with my hair, and I'll be down."

The sound of a loud bang comes from down at the bottom of the stairs, and a rush of cold air follows. It glides over my skin, making me want to draw back into the bathroom, where it's still steamy.

"Hey, Ma?!" Ian's shouting loud enough to be heard from one corner of the house to the other. He must be standing in the foyer. "That city girl up yet?"

The smile takes over my face before I have time to school my features, and Maeve catches it. She smiles too as she shouts back down the stairs. "Yes, she's all bright eyed and bushy tailed, as a matter of fact!"

"Good! Tell her to get her buns down here. I got something to show her."

"I guess you're getting a tour of some sort," she says to me in a low tone before leaving to go down the stairs.

"I'll be done in ten minutes!" I yell.

"You've got one!" Ian says back. "I'm not waitin'!"

I slam the door and drop the hair dryer on the floor in my rush to make myself presentable. The plastic end of it goes flying off and hits the wall, but I ignore it. If I had a nickel for every time that happened in my life, I'd no longer have to go to work on Tuesdays. My hair goes up into a knot with an elastic holding it in place, and my makeup is limited to mascara and eyeliner.

Boom. Done. Who says I'm high maintenance?

Wrapped in my short silk robe, I sprint on tiptoes from the bathroom to my bedroom and throw on pink thong underwear, matching lacy bra, jeans from yesterday, and a college sweatshirt that has seen much better days. Since I spent so much time on the ground yesterday, I figure I'd better be prepared for more of the same today, especially when Ian's going to be my tour guide.

I wonder what it is he wants to show me. I hope it's him naked. I'm totally ready to melt some snow. I'll show him to give me sneak-attack, orgasmic foot rubs. He has no idea who he's messing with.

My new boots slide on with a whisper, and I'm ready to go. I don't know how serious he was about that one minute, but I don't want to chance missing out on whatever this is. I grab my purse and throw it over my shoulder as I run out of the room.

Dashing down the stairs, I stop at the bottom, realizing as I look at the coat hooks next to me that my leather bomber is out in the bed of the truck and covered in amniotic fluid.

The front door opens, and Ian sticks his head inside the house. "Well, come on, I don't have all day."

"I don't have a jacket. Andie got her goo all over mine yesterday."

He pushes the door open and steps in far enough to grab a big camouflage jacket off a hook. "Wear this one." Tossing it at me, he doesn't even wait for me to respond. He's out the door and gone, leaving behind some melting snow on the floor and a whole bunch of seriously cold air. My nipples turn into pebbles and not for the good reason. I hope they don't break off when I get outside.

I hold the coat out in front of me and speak loud enough to be heard through the closed door. "This thing is fugly. Whose is it?"

"It's mine," he says from the porch. "Come on! You're going to miss it!"

I throw my arm through one of the holes and grab the door, hurrying to catch up to him. The little high school girl in me is thrilled to be wearing Ian's coat. It's almost as good as a letterman's jacket. Hello, *Grease* throwback! I could totally do Sandy, and Ian wouldn't make a bad Danny now that I think about it.

"Whooo!" I yell, as the air is stolen from my lungs by the cold. Visions of Ian and me doing a musical together vanish from my

brain. I'm suddenly stuck in place. I have never felt anything so awful in my entire life. My nostril hairs are now frozen thorns inside my nose.

"Get your jacket on, fool," he says, halfway across the yard walking backward. "It's below zero out here."

"Ho . . . leeee . . . . sheeee . . . *it!* It is *cold* out here, mother *fudger*!" I jam my other arm into the jacket and gather it around me, wrapping it as tight as I can. Thankfully, it's way too big, so my hands are out of the cold and stuck up in the sleeves, and there's material over my neck and down to my knees. Still, I'm shivering. I'm afraid my hair is still kind of wet. Is this how hypothermia starts? I hope not.

I reach the truck he's standing next to and peek out from between the folds of cloth. "Where . . . are . . . we . . . going?" My teeth are chattering.

He reaches down and pushes my hands apart. I protest until I realize he's looking for my zipper.

"We're going to look at something I think you'll like, if you can ever get your butt in the truck."

"It's not even six in the morning yet, Ian. And you gave me no notice at all."

"High maintenance," he says, shaking his head as he zips up my zipper. He reaches into an outside pocket of the jacket and pulls out a lump of black leather. "Put these on."

I've never been so happy to see a butt-ugly pair of gloves in my life. I can already feel the warmth they're going to bring to my aching fingers.

I drop one trying to get it on too fast, and we both bend over at the same time to get it. Our heads knock into each other like two coconuts, and I fall backward trying to escape the pain.

"What in the Sam Hill . . ." Ian stands there holding his head, staring at me.

I lie on the ground, looking up at him as I hold my forehead. "Ow. Headache."

"You have got to be the least coordinated person I have ever met," he says, holding out a hand.

I roll over onto my side and get up on my hands and knees. "Go away. I don't need your help." When I finally stand, I spin around to stare him down.

He jumps with fright and then looks guilty, like I caught him at something. He stares at the ground, his face a little pinker than before.

My hands go to my hips and I use the opportunity to pull my pants up a little. It's possible I just gave him a plumber-crack flash in my efforts to stand. *Oops.* Good thing I have my cute thong on and not my granny panties. "Listen, Ian . . . if you and I are going to get along, you're going to have to stop insulting me."

"Insulting you?"

"Yes. You've called me high maintenance and klutzy. It's not nice to say that to girls. Didn't your mother teach you to be nice?"

"I suppose she did." He pushes his lips together and nods once.

"Good. So make your mother happy. Be a nice boy." I pat him on the cheek a couple times, maybe harder than I should, but he needs a little wake-up call. "Now be a gentleman and get my door for me."

He looks like he's about to say something smart back at me, but instead, he moves to the side and opens the passenger door of the big black truck we're standing next to. "Can I give you a hand?" he asks, holding out a gloved palm.

"Thank you," I say, grinning. I'm so happy he's behaving himself. Maybe he really does want to get along with me.

"You have a nice smile, you know that?" he asks. He's staring at me. "You've got a dimple right *there* in your cheek." His other hand reaches up and pokes me in the face. Firmly. Then he smiles.

I grit my teeth together to keep from saying something I'll regret. He is totally baiting me right now, waiting for me to fight back, which is exactly why I'm not going to do that.

Today, the tables will be turning—and not on me. Ian will be getting a taste of his own medicine if it's the last thing I accomplish before I leave. I hope it doesn't take me the whole vacation to do it, though. I'm really looking forward to seeing it happen.

CHAPTER SIXTEEN

"So what are we going to see?" I ask once we're both settled in the cab of the truck, with my purse on the floorboard at my feet.

"Just you wait and see," he says, shifting the truck into drive.

I had expected him to go reverse out of the driveway, but instead, he leaves off the back of the property. He's using a tiny shifter instead of the larger, regular one.

"What's that one for?" I ask, pointing to the smaller thing.

"Four-wheel drive. We're going off-road."

"Is that safe?" A whisper of fear runs through my body.

He glances and me and wiggles his eyebrows. "Probably not."

Warmth rushes into my heart. I don't doubt for a second that I'm perfectly okay with Ian. I stare out the side window for a moment to get my girly feelings under control. I can't let him know he affects me so easily. Resting my nose on the material of his jacket, I breathe the smell in. It's so Ian. *Delish.*

"What are you thinking up there in that bean of yours?" he asks.

"What bean?" I shift my gaze to the non-road in front of us. There are dirty tracks leading away from the house, going up toward the mountains that we're at the base of. I hope we don't fall off anything steep. How good are four-wheel-drive shifters with ice on the road? I can't imagine it's much better than a regular shifter.

"The Mexican jumping bean that's your brain. Always jumping from one crazy thing to another."

I glare at him. "First of all, the things I think are not crazy—they're interesting. And second, I was thinking . . . that the weather is nice today." No way am I going to tell him that he makes me feel safe. His head will blow up so big, it'll explode.

He laughs. "That's a lie. You hate the snow."

I sigh loudly, staring out at the bright white expanse in front of us. The snow never stops out here. I think it would drive me crazy to stare at it all day. "I'm trying to get over that."

"Some people never do. I'm not much of a fan myself, to be honest."

I look at him, suspicious. This statement seems very disloyal to the family for some reason. "How can you live here in Baker City and not be a fan of snow?"

He shrugs. "I didn't pick this place. My family did. Doesn't mean I have to like it."

"But you're a grown man. You're an architect. You could move anywhere. Why stay if you're not happy?"

He loses his happy face. "It's not that easy."

"Sure it is. You pack your bags, you say good-bye, you go. Done."

He looks sideways at me for a second before going back to facing the road. "You make it sound easy, that's for sure."

"Tell me what's so hard about it."

"How about if I just show you?"

A smile turns up the corners of my mouth. "Hmmm . . . I'm intrigued."

He grins, still facing out the window.

"Fine. I'm convinced. Show me what makes it so hard to leave here."

"Almost there," he says, turning the truck around a wide bend in the road. There's a large tree in the way with loads of snow balanced on its green branches. I cringe a little as we drive by, wondering if it's enough to qualify as an avalanche.

Our previous conversation in the gun store comes back to me, and my happy feelings dissipate. Maybe this is a setup so he can really get me good. "Are you going to show me a dead animal? Because if you do, I'll never forgive you. I'm not kidding, Ian."

He frowns, downshifting the truck to get it to go up a small hill with more power. "Now why would I do that?"

I shrug, feeling a little ashamed now that I even considered it. He might be a pain in the butt, but he's never struck me as mean-spirited. I'm going to go ahead and forgive myself, though, because I'm running on two hours of sleep. No one can think straight without some good REM.

"You said you like to hunt," I explain, hoping he won't hold my near accusation against me.

"Yeah, but not for sport. I eat what I hunt, plain and simple."

I don't have enough Google research ammo to have the grocery store versus wild game argument with him right now, so I keep my mouth shut. Later I'll explain in a way we can both understand. After I've had some REM and some time in front of the computer.

"Here we go," he says, coming over the top of a hill and putting the truck into park. Stomping down on the emergency brake, he cracks open his door. "Just walk quiet and stay kind of behind me."

I throw my purse strap across my body and follow him out of the truck. I have to wade through snow up past my knees to get to him.

He reaches a hand out behind him and I take it, thrilled that we're actually holding hands. My inner high school girl nearly squeals with delight.

"See over there?" He points to a black blob out in a flat area of snow. There's a lot of mud showing through the drifts of the frozen stuff, and for a couple seconds I think he's brought me out here to show me a big rock. But then I realize the rock is moving.

"What is that . . . ? Is that a cow?"

"Yep. She's calving."

"She's what?" I move closer, peering at the event over his shoulder.

"She's having a baby."

Movement out of the corner of my eye draws my attention away. There are actually several cows standing around, some with small calves next to them and others just hanging out alone.

A loud moo in the center grabs my attention back. "She's having a baby out here in the snow? In the mud?"

"Yep. Can't stop Mother Nature."

He starts to walk again.

"Are you sure we can go that close?" I'm holding onto both his hand and his arm with an iron grip. My purse bangs against my leg.

"Yep. She might need some help. She knows me, though. She'll be fine."

I start a whispered chant without really thinking about it. "Oh my god, oh my god, oh my god . . . this is crazy, this is crazy, this is crazy . . ." I slip a few times, but Ian's as solid as a brick house. I just hang onto him for dear life, and before I know it, we're standing just feet away from her, and my butt is still dry. It's some kind of Christmas miracle.

The cow is standing too.

"Doesn't she want to lie down?" I ask. Her sides are heaving, and she looks really uncomfortable.

"Yeah, just watch."

About a minute later, the cow moves down to her knees and then flops down onto her side. Something is sticking out of her back end. Something . . . gooey. And *big*.

"Oh, my . . . that's gross."

"Shhhhh, just wait."

I'm not sure how much time passes, but however long it is, I spend the entire period feeling sorry for that cow. Andie was right. The only way to do this whole birth thing is in a warm hospital bed with nurses and doctors standing all over the place with blankets. I can't feel my toes or my fingers anymore.

The cow stands when I think it couldn't be possible because she has this giant *thing* hanging out of the back end of her, and then this big blob just slides out. The baby falls right out onto the ground, a white sheet of something-I-don't-want-to-know-what covering its face. It lies there in the snow, not moving.

"Come on, come on . . ." Ian sounds worried.

"What's wrong?" I look from his face to the cow. The baby still isn't doing anything. In fact, if I hadn't seen it come out of the mother cow, I wouldn't even know it was a cow. It looks like a giant, gooey alien on the ground.

"Quick!" he says in a loud whisper. "Get the towels out of the back seat!" He takes off toward the cow and leaves me standing there.

I want to ask him a thousand questions, but I don't. Instead, I go as fast as I can through the snowdrifts back to the truck. I only fall once trying to get inside.

There's a stack of old-looking towels neatly folded on the seat. Grabbing them, I struggle to turn around and find Ian again.

He's kneeling next to the calf, wiping muck off its face. The mother cow is licking the baby's back legs, but it's not having any effect that I can see.

I think my heart has turned into a lump of iron, it feels so heavy in my chest. The baby definitely looks dead. "Oh my god," I whisper as it settles into my brain that I could be witnessing the death of a newborn baby. "No, no, no, no, nooo!" I sound like I'm crying. I can't get there fast enough. It's like one of those nightmares where I have to run in deep water. "Ian! I'm coming!"

I face-plant into the snow, landing on the towels. Getting up as quickly as I can, I take them into my arms again, letting the bottom one drop a little so I can try and shake off the snow that's clinging to it.

As I get closer to the cow, it becomes easier to walk. The animals have trampled down the ground and turned it mostly to muck. But now I'm afraid there's a bull around ready to hook me with his horns.

"Come on, stop dinking around!" Ian's waving me over, with his arm going in big circles.

"Where are the bulls?"

"There are no bulls out here; they're all cows. Come on!"

I see some horns, but instead of arguing, I run over with tiny steps, trying to minimize my chances of biting the dust again. Ian grabs the top towel from my arms as soon as I'm close enough and starts rubbing the calf all over with it.

"Come on, do it," he demands. "Rub!"

I drop the towels on the ground and take one, moving over to the other side of the baby cow. "Just rub?" I ask, moving closer.

"Rub. Stimulate her. Wake her up."

I put the towel on her butt and start rubbing. Tears are sliding down my cheeks as I feel her lifeless body wiggle beneath my hands. "She's a girl?" I ask. All I can think about is baby Sarah in the hospital.

"Yeah, she's a girl, I think. Come on, girl, wake up. Wake up. Breathe. You can do it."

I start rubbing with two hands. Her little body squishes around with our combined movements. "Come on, baby cow, wake up!" I say, trying to talk around my tears. "Don't you dare die. No cows die on my watch, you hear me! No cows die!"

The mother lets out a moo that just breaks my heart. She leans down, takes one more lick of the baby, and then walks away.

"She's leaving!" I cry, freaking out over the idea.

"Just keep rubbing," Ian says, focusing on the baby.

I crawl in the mud and snow up to the calf's head and rub around its ears and eyes and nose. "Come on, baby cow. Don't you dare die."

Then a flash of memory comes to me, and I pause as I consider it. There was this guy once on YouTube and this baby deer that needed resuscitation on the side of the road . . .

I grab the cow's head and turn it to look up at me. "Might as well give it a try," I say to no one in particular. Clamping the calf's mouth closed, I lean down, preparing to lock my lips to its nostrils.

"What in the Sam Hill are you doing?" Ian asks, ceasing his rubbing.

I don't look up at him, all my attention focused on the disgusting good deed I'm about to do for this ranch. They'd better appreciate it, that's all I can say.

"I'm going to give it CPR."

Before Ian has a chance to respond, the calf's body bucks up in some kind of seizure, and a big glob of something warm hits me in the face.

I'm suddenly blinded, afraid to open my eyes. Whatever it was she projectile vomited begins to slide down my forehead.

"That's-a girl!" Ian yells, his voice full of joy. He claps me on the back several times. It makes me burp once. I would probably care enough to respond if I could open my eyes, but I can't see a thing. My eyes, nose, and mouth are covered in what I can only assume are cow loogies.

"Oh . . . Jesus, Mary, and Joseph . . ." Ian says in a low voice.

And then he starts to laugh.

Keeping my eyes closed, I spit out everything that's anywhere near my mouth and say in a very calm voice. "Ian. Get me a towel."

CHAPTER SEVENTEEN

"So what you're saying is that you stay here in Baker City because there's always a chance that you'll be covered in cow loogies." I nod as I use the only remaining nondisgusting towel to remove crud from my hair. I'm sitting in the front seat of the truck, and we're headed back to the ranch. "Yeah. I can see why you don't move away. Who'd want to miss that?"

"Don't try and lie and say that you're not happy as a pig in mud right now." Ian's poo-eating grin is almost unbearable. Almost.

I look over my shoulder at our back-seat passenger. "I'm not saying anything about anything." The little black heifer is blinking her eyes, looking at me. It's like she knows she goobered on me, and it somehow connects us. We've bonded on an elemental level. Maternal feelings I've never had before well up in me.

For a cow.

I must be crazy.

I turn to look out the windshield, so I won't get suckered into anything dangerous. "So where to now?"

"We've got to get her back to the barn. Bottle-feed her."

"Are you serious?" I look at him to see if he's laughing at me. "Why not just leave her out there with her mother?" I saw all those other babies out there. Seems like it wasn't too dangerous. They looked happy.

"I can't be sure the mother's going to take care of her or that one of the other cows will adopt her, and she's too little to fend for herself."

I look back again at the beautiful long eyelashes that are just starting to show as the goop around them dries. "You mean . . . she might die? After all we did to wake her up?"

"Nah, we won't let her die." He pats me on the leg. "Don't worry. She'll be fine."

I give up trying to ignore her and stare at her the rest of the way back to the ranch. She really is pretty beautiful, especially as she dries out. Her fur is all black except for a small white star shape on her forehead.

Ian parks the truck next to a big barn and slides her out of the back seat, taking her in his arms and bringing her inside. There's a stall with some straw in it, and he lies her down there, taking the ropes off her legs that he said were necessary to keep her from trying to stand up in the truck. He closes us inside with her.

"Go ahead, little Candy, try and stand up now. You can do it." He nudges her with his boot as he steps back.

"Candy?"

He looks at me and grins. "Yeah. Pretty cute, right?"

"You named a cow after me?"

He shrugs. "You mad at me for it?"

My emotions are a whirlwind. This is completely crazy. I can't tell if he means it as an insult or a compliment, but I feel like crying with happiness.

In the end, the little cow baby standing up and wobbling around on her spindly legs wins me over. "No, I'm not mad." I cannot wipe the smile off my face.

Ian leaves me there to ogle her. She appears unsteady for a while, but then she starts acting like an expert cow. It doesn't take long before she looks like she's ready to try running. Cows are way more coordinated than humans, apparently.

"Here," Ian says, bumping me on the arm with a big white plastic thing that has a giant brown nipple on it. "Give her some of this."

I stare at it and then him. He doesn't look like he's messing with me. "Seriously?"

"Yep. It's all on you. Feed her and she lives. Don't and she dies."

My jaw drops open. "Harsh!"

"That's life on the ranch." He leaves me there holding the bottle.

I look at Candy and she looks at me.

"You want some of this?" I ask her.

She takes a couple steps in my direction and stops. I take one toward her and stop, holding it out.

She touches her nose on the end of it and bumps it. I almost drop it.

I giggle. "Hey. Easy, little girl. Don't be so pushy."

She walks closer, and I hold onto the bottle with two hands. "Easy does it," I say.

A big tongue comes out and swipes at it.

Wow. That's a long tongue.

I hold it steady, ready for anything. I hope she's not going to loogie on me again, but if she decides to, I'll probably let her. I'm her momma now.

She opens her mouth, takes the end of it, and then it's a tug-of-war between us. She slurps and sucks and goobers all over the place as she drinks every last drop. I feel so proud, like I'm the one doing everything.

When she's done, she dances around in the straw, even kicking up her back legs a little, only falling twice. She couldn't possibly be any cuter. I cannot stop staring at her. I wonder if they'll let me sleep out here with her tonight. I probably should. Don't babies need to eat every couple hours?

"You ready to head out again?" Ian's hanging over the top of the stall door, looking at me.

It takes a few seconds for me to get my head out of the clouds. "Huh . . . what? Out? Out where?"

"I've got to go do a headcount. If you'd rather stay . . ."

The idea of having Ian leave my side is unacceptable. Candy is sweet, but Ian is . . . sweeter. Plus he might need me to do CPR again. "Could there be more babies out there?"

"Possibly. You never know."

I jump to my feet. "I'll come." I pause in the doorway. "See you later, Candy. Take a nap while I'm gone."

I nearly melt when she turns a few circles and flops down in the straw.

Ian chuckles as we leave the barn.

"Don't laugh at me," I say, feeling self-conscious. I try to toss my hair over my shoulder, and it's then that I realize I still have cow goo stuck in it. Oh, how far I've fallen. If the girls at the salon could see me right now, they'd take pictures, Facebook them, and never let me forget it.

"I'm not laughing," he says.

I look over and see the smile on his face. "What's that grin all about then?"

"Nothin'." He gets in the truck and leaves me to open my own door.

I sigh, knowing that there are things about Ian that are pretty much hopeless, but that one of them is *not* the fact that he's a hunter. He can't possibly enjoy killing animals . . . not when he gets so much joy bringing them to life. This makes me way happier than I have a right to be.

CHAPTER EIGHTEEN

I feel like an old pro this time out in the truck. We bounce over rocks and ruts like it's nothing. I don't even have to hold onto the oh-shit handle up by the window anymore. All I can think about is Candy. She kind of looks like me, and her name couldn't be more adorable. I'm like a rancher now.

Ian stops the truck and stares out into the field we were in earlier. He doesn't say anything; he just looks at the cows.

His sigh of frustration is the first sign that there might be something wrong. The second is when he bangs the steering wheel with the heel of his hand. "Dammit!"

"What's wrong?" I ask.

"We're missing one."

"What?" I lean forward and look out the windshield. "A baby?"

"A pregnant cow. She might've gone off to have the calf somewhere, but I don't see where she could be." He opens his door a crack and looks at me. "I should've counted when we were out here before. Wait here. I'm going to see what I can find."

"No way are you leaving me here!" I grab the handle of my door.

"It's cold outside. If I need you, I'll call." He takes his phone out of his pocket. "Put your number in here."

I do as he asks and then call myself with his phone, logging his number into my list of contacts.

"Okay, but call right away," I say, hating the fact that he's leaving and I'm staying. "I can bring towels and whatever you need."

He winks at me as he takes his phone back. "Gotcha. Now stay out of trouble. I'll be back soon."

"If you're not back in an hour, I'm coming to find you."

Ian looks up at the sky. "If I'm not back in a half hour, call my dad. I'll text you the number."

He leaves me there in the truck, and when he's around the corner, out of sight, my phone beeps. The text from Ian glows out from my screen.

Here's my dad's number. And remember. Stay in the truck, stay out of trouble.

I text him back. *Ha. Like that's going to happen.*

He sends me back a smiley face, and I can't stop grinning. I think we're friends now. Why that makes me so deliriously happy, I can't say. I have lots of friends, both men and women. I don't really need any more; my funeral's going to be standing room only as it is. But none of them have been able to make my blood boil one second and my panties get all twisted up the next. Not like Ian.

My mind wanders as I stare out at the white expanse before me. I've had a few boyfriends I might call serious. None that I've lived with, but two that I considered being with long term. But for one reason or another, I always broke it off with them. It wasn't a fight or a major upset that caused it. I guess I just got bored or restless. Andie says I need a man who can keep me guessing, keep me laughing, make me feel like I've met my match. She's always said that one day I would meet him . . . my match, whatever that means.

I wonder if it could be Ian. That would be mighty inconvenient with him being here in the top left of the map and me being in the bottom right.

And if it could be him, is that what I'd want? He lives in the middle of cow patty central, and I live in the city. He sleeps three hours a day, and I need at least eight. He's fashion challenged, and I'm completely coordinated. I get the impression he's not much into commitment now that he's been burned, and I'm looking for that, especially now that I've seen Andie lying there in that bed with Sarah in her arms and Mack hanging over them.

I want that. I seriously, really truly do. For the first time in my life, I want to be part of something bigger than just my daily grind. I want a family I can call my own, people who will be waiting for me at home, who will celebrate with me and google stuff with me and laugh at all the crazy things life has to offer with me.

I frown. The conclusion after examining all the evidence is that this relationship with Ian would be doomed from the start . . . if we were planning on getting serious. But that *wouldn't* be the case if we were just going to have some fun, right? I mean, we could go out to that party, maybe on a couple actual dates, sleep together a few times . . . that wouldn't ruin things. It would be fun. Then when my vacation is up, I'd leave.

Maybe we'll email or text once in a while once I'm back home. And when I visit again, if he's still single, we could have some more fun, pick up where we left off. Or maybe by then I'd have found my one true love and I'd be having babies. Ian could just be my friend then. A great memory of times gone by.

It's like I'm convincing myself to be happy with this idea. I know for a fact I wouldn't be okay with doing nothing, just ignoring him for the rest of my trip. Too much has happened between us for me to walk away like that. We just brought a baby cow back to life! But for us to someday be in a family together? No. Not realistic.

Sigh. Talk about a sad face.

It's not like I really have a choice in the matter, though. Life is what it is, and I just have to adapt.

I nod my head, officially making the decision. If Ian's willing, we're going to hang out, drink a little, dance a little, and get naked a little. And then I'll go home and we'll text a little. After that, I'll focus on finding the guy who I can build a family with. My match.

A text comes over my phone, distracting me from my plan making.

Don't get out of the car. There's a big cat nearby.

A cat? In my brain a picture of a giant Persian cat pops up. It looks exactly like my neighbor's cat, but bigger. Then I realize that Ian isn't talking about an over-sized house cat, and my heart seizes up.

I text back with a speed I've never possessed before. *How big?*

Cougar size. Don't get out of the truck.

Ack!

My fingers fly over the keypad. *But you're out there!*

I'll be fine. Stay in the truck.

"Oh my god, oh my god, oh my god . . ." I stare at my phone. Ian's out there with a fucking mountain lion, and I'm inside the truck with my gun. I'm safe, but is he?

Do you have a gun? I ask.

No. Stay inside the truck.

Now he's just pissing me off. *Stop telling me to stay in the truck. I heard you the first time.*

My phone beeps with his next message: *Stay in the truck.*

I dig through my purse and find Millie. Weighing her in my hands, I stare out the window. My heart is racing and so is my mind. Ian's out there without a weapon. A cow is missing. There's a cougar out there too. And how does Ian know it's out there? Did it eat the cow? Did he see footprints? Is he staring it down right this very second?

I put the gun on the seat and pick up my phone. *How do you know it's a cougar?* I ask.

I wait precious seconds for an answer that doesn't come.

Ian?

My hands start shaking.

Ian, that's not funny. Answer me.

Nothing comes. No beep, no text, no nothing. I crawl over to his side of the car and look out his window, shaking all over. Snow is starting to fall, obscuring my view. The cows I could see before are now veiled. I can't see very far down the road behind us anymore either.

Ian, so help me, if you don't answer this text, I'm getting out of the truck.

I'm giving him ten seconds.

10 . . . 9 . . . 8 . . . 7 . . .

I'm not kidding, Ian. Don't be a dick.

6 . . . 5 . . . 4 . . .

I'm getting out!

3 . . . 2 . . .

Right now! I'm getting out!

1.

He'd better be fighting off a cougar right now, that's all I have to say. I zip my coat up, put on my borrowed gloves, grab my gun, and throw open my door.

"Don't worry, Ian!" I yell. "I'm coming!"

CHAPTER NINETEEN

I hold the gun pointed at the ground, worried any sound will make me freak and pull the trigger. If I accidentally kill a cow out here, I will die of a broken heart. Candy would never look at me again if I took her momma out, even though her momma did kind of reject her. And Ian will never forgive me if I graze him again.

Ian's boot tracks are all muddled in the center of the field, but as they move out toward the edges, they become more clear. He's left the clearing for a wooded area. I'm terrified, but I keep going. Ian needs me.

"Ian?!" I shout out into the woods. My voice sounds muffled. I expected an echo, but it's more like I've yelled into a pillow.

"Ian! I'm coming! Where are you?!"

"Get back in the truck!" He sounds mad and a little desperate.

His voice came from my left, so I alter my direction. My legs are quaking with the fear and the cold. There's a ringing in my ears too, which may be the result of my blood pressure being off the charts.

"I'm already out!" I yell, trying to use the same footsteps he already made. It's way better than fighting the snow drifts. Under the trees it's not as bad, but it's still way worse than any street I've ever walked in Florida. I'm never going to complain about a silly rainstorm ever again, I swear.

He shouts again. "Heeyah! Get outta here! Yah!!"

"You don't have to be rude about it!" He needs a serious lesson in manners.

"I'm not talking to you! Heeyah! Beat it! Yah!!"

Either Ian's having a seizure, or something is very wrong. My brain won't let me analyze what that wrong thing is or could be. I've suddenly lost the ability to reason. Ian sounds like he's riding a horse that won't move. His voice is getting louder, though, so I'm confident I'll get to the bottom of this mystery very soon. *Please God, don't let there be a lion there. Let it be . . . paw prints or . . . a fox or . . .*

"Where are you?!" I yell, falling into full-on panic mode, knowing I'm just fooling myself. This shit is real, and it's going down right now, with Ian in the middle of it and completely unarmed. "I can't see you!"

"Goddammit, Candice, I told you to stay in the damn truck!"

I see some movement behind a thick grouping of trees and smile. "Ah-ha! Found ya!" I come from between two of the trees to walk up behind him. I feel much better seeing him standing there in one piece. Just being in his presence makes me brave. I am She-Rah! *Rawr.*

"Congratulations," he says, out of breath and obviously angry. "Look who else you found."

He has a giant stick in his hand—more a small log, really—and he's pointing it at something on the ground.

It makes no sense, but I expect to see a cow. The concept of a mountain lion being anywhere but behind zoo bars is too foreign for my brain to process. But instead of seeing a cow, I see a cat. A really, really *big* cat.

And it ain't no Persian one either.

"That's a . . ." My empty hand goes to my mouth as I try to process what I'm seeing. Yes, I know he told me there was one of these out here, but reading that in a text and seeing one live are two totally different things. Cougars are waaaay bigger in real life than they are on Google, by the way. This one is the same size as Ian, pretty much.

As I take that into consideration, that's when it all becomes clear to me. Ian and I are probably going to die out here together in this fucking cold-ass snow. My life flashes before my eyes, and I ache from head to toe, knowing I'll never get the chance to find the happiness that my best friend Andie did. It's too late for me.

"That's the cat who took out a fully grown cow," Ian says, snapping me back to reality. "Now we just need to get out of here before she takes us out too." A tiny spark of hope comes to life in my heart at the idea that Ian has a plan to save us. My hero!

The cougar's ears are back, and she's growling low in her throat. My fantasy about surviving and that spark of hope both disappear in a puff of smoke. This thing is definitely going to kill us.

I've heard that expression where people say that the hair on the back of their necks stood up, but until this moment, I never understood how that could possibly happen. Well, let me tell you . . . it seriously does. The hair goes right up from the roots. Oh, and people can also pee themselves a little when terrified, that's a fact.

Ian talks softly to me. "We're going to just keep waving this branch and making noise and hope that scares her off. Look as big as you can."

"What?" I stare at Ian. He's talking crazy. This demon-possessed lion is going to eat us for breakfast. We are bagels and lox as far as she's concerned. There's blood all over her mouth already from her appetizer course of steak tartare.

"Cats respond to threats. Be a threat!" He waves the branch he's holding at her and yells again, some kind of caveman nonsense.

My hand that has Millie in it lifts of its own accord, without any conscious thought on my part. I see it coming up in my peripheral vision, but I can't bring myself to point it at her. I aim it to her left instead. "Go away, cat. I don't want to have to shoot you." My voice comes out weak and trembling, and my arm is weaving all over the place, left and right, up and down. At this point I'm sure I won't be able to hit even the broad side of a barn, let alone a slinky, crouching lion, so I pray she knows what a gun is and the fact that she should avoid having one pointed near her.

Ian stops waving his branch around. "What in the hell . . . ?"

"Go on!" I yell, wiggling my arm a little at the lion, getting braver since she hasn't yet killed me and Ian seems to have calmed down. "This is way more dangerous than that stick he has. Just move on and I won't shoot you."

She crouches lower and I lose some of the force in my voice. "Please? Pretty please with sugar on top?"

"You brought a gun?" Ian turns his head to look at me. He sounds confused.

The cat takes a slow, slinky step toward us, lowering herself really, really close to the ground. Her stomach is on the snow. I saw my neighbor's cat do this once, right before he attacked a butterfly. He moved so fast the poor thing never saw it coming. I don't want to be like that butterfly.

I point the gun at the cougar and try to imagine myself pulling the trigger. My hand is shaking so hard right now I could possibly hit Ian and he's still standing next to me. Efforts to straighten my hand out go nowhere. "Go away, cougar!" I yell, my voice bordering on hysterical. "I'm not kidding!"

"Give me that," Ian says, reaching for the pistol.

I shove him with my other arm, knowing we don't have time for him to play the man-hero with me. "Get off! It's my gun!"

It's at this point that things go a little blurry for me.

A seriously vicious cat scream comes from somewhere in front of me.

I pee some more.

Then I'm hit by a mini-bus.

At least it felt like a mini-bus. I fall backward, and I'm pretty sure Ian goes with me. My head clunks against something really hard, making me see stars. A headache blossoms from there.

Something heavy is on me, and the sounds—the only word I can use to describe them is *unholy*—fill the air around us. I can't see anything but a blur of color and motion sprinkled amongst the dancing, head-banger stars that were floating above my face, but one thing is very clear: someone is about to die. I'm pretty sure it's going to be me.

I pee a lot more.

CHAPTER TWENTY

My fists squeeze as I try to fend off my attacker, and a loud shot rings out.

Snow flies up, blinding me, and someone punches me in the gut, forcing all the air out of me.

I wheeze as I try to catch my breath. The stars are back, in place of my vision, when the oxygen isn't enough.

A heavy weight comes off me, and snow flies into my face again, freezing it, while something on my arm burns like a bejeezus. I can finally breathe again, though, so the stars go away. Unfortunately, the headache does not.

"Gimme that!" Ian yells, taking something heavy out of my hand. Was I carrying the log? When did I get the log from Ian? No, wait . . . it's my gun.

I hear two more gunshots and then mostly silence.

At least there's no more of that crazy screaming. Now there's just heavy breathing. I'm no longer panicked because I've decided I'm probably dead, or nearly so, and it's not as awful as I expected it to be. My lungs are finally functioning again, but unfortunately, my bladder is no longer up to the task. I have completely wet my pants. Not just a little, but a lot. Normally, I'd be embarrassed over something like that, but my head hurts too much to care. Besides, I'm going to die anyway. What's a little pee-pants problem in the grand scheme of things?

When I open my eyes, Ian's face is hovering above mine.

"Hi," I say, a little dizzy and definitely dazed. Everything is so bright around me. Maybe I'm not going to die.

"You okay?" He glances down at something in the snow near me.

"I think so. Aside from peeing my pants, anyway." I frown as I try to move my arm. "Something burns." Since death is supposed to bring relief from pain, I'm pretty sure I'm not on the death's doorstep now. If I had any more pee in me, I'd let it go now out of relief, but I don't.

"Let me help you up." He leans down and puts his arm behind my back, digging it into the snow.

"Where's the lion?" I ask, sitting up and looking around. Snow is covering my face and dripping from my eyelashes. I blink a few times to see better. There's red in the snow around us. *Blood.* I try not to let it send me into a panic. Whose blood is that? Is it Ian's?

I scan Ian's body to see if he's been shot or bitten. There are some red smears on the front of his coat. "Are you okay?" I sit up straighter and hold my palm out at his chest. "Did I shoot you?" My heart sinks as my fingers move to cover my mouth. *Please, God, don't let me have shot him!*

"No. Not me." Ian stares at my side.

I follow his gaze and see my arm lying there limp. The thick camouflage jacket I'm wearing has been torn and there's blood coming from the tear. I can feel myself go pale as I get dizzy again. My head is throbbing with pain.

"Did I shoot *myself*?" Oh my god! How colossally clumsy! Ian will never let me live that down. And the scar will be hideous. *Ugh.* Why did I think buying a gun was a good idea?!

Ian almost smiles. "No. Not you either." He points at my arm. "You shot the cougar who did that to you. I think. Can I look at it?"

I nod wordlessly. This is some kind of weird nightmare I'm having. No way is this real life. My vision goes blurry for a few seconds before focusing again. There are trees everywhere. And snow. And red. And Ian. He looks worried.

"Let's get back to the truck first. It's warmer there." He puts his shoulder under my armpit and lifts me to my feet. Then without any warning, he swoops me into his arms and carries me through the snow like a giant baby.

"I can walk, you know." I'm totally humiliated that he's carrying me and my pee-pee jeans in his arms. We are bonding way too much. How is he ever going to sleep with me now? Every time he looks at me, all he's going to see is the girl who wet her pants when a cougar showed up. That's not sexy. Not sexy at all. It makes my headache worse.

"It's probably better if you don't walk right now."

Something warm is trickling down my arm. *Please don't let that be my blood.* "Is that snow?" I ask. "I hope it's snow." I'm wet everywhere. It's probably snow.

"Never thought I'd hear you say that," Ian says, breathing hard with the effort of getting both of us across the field.

I'm about to correct him since he misunderstood me, but I'm distracted by the fact that we're alone in this place. For some reason, all the cows are gone. Maybe I'm just confused. Maybe none of this is really happening. Nothing is in focus, and those damn brain stars are back, dancing around my head. *Ping! Ping! Ping!* Fireflies in my skull.

"Where'd all the cows go?" I ask, trying to focus on reality.

"They're not fans of cougars. They beat it out of here. We'll round 'em up later."

"I can help." I really want him to put me down. Maybe he hasn't smelled my pee-pants yet.

"Nooo, I don't think so." He chuckles and then his expression shifts into something more serious.

"I have a gun," I say, wondering where it is. "I can help protect you."

He doesn't say anything for a few seconds.

I keep talking because I can't think of anything else to do. "I can, you know."

He sets me down by the passenger door of the truck and opens it up. "And so you did," he says, picking me up again and heaving me up into the seat.

I bounce up once before settling into the still-warm seat. Holy brain explosion. I push my hands down on the seat to steady myself. It's then that I notice how much my injured arm is throbbing.

"Did you say the cougar did this to me?" I look down at my arm. I'm afraid to touch it, not even sure it's my arm. This whole situation is ludicrous. Why am I wearing so much camouflage? Green is *so* not my color. How's Ian going to fall under my spell if I look like a zombie woman? I swear, green makes me look undead.

I'm sleeping in the truck, that's what's going on.

I let out a sigh of relief and smile. Perfect explanation. Ian went out to check cows, I fell asleep waiting for him in the truck, and this is the dream I'm having. I have very realistic dreams that I could swear are real until I actually wake up. I can't wait to tell Andie about this one. She always finds great entertainment value in my dream stories, and this one's a doozy. I'm not sure I've ever had one where I suffered actual injury pain.

I'd pinch myself to be sure, but this fake lion injury is stinging badly enough that a pinch wouldn't make much of a difference. As I try to noodle that through, Dream Ian moves around the front of the truck and climbs in on the driver's side. He turns the key and gets the heater going.

My body trembles as the warmth starts to sink into my frozen bones. My teeth chatter, and it makes my head throb even more. I feel like letting my eyes cross just to take some of the pressure off.

"I'm going to take your jacket down from your arm. I don't think it's going to be too bad. There's not too much blood."

"This dream seems super real," I say, smiling at him as I tip my head back to rest on the seat. I have to move it sideways to keep the lump back there from hurting too much.

"Keep telling yourself that," he says, helping me out of my jacket.

I slide my eyeballs sideways to look out the windshield, not interested in what my crazy brain has cooked up for me in the form of a dream injury. For all I know, there'll be robotic arm parts in there. Sometimes in my dreams my brain turns me into one of those Austin Powers fembots. Normally, I like being a fembot shooting bad guys with my boob-guns, but not today. Today I just want to be awake, hanging out with Ian, rescuing cow babies. I hope Candy wasn't part of this dream too, but now that I think about it, she probably was. It's kind of hard to believe I bottle-fed a gorgeous baby cow named after me. That sounds more like something I'd make up. Maybe Ian was right about my brain being like a Mexican jumping bean.

"It's going to need stitches," he says. I think he's touching my skin there, but I can't really feel it, just the pressure as his finger pushes down. My head is getting all my attention right now.

"Are there robot parts in there?" I ask with a sigh.

"Robot parts?"

"In my arm. Am I a fembot? Just tell me." Sometimes my dreams are very dramatic too. I go along with this one since it's pretty unique. Maybe I should rustle up some tears to make it really good.

"You're going into shock, aren't you?" He puts his hand on my forehead. "You don't feel warm. And you're pale. That's probably a bad sign." His hand falls away as he places it on the wheel. "Come on—we need to get you to the hospital."

"Yeah. Let's go visit Andie and Sarah." I smile as I think about my little godbaby waiting for me. "I need to go bond. I'm her second-in-line momma, you know."

"Stitches and antibiotics first, bonding after."

"Whatever you say, bossy boss pants." I'm suddenly really tired. My vision goes a little blurry, but I don't fight it. The bouncy bouncing of the truck jerks my robot arm and makes me wince. Sleep will make that all go away.

"Don't go to sleep on me," Ian says, patting my leg.

"Juss a little . . ." My eyes fall shut and my head lolls to the side. Sleep. Sooooo nice. Just a little sleep . . .

"Ow!" I sit bolt upright and glare at him. Then I look down at my arm. My eyes bug out as I take in the edges of ragged flesh and the blood seeping out onto the jacket underneath my arm. "What did you just do?!"

"I told you not to go to sleep. Stay awake until we get to the hospital, or I'm going to poke your cut again."

"Poke my . . . ? Are you *serious*?!" I want to wrap my arm up in towels and hold it against me where he can't reach it, but those towels in the back seat look like they've already been used for a lot of gross stuff, and I don't want to ruin my shirt. It's an ugly sweatshirt, granted, but it is from my college days. I have a lot of memories of wearing this thing. It's bad enough that it has a rip in it now.

"Did you hit your head?" he asks.

He reaches over like he's going to touch my scalp, so I lean away. "No touching!"

"Does it hurt?" He glances at me before going back to staring out the windshield. He's leaning really far forward. The snow is making it very hard to see anything, even with the wipers going really fast.

"Like a bitch," I say, leaning the side of my head against the seat back. I'm staring at Ian's profile. "You are seriously good looking, you know that?"

Ian smiles. "You think so?"

"Yeah. I probably shouldn't say that to you because you'll get really stuck-up, but I just had to anyway. I'm tired of thinking it and not saying it out loud."

He laughs. "Head injuries are kind of crazy sometimes."

"So are dreams." Visions of him in a tux standing at the end of an aisle assail my brain. "You think you'll ever get married?" I feel like I'm drunk. There is no filter between my thoughts and my mouth. I probably should care, but I don't. I'm just dreaming anyway. He'll never know.

"Yeah, someday. I'd like to." He glances at me and then he's back to being a responsible driver. "I just need to find the right girl."

"It's not Ginny," I say.

"No, definitely not her."

"Is it The Banana?"

"The Banana?" He looks at me and frowns. "Are you okay?"

"Of course I'm okay. Don't I look okay?"

"Not really."

"Rude."

"You just asked me if I'm going to marry a banana. I think you have a skull fracture. You'd better not die on me."

"No, I asked you if you liked that girl, that banana girl at the diner." I squeeze my eyes shut, trying to focus. "I forget her full name. Hannahbelle Lecter or something."

He barks out a laugh. "Hannah? Are you talking about Hannah Banana?"

"Yeah, that's her. Girl with the chicken-fat yellow haystack on her head."

Ian's laughing too hard to respond.

"Is that a no?" I smile through my pain, opening my eyes again. His laughter is too infectious not to. He's so pretty.

"That's a definite no," he says. "No times a hundred. I've never touched her and never will."

"She says you've been getting it on." I keep smiling because I know instinctively that this will make him insane. I like seeing Ian go crazy.

He stops laughing. "That's not funny."

"Hey, that's what she's telling everyone. I didn't make it up. Don't shoot the messenger."

"You finally got that right."

"Got what right?" I wince as we hit a big bump and my head bounces against the seat.

"That expression. And don't worry. I'm not going to shoot the messenger, even though she shot me." He gives me a pointed look. I think it's supposed to make me feel guilty, but it doesn't. It makes me happy.

I grin. "I didn't shoot you, fool. Karma shot you." I'm so happy right now, I could pee my pants again and not even care.

"Don't go to sleep," he says, making me realize I'm staring at the inside of my eyelids again.

"I need to rest. I don't want to miss the party."

"What party?"

"Boog's party." I'm going to look extra hot at this party with my boob-guns on. I'm a fembot, and I'd be willing to bet they don't get fembots in Baker City that often.

"You aren't going to Boog's party or anyone else's party for that matter. You're going to the hospital."

"Bull honkey."

He laughs. "We'll see."

"Yeah, we will," I say. And then that's the last thing I remember of that car ride or that conversation. Everything goes black, and the warmth comes in and swallows me up whole.

CHAPTER TWENTY-ONE

I can hear sounds, but I can't see anything. My eyes are shut. I'm trying to open them, but they don't want to cooperate. Then the voices in the room stop me from trying too hard.

"Ma, anyone ever tell you you're nosy?"

"Not anyone who wanted to live to see his next birthday."

Ian hisses out a long breath. "Listen, I hear what you're saying, okay? I got it. I'm not going to do anything stupid."

"Looks like you already have. Andie's best friend is laid up in the hospital with a concussion and stitches from a cougar attack on her second day. Her *second day*, Ian, and I hold you responsible."

"Ma, she's a grown woman, and if you know her at all, you know that telling her *no* is like talking to a wall and telling the wall *no*. She did all this to herself. I was just an innocent witness."

"Innocent, my buns."

"I told you she shot me, right? I showed you the bruise."

"Son, knowing you, you deserved it."

He sputters. "How can you say that? I'm your son!"

"I can say that because I know you. You've been looking for trouble for going on three years now. And while you may be bound and determined to screw things up for yourself, I'll not have you doing it to Andie's friends."

"I ain't."

"Don't use that word with me. You know I don't like it."

"I know. That's why I said it. I'm trying to get you to stop nagging me."

I can't help but smile. At least he's honest.

"Hey," Ian's voice goes suspicious. "I think she's listening."

I hear footsteps and then Ian's voice much closer than it was.

"Wake up, Sleeping Beauty. Time to face the music."

"I'll be outside," Maeve says, her voice softer, kinder. "Let me know when she's ready for a visitor." A door closes and there's silence.

I open my eyes to find piercing green ones staring down at me. My heart flips over once when I take in how beautiful he is. There's stubble growing in on his chin and cheeks, and his hat is a different color than the one I remember him wearing. This time he's wearing the one I picked out that he threw on the floor of his room. It makes me go all gooey inside, thinking he might have done that on purpose. Does he like me?

"That's a good color on you," I say.

"That's what my fashion advisor told me." He grins. "You feeling better?"

"Better than what?"

"Better than a girl who pissed herself, got a slight concussion and an armful of stitches fighting off a mountain lion?"

I close my eyes as my face heats up. He knows about the pee-pants. "Go away. I'm unconscious right now." The room was swirling around a little when my eyes were open, so it feels pretty nice to go back to being half asleep. Avoiding humiliation seems like a great idea too.

"Doc's got you on some pretty good drugs, or so the nurse says."

"Sleeeeeeping . . ." I throw in a couple fake snores to drive the point home. I can't believe he brought up the fact that I peed my pants. Who does that? Now I'll never be sexy to him. *Dammit.*

"Want to know how many stitches you have?"

I sigh loudly to show my annoyance. "Want to get punched in the eyeball?" I ask.

"Not particularly."

"Then go away. I'm tired, my head hurts, and nothing makes sense anymore."

There's the sound of furniture being moved across the floor, but I refuse to open my eyes and figure out what that means.

Ian's voice is at the side of my head. "What doesn't make sense?"

When I feel his warm hand pick up mine and hold it, it causes my chest to tighten. "That's not helping," I say before I can stop myself. *Damn those drugs.*

"What? Me holding your hand?" He strokes my fingers. "I'm just being nice. Concerned about your welfare. Grateful you saved my hide."

I have to smile a little at that. "I did save your hide, didn't I?"

"Yep. Like the Lone Ranger. Rode in and saved the day with your little pistola."

I open my eyes to find him grinning at me.

"I don't trust that face," I say, frowning at him.

He goes all innocent on me. "What face?" He points at his chin. "This face?"

I pull my hand away from his. "Yes. Go away." I stare at the ceiling. Having him this close makes me sad for some reason. Must be the drugs again. I never did like being on them. Wine is way better.

He takes my hand back. "Don't be like that."

"Ian." I grit my teeth, trying to keep the pain back and my emotions down. "Don't play with me, okay? I can't deal right now. At least wait until I'm back on my feet."

He reaches up and moves some hair away from my face. "I'm not being like anything."

I lift my injured arm and swat his hand away. "Yes, you are. You are playing me like a . . . like a . . ."

"Fiddle?"

"No. Like a cello. More like a cello. And I don't like being played like a cello."

He laughs. "Why like a cello and not a fiddle?"

"Ian." I glare at him.

"No, I'm serious. I want to know."

"Because." I pause, wondering if he'll understand. "I'm way deeper than a fiddle."

He thinks about it for a few seconds and then nods. "I agree. But not with the fact that I'm playing you."

"You and I both know that from the very second you laid eyes on me, you decided you didn't like me and were going to mess with me. And so far, you've done a really good job. But I've got a monster headache, and I'm dizzy, and my arm stings, so it's really not very fair of you to do any of that while I'm suffering. Just give me forty-eight hours and you can restart your campaign."

He's laughing again. "My campaign? What campaign?"

"Your campaign of . . . messing with me."

He stops laughing. "You think this is just a game with me? That I don't like you?"

I roll my eyes, even though it hurts to do it. "Of course it is and of course you don't. Come on. Stop it. I told you, I'm on the injured list." I have to close my eyes to block out the light. It's just too painful to focus on him.

"Okay, if that's what you want, I'll leave you alone." His hand starts to pull out of mine and my fingers twitch uncontrollably.

He pauses. "What? You don't want me to go?" His teasing voice is back.

Time stretches between us. I'm not sure what to say. Should I lie or tell the truth? I decide on something in the middle.

"Your hand is warm, and I appreciate the company." I know Andie can't be here, and aside from her, I can't think of anyone I'd want here with me more than Ian. Stupid jerk.

His hand moves more deeply into mine and he smooths his thumb across the back of my fingers. "Okay, I'll stay. But only because it's part of my big campaign."

I smile as I drift back to sleep. "Good. I'm going to win, you know."

"Win what?"

"Win the war."

As I'm drifting off, I hear him say, "I'll let you win a battle or two, but I'll be the one winning this war."

CHAPTER TWENTY-TWO

The next time I open my eyes, it's Andie at the side of my bed in a chair, and it's just the two of us in the room.

"Where's the baby?" I ask, my voice raspy and not very attractive. I sound like I've been smoking three packs a day for the last thirty years. I have no idea what time it is or even if we're in the same day as I was when I arrived.

"She's with her daddy one floor above you. How are you feeling?"

"Good. Great." I try to sit up, but the pounding in my head makes it slow going. "Damn headache."

"You have a slight concussion. Maybe you should stay down." She puts her hand on my arm, and her expression is pure concern.

"No, thanks. I need to get out of here. My co-pay is outrageous."

"Don't worry about the co-pay. Just get better." Andie sits back in her chair and rubs her belly. She still looks pretty pregnant, but no way in the world will I tell her that.

"How's Sarah?" I ask, directing the conversation away from myself. I know once Andie realizes I'm okay, she'll start scolding me for having that gun. Better to divert her attention before she becomes fixated on things I'd rather not discuss.

"She's perfect. We're going home later today. Maybe we can all ride together. They said you don't need to stay another night. You just have to rest."

"Do I get to ride in the back with her?" I like the idea of making googly eyes at her for the thirty minutes it'll take to get back to the ranch. I need her to memorize my face before I leave, so when I call her on the phone, she'll know who's talking.

"If you want." Andie stares at me and then leans in closer, lowering her voice. "So what's going on with you and Ian?"

I look around the room, making sure he's not hiding in any corners. "What do you mean?"

"I mean, I'm gone for a day, and suddenly you guys are out getting into all kinds of trouble."

Something tells me the best plan of action here is to play the drama down as much as possible. I don't want Ian getting into trouble. He didn't do anything wrong. "I was just taking a ride in the truck while he was checking cows. It was no big deal."

"That's not the way we heard it." She frowns at me. "You know he's got a wild streak."

It makes me cranky just hearing her say that. "He wasn't doing anything wrong."

"Then what are you doing here in the hospital with stitches and a concussion?"

I struggle to sit up. I'm too angry to remain lying down for this conversation. "It's a *slight* concussion, not a full-on one. Besides, that has nothing to do with him, okay? He was perfectly nice. A perfect gentleman." I pause so she can see how serious I am. She just doesn't understand him like I do, apparently, which is pretty sad since she sees him every stinking day. "Have you ever checked cows before?"

She smiles vaguely. "A couple times. With Mack."

"Okay, then. So you know that you can sometimes have shit happen, and you just need to deal with it."

"So what happened?"

"Didn't Ian tell you?"

"No. He got mad at Mack and Angus and stormed off before they got the whole story from him."

"Probably because you guys were accusing him of something he didn't do." I try to cross my arms over my chest, but the IV in my arm gets in the way. I stare down at it, and it reminds me of a leash. "Someone needs to get this junk off me so I can leave."

"Where are you going?"

"I have to go find Ian, of course."

"Why?"

"Because!" Now that I think about it for a split second, I realize I don't have any reason to go find him. But I do have a reason for getting back to his house soon. Poor little Candy. What if she's starving? She needs me! "I have responsibilities back at the ranch."

Andie laughs.

"That's not funny. I'm serious." I lift my chin a little. It just so happens I have a newborn to take care of, not that it's any of her business. Or maybe it is, but now I'm too mad to tell her about it.

"Okay, I'll bite. What are your responsibilities? Are you in charge of wardrobe selection?"

"No." Her statement makes zero sense. I'm staring at her like she's stupid.

"Do you need to do someone's hair?"

"No. Why are you saying that?" I'm pretty sure she's mocking me right now, but that's not something that Andie would ever do before. It makes my chest hurt to think she's doing it now.

She shrugs. "I'm just trying to figure out what you could possibly need to do back home, that's all."

I feel like crying. "For your information, I'm needed for a lot of things, not just color matching and hair." Now I am, anyway. Thanks to Ian. My heart fills with warmth just thinking about what he did for me today. He made me a cow momma.

Andie's face falls. "I didn't mean it like that."

"Yes, you did. You meant it *exactly* like that." I press the red button on a wire looped around the edge of my bed.

"What are you doing?" she asks as I swing my legs over to the opposite side of the bed and move to the edge of it.

"I'm leaving."

"What do you mean, you're leaving?"

"Where's my phone?" I ask, looking around.

"In a plastic bag in your top drawer over there." She points to the side table next to my left leg.

I stand and get into the drawer, finding my phone. When I turn it on, I'm relieved to find that it still has a charge. I send off a quick text.

"Who are you calling?" Andie asks.

"I'm not calling anyone. I'm texting." My clothes are in the bag too, but I can't very well wear the jeans. They smell rancid. I keep them in the bag with the rest of the stuff, and send another text.

"Who are you texting?"

Before I can decide how to answer her, I get a response.

Be there in a few. I'm in town. What size are you?

I text him back the details and then sit on the bed, looking over my shoulder at Andie. "Do you have a brush?" I ask.

"Sure." She pulls one out of her purse and hands it to me. "What's going on?"

I take my time brushing my hair, not saying anything. I need to figure out how I'm going to handle this situation without making Andie freak out. She has the baby to think of, and I don't need her worrying about me. I can handle this, no problem.

The nurse comes in as I'm stalling for time. She's not the same one who was taking care of Andie, but she has the same expression on her face. Why do all nurses act like they hate me?

"Did you need something?" she says, her mouth all twisted up and wrinkly when she's done talking and is waiting for my answer.

I hold up my arm so she can see the IV needle. "Yes. I need you to take this out."

"I'm sorry, but I can't do that right now."

I give her a tight smile. "Either you do it or I will."

She glares at me. "The doctor is the one who gives the orders around here, missy, and he says you need the fluids and the meds." She looks up at the clear bag hanging above me. "When that's done, we'll come back and take a look."

"Wrong-o, Nurse Ratched." I pull at the tape on my arm, wincing when it yanks a few of my fuzzy arm hairs out. "I say I'm done, so I'm done. My body, my decision."

Andie stands and leans over, putting her hand on my shoulder. "Sweetie, maybe you should wait."

I shrug her off. "Nope. I'm not waiting. I have to get my hair brushed out and my face fixed before Ian gets here. I can't do that hooked up to this contraption."

The nurse walks over and tries to get in my way. "You need to wait."

I pause and glare at her. "You so much as touch me, and you will be one sorry mofo." I want to tell her that I wrestle with mountain lions and win, but I keep it to myself. It probably won't help to convince anyone I'm ready to be discharged.

The nurse stops trying to touch my arm. "Are you threatening me?" she asks. "Because I can call for security."

"Oh, it's not a threat; I'm making you a promise. Touch me and you will feel the pain, guaranteed." I stop messing with the tape and stare her down. "You can't keep me here, and you can't force treatment on me. I know my rights. So either you help me get out of this, or you get the hell out of my room. That's your choice: take it or leave it."

See, what's happening here, I think, is that I fought off a mountain lion and lived to tell about it. I am badassery personified. On top of that, everyone thinks the stuff that went down was Ian's fault, which is totally not fair. I mean, maybe it was kind of his fault, but not in a bad way.

The things that happened to me today were awesome in an I-faced-death-and-kicked-its-ass kind of way, and I have Ian to thank for that, not to mention the bond with Candy. I feel like I need to tell him right now how grateful I am before anyone else gets near him and fills his head with nonsense that makes him feel bad. Today I was the best version of myself—strong, brave, resourceful. I never would have met that me without Ian there to bring her out.

"I'm going to call for security," the nurse says, leaving us in the room.

"Go ahead!" I yell after her. "Tattletale!"

"Candice, I'm really worried about you," Andie says, coming around the bed. "Seriously, would you please just calm down and leave that alone?"

"Hand me some paper towels," I say, ignoring her. I have all the tape off and just the needle to get out. I'm afraid this sucker is going to bleed. The needle looks really thick.

I lean down and look at it closer. What is that, a frigging garden hose they put in my arm? Probably that rude nurse picked the biggest one they have because she's jealous of my hair. Wench.

"Here." Andie hands me a wad of towels from the bathroom and one gauze pad she found somewhere and pulled out of its wrapping.

I push the whole pile of it against my arm, using my stomach to press on it as I slide the needle out with my free hand. And damn, does it burn like . . . ooooh . . . *fire*! My arm is on fire! *Gah!*

I drop the needle on the floor and do a little jig to try and ease the pain. Andie waits patiently as I do the cha-cha, the one-woman abbreviated tango, and a short waltz. It does wonders for the pain.

As I hold my arm up and put direct pressure against the garden hose hole with my opposite hand, I smile at Andie. And I keep on grinning, right through the fire burning up my arm and the nausea that threatens to overtake me. I swallow, fighting back against the bile that keeps trying to come up. "See? No big deal."

"You are insane," she says, almost smiling. "What's gotten into you?"

"Nothing." I shrug as I lean against the side of the bed, totally casual and in control—or so I want her to think because I don't want her trying to force me to stay here without Ian. "I'm just done with being here, and I don't like it when people don't listen to me."

"Sweetie . . . you were attacked by a *cougar*. You have stitches in your arm and a big lump on your head." She looks at the bandage on my bicep. "You need to be careful, or you could get an infection. Those cat nails are very dirty."

"So? I'll take antibiotics."

Andie looks up at the bag. "That's what you were doing before you pulled that thing out."

I look up at the bag and then at the needle that's dripping liquid on the floor near my foot. "Oh." My arm burns even more just seeing all that germ killer going to waste.

Andie sighs. "I'm sure we can get you some pills. I just want you to stop and take a breath and tell me what's going on." She shakes her head. "Ever since you met Ian, it seems like you've gone off the rails."

We both stop speaking for a while. The silence stretches to the point that it's becoming awkward. I have to say something.

"Ian has nothing to do with it."

She stares me down until I cave.

"Okay, maybe indirectly he has something to do with it. *Very* indirectly."

"Tell me." She sits on the edge of the bed next to me.

It takes me awhile to explain to her what's going through my mind and my heart. It doesn't make a whole lot of sense, the way I feel like killing her brother-in-law one second and humping his leg the next. How do I put that into words that don't make me sound nuts?

"I don't know. He just . . . he gets me all riled up. And he makes me laugh. He challenges me. I do things with him that I've never done before. I like it. I like this new me that I am with him."

"Oh," she says softly.

And then even more softly she says, "Oh my."

Fear trickles into my brain and my heart. Then the idea that I should be offended. "'Oh my'? What does that mean?"

"Nothing."

"Don't lie. You meant something with that 'Oh my.' What were you thinking? Because if it's something bad about Ian, I'm going to be mad at you."

"No, no, nothing bad. Well . . ."—she pauses—"nothing too bad."

I jab her in the rib with my healthy elbow. "Out with it."

She goes all serious and stern on me. "Have you slept with him yet?"

My jaw drops open with the suddenness of her approach. I lean back on the bed next to her. "Wha . . . ?"

"Don't play innocent with me. I've known you for way too long to fall for that."

"I'll have you know that I am an Ian virgin, okay? Geez. I just met the guy." I'm glad she can't read my mind; otherwise, she'd know that I'm fully prepared to sleep with him the very next time I lay eyes on his gorgeous self.

"Maybe you shouldn't. Sleep with him, I mean."

I look at her, trying to read her mind through her eyes. All I see there is sadness. "Why not?"

"Because. It could go bad."

"What could go bad?" I shake my head at her. "You're talking in riddles, Andie, and I have to tell you . . . it's annoying as hell. I'm injured, if you haven't noticed." I hold up my arm for confirmation. "*And* I have a headache. Just say whatever it is you need to say and be done with it."

She stares at the floor for a really long time. I'm starting to think she's fallen into a trance, when she finally lifts her head up and speaks.

"I can tell you like him. I mean, *really* like him. But sweetie, Ian's not into commitment. If you sleep with him, it's a guaranteed broken heart for you, and I'd hate to see that happen."

I scoff, trying to play off the way her words have made my heart leap and flip around. "Please. As if I'd fall for Ian MacKenzie."

A small knock comes at the door, and a head pops in. "You decent?"

Happiness fills me to the point that I feel like I'm about to choke on it. "Ian! You came!" He must have broken all land speed records to get here this quick. Maybe he was already shopping for me when I texted. Just the idea makes me go all warm and gushy inside.

He pushes the door open more fully and nods at Andie. "Andie."

"Ian," she says, standing. "Where'd you come from?"

"Store." He holds up a bag that has a big red circle on it. "Got what you asked for." Tossing it on the bed, he turns around to leave.

"Where are you going?" I ask, worried he's about to abandon me.

"Thought I'd wait outside 'til you're dressed."

I smile at Andie and give her the look. "Isn't that polite of you, Ian. Thank you so much."

"Sure." He's outside the door before Andie has a chance to say anything else in his presence.

She shakes her head. "You are seriously going to regret this. Mark my words."

"That is just mean, Andie." I shake my head. "I don't get you. Why are you being like this? Is it lack of sleep or something? Hormones?" I pause, suddenly remembering she just had a baby. Duh. "It's hormones, isn't it?"

Andie turns sideways and takes my hand. "Babe. Listen to me. Ian is a sweetheart when he wants to be. I'm not arguing that. But he is not into commitment—do you understand what I'm saying? He's had years to settle down, and he's done the exact opposite, okay? He's raising hell in town every weekend, he drinks too much, he sleeps around. He's not your type."

I pull my hand from hers and take the bag Ian tossed into the room, opening it up to see what's inside. "He hasn't slept with old Banana, I'll have you know. She was lying about that."

"Whatever. If it wasn't her, it was someone else. And I know you. You're not the fling type. You say you are, but you aren't."

I frown at her. Some kind of alien has taken over my BFF's body, apparently. Andie would know better than to say that about me. "What are you talking about? I have flings."

"Name one."

I lift my chin. This is an easy one. I fling around all the time. I'm the fling master. I'm a flinger of the highest degree. They call me the fling-dinger. "Matthias."

"You wanted to bear his children. You told me that after your first and only date. That is not a fling. It's an obsession and the exact opposite."

"I was only joking." He *was* super cute, though. He had awesome DNA. I could see it in his cheekbones. You can tell a lot from a man's cheekbones and other facial features.

"I still remember the baby names you told me you were going to use," she says frowning, giving me the Andie evil eye.

"Fine." She wins that one. But I have more. Lots more. "What about Jason?"

"When he didn't call after your third date, you practically stalked him."

I gasp. "I did not! I would never!"

"Okay, maybe *stalk* is a strong word, but you did friend him under a fake name on Facebook so you could check his relationship status and photos."

My face burns with the memory. "I had too much wine. I can't be held responsible for that night."

"I'm just saying . . . you're not the fling type. Your heart is too big for that kind of nonsense."

I think about her comment for a few seconds before responding. "I do have a pretty big heart, that's true. But I don't think it means I can't have a little fun while I'm here." I have plenty of other fling stories to challenge her with, but there's no point now. She's made up her mind about me and about Ian.

Andie pulls me into a hug. "Have fun. Just don't get your hopes up or your heart broken, okay? I don't think I could handle it."

I lean back to see her face. "Are you crying?"

"Of course I'm crying!" she shouts. "You almost got killed by a mountain lion for shit's sake, and now you're about to get your heart crushed by a player who I can't kill because I'm related to him!"

"Awww, poor baby . . ." I pat her cheek. "Those hormones are just kicking your ass right now, aren't they?"

She slaps my hand away. "No, stupid, it's not the hormones. It's *you*, taking risks you shouldn't. Now, where's the gun?" She holds out her hand as if I'm supposed to put something in it.

"What gun?" I'm all innocence.

"The gun you bought."

"I don't know what you're talking about." I'm not technically lying since I don't currently know where the gun is. I hope Ian has it in his truck or somewhere else safe. That thing saved our lives today. I think.

A knock comes at the door, and Ian's voice floats into the room. "You ready yet? I have to get going. If you want a ride, you'd better come now."

I cut Andie's next question off with a raised hand. "Save it for later. I have to get dressed and go before Nurse Ratched brings in the National Guard."

Andie watches me while I struggle into the outfit Ian bought me at the store. My IV hole is dripping blood, but as soon as I'm dressed, I slap the gauze back on it.

When I'm finally done and standing straight, I realize with the red plaid shirt and elastic waistband jeans Ian bought me, I look like a redneck slut from the nineteen forties on a bender. Andie and I stare at my sad self and then burst out laughing together.

"I'm not worried anymore," Andie finally says, still smiling.

"Worried about what?"

"Worried that Ian will convince you to run away with him."

"What's that supposed to mean?" I ask, a little confused.

She points at me. "If that's his idea of a cute outfit, he doesn't stand a chance with you."

Ha-ha.

I laugh right along with her, but inside I'm telling her she doesn't know diddly-squat about me or Ian. He did this on purpose, which is his way of begging me to come at him with everything I've got. I'm giddy inside, knowing that he thinks he's winning, but that he's wrong. I am seriously going to get him when he least expects it. He has totally met his match in me.

CHAPTER TWENTY-THREE

The ride back from the hospital is awkward. Ian's rescued me from Andie's interrogation, but now, as I think back on all the things I was saying to her and what was going on in my mind, I realize what I actually meant. I like Ian. I mean, I *really* like him.

Sneaking glances at him as he drives and hums along to the radio only confirms my suspicion. God, he's gorgeous. Sexy. Adorable. There's no way I can just sleep with this guy and escape unscathed. He's going to take a piece of my heart, and I'll have to leave it behind when I go. Do I want to do that? *Can* I do that?

"What's going on in that bean of yours?" he asks without looking at me.

"Just thinking about how sexy I look in these clothes," I say, glad he can't read minds. "I don't know how you're going to keep your hands off me now."

He chuckles. "Me neither. Thought those colors suited you."

I pull out the waistband. "And this elastic too. Sexy, sexy."

"Makes it easier to get in and out of 'em with a hurt arm."

I laugh. "Don't play. You know you bought these for me because they were the most hideous pair in the entire store."

"Wrong again," he says, pulling onto the dirt road from the paved one. "Trust me. There were way worse ones there I could've bought for you. I can go back and get 'em if you want." He glances at me and winks.

I just blow out some air and stare out the side window. I have no response for that. My brain isn't running on all cylinders. It sounds like he was being nice again, even though he dressed me like a drunken redneck granny.

"Want me to take care of Candy for ya?" he asks.

I look at him. "She's real?"

"Of course she's real." He frowns at me a couple times before going back to watching the road. "You sure you should be out of the hospital?"

"Of course I should be. I just . . . wasn't sure if I dreamed that part or not."

"No, you definitely didn't dream it. And she's probably pretty hungry right now."

My gut twists uncomfortably as I think about that poor baby starving without me there to feed her. "Hurry up, Ian, go faster."

"Just relax. I'm messing with you. She'll be fine."

I wipe the nervous sweat off my forehead. "Just hurry up."

The car goes quiet for a while, and then he speaks again when we're not far from the ranch. "You're really worried about that calf, aren't you?"

"Of course I am." I look at him and try to figure out why that's so surprising to him. "Aren't you?"

"I guess." He pulls into the parking space for his truck but doesn't turn off the engine. Instead he puts the truck into park and takes his seatbelt off. He stares out the window as he rests his arms on the wheel.

"What are we doing?" I ask.

"Just thinking."

I stare at the flakes of snow that fall lazily to the truck's windshield. They melt before they can build up, probably because Ian has had the heater blasting all the way here.

"Thinking about what?" I finally ask, almost afraid to hear the answer.

"Just thinking that you turned out different than I thought you would be." He finally looks at me, but I cannot read his expression at all. The waning light is not helping any.

"How so? I mean, what did you expect?"

He looks down at my clothes and then my shoes before coming back up to meet my gaze. "Not this." He turns off the truck, opens his door, and jumps out before I can say anything back.

I throw my door open and try to get out, getting tangled up when I realize that I forgot to take my seatbelt off first.

"I wouldn't look like this if it wasn't for you!" I shout at his rapidly disappearing back.

"You're welcome!" he yells over his shoulder.

"I didn't say thank you!" I yell back.

When I'm finally out of the seatbelt, my feet hit the snow, and by some kind of miracle, I don't fall. I walk with my legs kind of far apart so I have better grip on the ground. Following Ian's footsteps, I make it all the way to the barn without getting snow on anything but my boots. I'm practically a native now, the way I can negotiate these treacherous grounds. I'm grinning from ear to ear when I get in the barn.

"Yeah, yeah," Ian's muttering. "I hear ya."

"Are you talking to me?" I ask as I walk up to the stable box where the calf is. Ian's around the corner doing something.

My little baby is walking around, sniffing the straw and tossing it around. She's covered in little bits of it.

I open the door and go in, and she runs to the opposite side and stares at me. When I bend down and talk nonsense to her, she takes a few tentative steps in my direction.

"Here," Ian says, handing me a bottle over the door.

I take it with my good arm and hold it by my face. "Dinner tiiiime, little Candy girl. Come on over here and eat it up for momma so she can stop worrying about you."

She walks over like she understands every word I just said and then we play tug-o-war with the bottle again until she sucks it dry. My arm is on fire, but I ignore it. Every bit of pain I have to endure for her is worth it.

When she's done, she goes off and does her happy-milk-belly dance, and I stand in the corner watching. I don't realize I've got happy tears on my cheeks until Ian reaches over and wipes one away.

"You ready for dinner?" he asks softly.

"Yeah. No. Maybe." I can't focus on him. I can only stare at this little miniature cow and revel in the miracle that is her. I can't believe Ian and I actually brought her back to life. If we hadn't shown up when we did, she'd be frozen solid right now, and her real mommy would be mooing while her heart broke. I feel like a superhero.

"Want me to bring it out here?" he asks.

That gets my attention. "Could you?"

He smiles. "Yeah. Be right back." A second later he's handing a short stool over the door to me. "Here. Make yourself comfortable."

I put the stool in the corner of the stall and sit on it. Candy comes over to check things out and lick me with her really rough tongue before I push her away, and she goes back to ruffling the straw around. It's only after I've settled in and she's going back to sleep that I realize how frigging cold it is out here. I wiggle my toes over and over, trying to keep the circulation going in my feet.

Ian shows up a few minutes later with a blanket that he throws over the door on top of me and something covered in tin foil. He opens the stall door and comes in, sitting down in the straw next to me as I settle the warm wool on my shoulders.

"What's this?" I ask as he hands it over. He keeps one for himself and tears the top of the foil off.

"Burrito. Fresh frozen and microwaved by yours truly."

"Wow," I say, taking a bite of it, failing miserably at looking like a girl with manners. "You have so many hidden talents."

"You know it," he says, eating a third of his burrito in one bite.

I laugh as a bean rolls out of his mouth and sits on his chin.

"What?" he asks, all innocence, even though I know he has to feel it sitting there. "What's wrong?"

I shake my head. "Nothing. Nothing at all."

"You sure?" he moves his head left and then right, showing off his new bean mole.

"Positive. You're perfect exactly like that. Best you've looked all day."

He turns his head sideways and in one quick movement flicks the bean off his face. It lands in my hair.

I sigh through my nose and just sit there, chewing my burrito, reviewing the tragedies of the day. I've had cow loogies all over my face. I've been scratched by a lion and now have stitches and a future scar that will show every time I wear a sundress or a T-shirt. I've contributed to the death of said lion. I've pissed off my best friend and pretty much her entire family. And now I have a burrito bean *in my hair*.

A great big smile breaks out over my face.

"You're smiling," Ian says. He sounds worried.

"Yes, Ian, I am."

"I'm a little scared."

I keep staring out into the stable. "You should be."

"Really?"

Without warning, I dive to the side, effectively tackling him into the straw. My burrito goes flying. "Yes! Really!"

The baby cow jumps up on wobbly legs and runs to the far corner.

I'm on top of Ian, staring down into his surprised face.

A few seconds later, a weird smell comes wafting up into my nose.

Ian's expression goes dead.

"What's that smell?" I ask.

Ian closes his eyes. "Can you let me up? I think I'm lying in cow shit."

CHAPTER TWENTY-FOUR

I cannot stop laughing all the way to the house. The back of Ian's head is covered in cow poo. And I thought my hair was bad with some loogies and a burrito bean in it.

"Don't say it," he warns as he goes up the front steps.

I'm gasping for air, bent over as I hold my stomach. Oh, it hurts so much. I can't stop laughing.

"I'm hitting the shower." He throws open the front door and drops his jacket on the ground just inside the entrance. "Don't flush any toilets while I'm in there."

I pause in the foyer, my laughter drying up with the confusion of his statement. "What?"

He clomps up the stairs. "Don't flush any toilets while I'm in the shower."

"Why not?" I yell up after him.

The door to the bathroom slams shut without him giving me a response.

I wander into the downstairs powder room to check my face and hair. That was my first mistake.

I stare in horror at the image reflected back at me. I can honestly say that I have never looked so bad in my entire life, even after once getting wasted back in college and ending up at some guy's house whose name I couldn't remember, waking up with my face pressed into his living room carpet. That was a bad day, but this is a worse than bad day.

I lean in to get a closer look and then just as quickly back up. Oh. My. God. I've spontaneously wrinkled out here on this ranch! I look ten years older!

Maybe it's the clothes. Maybe it's the food.

I hold my stomach as it turns over and grumbles. That burrito is not going down well. Nature is calling.

I sit down on the toilet and think back on my day as I take care of business. My stomach continues to express its discontent as I wander through my memories. I'm really glad it's just Ian and me here in the house. I'm making a lot of noise in this little room. Wow.

Ian and I did chores together. He came to *get* me this morning so I would do them *with* him. He wanted to show me baby cows and stuff. That was probably a big hassle for him to do that. Was he just being polite? I doubt it. It seems like something a guy would do if he liked a girl. Does Ian like me?

Or maybe he just wants to make fun of me, laugh at all the times I fall down on my ass and make a fool of myself. And he has laughed, that's for sure. The jerk probably has sore abs from all the gut busting he's been doing. But he's also been really nice and even polite sometimes. He said I'm not like he expected me to be. I can't be sure, but I think he meant it as a compliment. That's a good sign, right?

There's always the chance that he could just be trying to get in my pants. He's being creative about it—I'll give him that. I can honestly say that I've never had a guy try to woo me by having me take part in a cow birth. The best I've ever had prior to this was a date at the zoo followed by a candlelight dinner. At the time I thought that was pretty creative, but it pales in comparison to this day.

That's when it hits me. *My god,* I have a baby cow to take care of! How often does she eat? What exactly does she eat? I need to get googling!

I finish up, using copious amounts of two-ply, and stand, pulling my elastic granny pants up to my waist. I need to find out how often Candy needs to be fed and what goes in that bottle. Will I have to sleep out in the barn tonight? No one but Ian is home. I need to go ask him and figure out how I'm going to do all this and keep up with my social schedule, visiting with Andie and going to Boog's party and all that.

I flush the toilet and leave the bathroom after washing my hands. I'm not two steps into the hallway when a loud roaring comes from upstairs.

I take the stairs two at a time. It sounds like Ian is dying up there.

"What's wrong?!" I shout at the top of the stairs. When I reach the bathroom door I pound on it. "Are you okay?!"

"I told you not to fucking flush the toilet!"

I bite my lip as his meaning sinks in. "Oh."

"Yeah, *oh*. Don't act like you didn't do that on purpose!"

He's really mad. It kind of makes me angry that he's so mad.

"I didn't!"

"Liar!"

"I'm not a liar."

"Yes, you are. You're a *damn* liar. You flushed on purpose to freeze me out. Probably trying to see me naked or something, thinking I'll come running out of here."

My eyes narrow as I picture him standing there accusing me of something I didn't do. And seeing him naked kind of sounds like a good idea.

I turn around and run down the stairs, just as fast as I ran up. Maybe faster. Into the powder room I go, flushing that toilet for all I'm worth. I also turn on the sink faucet just for good measure.

I giggle like an insane person when I hear him roar again. Running into the kitchen, I turn on the faucet there too and then press the buttons to turn on the dishwasher.

I hear a pounding of feet but ignore it. He's probably jumping around up there like a deranged monkey. Now all I have to do is find their washing machine. Ahoy! Super big load of laundry needing massive amounts of hot water, coming right up!

I'm running around the corner into the hallway when I slam right into something big and hard and wet. It's breathing heavily.

"Caught ya!" Ian shouts in my face, throwing his arms around me.

"Ack! What are you *doing*?!" I scream. He's wet. And naked. Like, really, really naked. I start yelling and laughing at the same time. I can't help it. The adrenaline has exploded in my heart, and I'm completely out of control.

"Just giving you what you asked for!" He picks me up and starts walking toward the front of the house. We make it to the foyer before the doo hits the fan.

Neither of us is prepared for the front door to fly open and for Mack and Andie to be standing there on the doorstep, with Angus and Maeve right behind them.

Ho. Lee. Shit.

CHAPTER TWENTY-FIVE

"Uhhhh . . ." Ian puts me down in front of him. A freezing cold burst of air hits me in the face.

"Uhhhh, hi," I say. My face is on fire despite the sub-zero temperatures.

"Ian Michael Angus MacKenzie . . . of all the . . ." Maeve is rendered speechless apparently, because that's all she has to say.

"I'll . . . uhhh . . . just hop back in the shower." Ian leaves me standing there in the foyer staring at the entire MacKenzie family in shock. His pounding footsteps fade in the distance. A door upstairs slams shut.

Andie looks up at Mack. "I told you something like this was going to happen." She shifts her arms, and for the first time I notice there's a baby there.

"I'll talk to him," Mack says, without looking at me.

My face goes even redder as I realize how awful this looks. I try to explain. "I flushed the toilet."

Maeve comes in and pats me on the arm. "That's nice sweetie. Maybe you should get in bed. You've had a long day."

Angus breathes out heavily but says nothing. Mack walks around me to the kitchen, and his father follows. Andie and Maeve just look at me.

"Yeah. I think I'll go to bed." I turn to go up the stairs.

I've never been so humiliated in my entire life. I used to be a mature, adult woman with a degree in fashion design and a thriving salon business in a metropolitan city. Today I'm a moron in granny jeans with cow loogies and a burrito bean in her hair being chased by a naked maniac in his mother's house. Good. Lord. Have. Mercy.

"We'll discuss this in the morning," Andie says. It sounds like a warning. Somehow she's shifted from being my BFF to being my mother.

"Okey-dokey," I say, acting like I don't have a care in the world, even though my insides are back to being a mess, and my head feels like it's about to pop right off my shoulders. I'm pretty sure I've never been so embarrassed in my entire life, even when I accidentally turned my business partner's hair green. He still hasn't gotten over that, and neither have I, but right now I'd happily trade another one of those incidents for this one.

Going up the stairs is like taking the walk of shame or something. I can feel Andie's stare boring into my back. I know exactly what she's thinking too, but tomorrow I'm going to set her straight. There will be plenty of time to do it then. Tonight I can just go to bed and try and forget for a few hours that any of this happened. Hopefully, Candy won't get too hungry in the meantime.

I walk past the bathroom that Ian's still showering in and go into Mack's bedroom just across the hall from it. Closing my door, I try not to let my mind wander into that place where it imagines what's going on inside that bathroom, what Ian might be doing right now, what he might look like.

Oy. I'm in so much trouble. I caught a glimpse of him naked and . . . hooey! . . . It was way better than my imagination. Talk about a swinging dick.

Sliding out of my granny jeans is way easier than I thought it would be. Ian was right about that. It makes me wonder if he really did buy these because I'm on the injured list and not because he was trying to make me look insanely ugly.

Deciding that my lacy pajamas are going to be a little harder to get into, I abandon them for the flannel shirt Ian bought me today. I lie down on my back and slide under the covers, wearing nothing but the shirt and my underwear. The room is dark, but I have no idea what time it is. I can't hear anything but the sound of water in the bathroom across the hall. It gradually puts me to sleep.

CHAPTER TWENTY-SIX

A bright lightbulb going on and shining through my eyelids brings me back to the land of the living and forces me awake. I squeeze my lids shut tighter, trying to block it out.

"What the fudge . . ." I say, my voice sleep-rough and barely there.

"You awake?" Ian asks.

I crack one eye open. He's wearing a T-shirt and shorts. It's dark outside.

"I am now, fool." I close my eye and try to fall back to sleep. My head is killing me.

"The discharge instructions say you need to take these pills every six hours."

I open an eye again and find him standing there with his palm up and a glass of water in the other hand. There are three pills waiting for me.

Sitting up gradually, I wince at the pain in my skull and the burning in my arm. *Youch.* Fighting cougars is painful. "What are they?" I ask.

Ian sits down on the edge of the bed and hands the pills to me. "Antibiotics and pain meds, I think."

"You trying to slip me something so you can take advantage of me?" I ask before throwing them into my mouth and chasing them down with the water.

He grins. "I notice you didn't wait for my answer before you took 'em."

I shrug and hand him back the glass. "Whatever. Take advantage of me if you want. I'm too tired to fight you off." I close my eyes and try not to scowl too hard over the pain the lump gives me when I'm lying down again. Turning my head to face the wall only partially relieves my misery.

"You in pain?"

"What do you think?" I ask.

"I feel bad."

That makes me open my eyes. I flip my head over to the other side so I can look at him. "Why would you feel bad?"

"Because this is my fault, and I apologize for that."

I reach up and slap his arm. It's not a very powerful slap, but it's the best I can manage right now. "Shut up. Don't you dare apologize."

"Why not? If it weren't for me, you'd be your regular self and not sporting a scarred-up arm and a lumpy head."

I blink slowly a few times, letting that image settle into my brain. "Thanks for that description."

"You're welcome."

"But even though I'm now hideously ugly, I'm still not accepting your apology."

"Why not?" He sounds cranky.

"Because you never should have given me one in the first place. This wasn't your fault. Plus, I have no regrets, so . . . yeah. Keep your apology. Use it on someone else."

"You have no regrets."

"That's what I said." I close my eyes and roll over onto my side, facing away from him. "I'm going to sleep, so unless you're here to rub my back, you can leave."

There's silence for so long I think he's left me and I begin to drift off. But then I feel his hands on me.

"You're pretty cool, you know that?" He's rubbing my shoulder. It makes me tingle.

"Yeah, I've heard that about me before." My words come out all mumbled. I sound like I'm drunk.

"When I first met you, I thought you were a pain in the ass. All high maintenance and shit . . . stuff, I mean."

"That's nice." My mind is spinning very slowly, slowly, slowly. His words and his hands are working some kind of magic on me. Maybe the pills too. I feel like I'm falling into a dream world.

"But you're really not. You're actually smart and funny and someone a person can count on when stuff gets real."

"Thasss meee," I say lazily. "Fuggin' superhero. They call me Wonder Bitch." I giggle at my new name. I could totally see me in spandex with a cape and a big letter B on the front of my chest. I'd be in a bustier, à la Wonder Woman, naturally.

"You're not a bitch. I think you're actually kind of a marshmallow under all that noise."

I lift my arm as high as I can and wave it in his direction. "Go 'way. I'm sleeping."

His hands leave my back, and the bed shifts. Something heavy and warm is behind me now. I realize just as I'm drifting off again into la-la land that it's Ian. He's lying beside me and his arm is over my hips.

Or maybe I'm just dreaming.

CHAPTER TWENTY-SEVEN

Andie claims she woke me up to give me pills and that I actually sat up and took them, but I have very little memory of that. It all just feels like a dream. Especially that part where I dreamed Ian was sleeping with me, keeping me warm, snuggling up behind me. I guess a twelve-hour nap will cause a person to kind of lose touch with reality.

"You're not going anywhere," Andie says, frowning at me. "You have a concussion, and you've slept for twelve hours."

"I have a *slight* concussion, first of all, and as you said, I've had plenty of sleep. I'm just going to tag along with Ian for an hour or so, and then he's going to bring me back home."

"I am?" Ian says, walking into the kitchen and going to the refrigerator.

"Yes."

"Where exactly are we going?" He takes out a jug of milk and pours himself a giant glass of it.

"To Boog's party, remember?"

He pauses with the glass halfway to his mouth. "Uhhhh . . . say what?"

Andie sits back and smiles, adjusting Sarah on her boob for the hundredth time. "See? He wasn't even planning on going."

I give Ian my death-is-coming-for-you stare, and he blinks in response. Then he drinks the entire glass of milk in one large swallow. It leaves a big milk mustache above his lip that he ignores.

"He was too planning on going—right, Ian?" I raise both eyebrows into my hairline.

He looks at Andie's scolding gaze and my unspoken threat, and he nods. "Yes. Absolutely. Leaving in a half hour." He couldn't be more adorable than he is right now, being my slave with that milk on his lip. I want to eat him up.

I smile and nod. "See? We won't be gone long."

"Nope," Ian agrees, wiping his mouth off with the back of his hand. "We have to get back to feed the calf, so we can't stay out late."

Andie shakes her head. "You two are just bound and determined to get yourselves into trouble, aren't you?"

"Who, us?" Ian asks.

I stand up. "Yeah. Who, us?" My best innocent expression jumps in to save the day. "I'm just being social, getting out of the house, meeting some of Ian's friends." I back out of the kitchen down the hallway. "You can go with us if you want, Andie." It's mean, but I'm hoping she'll decline my invitation.

"No, thanks. You guys go ahead." She says something in a lower tone to Ian, but I don't hear it. I'm too focused on getting upstairs and finding something decent to wear. I ignore the pain in my head and arm as I mentally comb through the wardrobe I brought with me. Thank goodness I already did my hair and makeup.

I'm inside Mack's room, changing, when Ian knocks on the door.

"I'm not dressed. Just wait a second." I shove my legs into my jeans, breathing hard when it makes my stitches pull and sting like a bejesus.

"You sure this is a good idea?" His muffled voice comes through the door. "I don't think we should go. You're still messed up."

"No, I'm not still messed up. I'm doing just fine, thank you very much." Everybody is treating me like a baby here. I have fifteen stitches and a bump on my head. Big deal. I burn myself almost daily at work and stand on my feet for twelve hours at a time with my arms up like bird wings. This is nothing.

"Boog's parties aren't fun."

"Boog's parties have never had me there."

"You gonna wear your new pants?"

I throw open the door and let him take a long look at me. "You wish." I know I look amazing. I have my best cleavage shirt on and a pair of skintight pants that have the pockets bedazzled just the tiniest bit. *Ka-chow!* Cowgirl awesome? Yes, ma'am. I define the look.

His jaw goes off center, and then he backs up. "I'm gonna change my hat."

I laugh. "Don't you dare wear that ugly green one." I actually like the green one, so I'm testing him to see if he rises to the bait.

When I meet him down in the foyer two minutes later, I go all warm inside. He has a black cowboy hat on and a black dress shirt tucked into jeans that were absolutely made for his butt.

I have a hard time breathing. Seriously. This man is dangerous. I'll bet he has all kinds of stalkers, and he probably doesn't even know it. I'm going to be paying extra special attention to the chicks at this party to see who's giving him those kinds of looks.

"Ready?" he asks.

"Ready." I look at the coat hooks and frown, distracted from admiring him by my minor wardrobe malfunction. "I don't have a jacket again."

He nods. "You're kind of murder on coats, aren't you?"

"Superheroes do what they have to do; what can I say."

He takes a puffy black one off the hook. "Here. This is Andie's. She won't mind. Try not to get attacked by a cougar in it."

I put it on and admire myself in the hallway mirror. I do look pretty cute, if I do say so myself. It cheers me up even more. I'm so ready to have a drink and share some gossip. My plan is to get one of these chicks from Baker City to spill the beans . . . figure out what Ian's deal is and why Andie doesn't have any friends here. Kill two birds with one party.

"How's Candy doing?" I ask as I trudge through the snow to the truck. The knit hat I found in the pocket of Andie's coat is making me a lot warmer than I expected. Maybe it'll be worth messing my hair up a little bit to stay warm on some part of my body. My hands are jammed in the pockets, but already freezing cold.

"She's good. She misses you, though."

I look out toward the barn, feeling like a really bad cow mommy. "Ooh . . . maybe I should go say hi before we leave."

He opens my door for me. "You can say hi when we come back if you want. We need to get to Boog's sooner rather than later."

"Why?" I ask, trying to read his expression as I climb up into my seat. As usual he's got his poker face on.

He slams the door shut and comes around, getting in and buckling up. "Because. People get drunk and stupid after ten."

"I hear that's your style of partying," I say, not looking at him.

"Who says that?" He pulls out onto the rough road that leads to the highway. The headlights make the drifts of snow look like lions. Lots and lots of lions. It makes me break out in goose bumps, which then makes my stitches burn.

"Ohhh, people. Where's my gun, by the way?"

"Under the seat. Don't take it into the party."

"I wasn't going to." I roll my eyes.

"Who says I do that?" he asks again.

"Is it true?"

He pauses before answering. Then he shrugs. "Maybe."

"Why?"

"Why what?" He's playing dumb.

"Why do you do stupid things like that?"

"It's not stupid to have fun."

"Are you really having fun, though?"

He doesn't say anything for a long time. Mostly he just stares out at the road, scowling.

"I guess things have kind of sucked for you since your wedding was called off."

"You could say that."

"I just did." I smile at him, trying to ease the pressure off the conversation. I love talking to him, and I want to know all his secrets, but I know that won't happen if he knows I'm digging into his life. I have to be stealth about it.

He smiles vaguely and then goes back to scowling. I can't tell if he's doing it because he's mad or because the snow keeps falling and making it hard to see the road.

"Have you had any girlfriends since Ginny?"

"Define *girlfriend.*"

"Girl you spent time with not drinking and screwing. Girl you hang out with when you could have been doing something else. Girl you spent quality time with. Girl you do nice things for. Girl you want to smooch all night."

He laughs once. "I guess that makes you my girlfriend."

That renders me speechless for all of about ten seconds. "Ha-ha, you wish."

He shrugs. "Hey, you're the one always trying to see me naked. I figured the feeling was mutual."

My jaw drops open. "What? You're crazy. Nobody's trying to see anybody naked." My ears are burning. Maybe Ian does read minds after all.

I let the conversation subside after that. I thought I was going to have to use a crowbar to get him to talk, but all of a sudden he's jumping into me liking him and trying to see him naked. I can't show up at this party not a hundred percent on my game, and talking to him about these dangerous topics definitely throws me off. My ears will not stop burning.

"What's the matter?" he asks when we're finally on the highway. "Cat got your tongue?"

"Nope. Just done talking." I stare out the side window, even though there's nothing to see.

"Conversation get a little too hot for ya?"

I snort. "As if."

"So you admit you've been trying to see me naked."

I have to laugh at his gall. "No. I admit nothing."

"See, you just admitted it right there."

I slap him with the back of my hand. "Watch it or I'll get my gun out."

"Man, you're dangerous."

"You got that right." I love being called dangerous. That's probably a bad sign, but oh well.

"And here I thought you were some fluff-headed girl from the city, softer than a lamb's belly."

"I am from the city, my hair is fluffy, and I am definitely soft. Not sure how soft a lamb's belly is, but I moisturize every day, so . . . yeah. You've got me pegged."

He laughs. "Sometimes I can't tell if you're messing with me or not."

Likewise, my seriously hot cowboy crush, likewise. But I'm not going to tell you that.

The lights of the town are coming into view, so I use the opportunity to change the subject. I don't like it when he talks about his impressions of me. They never sound very complimentary.

"How far into town does Boog live?"

"Not far. We're just five minutes away now. You chickening out?"

"Hell no. I don't chicken out."

"I noticed that about you." He stops at a red light, the first stoplight off the exit. "You're pretty damn brave, actually."

"I am?" I look at him to see if he's joking.

"Hell yeah, you are. You killed a cougar. Saved my ass."

My heart drops. "Did I really kill it?"

His voice loses its excitement. "Well, no, you just tagged it. I did the killing."

I can't help the tremor in my voice. "Are you just saying that to be nice?"

He lowers his chin and looks up at me. "Does that sound like something I'd do?"

"Yes."

He goes back to driving, the light now green. "I thought I was a hell-raising, bad-news kind of guy."

"You are a hell-raiser, or so I hear. That doesn't make you bad news or not nice."

"Tell that to Andie."

"Tell her yourself. You just sit there and let people believe what they want to believe, so you can hardly fault them when they jump to the wrong conclusions about you."

"Who says they're wrong conclusions?" he asks, turning right into a neighborhood of small houses with large front lawns.

"Me. I say it."

He pulls up to a curb and shuts off the engine. "You don't know me well enough to say that."

"Oh, yes I do." I unbuckle. "Are we here? I need a beer."

He smiles. "One beer, coming up." He opens his door and jumps out. "Hang on, I'll get your door." His door slams shut, rocking the whole truck, and then he's at my window. "Watch your step," he says. "Ground's real slippery."

I'm warm from my head to my toes, but not because of my jacket or my boots. Ian's being a total prince, and the connection between us is undeniable. I know he feels it too. It's almost like we're a couple, and we haven't even really officially kissed yet. *Yet.* That one in the hospital didn't count since it was fake, not fueled by passion. I fully intend to kiss him at or after this party, though. I can't wait anymore.

He holds out his elbow so I can hook my hand through his arm. I do it not only because it helps me walk over the slippery ground without falling but also because I want all the chicks in this town to know that for as long as I'm here, he's mine. Mine, all mine, all mine.

The snow crunches under our feet as we walk across someone's front lawn. "I hope you aren't expecting anything too fancy," Ian says. "Boog isn't the most sophisticated guy in town."

"Oh, don't worry about me. I can party with anyone." The hair and beauty business attracts all types of people, and I've never been one to discriminate.

The sound of heavy rock music comes from the house, even though it's shut up tight. "This is it," Ian says, stopping just at the bottom of the front steps. "Last chance to turn back."

I stop, facing him. "You can't scare me away from this, Ian."

He looks down at me and smiles. I can't see his eyes very well, the shadow from the brim of his hat making them pure darkness, but I know they're twinkling. "Not trying to scare you. Just giving you a chance to change your mind. I hear most women do that a lot."

"I'm not most women. Once I decide to do something, I do it."

"Well, you're right about one thing," he says, walking up the stairs and letting go of my arm to take the door.

"What's that?"

He pulls the door open, letting the heat and the noise blast into me. "You're not like most women, that's for sure."

CHAPTER TWENTY-EIGHT

We walk into the house, me first and then Ian, who shuts the door behind us. The warmth hits me all of a sudden, like I just walked into a sauna, but fully clothed in way too many layers. I hurry to get out of my borrowed coat, so I don't start sweating. Several guys stop talking and watch me, so I make sure to arch my back a little and give them a good show. I paid for these boobs, so I like to make sure I get my money's worth.

I'm smiling at the attention, but it doesn't last long since Ian decides to walk around me and block my view.

"Watch it, Ian. I can't see."

"Come on, let's go get a drink." He takes me by the hand and starts pulling me through the front room.

Part of me is thrilled that he's holding my hand in front of strangers, but the other part is getting cranky that I'm being dragged past a whole group of people like some sort of dog on a leash.

Slowing down, I use his forward momentum to break our hands apart. He gets a few more steps toward another room before he stops. Before he can turn all the way around, there's a guy standing at my side.

"Hey there. You the girl staying up at the MacKenzie place?" he asks. He's tall and lanky, dressed in a T-shirt and jeans. His belt buckle is the size of a bread plate, but he's cute. His hair is short like he's in the military, and I see the bottom of a tattoo just visible beneath his shirtsleeve.

I smile as big as I know how. "I am. And you are . . . ?"

He puts his beer bottle in his left hand and holds out his right. "I'm Mike. Friend of Ian's. Nice to meet you." He lifts his chin at Ian, who stops at my side.

"Mike," Ian says, shaking his hand too.

"Heard today you got into a little wrestling match with a cat," Mike says, smiling when he's done. He has the most charming dimples on both cheeks; I totally want to squeeze his face.

"How'd you hear that?" I ask, mystified since it's been only a day since it happened.

"Stopped by the diner. Heard it from Hannah." He takes a drink of his beer without taking his eyes off me.

"How does Hannah know?" I ask, looking from Mike to Ian.

Mike shrugs, looking at Ian. "I figured Ian told her."

I feel a little sick over the idea that Ian might have been hanging out with her when I was in the hospital, but it's not like I have any claim over his time. Some of the excitement of coming to this party with him fades.

"I haven't talked to her or anyone else about it," Ian says. "Why would you think I did?"

Mike takes a long drink from his beer again before answering. "Don't know." He lets out a burp that he tries to keep somewhat not loud by covering his mouth with the back of his hand. "I suppose because she likes to talk about how much you all hang out." He shrugs.

Ian lets out a hiss of air. "Man, you know she's full of it. You know I don't hang out with her."

Mike kind of laughs. "So? What's the big deal whether you do or not?" He looks from Ian to me and then back at Ian. Before Ian can respond, he speaks again. "Oh."

"Oh, what?" I ask.

"Nothin'." He backs up a couple steps. "You guys have fun. I gotta go talk to Boog."

He turns around and leaves us standing there.

"What was that all about?" I feel totally rejected. Reaching up, I casually wipe at my nose. If I have a booger hanging out, I'm going to die of mortification. Talk about making a big first impression.

Ian rubs his nose and sniffs loudly. "I don't know. He's crazy."

I panic when I see him staring at my face. My nose twitches, and I have to wipe it again, this time harder. The way Ian is staring at me with that concerned expression, I know there's something amiss up there.

He grabs his nose with two fingers and wiggles it around. "I'm going to get us some beers, okay?"

I nod, pretending I'm not totally covering my nose with my entire hand now. My eyes dart left and right, trying to locate a bathroom.

"Be right back." He turns away and sniffs really loudly.

I turn to the right, sure I'll find a bathroom near the front door, and accidentally bump into someone. I have to get there before Ian gets back! Emergency dangler alert!

"Well, hello there. I didn't expect to see you here."

I'm looking Hannah the Banana right in the eye. We are the same height in snow boots, only a foot apart. I tip my head down so my tragedy won't be as easy to discover.

"Hi." Looking over her shoulders, I still don't see anything that looks like a place that might have a mirror.

"Who you here with?" she asks.

I sigh out my annoyance. "Ian." A glance at the kitchen area tells me he's about to come back. Panic sets in. I cannot let him catch me with a dangler!

"Oh. Did he just give you a ride or . . ."

I put my hand on her arm to stop her, no longer tipping my head down. She's my only hope. "Listen. I know you don't know me very well, but I need your help."

"Okaaay . . ." She looks around the room, as if seeking assistance from someone to help her deal with a crazy person. "What do you want me to do?"

I tilt my head back a little. "Do you see anything? On my nose?"

She frowns and backs her head up a little. "Say what?"

"On my nose." I point to it urgently. "Do you see anything . . . dangling or whatever?"

She kind of looks but then scowls again. "*Ew*, no. Why are you asking me that?" She takes a step back.

I put my head back down and let out a long breath, so relieved. If she's lying to me I'm totally going to shoot her, because Ian's walking toward me with a bottle of beer in each hand, and it's too late for me to do anything else. "Sorry. I just had an emergency situation there. Thanks for your help."

She's still frowning when Ian arrives. He hesitates for a few seconds a couple feet away, but then he continues toward us until he's on my left.

"Here you go," he says, handing me a beer.

"Oh, that's so nice," Hannah says, taking the other beer from his hand. "You're always such a gentleman with me, Ian." She tilts her head sideways to be cute and then starts to lift the bottle to her lips.

Before she gets it two inches up, I snatch it from her hand. I wasn't thinking, I just did it. It's annoying the ever-loving crap out of me that she's just taking over like this. Plus, I saw him take a sip from the bottle already as he was approaching us, and I hate to think about her and Ian swapping spit, even if it's just on the rim of a beer bottle.

"Hey!" she says.

I hand it to Ian. "Get your own beer. This one has cooties on it. Ian cooties."

She gives me a hard look and then shakes her head, turning her attention to Ian. "This girl is crazy with a capital C, Ian, sweetie. I'd stay away if I were you."

Ian's slow smile makes me go all gooey inside, and all my anger dissipates when he turns his gorgeous green eyes on me. It's like everyone else in the room has ceased to exist, and he only sees me.

"That's why I like her." He moves closer and throws an arm up over my shoulders before turning his attention back to Hannah. "How've you been, Hannah? I hear busy . . . starting rumors."

She gives him a bitchy smile. "I've been fine, thanks for asking. And I don't know what you're talking about. I'm not a gossip."

I snort, choking a little on the beer I just sipped.

Hannah ignores me.

Ian gestures in my direction with his beer bottle. "Candice told me you've been telling people you and I are getting together."

She laughs. "You wish we were." Then she scowls at me. "Why would you lie to Ian like that? That's not very nice. We're not really those kind of people here in Baker."

Ian and I look at each other and smile like idiots. I can't stop staring at his deep green eyes. I see flecks of blue in there too, this time. They remind me of the color of the sea off the coast of Mexico where I went one spring break during college.

And that hat! Holy panties on fire! I never thought a cowboy hat could be hot, but yes, this one is most definitely hot when it's on his head. My underwear is about to burst into flames over it. I can feel my nipples hardening under the lace of my bra.

"Okay, well, whatever. You guys are boring. See you later." Hannah leaves us standing there.

"Is she gone yet?" Ian asks, his eyes rolling around kind of crazy.

I can't help but laugh. "Yes. Thank God."

He lets out a long sigh of relief. "Good. Man, that girl . . . she's a real piece of work." He drinks from his beer, and the moment we were having fades away.

CHAPTER TWENTY-NINE

I can finally breathe normally again. Searching for something to say that sounds cool, I blurt out the first thing that comes to mind. "I'd love to hook her up with Bradley. Andie's ex. They'd make the perfect couple." *Where did that come from?* I have no idea, but I'm going with it. My super-brain is on autopilot again, and that's always a good thing.

"Do it. Then she'd finally be out of our hair."

"Yeah, she could move to my town." I pause to think about that. Maybe my super-power brain is malfunctioning a little after all that medication. "On second thought, never mind. I don't want that girl anywhere near my city."

Ian turns us around so our backs are to the wall and we're looking out at the groups of people standing and sitting around the room. Every single person has a longneck bottle of beer in their hands. Some have one in each hand. Several of the girls have cowboy hats on, and some are dressed like country prom queens in the off-season. Hannah is one of the latter group.

"What's your city like?" he asks.

"West Palm?" I shrug. "It's hot a lot of the time. Humid. But it's a nice place. They've put a lot of money into their two main downtown areas. There are lots of places for people like us to hang out, have fun."

"If I came to visit, what would we do?"

My heart does a triple flip inside my chest as I think about what he might be suggesting. But instead of letting my heart get ahead of reality, I keep my voice calm and answer.

"Well, first I'd take you to my salon so I could get my hands on your hair."

"Oh yeah?" He takes his arm from my shoulders and lifts his hat up, rolling his eyes to his forehead as if he can see his hairdo without a mirror. "Something wrong with my hair?"

Another heart somersault. This time it's a little painful. "No, your hair is gorgeous. Hair is my thing, so when I see a nice head of it, I want to get my hands on it." I shrug. I know it makes little sense to someone outside the business.

He puts his hat back on, and I nearly melt with happiness when his arm goes back across my shoulders. After taking a swig of his beer, he smiles at me. "I do love me a good shampoo massage."

"I have good hands," I say in a low voice.

"I'll just bet you do," he says back.

Aaaaand cue the mood breaker . . .

"Hello, Ian."

A girl's voice breaks apart the sexy cloud I was falling into with Ian. I look up at her, dazed, my blood going cold when I see who it is.

"Hello, Ginny. You remember my girl, Candice." Ian tips his bottle toward me. It makes me feel kind of cheap the way he does it.

Before she even answers, the echo of his words brings back the scene in the hospital with her, and then everything comes crashing down on my head. Flashbacks of him flirting with me here and being so nice, and then how we ended up coming here in the first place. The scene with Ginny in the hospital cafeteria is why we're here. Oh my god. *This is all just an act!*

I pull to the side a little, enough to make Ian's arm fall off my back. "Hi, Ginny," I say, holding out my hand. "It's nice to see you again."

"You too," she says, shaking my hand. Her grip is firm. "Are you enjoying our little town?"

I laugh through the pain that's beating me up inside. "Oh yeah. Except for the lions and stuff."

"Lions?" She turns her questioning gaze to Ian. Her ex-fiancé. The guy who is trying to trick her into thinking we're together.

Dammit, how could I be so stupid?! I forgot he was doing this on purpose, that this was why he agreed to come to this party with me and the reason why he's hanging all over me. *Stupid, stupid, stupid.*

"Yeah, we were out checking cows early yesterday, and we ran across a cougar." Ian sounds like he's talking about the weather, he's so cool. "But we took care of it." He points at my arm with the edge of his bottle. "My girl took a hit, though. Had to get some stitches."

"Really?" Ginny nods at me slowly. I can't tell if she's feeling some respect or hates my guts. "Impressive. And on your second day here too."

"Yep." I have nothing else to say. I'm too sad to put the words together. One-way crushes suck big dicks.

"How long are you staying again?" she asks me.

"Two weeks." Before, when Ian and I were getting along and I was pretending it was all real, I was wishing it was three weeks. Now I wish I had a flight out tomorrow.

"Two weeks, huh? Imagine what kind of trouble you could get into in all that time." She smiles warmly.

Ian and I answer at the exact same time.

"A lot," he says. "None," I say.

I hurry to explain. "I'm going to be focusing all my attention on Andie and the baby. Plus I have a calf I'm taking care of, so that's going to be a lot of work. I don't have time to get into any more trouble."

I feel sick inside. Silly me, thinking I could play this sexy game with Ian and not let my heart get involved. Turns out a high-school-girl crush also comes with the high-school-girl broken heart when the girl realizes she's been played. Andie was totally right about me. I don't do flings very well, if this heartache is any indication.

"Wow. A calf? Are you into ranching, then?" She tilts her head to the side a bit, acting like my answer really matters. I feel like I'm being interrogated in a very polite way.

"Parts of it." I'm supremely uncomfortable right now. All I want to do is bail. "Will you excuse me for a second?" I say, separating myself from the two of them. "I need to go into the kitchen for a minute."

I take off before either of them can react, and I don't stop until I'm standing in the corner of the room in front of the fridge. I'm staring at a calendar that has days marked off when someone speaks from behind me.

"Is this the girl who shot Ian MacKenzie? Because if so, I wanna shake her hand."

I turn around and find myself facing a six-and-a-half-foot-tall man. Or maybe he's a bear. He could possibly also be a giant, upright wild boar. A lightbulb goes on in my head. *This is the man-bear-pig that Andie told me about!* I'd met him once before at her wedding, but his hair had been brushed and his beard half this size and neatly combed.

Wow. He looks like a total savage right now in a kind of wild Sasquatch biker sort of way. It's not totally awful. I wonder what he'd look like with a shave and a nice cut. I'd bet pretty hot, actually.

I hold out my hand and smile. "I am she. And you must be Boog."

He smoothes his beard out with one hand, which really does nothing to tame it, and shakes my hand with the other. "Honored to meet you. It's about time someone shot that rabble-rousing degenerate."

I totally love this guy already. "Actually, it wasn't me; it was Karma, but same result."

"Come again?" he asks.

I wave the conversation away. "Never mind. Hey, thanks for inviting me to this party . . . or letting me come . . . or not kicking me out." I realize as I'm talking that I'm kind of a party crasher. "Ian's my ride, so please don't kick me out."

"Don't be silly. You're the guest of honor here."

"I am?" I blush over his attempts to make me feel better, even though he's totally lying. This is way better than my earlier act where I was busy fooling myself with a guy way too hot for my own good in front of way too many witnesses. I'm back on solid ground now, for the most part. Boog is an easy person to talk to.

"Yep," he assures me. "What can I get you? You hungry? I got some pizza and wings in the other room."

"No, thanks. I don't have much of an appetite right now." Something about a guy named Ian and being his fake girlfriend upsets my stomach.

Boog grins. At least I think that's what he's doing. His eyes crinkle up in the outside corners, but his mouth is too covered in black, pube-like beard hair to see it very well. "How about a little chocolate?" he asks. "You like chocolate?"

I snort. "Do cougar scratches burn like a bejesus?"

He laughs really loud and long, holding onto his impressive belly. "I don't know," he finally says. "You tell me."

"Hell yes, they do." I smile. "Where's your stash?"

He moves over to a cupboard and opens it up, pulling down a Tupperware container full of chocolate bars. "Don't tell anyone," he says conspiratorially. "I'm not supposed to eat the stuff."

I take a bar and rip off the wrapping. "You on a diet?" I bite into it and almost melt with the happiness that's on my tongue.

"Should be." He takes a bar too and puts the container back.

"What're you guys eating?" Ian asks, walking up behind me.

I turn around in mid-chew. My arm goes behind my back in a sad attempt at remaining stealth.

"Nuffin'," I say, working hard at swallowing the evidence.

"Liar." Ian looks at Boog, who's making no attempt to cover his tracks. "Cheating on your diet again?"

Boog eats half the bar in one bite. "Nope." When he's done chewing, he continues. "Just getting my daily ration of antioxidants, flavonoids, and theobromine."

It's kind of fascinating how Boog looks like a man-bear-pig but talks like a professor. It makes me want to spend more time with him to see what kind of secrets he might be keeping.

Thinking that reminds me of Ian and all the secrets he's keeping, not only from me, but from Ginny. Storm clouds move in over my mood.

"You ready to leave yet?" Ian asks.

"Nope." I keep eating my chocolate, out in the open now since Boog didn't try to hide it. "I'm just getting started." Pushing myself off the counter, I hold up my chocolate bar in a salute to Boog. "Thanks for the energy boost."

As I'm leaving the kitchen, I hear Boog's response. "Anytime. *Mi casa, su casa.*"

Ian says nothing, and I don't stick around long enough to see if that changes.

CHAPTER THIRTY

Walking out into the main room again, I'm conscious of several pairs of eyes on me. The female ones look suspicious; the male ones look interested. I stop near an armchair and wait to see who might approach me first. I'm not surprised when it's one of the guys.

"Hey there," he says, sporting a big smile. He has nice teeth and a big cowboy hat that's the color of straw, but made of much finer stuff, I think. The sleeves of his navy-blue button-down shirt are rolled up a couple times, and his belt buckle is big, but not as big as some I've seen around here, meaning I could probably fit a few carrot sticks on it instead of a full meal. Tall and broad shouldered, he has very tanned forearms, for winter. The scars on his knuckles tell me he likes to fight.

I sigh. He's way too handsome for his own good, and he knows it. I can tell by the way he walks, like he knows every girl in the room is looking at him and getting all revved up over what she sees. What a disappointment. I so prefer guys who are oblivious to their powers.

I know his type well; I call them roosters. They like to strut around and show off their feathers, and after they scratch out their territory, they have no problem fighting for it. But the fact that Ian was playing around with me earlier has me considering a conversation with this guy, someone I normally would avoid.

"Hey there, yourself," I say back.

"You the new girl in town?"

"I guess I am. Just here temporarily, though."

"Mack's sister-in-law or something, right?" He takes a drink of his beer and grimaces after he swallows.

"Kind of. Who are you?"

"Sorry, I should have told you sooner." He lifts the front brim of his hat and dips his head a little. "Tate Montgomery, at your service."

I don't know what it is about getting a cowboy hat salute, but it does something funny to me inside. I think I like it. I can't stop smiling in response, even though I had decided just a couple seconds ago that he wouldn't be worth my time. When he winks, I smile even harder. Yes, I definitely like the cowboy salute thing. And the cowboy who's doing the saluting. He's not as roostery as I first thought.

"Can I ask you a question, Tate?" Since my plan to get in Ian's Wranglers is all but busted, I decide to move on to my next order of business.

"Sure can. Ask me anything." He takes a small step closer to me, and I don't back up. He smells nice, like man-soap.

"How hooked into the gossip grapevine are you?"

He shrugs. "I don't do too much of it personally, but I suppose I know what's on the wind. Kind of hard not to, living here."

"I've only been here a couple days, but I was just wondering . . . how come Mack's wife, Andie, doesn't have any friends here?"

His face twists up a little, and then he casually looks around the room before answering. He seems uncomfortable, but it's difficult to tell whether it's because he doesn't like gossip in general or he doesn't like the answer he's about to give.

"Could be there's stuff being said about her. Don't know as I believe any of it, though."

My heart starts hammering in my chest. People are saying crap about Andie? *My* Andie? I force myself to remain calm. He probably won't tell me anything if I go all nuts on him. That kind of thing makes guys nervous.

"What kind of stuff and who's saying it?" I ask.

He shrugs. "It's really no big deal. She should just ignore it. It doesn't matter now."

I'm afraid he's going to back off and tell me nothing if I act too eager, so I take his beer from his hand and help myself to a swig of it.

He smiles and moves in even closer, the heat from his body coming off him like he's a human radiator. It's nice on a cold winter's night like tonight, and with a room full of strangers around us, I have nothing to fear, so I stay right where I am.

"I was just worried about her," I say, trying to be cool. "She's my best friend, and she's all alone out here in Baker City. I'd love to know she has some friends she can count on."

"Any friend of yours is a friend of mine," he says. He reaches up and takes his beer back, placing the top of it at his mouth. He hesitates with it like that for a couple seconds looking at me. Just before he pushes it harder against his mouth for another sip, the tip of his tongue comes out and hits the glass rim.

I know he didn't mean it to be sexy, but *whoa*. Now my brain is going a little haywire. I look around the room to see if anyone else noticed. Several girls are giving me looks that make me think they want to harm me physically.

I back away a half step, not because I'm afraid of anyone, but because this feels wrong. I know Ian's not really interested in me, but I did come here with him, and I'm not in the mood to complicate things more than they already are, even though it's a little tempting with this guy Tate.

If I hadn't met Ian, I'd definitely be all over this opportunity, but now that Ian's gotten into my brain, Baker City is ruined for me as far as men are concerned. If I can't do Ian, I won't do anyone. Decision made. Sorry, Tate.

"You worried about something?" he asks me, following my gaze.

"Oh, no, not really. Just some of the girls here look like they want to scratch my eyes out."

He laughs and moves closer, putting his hand on my hip. "Don't worry about them. It's just small-town bullshit. Same as everywhere else."

I don't move away from him immediately because I want to get more information from him. "So, what are they saying? About Andie, I mean."

He sighs. "You're going to make me tell you, aren't you?"

I grin, seeing the defeat in his eyes. This was way easier than I thought it would be. "Yes. Don't try to defy me. I can be very stubborn when I want to be."

"I'll tell you what," he says, a twinkle in his dark eyes. He leans down closer. "You agree to go out with me one time, and I'll agree to tell you what I know. How's that sound?"

I chew on the inside of my cheek for a few seconds, considering his offer, acting like him being this close is no big deal. "Lunch or dinner?" I'm stalling, trying to decide how this might play out with Ian. Will he be jealous? Mad? And what do I care what he'll be about it? He's just playing around with me to get back at Ginny. Maybe he even wants to get back together with her. He denied it, but guys do that crap all the time.

"Your choice," Tate says. "Any meal, any place, any time, my treat."

My eyebrows go up. He's eager and somehow available at all hours of the day and night. Maybe he's a rancher too. I find I'm kind of partial to that breed right now.

Since I have no other plans and the idea of hanging out with Ian anymore just feels like a recipe for heartbreak, I decide to go full speed ahead with my plan to solve the Andie-has-no-friends mystery.

"Breakfast," I say. "Tomorrow morning at nine, the diner in town where Hannah Banana works." I have no idea why I picked that place other than the fact that I don't know any other spot in town besides the gun range and the hospital. Somehow neither of those venues seems to have the right atmosphere for giving him the third degree. Plus, at the diner I can mess with The Banana, which has proven to be pretty fun. That wench, trying to deny my pregnant BFF her herbal tea. *Grrrr.*

He narrows his eyes. "You look like pure trouble right now, you know that?"

I hold my hand out for him to shake it. "Good. Because that's what I am if you don't keep your end of the deal."

He takes my hand but then leans down and gives me a soft kiss on the cheek. "It's a deal. Sealed with a kiss."

I'm about to smile and answer him, but he's suddenly yanked from my grip.

"What the hell are you doing, man?!" an angry guy yells.

It takes me a split second before I realize it's Ian, and he's got Tate by his shirt at his shoulder.

"What the hell?!" Tate stumbles but then quickly rights himself. Glaring at Ian, he jerks his arm really hard to pull himself out of Ian's grip. "Get off me, man!"

I back away until my legs hit the edge of a couch behind me. Boog is striding down the hallway from the kitchen in my direction.

"How 'bout you get off my girl?" Ian says in a deadly calm voice. His face is beet red.

Tate stands up straight and fixes his shirt. Then he looks at me. "Funny . . . she didn't mention being your girl when she set up a date with me."

Boog stalls in the opening to the living room. He starts with what sounds like a warning, "Ian . . ."

Tate smiles, interrupting Boog so he can continue taunting Ian. "Sorry to break it to you, man, but she's done with you. Can't say as I blame her."

I hold out my arm to stop what I see coming, but it does no good. Ian's a couple feet away and then a second later he's tackling Tate to the ground.

They smash into a television and bring it to the floor in a mighty crash of broken glass and plastic. Girls nearby scream and jump out of the way. The guys stand their ground or move to better sightseeing positions, their overriding goal to not spill their beers. Tate and Ian are both roaring insults at each other.

Boog comes over to me with his phone at his ear. "You ready to go home?" he asks, putting his conversation on hold as he waits for my answer.

"Um . . . yes?" I look at Ian and know that he's not going to be ready to drive me anywhere for a while. He's too busy trying to fight his way out of a headlock.

"She's ready to go," Boog says into his phone. He nods a few times while he listens to whoever is on the other end of the line, and then looks at me. "I'll tell her. Bye."

I lose all interest in Ian and focus on Boog. "What's up?"

"Mack's outside waiting for you. Get your coat and I'll walk you out."

I look from Boog to Ian, the latter now in some kind of wrestling position on the floor, legs all tangled with Tate's.

"What do you mean, 'Mack's here'?"

"He's out in his truck. Come on." Boog takes me by the upper arm and guides me over to the front door, where my borrowed coat hangs.

I feel terrible. "I'm sorry about all this," I say, gesturing back toward the other room where I can hear grunting and then another crash.

"Don't worry about it. This is status quo for Ian. This'll be the third TV he's bought me."

"And he's still your friend?" I'm bewildered over Boog's casual acceptance of the destruction of his property.

Boog's eyes crinkle up at the corners. "I've upgraded after each fight. This time I'm going for the fifty-inch, high-def model."

I laugh at the obvious excitement in his voice. "You're kind of crazy, you know that?"

His smile fades. "You're kind of beautiful, you know that?"

I'm too stunned to respond, but he keeps on going.

"Just be careful. With Ian, I mean."

"What? Ian? He's harmless."

"I don't mean be careful as in he's dangerous . . . I mean be careful with his heart. It's pretty tender."

I snort, so fed up with all the pandering I see going on here. Boog's getting free TVs when it's practically his fault the fighting keeps happening. They're all codependent sorrow addicts. "Please," I say with as much scorn in my voice as I can manage. "You guys are all just a bunch of enablers."

Boog stands up straighter and looks confused. Maybe a little mad too. "Come again?"

"You've let him act like a giant baby for the last three years instead of kicking him in the butt and telling him to grow up and get over it. That's not on me—that's on you."

And they have the nerve to warn me away. *Ha!* They should warn themselves away. They're doing more harm to Ian than I ever could.

I grab the front door handle, more than ready now to leave this lame party. Boog just went from cool guy to butthead on my list. I don't care if he gave me free chocolate.

His hand on my shoulder stops me just before I pull the door open.

"I didn't mean to insult you. I think you'd be good for him. But only if you're committed to seeing it through."

I don't turn around when I answer, my voice going out into the cold as I open the door and step outside. "You don't need to worry about any of that. I'm over him." Just saying the words makes me hurt.

The truck that Andie was driving before is parked at the curb, the engine rumbling and smoke coming out of the tailpipe. I trudge through the falling snow to the passenger side and get in next to Mack, ignoring anything Boog might be saying or thinking behind me.

CHAPTER THIRTY-ONE

The truck is warm, but the reception cold. Mack says nothing for a few blocks. It's so quiet in the car I can't stand it.

"So, thanks for the ride," I finally say, trying to break the ice. It's horrible to think that he's blaming me for the fight at Boog's. And how did he get here so quickly? Was he already in town? Why not with Andie? I want the answers to all these questions, but I'm too embarrassed to ask them.

"No problem." After a few seconds, he glances over at me. "You okay?"

I shrug, not returning his gaze. "Yeah, I'm fine. Just . . ." I can't say the rest.

"Just . . . what?"

I give up quickly on the idea of confessing to Mack. He's not the confessor type. "You don't want to know."

He makes a right turn, and the back end of the truck slides a little. He gets it under control before responding. "I wouldn't ask if I didn't."

I'm debating whether to tell him what's really on my mind or to make something up when he continues.

"Andie asked me to talk to you about Ian," he says before I can decide what I'm going to say.

I'm instantly on the defensive. "What about Ian?" I'm kind of offended that she didn't just bring it up with me herself. Since when does my friend have conversations with me through her husband? That's not cool. That's not cool at all. It makes me angry at him that he thinks he can be that person, that intermediary in our friendship that was in place long before he came sauntering into her life, and it makes me doubly angry at Andie. It feels like our friendship is taking a very distant position behind her entire family. And maybe that's the way it's supposed to work when a girl gets married and has a baby, but it feels pretty terrible, and I don't like it one bit.

He sighs. "I suppose she's worried you'll get hurt."

"Me? Or is it Ian she's worried about?" I roll my eyes as I look out the side window at the snow falling in the glow of the streetlights. "Like everyone else in town seems to be."

"Oh, it's you she's worried about. Definitely not Ian, believe me."

I look at him sharply over his tone. "What's that mean? You don't agree with her?"

He taps his thumbs on the steering wheel. "I guess it's a little complicated where Ian's concerned."

"Uncomplicate it for me." I really want to get to the bottom of this thing for Ian. It's so stupid how he's gotten stuck in time like he has. Even though I'm no longer planning to get into his Wranglers, it doesn't mean I don't want to help him.

"I wish I could."

"Try." I'm getting crankier by the second. It's like Ian is a lost cause to everyone or something, which he totally isn't.

Mack starts talking, but he doesn't sound all that tough or confident like I expected him to. He sounds . . . sad.

"My brother has had a hard time of it lately."

I resist the urge to snort my disbelief. Ian being the baby of the family has taken on the worst kind of meaning. They totally treat him like he's ten.

"He finally made the decision to leave town and strike out on his own, which is a pretty big deal around here but even more so in my family, and everything got messed up."

"So?" I counter. "You move on from stuff like that. You don't wallow in it for three years."

Mack shakes his head. "No, it's not that simple. See, he's been living in my shadow his whole life. I don't like it any more than he does, but it's a fact. Getting into architecture was his way of trying to distance himself, to be his own person."

"Well, it *is* very different from ranching."

"Yeah. The problem is, he's not really interested in doing architecture. Not at all, actually."

I frown. This is the first I'm hearing of this. "What? He didn't say that to me."

"How much has he told you?" Mack looks at me for a moment before going back to focusing on his driving.

I shrug, trying to remember. "Not much. Just that he's not a fan of the winters here, but he likes taking care of the animals. I think that's what he was saying, anyway."

Mack nods. "That's about right. Fact is, he was all set to move to Portland and be this person he really didn't want to be, just to get out of here."

"Sooo . . . Ginny messing that up wasn't really a bad thing is what you're saying."

"Weeelll, it was and it wasn't, depending on your perspective."

"How so?" I feel like I'm being given the keys to the kingdom here, learning all Ian's secrets.

"It was good in that it kept him from making two mistakes. Ginny being number one, and starting a career he doesn't really like deep down being number two."

"And what's the bad part?"

"He had to start all over. Back under my shadow with the added rumors going around that I destroyed his marriage and chance at life."

"He doesn't believe that garbage." I'm mad at the people who are saying those things, whoever they are.

"Not on the surface, but I'd be willing to bet there's a piece of him that does believe it . . . the piece that doesn't want to get up and start over."

"See? That's what I'm saying." I'm getting all excited. "You get it, Mack. He's totally wallowing in the past. He just needs to forget all that and move on. I mean, all of it. Being under your shadow, Ginny, the architecture thing—everything."

Mack chuckles. "You got it all figured out."

"Of course I do. That's my special talent you know . . . solutions. You've got problems, I've got solutions."

"So what's your solution to the problem of an almost thirty-year-old guy who doesn't want to move on? What's the solution there?"

I chew on my lip as I consider what my plan of attack would be, if I were still into Ian, which I am not.

"First, I'd talk to all his friends and family and tell them to stop feeling sorry for his sorry, pity-partied-out butt."

"Then what?" Mack's voice has laughter in it, but he's holding back, so I continue.

"I'd sit him down and ask him what he really wants to do with his life. If it isn't ranching and it isn't architecture, it has to be something."

"Okay, sounds reasonable. And then?"

"And then I'd kick him in the butt until he went after it. Went to school or started doing that thing, whatever it is." I smile and look at Mac. "See? Simple."

He nods. "I agree. When do we start?"

I blink a few times as his words sink in.

The truck goes silent.

"Well?" he prompts. "When? Tomorrow?"

I shake my head. "No, not me. Someone else has to do all this."

"Why not you?"

"Because."

"You like him—I know you do."

My face goes red, but he can't see it because it's too dark, thank goodness. "Sure, I like him. As a friend."

He chuckles. "You always chase your friends around the house naked?"

"Maybe." Now my face is on fire. His whole family saw that, and now my humiliation is back full force with him bringing it up.

"I doubt it. Andie says you like him, so I know you do."

"Andie's wrong a lot; you should know that about her," I say.

"Oh, I don't think so. I'm pretty sure she's right a hundred percent of the time."

I look over to catch him smiling. It's sweet and annoying all at the same time.

"You are so whipped it's not even funny." I try to sound disgusted instead of jealous. I'm happy my friend has Mack beside her, when he's clearly awesome, but it makes me acutely aware of the fact that I don't have something like that, and I want it. I want it bad.

"Whipped and proud to be." He looks over, catching me scowling at him. "Ian's the same kind of guy, you know. Once he loves a girl, there's no going back. He's in for life, and there'll never be another one for him."

I swallow with effort, the feeling inside me difficult to understand. It hurts way too much. "That's why he's so messed up over Ginny—is that what you're saying?"

"No, that's not what I'm saying. Not at all. He never felt that way about her."

I look over to see if he's joking, but he seems serious. "I find that hard to believe. They were together forever."

"Yeah, but Ian wasn't *there*. The real Ian was never there with her. He was always acting like the guy he thought she wanted him to be."

"The architect," I say.

"Exactly. Did he ever tell you that it was her idea?"

"What?"

"Yeah. She was with him in high school. She controlled his class schedule, told him she thought he was suited to drawing buildings and stuff. She always wanted to leave this place." He sighs. "Called it a hick town."

"She sounds like a manipulative bitch."

Mack sighs. "He was her way out. I can't blame her for seeing her opportunity and taking it. I just wish it wasn't on my brother's back."

"But she's still here. I'm sorry, Mack, but this makes no sense to me. This isn't the eighteen hundreds. If Ginny wanted to leave, she could easily do that. And you're telling me Ian was a pushover? I don't think so. He's totally bullheaded."

"Ian may be bullheaded on the surface, but when he's with a girl, he's different, focused on making her happy. That's what we were taught by our father, so that's just how we do things. The reason Ginny's still here is she hasn't found someone to hitch her wagon to yet that's leaving. But she will someday, believe me. She wasn't meant for this place."

The idea of Ian being putty in my hands when to everyone else he's a pigheaded jerk has enough appeal that I'm starting to think about his Wranglers again and seeing them in a pile on the floor. It's that bad-boy syndrome thing again. *Argh*, I totally hate my hormones sometimes.

"What was that like when Ginny made a move on you?" The question just pops out of my mouth without any warning, but now that it's out there, I'm curious enough to hear the answer that I don't correct myself and withdraw the question.

"Awful. Terrible." Mack's hands squeeze the steering wheel so hard his veins pop out. "One of the worst days of my life, actually."

"Why?" It's kind of fascinating how worked up he is over it, even after all this time. Most guys are flattered when a girl goes for it, even if it is inappropriate . . . sometimes more so when it is.

"Because it was so *wrong*. I knew as soon as it happened that it would destroy my brother. And I didn't ask for it. I didn't even see it coming. I keep thinking maybe I should have, and if I had, I could have stopped it."

That answer annoys me. "So essentially it's your fault that Ian's life is destroyed." More of this enabler stuff. No wonder Ian's so messed up.

Mack takes awhile to answer. "No, not exactly." He looks at me, his expression serious and possibly tortured. "Haven't you ever made a huge mistake in judgment, not seen something coming to be able to stop it, and lived to regret it? Seen someone's life changed, irreparably changed, and known that you had a hand in it?"

I think on that for a while before I answer. "No, I haven't. But I can imagine that it would suck."

He nods, back to looking at the road. "Yeah. It sucks. That's a fact."

I'm so confused. I wanted to be over Ian and not caring about his life, but now Mack has me thinking about him again, wondering about how the course of events in Mack's world altered Ian's life so drastically. Little things became big things, and what was wrong became both right and then wrong at the same time. No wonder Ian doesn't know up from down or in from out. I'd be dizzy too if I were him. There's not just enabling going on here. There's guilt and blame and . . . love.

I look at Mack, and my heart kind of melts over how upset he is. He really loves his brother a lot. It makes me wish I had a big brother like him.

"You're a good guy, Mack. I'm glad you and Andie found each other."

"I thank God every day that He put her in my path."

I laugh. "Even though you got doused with a cocktail?"

He laughs with me. "Yeah, even though. I still have that shirt, you know. Haven't washed it."

"I don't know whether to find that charming or disturbing."

"Andie says it's charming."

"She would." I say that as if I'm insulting her, but really I'm just jealous. Every girl should have a guy like Mack, saving his dirty shirts for the memories they hold.

The truck goes silent until we're nearly back at the ranch.

"So when do we start the plan?" Mack asks as we pass through the archway leading into the ranch property.

"What plan?"

"The plan to get Ian back on track."

My heart skips a beat as I imagine my role in that whole scenario. "Whenever you want, I guess. I'm not going to be a part of it. I'm leaving in less than two weeks."

Mack slows to a stop and puts the truck in "Park." He looks at me, leaving the engine running. "It won't work without you, Candice."

I pause, my hand on the door, ready to open it. "Why not?"

"Because. You're the only girl he's had any interest in since he was thirteen years old, and he needs a reason to change. You could be that reason. I think he needs you."

My jaw drops open. Is this really Mack sitting next to me, or has some alien who's watched too many soap operas from the eighties invaded his body?

"I have to go," I say, opening the door and sliding down to the snow. I only slip a little when my feet hit the ground, but since I've learned to hang onto doors and seats until I have a steady grip, I'm okay. My jeans stay dry.

"Think about it!" Mack yells as I slam the door shut.

I trot across the ground, anxious to put some distance between us. There's no way I can respond intelligently to his ideas because my head is just a giant tornado inside.

Around and around the thoughts and emotions go, getting all tangled together. Could I help Ian without falling in love with him? And if I did fall in love with him, could I leave him behind and go back to my old life? I'm afraid the answer to both questions is *no*, so as I mount the stairs to my temporary room, I try to think of another way I can help him move on, while not destroying myself in the process.

CHAPTER THIRTY-TWO

Sunday morning dawns bright and ass-biting cold. My brilliant plan to open my bedroom window to check the temperature results in me getting frozen nostril hairs before I'm even out of my pajamas. I layer myself in half the clothes I brought from Florida, just trying to keep my nipples from breaking off, before heading downstairs.

"Where are you off to so early?" Maeve asks me as I walk into the kitchen, my boots making clomping noises on the wood floor.

"Breakfast with Tate Montgomery." I grin big, trying not to reveal the fact that I'm on a very specific mission to fix Andie's life. "Can I borrow one of the trucks outside?"

Maeve's smile slips a little. "I could get Ian to drive you into town if you'd like."

I heard him come in several hours after me last night, but I haven't seen him since he started wrestling all over the floor, nor do I want to. I'm not ready to face him and my confused feelings yet. I have to get this business about Andie taken care of first. One disaster at a time.

"No, that's okay," I say. "I know he's busy."

"He said to tell you that he'd meet you in the barn when you get up, to feed the calf."

My heart pretty much gets a crack in it at that little statement, but I keep up the strong front. I'm not abandoning my cow baby or allowing her to starve. I know Ian's there for her. And I'll pick up where we left off when I return from breakfast.

"I'll just text him and tell him to start without me. I'll be back in a couple hours."

Maeve shuffles over in slippers to her purse. "Okay, that's fine by me. Here. You can take the smaller S-10 out there. The green one."

I take the keys from her and give her a hug, trying to express without words the fact that I mean her family no harm. "Thanks, Maeve. Can I get you anything while I'm in town?"

"No, that's all right, dear. I have to go in later for several things myself, so I'll wait."

"Okey-dokey. Tell Andie when she's up that I'll be home in time for lunch."

"Will do. Mack stopped by and said they had a long night, so I don't expect her up much before then."

"Okay, good. That works out perfectly. See ya."

I leave the house, relieved that I don't need to stop in and see Andie just yet. I'm anxious to hold Sarah again and get her imprinting on me, but I have this not-a-date to keep, and I have a feeling I'm going to get a lot of good intel from Tate. He definitely knows something. Maybe I'll come back with everything already worked out for her, and we can celebrate over some tea and backwoods cappuccino.

The Chevy is pretty easy to drive, even though the back end of it likes to fishtail around sometimes. I make it into town in forty-five minutes, which puts me exactly ten minutes late for breakfast.

Walking into the steamy diner, I scan the room. It's packed, but there's no Tate anywhere that I can see.

"Meeting someone?" asks a girl to my left. I recognize her voice immediately.

"Hello, Hannah Banana," I say, my tone full of sugary sweetness. I really just want to squeeze her until her silly head pops off, certain she's the root of a lot of Andie's problems.

She loses her smile. "It's just Hannah."

I ignore her and scan the room once more. "I'm supposed to meet Tate Montgomery here, but I'm a little late."

She cocks her hip, a coffee pot dangling from her hand. "He was here, but he left."

"Dammit." I bite my lip, wishing I had his number or a way to get in touch with him. Now what am I supposed to do? Buy another gun? More boots? I scratch at the stitches on my arm, trying to ease the itch that's settled in. I wince when I accidentally bump the stitches. *Damn mountain lion, ruining my perfectly unblemished arm skin.*

"I could call him for ya," Hannah says. She's smiling way too much for me to feel comfortable.

"Okaaay . . ." I want to ask, "What's the catch?" but she pretty much fills me in on that particular catch when she whips out her phone, presses some buttons, and starts talking.

"Hey, Tate? Yeah, it's me, Hannah. Your date's here waitin' for ya. Does Ian know you're meeting her here?"

Total troublemaker. Her next call is probably going to be to Ian, telling him exactly what I'm doing and who I'm doing it with. I got the impression last night that he's not much of a fan of Tate, and who knows what Hannah's ultimate motivation is.

She pauses and then looks up at me. "You going to wait for him?"

I nod.

"Yeah, she'll wait." She winks at me. "Okay, I'll tell her. See ya." She hangs up and points to the counter at the far end of the restaurant, just to the right of the fry-cook window. "Have a seat. He'll be here in two seconds."

Making my way from the front door to the farthest seat in the entire place reminds me of a recurring nightmare I have, where everyone in the room stares at me and says nothing. There must be fifty people in here, and apparently nothing they were talking about before I got here is as interesting as I am.

Yes. It's true. I am a human silencer. No one speaks when I draw near, but unlike my nightmare, I am wearing pants, so the sensation isn't as horrible today as it is when I'm sleeping.

When I sit down on the stool, it starts to tip to the right and then stops. I'm stuck at a thirty-degree angle. Whenever I try to straighten it out, it makes a horrible squeaking noise and then flops to the other side.

Squeeeak . . . bonk! Squeeaak . . . bonk!

Hannah puts an empty coffee mug down in front of me. "Regular or decaf?"

"How about a new chair?" I get up to look underneath the seat. What I see immediately makes me wish I hadn't bothered. Talk about nasty dirty. *Surely they've heard of bubonic plague in Baker City?*

I get back up on the seat and try to smile as I tip sharply to the right, but it's kind of difficult considering the hairy gray goop just under my butt. I put my hands on the sides of the chair cushion to help me balance, but I keep my fingers pointed at the ground so they don't accidentally touch any of the plague germs underneath me.

Squeeeak . . . bonk!

I hope this seat really is covered in genuine vinyl and not some other more porous material.

"Can't get you a new seat—sorry. Got a full house, as you can see." She sighs, like I'm annoying her. "So? Regular or decaf?"

The door opens and bells jangle. Turning around, I see Tate standing in the entrance, taking his hat from his head. Several people call out to him, and he nods or waves as he makes his way toward me, his hat poised in front of him near his waist.

He's even better looking in the full light of day than he was at night, which I'm pretty sure violates some very important laws of optical physics. At this point I'm starting to question whether there are any ugly cowboys out here in Oregon.

"You made it," he says, grinning as he approaches.

"Sorry I was late. I've never driven in snow before."

Squeeeeak . . . bonk!

My chair tips to the other side, and I grab both the counter and his arm to keep from falling off. "Damn chair's busted too. I guess today's not my day."

"Don't worry about it. I wasn't far away." He looks out over the room as he steadies me at my hip with a big, strong hand. "Hannah, you got any other seats?"

"For you, Tate? Any day. Just hold on a sec, and I'll go get rid of someone for ya."

I turn back to find Hannah winking at him.

Ugh. I really just want to slap her right now, even knowing she's rescuing me from this wonky, effed-up carousel chair that she took way too much pleasure in offering to me.

Two minutes later, Tate and I are sitting in a booth, facing each other, and I'm trying to act natural. It's hard when I know he likes me but that I'm only there to pump him for information. It feels dishonest and makes me nervous as a result. Yes, he's cute, but the fact is, he isn't Ian. I've only got eyes for the one guy I can't really have.

"Tell me you're not one of those girls who doesn't eat real food," he says, smiling in a teasing way.

"No, that's not me. I'm getting a waffle and some bacon."

He smiles bigger and looks down at the menu. "That's what I'm talking about. We'll get two of each and I'll have some eggs also, I think."

After Hannah takes our order, he leans back against his seat and rests his arms across the back of it on either side. "Go ahead, then. I know you just came here to interrogate me."

I grimace, totally busted. He's way smarter than I expected him to be for as good looking as he is. "That sounds terrible."

He waves me off. "Nah, don't worry about it. I know my place now. Ian squared me up. Just tell me what you want to know, and I'll see what I can tell you or find out for you."

I ignore the Ian-squaring-him-up comment in favor of the open book he's offering me. *Andie first, Ian later.*

"Okay, so what are the rumors about Andie? Why doesn't she have any friends here?"

He reaches up and spins his knife around on the top of the table, staring at it as it goes around. "I suppose it could be a combination of things."

"Like . . . ?"

"Well, maybe the circumstances of her being here to start with." He stops the knife spinning and then starts it again in the opposite direction.

"Which are . . . ?"

He shrugs, still not looking at me. "Mack leaving the bachelor party to be with her, and then Ginny jumping to the wrong conclusions, and her and Mack . . ."

"Her and Mack? You mean her and *her*. Mack had nothing to do with it."

Tate shrugs. "Believe what you want. Some say he did; some say he didn't." He looks up at me.

I'm instantly enraged. "How dare they!"

When he doesn't jump to agreeing with me, I notch down my righteous indignation. "What do you think? Do you think he asked for it?"

He shrugs again. "Probably not. I haven't thought that much about it, to be honest. I could care less what the MacKenzies do or don't do."

"But knowing Mack as I assume you do, is he the type to go after his brother's fiancée?"

Tate shakes his head. "Nope. Not that I can see."

"Good. But I know that's kind of past history, so what does that have to do with Andie now?"

Tate glances over at Hannah before he answers. "I'm not sure you'd understand this coming from a big city like you do, but here, things are kind of different."

I lean in closer and lower my voice. "How are they different? Explain it to me."

He leans in too. "For example, people get ideas in their heads about other people, and even when things aren't going according to plan, they have a hard time accepting it."

"Give me something specific." I'm keeping Hannah in my sights, using my peripheral vision. If she tries to come over and interrupt us, I'm going to have to cause a distraction or something. Maybe I'll throw something across the room. That should work. I could probably bury one of these butter knives in the wall if I had to.

"Take Ginny, for example. She's one of those girls who had it in her head that Ian was hers—lock, stock, and barrel—from the time they were kids. But he was never that into it."

"How do you know that?" It's like everyone but Ian and Ginny knew that Ian wasn't in love with her. I guess that's not too unbelievable, though. I've seen it enough times with my own friends. It happened with Andie and her ridiculous boyfriends all the time. She could never see what total d-bags they were, even when it was pointed out in very plain English, like me saying the more obvious things like "Hey, Andie, a guy who buys you plastic surgery gift certificates for Valentine's Day is a total dirtbag." Bradley was nearly the cause of the end of our friendship. Thank God, Mack came along when he did . . .

"How did I know?" He shrugs. "I don't know. You could just see it. Everyone could see it, not just me. Whenever she was around, he would just kind of disappear. I mean, he was *there*, but not there. Know what I mean? Like a ghost. The ghost of Ian MacKenzie."

"Yes, I think so." It sounds very much like what Ian was trying to describe to me himself, how he was always in the background, with Ginny out in front.

"But did that stop her?" Tate asks. "No. It just made her more determined. Kind of like Hannah is with Mack."

I look over at her and see her sending nervous glances our way.

"Tell me," I urge him. "All of it."

He shrugs. "I'm sure you know it. She had her hooks in Mack from the start. He never gave her the time of day, really. I mean, he was polite and all, but never encouraging. Hannah figured he was hers, and since he never dated anyone around town, people thought she had a right to believe that. She moved into his place sometime after he came back from Vegas and lots of people just assumed they were a couple."

"They weren't. He was just being nice."

"That's what he says. It's not what she says."

I glare at him and then Hannah. "She's a lying little bitch is what she is." If I had lasers in my eyes, she'd be smoke right now.

Tate puts his hands up. "Hey, don't look at me. I'm just telling the story."

"Don't shoot the messenger," I say, nodding at him.

"I hear you shot Ian." Tate smiles. "Pretty funny if you ask me."

"Don't change the subject. How does all this relate to Andie?"

He sighs. "The way people see it around here, she's the reason for all of it. If she hadn't come into the picture, Ginny would have her man, Hannah would have her man, and everyone would be happy."

"Not Ian or Mack!" I say way too loudly.

Tate glances around nervously. "Relax, okay? I told you you wouldn't understand."

"Oh, I understand perfectly." I shake my head. "Some people are just clueless."

"It's not that easy, really, though is it?" Tate's staring at me, all seriousness in his expression. It calms me considerably.

I shrug, not understanding what he's trying to say. "Why not? Seems pretty easy to me. Someone doesn't like you, move on. Game over."

"Maybe in a big city where you have a thousand guys to choose from, but around here it's not that way. You have your eye set on one guy for more than half your life, and then he kind of lets you know it's on, that's what you focus on. And when it's not good, you just keep focusing on it. It's not like you have a lot of options. Being alone is . . . lonely."

I roll my eyes. "In case you haven't heard, Tate, there's a whole world out there just waiting for you." I look around the room. "Any of you. Ginny, Hannah . . . if they're not happy here, they could move."

"Easy for you to say. But most of these people have never left here. Not even for a vacation. Their families have been here for generations, working the land and ranching for hundreds of years. And our families have big expectations that are hard to get out from under."

It all sounds so depressing, not to mention eighteenth century. "Did that happen to you? Are you happy?"

He grins in a nice, easy way. It makes him beautiful, and it's almost as if the sun has come right into the diner to be with us. "Oh, I'm happy enough. And I enjoy my life, even though I admit it can be lonely sometimes."

I tilt my head to the side, suddenly realizing I've done a really poor job of having a conversation with him. "What is it that you do, exactly?"

"I'm a mechanic. My garage is on Main Street."

A sign with a handsome face flashes up in my memory bank. "'First-Rate Tate'?"

"That's me."

I smile back. "Nice to me you, First-Rate."

"Just Tate'll do nicely, thanks." His face goes charmingly pink.

Two plates bang down in front of us with no warning. "Two waffles with bacon, eggs on the side."

Hannah's there and gone before either of us can respond.

He nods at me. "Now you've done it."

"Done what?" I look from him to my waffle, to Hannah, and then back at him.

"First you stole Ian from Ginny, and now you're stealing me from whoever has me in her sights."

My eyes go wide in jest. "Wow. Should I be afraid?" I look around the room, trying to find his stalker. I don't see anyone looking at us but Hannah.

He leans in close and give me the scary face. "Yes." He wiggles his eyebrows. "Be afraid. Be very afraid."

We both laugh it off and dive into our waffles.

CHAPTER THIRTY-THREE

I have a lot to think about on my drive home. As I pull into the driveway at the ranch, my plan is almost fully put together. If Andie could see me now, she'd probably say my hamster's about to die of a heart attack, but she'd be wrong. My hamster could compete in the Ironman competition if they'd let him. He'd totally win too.

"Back so soon?" Maeve asks me as I stomp the snow off my boots in the front hall.

"Yep. Hannah got me a seat right away, and I wolfed down my amazing waffle in record time."

Maeve looks a tiny bit uncomfortable as her gaze shifts away from me to rest on the floor. "I thought you were having breakfast with Tate Montgomery."

"Oh, I did. And I wanted to talk to you about that, if you have a minute."

She's back to looking at me. "Okay. Shoot."

"How about over coffee?"

She smiles. "Great idea. I just came in from gathering eggs, and my fingers could use a good thawing out."

She puts the coffee pot on in the kitchen as I take a seat and do a few leg stretches to keep my mind off the fact that her fingers have just been in places mine will never go.

Chicken butts. *Shudder.*

I'm distracted by this distasteful idea by the state of my muscles. I'm not even sure if I could do a high kick right now, the way my legs feel. All this cold is shrinking my body, turning it into a clamped-down mess.

"So you enjoy the waffles in town, hmm?"

"Delish. I'd come back here just for those even if Andie didn't live here."

She laughs. "Well, I suppose I'll have to try them then if they're that good."

"Don't you ever go in there?" I'm starting to wonder if this is some sort of town epidemic, this Hannah avoidance-itis.

"Not often and never for the waffles. We have a ranch women's meeting at the diner once a quarter that I attend, but I usually stick to coffee."

"Definitely try the waffles next time. They're totally worth the trip, even in this snow."

"So how did you meet Tate?" Her back is to me as she gets mugs and sugar out.

"Last night at Boog's party. He and I had a deal, and my end of the bargain was having a meal of my choice with him. I chose breakfast."

"Hmm . . ." Maeve says.

I get the feeling her response actually means something, but it's all she gives me.

"I had this idea that maybe he might be able to tell me some things . . . shed some light on a particular mystery I've stumbled across." I try to make it sound intriguing. She's a critical part of my plan so I need her buy-in.

"A mystery, eh? That sounds very . . . mysterious." She laughs, turning around with mugs and sugar in hand.

"Is Andie around yet?" I ask. She's not where I can see her, and there are no baby sounds cluing me in to her presence, but I want to be sure that she's not within hearing distance.

"No, but she should be here in an hour or so. It's taking her a bit of time getting used to the whole rhythm of things."

"Maybe we should go over there."

"We will. I plan to go do a little cleaning, some laundry, and some cooking. You're welcome to join me. I hear you're an amazing cook."

My face goes a little red. "You did? From who?"

"Ian. I'm sorry Angus and I missed out on your spaghetti. Maybe you can make it again before you leave."

"Sure. Anytime." Aaaand the panic sets in . . .

The pot of coffee is dripping, filling the silence. It does nothing to calm my nerves now that I know my nonexistent cooking prowess is about to be tested once again, only now by the entire family. Andie will totally poop a brick if she finds out what I've been telling these people about my skills. I better warn her ahead of time. *Note to self: Pay Andie to say I'm an expert chef.*

Maeve breaks into my thoughts. "So, do I get to know what the big mystery is, or is it a secret?"

"Actually, I'm glad you asked, because you need to know the mystery in order to help me fix things."

She wraps her hands around her mug and smiles. "Ooh, this sounds good."

She glances up at my forehead. I try not to look up to see what has her attention, but I can't help it. It's possible I'm going cross-eyed as I start telling her my plan.

"It is good. I think. Anyway, I've noticed since I've been here that Andie doesn't exactly have many friends."

Maeve loses her smile. “Yes, I’m afraid that seems to be the case. I’ve never seen her spend time with anyone but us.”

“There’s a reason for that.”

Maeve’s eyebrows go up. “There is?”

“Yes. Apparently, there are rumors going around town that Andie is the reason why Ian lost Ginny and Hannah lost Mack. I guess Andie’s the town harlot or the town husband stealer or something.”

“That’s utterly ridiculous!” Maeve’s pissed. “Neither of those women had a claim on my boys. Andie had nothing to do with either of them missing out on whatever they felt entitled to.”

“You must have heard this stuff before, though, right?” I ask, kind of pressing her. “I mean, you live here. You belong to that rancher lady club or whatever. This isn’t news to you, I’ll bet.”

She stands to get the pot of coffee, a lot less relaxed and calm than she was two minutes ago. She might even be shaking a little. I’ve never seen her like this. She’s always so self-possessed.

“I hate to say it, but I’m about as friendless as Andie at this point.” She brings the pot over and fills our mugs, letting out a long breath of air. “I lost my two best friends to cancer. Another good friend left and moved to Seattle with her new husband. As for the rest . . .” She shrugs as she adds two lumps of sugar to her mug. “. . . I suppose we don’t talk about those things relating to Andie. Probably because they worry about what I’d think.”

“You’re not much of a gossiper, I take it.”

“No, not at all.” She smiles but doesn’t look that happy. At least she’s not shaking anymore. “I don’t have time for it. And it’s all a bunch of nonsense anyway. I’ve got better things to do with my time.”

“Well, no need to worry. I’m an expert gossiper, and I’ve got the scoop.” I wink at her to assure her that she’s in good hands. “My guess is that Hannah the Big Butthead Banana has been spreading lies around, either because she's just bitter or because she's fooled herself into thinking that Mack will break up with Andie eventually, and then he'll be free again. Either way, we're going to put an end to it and find Andie some friends."

"We are?" She doesn't sound very enthusiastic, which is disappointing since she was going to be a major player in my scheme. I'm going to have to go for the hard sell.

"Yes. We most definitely are. I can't leave Baker knowing that my best friend is going to be all alone out here in coyote-lion-rattlesnakesville without someone to chat with or talk baby stuff too. I'm not always available by phone, you know."

Maeve smiles. "I hear you're quite busy at your salon. Do you like having your own business?"

Any other day of the year before I came here, my answer would have been an enthusiastic yes. Now, this lukewarm feeling comes over me and it bleeds into my answer. "Yeeeesss. I mean, I do love it. It's just . . . it takes a lot of my time away from other things."

"Other things? Like what? Hobbies?"

"Well, no. I mean, hair and fashion are my hobbies. It's just . . ." I stare at the floor as I try to put into words what's going on in my heart. "I guess since I've been here I've never really thought about what else I'd like to have in my life, but now I'm starting to think of those things."

"What kinds of things? Cows?"

I laugh, but then images of my baby cow Candy come to mind, with Ian and me wrestling around in her stall, and it doesn't seem so silly. "Kind of. Maybe more the way of life you have around here. With husbands and babies and chickens and stuff." My future husband can be the one to touch their butts; I'll just make omelets. I'm sure there are recipes online I can follow.

She laughs. "You have pretty much just summed up my life in one sentence."

My hand shoots out to rest on her forearm. "No! I didn't mean it like that. I didn't mean to sound like I was demeaning it or anything."

She pats my hand. "Not to worry. I didn't take offense at all. I love my life—cows, chickens, babies, and all."

"Don't forget the husband part," I say kind of softly.

"You looking to get married?" she asks, taking a sip of her coffee as she waits for my answer. She's staring at me over the rim of her mug.

"Yep. Definitely. Before I wasn't sure, but now I am."

"Before what?"

"Before what?" I ask her, playing stupid. My heart rate has picked up. Dammit! My mouth got ahead of me there.

"Well, you said before you weren't sure of wanting to be married, but now you are. I was just wondering what event or . . . person . . . might have changed your mind."

Busted! Obviously my hamster is way more fatigued than I originally thought. I walked right into a trap of my own making. Quick! Think of an answer that doesn't involve Ian!

"Andie having a baby, I guess. I never thought that could be me, but now I do. And seeing Candy be born and me and Ian helping her survive—that was amazing." Dammit! Ian made his way into my answer after all. My hamster needs a serious nap.

"Are you seeing anyone back home?"

"No. Not at the moment." Just the idea of leaving all these gorgeous cowboys behind is kind of depressing. It's not that West Palm doesn't have its fair share of hot guys; it's just that they aren't . . . Ian.

Damn you, Hamster! Stop making me think about him! Go to bed!

"Maybe you'll fall in love with someone here and then you'll want to stay." She winks at me and takes another sip of her coffee.

The sheer impossibility of it makes me sad. "Nah. I can't move my business. I mean, I could sell it, but I wouldn't want to. I've spent years building up my clientele. And I have a partner. His name is Jorge, and he'd kill me if I left him."

"Have you ever dated Jorge?"

I laugh at how ridiculous that would be. He in his red skinny jeans and me in my Diesels. We'd definitely turn heads if we started kissing. I think it would be more confusing than anything else. "No, never. He's not really into girls. More like rugby players."

"Oh." Maeve's face goes a little pink. "That must be hard on him."

"Seriously, it is. There aren't many rugby players who are gay. At least not that many that admit to it." I sigh, thinking of poor Jorge. He's even worse at dating than I am. The bright side is that it's given us plenty to commiserate about over the years, and it has given us lots of free time to throw into our business. Now neither of us has to even work a full day if we don't want to, but we do because there's nothing else to do. We've sacrificed a lot to be where we are now. I used to be proud of that. Now I'm not so sure it wasn't a mistake.

"So back to your plan," Maeve says, relaxing in her chair. "I'm all ears."

My conflicted feelings over Ian fly out the window as my plan emerges for Maeve's appreciative ear.

"We're going to have a baby shower."

"A baby shower?"

"Yes. A baby shower. And we're going to invite anyone in town you think might be in Andie's circle of friends, but not Hannah."

Maeve looks as if she's shrinking. "Not Hannah?"

"Nope. Not Hannah. I want everyone to see Andie as herself and let them decide who she is without listening to The Banana's nonsense."

"But won't Hannah feel left out? She's not the nicest of persons when she feels she's being cut out of things. You can ask Mack about that."

"I don't care how she feels about it. What's important is that Andie forges some bonds with some girls out here. Maybe even some that already have kids, who can help her when she has questions."

Maeve frowns.

I reach out and put my hand on her forearm. "It's not that you aren't enough for the advice and stuff, but sometimes it's nice to hear from more than one source. And Andie's not much for googling."

Maeve smiles. "Oh, no offense taken. I was just trying to think who we might invite. There are a couple girls, daughters of some of the ladies in the ranch women's club I'm in . . ."

"That would be great!" I'm feeling pretty full of myself right now. "How many do you think you could invite here?"

"Five? Maybe six?"

I'm grinning from ear to ear. "Perfect. That'll get the ball rolling. We can do a lunch, here at your place."

Maeve smiles back, but it's missing some of its usual spark. "If you think that's best."

"Of course it is." I pat her on the hand. "You just make the phone calls, and I'll plan all the rest."

We finish our coffee, talking over food possibilities, and because I'm practically a professional chef at this point, I'll be the one doing all the cooking. Swedish meatballs can't be all that hard to make, right? I mean, I made spaghetti sauce and that had meat in it.

Maeve stands and takes our empty cups to the sink. "Why don't you see about feeding your calf, and I'll make a few phone calls?"

"Good idea." I stand, ready to face the day, armed with the knowledge that when I leave here, even though I'll be doing it with a broken heart for leaving Ian behind, Andie's life will be back on track. Nothing but the best for my BFF and my godbaby.

CHAPTER THIRTY-FOUR

I'm staring over the stall door at my cow baby when I sense I'm no longer alone in the barn. It's not too difficult to do, seeing as how this person lets in a huge gust of chilled air with him that turns my nipples into stone.

I put my arms around myself to try and stay warm. My breath comes out in big white puffs, making it look like I'm smoking.

"I already fed her," Ian says. He sounds grouchy.

I turn around to respond, but I'm too shocked by his face to say anything.

"Oh my god. Does that hurt?" I reach out and touch the blue spot under his eye.

He jerks back. "Yes, it hurts! Jesus, don't touch it."

I reach out again but stop with my finger a couple inches away.

He doesn't flinch this time. "You better not."

My finger moves forward a little more. I'm not in control of it. I'm being possessed right now by some woman who wants to get under Ian's skin. He's so damn teasable, it's not even funny.

"I'm not kidding, Candice. Don't touch me."

I frown. He doesn't want me touching his eye—or him in general? My finger moves lower. Now it's aimed at his throat.

"You'll be sorry," he warns.

"I highly doubt that," I say, moving even closer.

We're both staring down at my finger that's centered on his chest.

"Trust me," he says. "You'll be very sorry if that finger makes contact with any part of me."

Without warning, I quickly flick my hand up, bonking him on the nose. "Made ya look!"

Without warning, he grabs me and picks me up, throwing me over his shoulder.

"Whooop!" A scream leaves my lungs along with the rest of my air.

He smacks me hard on the butt. "I warned you, woman!"

"Ian!" I screech. "Put me down right this minute!"

"Oh, I'll put you down, alright!"

For the next few seconds all I can feel is his solid shoulder digging into my gut. Then I'm flying through the air.

"Aaaaaack!" I yell, just before I land on my back in a big poof of something crunchy.

A bunch of dust and bits of hay fly up over me as Ian stands spread-legged at my feet.

"What the hell . . . ?" It takes me a few seconds to figure out where I am. My arms go out to test my theory. "Did you just throw me into a pile of hay?"

"No. I just threw you into a pile of straw, City."

"Same thing. Now help me out of here. My hair's going to be ruined." I hold up both hands for him to take.

He scowls. "Worried your new boyfriend won't like it?"

I pause my struggling and let my arms fall to my sides. "My new boyfriend?"

"Tate. I heard you had breakfast with him today."

A slow smile breaks across my face. If this isn't jealousy in his expression and tone, then I'm a talentless hack in the beauty department. The question is, do I tease Ian about this or soothe his hurt feelings? *Hmm . . . what to do, what to do . . . ?*

"Don't try to deny it. Everyone in town saw you."

I lift an eyebrow. "You didn't."

"No, but other people did."

"How'd *you* find out about it?"

"Never mind about that. Point is I did. And you should be careful around that guy. He's got a bad reputation in town."

"Awww, isn't that sweet? You really care about me, don't you, Ian?"

He scowls some more. "You're my sister-in-law's friend. I suppose I feel obligated to make sure you don't get talked bad about while you're visiting."

"So that's what this is? Friendly concern? An obligation?" Now I'm mad. Why can't he just be a grown-up and admit his feelings? He obviously wants to get in my Diesels. I'd have to be blind not to see that.

"Yeah. Exactly. And now I've met my obligations." He turns around and starts to leave.

I scoff. "So you're just going to leave me here in this hay?"

His voice sounds muffled as he gets farther away. "I told you it ain't hay. It's straw."

I'm infuriated on two levels. First, he actually *is* leaving me here, and second, he's using that word I know for a fact he uses just to piss his mother off.

"*Ain't* isn't a word!" I yell, but he ignores me.

I climb out of the hay or straw or whatever the hell it is with two fists full of the stuff. Running up behind him, I wait until I'm practically on top of him before I let loose.

I fling that hay stuff as hard as I can at the back of his head. As it surrounds him in a giant mushroom cloud of yellow, I stop, admiring the view.

Wow. I had a lot more of it in my hands than I realized.

He slowly turns around, and I back away. His head and shoulders are covered in crud, and he looks very confused.

"Did you just throw straw at me?" he asks, incredulous.

I cross my arms. "I'm pretty sure it's hay."

He takes a step toward me. "That was a bad move, girl."

I take another step backward to keep some distance between us. My heart is racing now, and not from the exertion. It's more from the danger I see in his eyes. But I can't let him know he intimidates me. "Not from my point of view, it wasn't."

He lowers his shoulder like he's about to tackle someone.

I realize too late that someone is me.

Screaming, I turn around to run, but that only makes it easier for him to take me down. Two seconds later, we're both buried in straw.

"Get off me, you idiot!" I yell, trying to throw some into his face.

He dodges me and buries his face in my neck. "Stop throwing that shit everywhere! It's itchy!"

I pause to catch my breath and to see if he's telling the truth. I don't know if it's an actual fact or just his suggestion working its magic on me, but I am kind of feeling uncomfortable.

"You're the dumbass who threw us in here."

"You asked for it." He lifts his head and stares at me.

Our bodies are pressed together from our stomachs to our chests. I can feel his heart beating rapidly through my coat, the rhythm matching mine.

"You wish," I say, my voice going way down in volume. I can hear the swishing of straw in another part of the barn, which

I write off as coming from Candy the baby cow. We're alone, but not really alone. It's strangely sexy.

"Maybe I do wish," he says.

My heart does a double back flip.

He shifts his weight so more of him is on me. I can feel his waist there against mine, and his dick is as hard as a rock.

Oh my god, oh my god, oh my god . . . What's happening?! My brain is spinning out of control. I can't think straight. Are we about to do it in the hay?

"I don't get it," I finally say. When in doubt, just say what's on your mind, that's my motto. "What's happening here, I mean."

"I don't get it either." He's not smiling.

"Are you mad about that?" It seems kind of silly to be mad at your own feelings, so I smile.

It seems to take some of the anger away for him. His expression relaxes. "Maybe. I'm not sure."

I wiggle around a little, trying to get a thing in my back to stop poking me.

"You better quit moving around like that," he warns.

The devil in me sparks to life. "Why?" I wiggle around some more. "What'll happen to me if I don't?"

He pushes his hips into me and settles his hard length into my softness. "You'll be sorry because I won't be able to control myself anymore."

"Who said you have to control yourself around me?" I move my hips in a slower rhythm, but one he won't mistake for irritation at pokey straw.

We stare into each other's eyes for what seems like forever. Then I move my hips some more, and he closes his lids, pushing into me in response.

"You are in so much fucking trouble," he whispers.

"You're the one who's in trouble, not me," I whisper back, opening my legs to give him better access.

His eyes come open really slowly, and then his lazy smile is back. "I'm not sure I'm hearing you right. Are you saying you want a little roll in the hay? With me?"

I giggle. "I'm pretty sure we're already doing that." I move my eyes around to emphasize the fact that there's nothing *but* hay around us.

He grabs my left hand and puts it up above my head, trapping it there under a hard bale of the yellow stuff. "I told you, Candice . . ." he lowers his face until our lips are a hair's breadth apart, ". . . it's not hay. It's straw."

And then he's kissing me.

CHAPTER THIRTY-FIVE

He reaches down and unbuttons my jeans.

"I could help you if you'd let go of my arm," I say.

"You just keep your hands where I can see 'em," he says, a warning in his tone. He takes my other, stitched-up arm more gently and places it above my head too. "Leave 'em there."

He gets up on his knees and pulls my pants down.

"Oh my god, it's so cold in here!" I say with a squeak.

"Don't you worry, baby—I'll get you warm real quick."

I open my mouth to ask him how, but stop when he starts showing me. He lowers his face to my panties and kisses me through the thin material.

"Oh my," I whisper. I'm already wet, and all he's done is this. I am in so much trouble.

He licks around the edges of the cotton and then slides a finger under the edge of it near my inner thigh. He's still kissing, pushing hot air through the material as his finger slides inside my panties.

My breath comes in gasps and my hips move a little, first left, then right. His light touching is killing me.

"Easy now," he says, rubbing my thighs up and then down as he pushes his face into my soft parts.

His hands come up and pull my panties down, slowly, slowly. He looks at me with a dark expression before putting his mouth to my folds.

When his hot tongue comes out and goes inside me, I nearly scream with delight. My legs tremble with need. I have to bite my lip hard to keep from telling everyone in a quarter-mile radius what we're doing.

"You're so wet," he says, looking up at me. "I'm not going to last very long. It's been awhile." He's apologizing to me for being too turned on. At this point, Ginny is the dumbest woman on the planet as far as I'm concerned.

"We'll go slow," I say, holding out my arms. "Have sex with me now."

"But you taste so good," he says, putting his mouth on me again.

I moan, torn between wanting more of this and needing to feel him inside me, more of him, the part that will bring us both pleasure.

"Ian, please . . . I'm not going to last very long either if you keep doing that."

"Are you complaining?" he asks, a low chuckle coming from deep in his chest.

"No. I just want to come with you."

He reaches into his back pocket and pulls out a condom from his wallet. "You don't have to tell me twice."

He pulls his jeans down and I finally get a look at that package I've been admiring for days. Seeing him running out of the shower didn't do him justice. When he's hard, there's some sort of nature's miracle going on down there.

"You ready for me?" he asks, back on his knees and poised between my legs, his hand on his dick.

"Are you ready for me, is the question." I open my legs wider and move my hips a little, ignoring the straw poking me everywhere from the waist down. I must look ridiculous with my jacket still on but bare parts below, but I'm not willing to freeze my boobs off to look a tiny bit sexier.

Ian moves in closer and guides the head of his dick to my folds. He's concentrating on being careful, but I can see the instant he finds the warmth that is me. His face relaxes and pleasure takes over.

"Oh, baby," he says, "you feel so good."

I hold my arms out. "Come inside where it's warm."

"Don't mind if I do," he says, lowering his weight down on me and pushing the rest of his length inside.

I moan with happiness. This is heaven, right here in this pile of straw.

He moans too and starts moving in and out. I meet every gentle thrust with one of my own. It's tender but demanding. Intoxicating. I'm so close to orgasm, which makes no sense since we just started, but it's a fact. It's because it's *him*. It's Ian on me, the man who makes me crazy, who I want to hit with snowballs and piles of hay. He's on me and in me, and he wants to make me come. He claims I make him crazy, but he wants me. He wants to possess me, to have sex with me. It's blowing my mind, making me question everything. What does this mean? Will we be a couple now, or is this just a game? I hope it's not a game to him because it's not to me.

His rhythm picks up, and every muscle in his body is tensed. "Babe . . . I'm sorry . . . I'm going to come . . ."

"Me too!" I gasp, suddenly aware of the fact that I've lost control of everything . . . my thoughts, my body, my desires. I'm hanging onto him for dear life, ready to cry with need. "Me too!" I try to catch my breath. What's happening?! "Oh my god!"

Waves of pleasure are coming for me. I can feel them. Approaching, building . . .

"Candice!" he yells. "Dammit!" And then a series of grunts and growls come from his throat as he slams into me over and over.

I lose it when he's halfway done. Sounds are coming out of me that make no sense. They sound like they should be words, but they're not. I hang onto his jacket for all I'm worth, riding this crazy merry-go-round until it finally stops spinning.

He goes still, collapses his entire weight on me, and we both sink deeper into the straw.

As I'm coming down off my sex high, I start to notice straw bits poking me in parts that are really uncomfortable. Like, really, *really* uncomfortable.

"You okay?" he asks.

"Kind of squished, actually." I try to laugh, but it comes out kind of wheezy.

He rolls off to the side, pulling out in the process. "Better?" he asks.

I nod.

He closes his eyes and flops back over on top of me.

I can't help but smile.

"Ian?"

"Yes?" he moans into my neck.

"You said I was going to be sorry." I'm practically breathless which makes talking difficult.

"Yes, I did."

"Guess what?" I ask.

"What?"

"I'm not. I'm not sorry one bit."

He lifts his head and looks into my eyes. "Neither am I."

We're both grinning like fools. I feel like I could jump off this barn and fly back to the house. Now I know what that expression "Love gives you wings" means.

"Wanna go again?" he asks, the devil in his expression.

I open my mouth to answer, but then the sound of a very unhappy cow baby interrupts me.

Ian rolls his eyes. “Hold that thought.” He kisses me hard and then gets up on his knees. “Gotta feed the calf.” He pulls the rubber off and stuffs it in a tissue he takes from his pocket. Getting to his feet, he pulls his jeans up and buttons them. He has straw bits everywhere.

“I thought you said you already did it.”

“I lied.”

“You butthead.”

“Yeah, what can I say?” He gives me his most charming grin. “I’m a butthead sometimes.”

“I want to do it!” I say, struggling to get up out of the mess. My butt is quickly losing the warmth it gathered from our exercise. “Holy mother, it’s cold in this joint.”

The sound of a door rolling open interrupts my next thought, and then Maeve’s voice comes from around the corner. “Candice are you in here?”

My eyes bug out and I freeze. Ian does too.

“She’ll be out in a sec, Ma!” he yells. Throwing me my pants, he scrubs his hair, trying to dislodge all the straw from it. He’s only partially successful.

“Okay,” Maeve says. “Tell her to come to the house. I have some responses for her we need to discuss.”

“Responses?” Ian looks at me. “What’s she talking about?”

I’m finally on my feet and mostly dressed, pushing him out of the way. “Nothing you need to worry about.” I zip and button my jeans as I try to get out of the pile.

He grabs me before I can get past him.

I’m all set to complain, but then he’s leaning down and kissing me warmly on the lips. It kind of puts a spell on me, and I forget that Maeve wanted me for something.

“Tell me all your secrets,” he says playfully.

I sigh in defeat. That’s all he needs to do is give me that look, and I’m ready to surrender. “Fine.” I blink a few times trying to remember what the secret is. "Oh, yeah. So I'm putting together a baby shower for Andie."

"What for?"

"To try and help her get some friends."

Ian detaches himself from me. "Say what, now?"

I sigh out heavily, annoyed that I have to explain myself when Maeve needs me. "She doesn't have any friends in town if you haven't noticed. And that's all because of Hannah spreading rumors around town. I'm going to fix all that."

"How are you going to do that? And how do you know all this shit anyway?"

"Tate told me all I needed to know. And I've decided that all Andie needs is an opportunity to meet with these girls on her home turf and they'll all see what a great person she is and want to be her friend."

Ian snorts. "You think so, huh?"

I cross my arms as the fever from our sexy time dissipates quickly into the freezing cold air. "Yes, as a matter of fact, I do."

He lifts an eyebrow. "You're getting that look on your face again."

"What look?"

"The one that begs me to take you down into the straw again . . . calm you down."

I reach out to hit him, but he catches my wrist.

"Calm me down . . . who do you think you are?"

He pulls me close, until our chests are touching again. "I'm your guy, that's who."

"My guy?" I suppose it's kind of silly, but it makes me go all warm inside to hear him say that. I can't feel the cold anymore. Even my nostril hairs have thawed.

"Yeah. If you want me to be." He looks down at my chin, like he's afraid to look me in the eye.

I sigh with a mixture of happiness and sadness. "I'd love for you to be my guy," I finally admit. "The only problem is that we live a million miles apart." I'm not even sure that I'm talking about actual distance or the fact that we come from different worlds.

"So? You're here now, right?"

I know his words were meant to be encouraging, but all they do is remind me that I won't be here for long. I move away from him and smile. "Yeah. I'm here now. But I have to go talk to Maeve."

He gestures toward the barn doors, his voice sounding resigned. "Go ahead. I'll feed Candy for ya."

"Thanks, Ian." I walk away and leave him there to take care of my chores once again, because being around him anymore is going to start making my heart hurt.

CHAPTER THIRTY-SIX

"What do you mean 'none of them can come'?" I ask, hands on my hips.

Maeve tries to smile, but it looks more like she has a stomach cramp. "No matter what date I mentioned, they all said they were busy. I got the impression that they weren't really, though."

"How? How did you know?"

Maeve sighs heavily and sinks into a chair at the kitchen dining table. "I talked to Janet, one of their mothers, first. She assured me her daughter was free, but then when I talked to her daughter, she told me she was going to be at Janet's for the entire day. I called Janet back, and she said it was news to her."

My eyes narrow to slits, and I shake my head as I realize how far Hannah's poison has spread into the town. "She is going to be so sorry . . ."

"Who?"

"Never mind." I grab my jacket off the back of my chair and put it on as I head down the hallway.

"Where are you going?" Maeve asks, calling out from the kitchen.

"Into town. I'll be back in an hour or so." Storming out of the house, I head right for the barn. Ian is coming out the door when I get there.

He takes one look at me and goes on the defensive. "Whatever it is, I'm not responsible for it."

"I need you to take me into town and back me up if necessary."

"Back you up?" He laughs. "You want me to bring my rifle?"

"Yes, if you think it'll help."

Ian grabs my hand as I try to walk by.

"Hold up there a second."

I stop, but only because he's making it impossible for me to get any traction on the snow. "What, Ian? I'm kind of in a hurry."

"That's what worries me. That and the Terminator look on your face." He pulls me into him and looks down at me. "What's going on? What can I do to help?"

Some of my anger leaves, replaced by more of those mushy feelings Ian keeps making happen inside me. I have to blink back tears that jump into my eyes for some reason. I'm so confused.

"You okay?" he asks.

"Yes," I say, pulling away from him. "I'm fine." I use the tip of my glove to wipe under my lower lashes. I can't have my mascara leaking all over the place when I'm about to throw down, country style. "I just need to go have a chat with Hannah."

"Hannah? Why? What about?"

"I'll tell you when we get there. Can you drive me?"

Ian looks out toward the back pastures and then at the trucks. "I suppose, if it won't take too long."

I turn to go to the truck. "Won't take long at all. Just take me to the diner, and we'll have our little chat, and then you can take me home."

Ian looks at his watch as he draws up next to me. "It'll be lunchtime then. They get slammed every day at noon. She probably won't be able to talk to you until after two."

"Oh, don't worry. She really just needs to listen, so we'll be fine."

I get to the truck and climb in without thinking about it. I'm too focused on teaching Hannah a thing or two about city girls to worry about falling or looking graceful.

Seconds after, Ian and I are sitting side by side in the truck. I'm staring out the window, waiting for the truck to start, but it doesn't, so I look at him and ask, "What's the holdup?"

"You sure look cute climbing up into my truck," he says, grinning.

More of my anger at Hannah and her b.s. falls away. "Stop trying to manipulate me into doing what you want."

He laughs. "Is that even possible?"

"No. So stop trying."

He chuckles halfway down the road leading to the highway as I work on getting all the straw out of my hair.

CHAPTER THIRTY-SEVEN

The diner is packed. Several people are waiting for tables by the time we walk in at twelve thirty. I don't bother standing behind them, though. I'm not here for waffles this time.

I scan the space and find Hannah behind the counter, serving someone some coffee. It's decaf, and that pisses me off probably way more than it should. I knew she was lying before when she said they didn't have any. That wench.

Striding over, I ignore the looks of interest that come at me from everyone in my path. I stop when I'm in front of Hannah, behind the broad back of a very big man with puffy dark hair.

"Hannah, I need to talk to you."

She looks up in surprise and then scowls. "I'm busy."

"So? I need to talk to you anyway."

I feel someone at my back and turn around. Ian's there, looking very worried. His presence reassures me and makes me feel bolder.

"Hey, Hannah," he says in greeting before turning his attention to me. He's talking barely above a whisper. "Maybe we can do this later, someplace else?"

"Nope, we can do it right now." I fold my arms across my chest and go back to staring Hannah down.

Several people have stopped eating to watch. The man in front of me turns around, and I notice for the first time that it's Boog.

"Hello there," he says.

I cringe at the food shrapnel in his beard. It might be egg.

"Hi, Boog," I say before turning my attention back to Hannah. "You and I need to talk."

She cocks her hip and slams the orange-topped pot down on the counter. It's a miracle it doesn't break. "Like I said, I'm *busy*." Some of the hot coffee sloshes out onto Boog's plate.

He stares at the brown pool in his plate along with Ian, but her violence with caffeine doesn't dissuade me from my mission one iota.

"I hear you've been starting up and spreading vicious rumors about my friend Andie all over town for the past year."

"Who said that?" Hannah asks, her face all screwed up. She looks at Boog. "Did you say that?"

Boog's mouth falls open, but before he can get a word out, I continue.

"Doesn't matter who said it. What matters is that it stops. *Today.*" I give her my most dangerous look.

"I know you're not talking to me," she says, taking her hand off the coffee pot and folding her arms across her chest. They push her boobs almost completely out of her top.

"I am most certainly talking to you, Hannah Banana."

She begins untying the apron around her waist. "I told you before, my name is Hannah. Just *Hannah*!" She finally gets all the straps from her apron undone. After crumpling the entire thing up into a ball, she throws it on the counter, covering half of Boog's plate.

Her attention is back on me. "You say one more word to me about that girl, and we're going to have a big problem," she warns.

She took her apron off, so oh yeah, it's totally *on*. I am so ready to teach his country bumpkin a lesson in how we city girls roll.

"That *girl* happens to be my best friend, and she never did anything to you, so you better stop talking about her *or else*."

Everyone in the restaurant has pretty much stopped talking or eating. All eyes are on us, and I totally don't care. I'm all fired up, seeing that Hannah somehow believes she's entitled to ruin my best friend's life.

"You gotta lotta nerve coming in here and talking to me like that," Hannah says, glaring at me. Her head bobs and weaves a little.

I lean over the counter a little and talk loud enough for the whole place to hear me. "You've got a lot of nerve making up lies about people you know nothing about."

"I don't make up lies," she spits back. "I just tell it like I hear it."

"Then you're hearing wrong."

"Says who?"

We're practically nose to nose right now.

"Says me. So you can stop telling people that Andie broke you and Mack up because everyone knows you guys were never together. And you can stop telling everyone that she broke Ian and Ginny up because Ginny did that all by herself. Mack had nothing to do with it, and Andie had nothing to do with it." I back up and let my words sink in.

"Well, guess what, Miss Know-It-All?" Hannah says, her mouth all twisted up, "I'm not the one saying all those things, so you can go sit on Ian's gear shift and spin as far as I'm concerned."

My mouth drops open as my face burns flame-red. Is it that obvious that I've sat on Ian's gear shift?

Before I can answer, Ian puts his hand on my shoulder and pulls me back from the bar. "Hannah, if it's not you saying that stuff, tell us who it is."

Hannah loses her angry expression and starts to pout. "Why should I?"

"Because if you don't, I'll tell everyone what I know about a certain drunken confession I heard on the Fourth of July last year."

She glances quickly at Boog and then at Ian. "You *wouldn't*."

Ian smiles. "Oh, you know I would."

Her nostrils flare. "Ian you are evil—you know that?"

"No argument here. You gonna 'fess up, or am I going to start talking?" He looks pointedly at Boog.

Hannah's face goes white. "No! No, I'm talking, I'm talking." She grabs her apron off the counter and turns to face the cook. "I'm taking a break."

"A break? You can't take a break now!" He's talking to her back, though, because she's already halfway down the counter on the way to the front door.

She only pauses to grab a red puffy coat off a hook at the door and then she's outside.

Boog just gives me a lifted eyebrow before going back to his lunch.

"Come on. Let's hear what she has to say," Ian says in my ear.

I ignore the whispers and stares from the patrons of the diner as we make our way out.

"She's not getting off that easy," I mumble as we walk through the door.

"Just let her talk," Ian says. He laces his fingers through my gloved ones and shoves both of our hands into his coat pocket.

I try to keep the grin off my face, but it's impossible. He's declaring to the world that we're together, and I couldn't be happier about it. Even though this is only a fling, it sure is a nice one. I can't remember ever being this excited just to hold someone's hand. Not even when Jimmy Cunningham grabbed my hand with his clammy one between forth and fifth periods in high school was I this thrilled. Maybe I'm coming down with something. I'm going to google my symptoms later. Breathlessness? Check.

Hootchie on fire? Check. Mood swings? Check aaaand double-check. One minute I want to laugh, and the next I want to bang heads together like two coconuts. I'm definitely ill, probably with something serious.

Hannah stops a few paces down the sidewalk outside the diner and huffs out a breath of hair, making white smoke go all around her face. "You got some nerve coming into my work and talking to me like that." She's glaring.

I can't tell if she's talking to me or Ian, but I answer anyway. "Stop spreading lies about people, and you won't have to worry about it anymore."

"How am I supposed to know they're lies?"

"Because they're about you, Stupid, and you know the truth."

"Don't call me stupid," she says, giving me the stink eye.

"Don't act stupid and I won't." I give her the eye right back.

Ian steps sideways so he's almost between us. "Come on. Let's just get this over with." He turns to Hannah. "Tell us who's making up the lies, Hannah."

"Not me."

"So you say." Ian glares at her.

"Isn't that good enough for you, Ian?" She pouts again, and I have to admit, she is pretty good at it. "We used to be friends, you know."

"No, Hannah, we were never friends. You've always been a pain in the ass."

"Well that's just plain rude." She tries to act all offended.

"Whatever!" I say, cutting in on their leftover high school drama. "Who's talking bad about Andie behind her back!"

She turns on me, looking ready to spit. "It's Ginny, okay?!" She turns her gaze to Ian, her expression going softer. "Sorry. I know you didn't want to hear that, but it's true."

Ian goes very still.

"So, Ginny's telling everyone that Andie broke you and Mack up and her and Ian up?"

"Yes." Hannah sighs and shoves her hands in her coat pockets. "She was pretty brokenhearted when Ian dumped her. She might be embellishing the facts a little, I admit, but it wasn't me who did it, okay? I tried to tell her to let it go, but she won't. She's super bitter. Like outer limits bitter."

Ian looks up at the sky and shakes his head for a few seconds. Then he growls and looks straight ahead out into the street. "That's pretty fucking rich . . . me dumping her? She's got to be crazy."

"You didn't dump her?" I ask, a sharp stabbing sensation inside my chest making my heart ache. Does this mean he never wanted to break up with her in the first place? Does he still love her? And if he does, why does that make me so damn sad? I'm leaving here!

"Of course I broke up with her!" he says, turning his ire on me. "But it wasn't *my* choice! It was *hers*!" He lets out a long breath and talks in a calmer voice. "She chose to throw herself at my brother. That's on her, not me."

"But she says you practically made her do it," Hannah says in a small voice. "She was just trying to get your attention. You didn't have to break up with her over it."

Ian glares at Hannah. "Do you seriously believe that crap?"

Hannah shrugs. "Kind of?"

"Well, quit doing it, 'cause it ain't true." Ian stands with hunched shoulders, blowing white smoke out with every breath, shaking his head.

"*Ain't* isn't a word," I say, trying to lighten the mood. I can't help but feel sad that maybe Mack was wrong about everything he thinks he knows about his brother. But that doesn't mean I want Ian to be sad. Maybe he still wants to be with Ginny, and if that's what he wants, then I'm going to have to like him enough to help him get it. That's what people do for people they . . . care about.

Ian glares at me. "I've got a word for you."

My jaw goes a little off to the side. "Let's hear it then."

Ian says nothing. We just stare at each other. I'm using every bit of willpower I have to not smile. He is so damn cute when he's angry.

"So you guys are dating now, huh?" Hannah asks.

I laugh a little. "Kind of hard to be doing that when you never actually go out on a date."

Ian frowns playfully. "What do you mean I never take you out on a date? We went to the shooting range together, where you shot *me* by the way; we went checking cows, feeding the calf . . ."

"You didn't take me to the range, you fool—I took myself. And I didn't shoot you either."

He looks at Hannah. "Did you see my scar? She shot me. I have witnesses."

Hannah laughs. "It's about time someone shot you, idiot." She starts walking away. "I have to go back to work."

I talk at her back. "Thanks for telling us about Ginny. But you better not keep talking about Andie like that. I'm serious, Hannah!"

She waves over her head, her bright red nails showing off well against the white snowy backdrop. "Yeah, yeah."

Ian wraps his arms around me from behind, trapping my arms at my sides. "You're my prisoner."

"I'm pretty sure it's you who's my prisoner," I say, smiling. People in the diner are probably staring at us, but I don't care. Let the world see that this man makes me completely silly.

"Do you always argue about everything?" he asks.

"No. Do you?"

"No. Never. Only with you. But I'm pretty sure it's not me actually arguing. It's you doing that." He kisses my neck and then snorts in there too like a wild pig or something, giving me goose bumps all over.

I turn around and fling my arms around his neck, hugging him tight. "Stop that, Piglet."

"I can't help it." He buries his face in my neck again. "You smell so good. And you taste good too." He pushes his hips into me a little, letting me know he's ready to go again for another roll in the hay or the straw or whatever that yellow stuff is.

"You're so bad," I say, smiling like a loony bird. I would totally do him standing up out here. I would.

A car drives by and honks several times. Then someone yells out the window, "Get a room!"

Ian lifts his head and then flips someone the bird. The guy honks some more.

"Come on. Let's go home." Ian puts our hands in his coat pocket again.

His choice of words makes me sad. *Home.* Home is where the heart is, but I live in Florida. Can I live in a different place than my heart? Talk about mood swings. I'm back to fighting tears off again. I must be ready to have my period or something. Maybe the jet lag is throwing off my calendar or something. I shouldn't be this moody until next week.

"What's wrong?" he asks me as we approach the truck.

"Nothing." I get inside with his help and wait for him to shut the door, but he just stands there instead, looking up at me.

"What?" I ask, avoiding looking into his eyes. I focus on his hair instead.

"You're sad or mad or something."

"No, I'm not."

"You're arguing again."

"It's you, not me."

He stands up on the running board of the truck and kisses me quick on the lips before I realize what he's even doing. "Liar," he says before he hops down and goes around the back of the truck.

I take four deep breaths, trying to calm myself down. Going all crybaby on Ian right now is the last thing I want to do. I have a life waiting for me in Florida. I cannot let this little fling get out of control.

We ride the rest of the way back to the ranch in silence.

CHAPTER THIRTY-EIGHT

I walk in the door and hear voices in the kitchen. Following the sounds, I find Andie there, sitting at the table and holding the baby. Maeve is hovering over them.

"Oh, Sarah's here!" I say, dropping my purse on the ground at the entrance to the room.

"Her mother's here too," Andie says in a wry tone.

I wave her off. "Yeah, yeah, but it's the baby that everyone wants to see—you know that. She's new, you're old. Get used to it."

Andie tries to kick me as I approach, but I'm too nimble for her post-pregnant butt. I jump to the side and keep coming until I'm able to crouch down by my goddaughter.

Sarah is completely wrapped up in a puffy blanket. The only thing showing is her tiny pink face. Her eyes are closed, and she's making sucking faces.

"Awww . . . look . . . she's dreaming about nursing. How cute is that?"

Andie smiles. "She's pretty cute, that's for sure. I can't stop staring at her. She's such a miracle."

I look up at the weird tone in her voice to see Andie crying.

"Why are you sad about that?"

"I'm not sad," she says, all weepy, "I'm so happy, I can't stand it. I never knew being a mother would feel like this."

I nod. "I know exactly what you mean."

"You do?" Maeve asks. "You don't have any children, do you?"

"Yes."

Andie's eyes bug out. "No, you don't." She's frowning in confusion.

"Yes, I do. Her name is Candy, and she's out in the barn." I lift my chin a little. "Ian and I are her foster parents."

Andie shakes her head. "You're crazy."

"Crazy like a fox." I look up and wink at Maeve.

"What was that?" Andie's pointing at my face.

"What was what?" I am innocence personified. There's no way she'll get anything out of me. All I have to do is play stupid for a few minutes, and this will all blow over.

"That *wink*." She's still pointing at my face. "You just winked at Maeve, and don't act like you didn't."

I blink several times. "I had a snowflake in my eye."

Andie narrows her eyes at me. "Snowflake, my ass. It's too warm in here for a snowflake."

"It was snowflake *residue*, silly. From all the pollution."

"You are so full of it." Andie turns her attention to Maeve. "Tell me what she's scheming about. I know she's got you involved."

Maeve's eyes open wide, and she looks from Andie to me.

I pantomime slicing my throat, but Andie turns really quick and catches me.

She slams her hand palm down on the table, startling the baby. "Tell me!" she insists.

"Whoa," I say, standing and backing up a little. "Hello, hormones."

She glares at me as she bounces the baby, trying to get the little thing to close her eyes again. From what I can see over here, she's too terrified to let her guard down, and I don't blame her. Andie's acting crazy.

"It's not hormones. It's me being cranky about being in the dark."

I pat her on the hand. "Never you mind. Auntie Candice has it all under control."

"Auntie Candice is going to get a chunk of hair cut out of her 'do while she's sleeping if she doesn't start talking," Andie says in a deadly calm voice.

I put my hands on my head in a protective gesture. "Holy *harsh*. What has Baker City done to my friend, anyway?" I feel like I've been accosted by a terrorist. What's next? My fingers? Is she going to lop those off too?

"It made me a no-nonsense person is what it did. Tell me what you've been up to while I've been up all night feeding this little monster."

I walk over to Andie slowly and reach down. "Give the babyyyy to meeee . . . there we gooooo . . . everybody's happyyyy . . ."

Andie slaps me away. "You can hold her after you've confessed."

My hands go to my hips, angry that I'm being not only threatened but thwarted. "Are you denying me my rights as a godmother?"

"I'll be denying you a whole lot more than that if you don't start talking."

I'm completely deflated. I barely make it into a chair before I'm totally boneless. I can hardly hold my head up to look at the shell of my former best friend. She looks like a pudgy Andie on the outside, but inside . . . ? She's pure demon.

"Don't you think you're being just a little . . . hard?" Maeve asks, acting like she's ready for Andie to blow. Andie is a grenade, that's for sure.

"Are you kidding me?" Andie looks at me and then Maeve. "This is the girl who two years ago single-handedly caused an entire city to stop serving buffalo meat because she convinced people that the animal was on the endangered species list."

I frown, recalling that little nugget from my past. I don't know why she always has to bring that up when things don't go her way. My heart was in the right place.

"It's not my fault Google lied," I say in my defense.

Andie bugs her eyes out at me. "Google is not a person, okay? I don't know how many times I have to tell you that."

I look toward the door, thinking a nap might be a good plan for me right now. A nap behind a locked door. I'm not sure I can manage Andie's mood swings with the grace that's probably called for in this situation.

Maeve cuts in to save me. "Well, buffalo aren't endangered exactly, but they certainly aren't as common nowadays as they used to be. And cattle are much more plentiful, so maybe it's not a bad thing if people give the buffalo herds a chance to grow bigger."

I point to Maeve. "Yeah, see? I was doing you guys a favor. Do you know how much business you'll lose if everyone starts eating buffalo? A lot, that's how much. And *then* how will you pay for Sarah's college?" I nod to drive my point home.

Andie looks at me with no expression, just blinking a few times. That scares me more than any mood she might have been in before. This is her lawyer face, and she's a really good lawyer.

Andie lowers her head a fraction, never breaking eye contact. "Tell me what I want to know."

I could fight her, but I realize it's pointless. She's like a dog with a tasty bone sometimes. One of those bulldogs that gets lockjaw.

"Fine. You want to know so bad? I'll tell you. Maeve and I . . ."

Maeve holds up her hand. "Just to be clear, I wasn't exactly part of the planning committee."

"Hey!"

Andie holds up her hand to stop us from having the side argument that I was planning to use to distract Andie. *Dammit.*

"I know, Maeve," she says. "She ropes people into her schemes all the time." Andie goes back to staring at me, waiting, silently demanding my explanation.

I am so ready to leave this place. Some mean bitch has taken over my best friend's body and turned her into someone I would never hang out with.

I stand, making the chair scrape across the floor. "You know what? I need a nap."

Andie grabs my wrist. "Sit. Stay. Have some coffee." Her voice is a tiny bit less mean, but it's still not good enough to make me want to listen.

"No, thanks. I'm all coffeed out for one day." I turn to go, but she still has me in her grip. I'd yank myself away from her, but I'm afraid Sarah will end up on the floor.

"Please? For me?"

I grit my teeth and glare down at her. "Your emotional roller coaster is giving me whiplash, Andie."

She starts crying. "I know." She's weeping as the words come out. "Me too."

"Oh, poor baby!" Maeve exclaims, rushing over to kneel down and pat her on the back. "It's okay, sweetie; everything is going to be fine!"

Andie looks down at Sarah, still holding me in her kung fu death grip. "I love her so much! Why do I keep crying about it?"

"Baby blues," Maeve says, smoothing her hair on her head. "It's totally normal. You're just hormonal. It'll go away on its own, or we can get you some medication. It's nothing to be embarrassed about."

I sit down across from her, feeling bad that I jumped to the conclusion that my friend was consciously being awful to me. She finally lets me go, leaving red marks behind on my skin.

"I'm sorry, Andie," I say, letting go of all my plans for future pouting. "Don't be mad at me."

Andie shakes her head. "I'm not mad at you. I love you. I could never be mad at you."

I try to smile. "Even though I tried to plan a baby shower for you, and it didn't work out?"

"You did that for me?" Her crying goes on pause.

"No, I just told you. I *tried* to do it, but it didn't work out." I give Maeve a knowing look. "But I'm pretty sure I know why now, though. And I'm on it, believe me."

Maeve lifts an eyebrow.

"Do I want to know what you're talking about?" Andie asks, sniffing as she wipes her nose on her sleeve. She sounds exhausted.

"No, you do not." I nod my head once for emphasis. "Ian's helping me, so don't worry." I look at Andie's mother-in-law. "Maeve, you're off the hook."

"Oh. Good. I think."

"So, do I get to hold that dang baby or what?" I ask, huffing out some air in annoyance. Time to change the subject.

Andie gives me a watery smile. "Of course you can. You're her godmother." She hands the bundle over to me and makes sure I have a good grip before she lets go.

"Good. Finally." I look down at Sarah, who has miraculously fallen asleep even in the middle of all the drama. She's already tough as nails, apparently. "Open your eyes, baby girl. You need to memorize my face before I leave."

Andie starts laughing, and then her laughter turns to tears again.

I shake my head in pity at my friend. "Don't worry, sweetie. As soon as I've got Sarah imprinting on me, I'm going to google that baby blues thing and get you all fixed up."

Andie laughs through her crying jag. "Thank you, Doctor Candice, Internet MD."

I smile back at her, happy now that she's acknowledging my skills. "You are very welcome."

CHAPTER THIRTY-NINE

I'm in my room after my fat nap, looking at the meager offerings my suitcase holds, when Ian comes in and shuts the door almost all the way.

"What are you doing in here?" I ask, turning around to face him. I'm instantly on fire, but there's no way I'm going to touch him in his parents' house. I hold onto the back of a chair behind me for strength.

He clears his throat. "I came to see if you want to go out with me tonight."

I blink a few times, letting that sink in.

"On a date," he clarifies.

I go all tingly inside, and suddenly I'm feeling kind of shy. "Sure. I'd like that a lot."

"In ten minutes."

I frown, no longer suffering that little shyness problem. "Are you joking?"

"No, I'm totally serious."

I fold my arms across my chest. "Do you have any idea how rude that is? To just assume I'll drop everything and go out with you . . . like I don't already have plans?"

"You were sleeping earlier."

"So?"

"And I thought you wanted to confront Ginny, but if you don't . . ." He turns to walk out the door.

I run across the room and grab his arm. "No! Wait."

He grins. "That's what I thought." His head tips down, and he steals a kiss before I know what's coming. "Be ready to go out to a bar."

"Out to a bar? It's not even dinnertime yet."

"Dart tournament. Ginny's entered to play. We should get there before too many people are eliminated. She's not that good."

"How'd you know she was doing that?" I go over to my suitcase and pull out the black cashmere sweater I was saving for a special occasion, wondering if a dart tournament qualifies.

"Got a text from Hannah, of all people."

I snort. "She's sucking up. She probably wants to sit on your gear shift and spin or whatever."

Ian comes up behind me and presses his whole body up against mine, so I can feel him practically from head to heel. "I was kinda hoping I could convince you to do that."

Half of me wants to throw him out of the room for being so rude, and the other half wants to go ahead and shove him down onto the bed so I can ride him like a bronc.

Instead, I do neither. I ignore his obvious invitation and hold up the black sweater. "Do you think this will work?" I ask.

"Sure." He nuzzles my neck.

"What about this?" I ask, holding up a nightgown.

"Sure. Perfect."

I sigh. "Ian, these are pajamas."

"Whatever. You look hot in anything." He's too busy sucking my neck to make any sense.

He tweaks my nipple and I jump. Spinning around, I detach myself from his grip, speaking in a loud whisper. "You're terrible! This is your parents' house!"

"So?" He comes at me with his hands open, like he's going to grab me by the waist. "They're grown-ups. They know what other grown-ups do."

"Not in their *house*!"

"Oh, you prefer the barn?" He's getting closer, and I'm running out of room to escape.

My legs bump up against the bed. "No, I don't, as a matter of fact. I'm still fishing pieces of hay out of my hair." The heat is building up inside me, and my panties are getting wet. Life is so unfair. All he has to do is look at me like that with those crazy, intense green eyes of his, and I go nuts inside.

He stops just in front of me and rests his hands gently on my hips. "Kiss me."

"Just once," I say in my best bossy tone. "Then no more. You have to leave my room."

"Okay, but it has to be a *good* one." He grins.

"All my kisses are good ones." My hands slither up his chest to go around his neck. We fit so perfectly together, like he was made for me, and I was made for him.

He lowers his head and says, "I'll be the judge of that," just before he presses his lips to mine. His mouth is so soft, not asking me for anything, but making me want to give it to him anyway.

We draw apart after just a couple seconds.

"There," I say, completely unsatisfied, but acting like everything is exactly how I wanted it. "Now you need to go."

He shakes his head. "Nope. Sorry. The deal was a *good* kiss."

"Excuse me, but that *was* a good kiss."

He screws up his face and shakes his head a little. "Naaah, not so much."

"What? How dare . . ." I huff out some air. "Fine. You want a good kiss? Here's a good kiss." I grab his head and pull him down to me, ready to make out with him like nobody's business.

He pulls away and holds up a finger. "One sec."

"What?" First he asks me for a good kiss, and then, when I'm finally ready to cave in, he leaves? What kind of messed up, mind-bending reverse psychology is that?

Walking across the room, he goes to the door and shuts it, locking it before he comes back.

I look at him sideways, happy that I'm not being abandoned but worried again that he's going to convince me to do something that feels naughty. Unfortunately, anything having to do with Ian feels like it can't possibly be wrong, even when it clearly is.

"Ian. I told you . . . no messing around in your parents' house."

He holds out his arms. "Just a good kiss. That's all I need."

He's standing there with a giant bulge in his pants, and all I can think about is seeing him naked. I look at the door and then at his pants again. The whole rule about not doing bad girl things in his parents' house is seeming sillier and sillier by the second.

"You're killing me, babe," he says, turning his smile upside down.

The look of pain on his face is what does it to me. I throw all my ideas about propriety out the window and spontaneously reformulate my ideas of right and wrong. *Boom.* Done.

"Take your clothes off," I say, seized by some demon slut who cannot control her libido. All I can think is that I need to get my hands on his dick.

He doesn't even question me. His shirt comes flying off along with his socks and then his jeans. He's standing in a pair of boxer briefs with a giant tent bulge in the front in less than a minute.

"Your turn," he says, looking me up and down.

I decide a sneak attack is the best way to handle this situation. This'll teach him to try and call the shots with me.

I walk up closer and act like I'm going to take my shirt off, but instead I get on my knees, pulling the top of his briefs down with me. His dick comes out and bounces up and down in front of my face, fully erect.

"What are you doing?" he asks, confused.

"Giving you a *good* kiss so you'll leave my room."

CHAPTER FORTY

I take Ian's rod in one hand and rest my other on his thigh. My mouth goes to the tip of his cock and I lick it with my tongue, once, twice, and then three times, bringing my lips in to slide around and accentuate the feeling for him.

His sharp intake of breath tells me I made the right choice.

"Fuuuuck," he says with a long exhale.

"No, not fuck," I say, and lick him again. "Just kiss."

He moans. His hands move to my shoulders as I begin to slide my lips over the tip of his dick and down the shaft. My tongue swirls around while my lips move forward and back. I use my hand to stroke the length of him, and his hips move slightly with the rhythm I've set.

"I had no idea . . ." he says.

"Mmm . . ." I can't respond—too busy reading his signals, taking him in deep, making sure to work the entire length of his cock.

He's getting bigger, thicker, so I know I'm doing what he likes. I'm trying to remain focused on his pleasure, but at the same time I wish I'd taken the time to remove my clothes too, so I could throw him down on the bed and climb on top before he finishes. I'm getting seriously turned on watching him start to lose it.

Sweat has popped out on his face and chest. He's breathing heavily, and his grip on my shoulders has tightened. "Oh my god, babe . . . oh fuck . . . yeah, that's it . . ."

My other hand comes up to cup his balls.

He moans and jerks back, pulling away from me.

"Is something wrong?" I ask, looking up at him from the ground.

"Yes," he growls, grabbing me by the armpits and hauling me to my feet.

I'm trying to decide whether to be mad or embarrassed when he grabs the bottom of my shirt and pulls it up over my head.

"What are you . . . ?"

"I need to be inside you," he says, still growling at me.

No way am I going to argue with that statement since I agree one hundred percent that it's the best idea for both of us. I help him get my pants and socks off, quickly followed by my bra and panties.

When I move to kiss him, he takes me by the waist and turns me around. My back is to his chest and his cock is pressing into my ass.

He pushes his dick to the side so he can get closer. His hands slide around to the front of me and go down, his finger sliding into my slit.

"Mmm, you're already wet," he says in my ear.

"You turn me on so much," I whisper back.

Then his finger is touching my clit and rubbing back and forth, sliding sometimes inside me and then coming out to rub again. The tingling starts immediately, and I open my legs, trying to respond to the need that's building but not quite getting me where I want to be.

He pushes my upper back down with his other hand and I bend over in response. Then his big cock is pressing against my opening from behind, and I gasp with how easily he enters me.

"Oh, babe . . ." he says, his voice hoarse.

"Shh," I warn, worried people will hear us, and then I moan too. So much for being discreet.

He takes me by the hips and pushes all the way into me, pounding a few times at the end and rubbing back and forth when he's fully buried.

I push against him, begging for more. My hands open and close on the bedsheets, twisting and turning them into wrinkled piles.

He builds a rhythm, going in and out, the friction growing along with my desire.

"Harder," I say, knowing I need to feel more of him.

He bangs into me so forcefully, my feet lose their grip on the floor and I fall forward onto the bed.

He crawls up behind me and pushes into me from above, quickly, like he can't wait for me to be ready.

I collapse onto the bed on my stomach, but he doesn't stop. He's going faster and faster, pushing, demanding, and I have to raise my ass off the bed as high as I can to keep him in the best position to go deep.

It's crazy the way we just keep going, not caring which end is up or who might hear. We just have this *need* to satisfy, and neither of us is willing to walk away from it. I've never ever been so carried away with someone before.

His hands come under me and pull my hips up even higher. I didn't even know I was capable of this kind of maneuver, but I'm glad as hell that I am. He is hitting me in exactly the right spot, the pressure pushing on my nub and making a tingle come from somewhere deep inside me, his long hard cock filling every bit of me.

He's going nuts, pumping so fast, I can't keep up with his rhythm. I don't need to, though, since my body seems to have gone into some sort of autoerotic state. I don't even know where I am anymore—some kind of dark sex pit, maybe. I could care less if the whole house hears us at this point. I just want him to take me all the way to the end of this crazy ride. It feels so good, I just hope it doesn't end too soon.

"Argh!" he yells, stopping suddenly. He's breathing so hard he sounds like a freight train.

"What's wrong?" I ask, also out of breath.

"Turn over."

"What?"

Before he bothers to answer, he pulls out, grabs me by the waist and flips me halfway over. "That's good, right there."

I'm on my side, and he's straddling one of my legs. The other one he's lifting to put over his shoulder.

"What are you doing?" I ask, scared and excited at the same time. I'm throbbing with need. I just want him back in there, making me feel like I'm on fire again.

"Fucking you." He gets low on his knees and guides his dick into me again. He's holding onto my leg with both hands as it rests against his chest and goes over his shoulder at the back of my knee joint.

I've never had anyone fuck me sideways before, but it doesn't take me long to figure out that I like it. Yes, please, Ian. Fuck me sideways.

"Oh my god," I say as he pauses to rub some circles around me with his pubic bone. I'm getting a massage on the outside and the inside at the same time. It crosses my mind that this is what heaven is like. Just exactly like this, only with unlimited cookies that don't make you gain weight.

"You like that?" he asks, putting his thumb on my nub, gently rubbing it as he pulls out and goes back in.

I nod, unable to speak.

He keeps rubbing me like that, pausing, starting again, going in and out, and I get closer and closer to the elusive orgasm that seems to be playing hide and seek with me today. I can't quite fall over the edge, but I try not to get frustrated by it. This feels way to good to worry about little details like that. I know that Ian would never leave me hanging.

He stops and pulls out.

"What's wrong?" I ask, worried we're done already.

"I need to go deeper. I want to see your face when you come, and I know you're close."

He gently pushes me onto my back.

I open my legs and arms. "Come on then," I say, smiling. "Gimme, gimme."

He grins. "Oh, I plan to, believe me."

And then he's inside me again. We stare into each other's eyes as the heat builds inside me again. He sinks into me slowly, carefully, making me happily aware of every inch of him.

The sliding gets slicker. Easier, as the heat builds. I feel parts of my body swelling down there, and the tingling comes from deep inside again. This time it comes faster and stronger. I imagine that I'm falling.

His expression goes dark and his nostrils flare. The muscles at his jaw begin tensing and releasing, over and over.

I start to close my eyes.

"No," he says. "Open your eyes. I want to watch you."

I do as he says and stare into his impossibly green eyes. It's intense feeling him in me and on me while watching him gaze at me so intently. It's like we're somehow being melded together, no longer two individuals, but one whole. It's scary, but I can't deny that it feels right. I want to watch him come too.

I can feel orgasms coming for both of us at the same time. Keeping his gaze is no longer an option. I have to keep my eyes locked with his or I'll drown. He's the only thing saving me from certain oblivion. I've never felt like I'm about to completely lose myself before like I do now. It's amazing yet disconcerting at the same time.

"Ian . . ." I'm desperate, holding onto him with an iron grip.

"You're going to come," he says.

I nod, my face contorting with the pleasure and the anticipation. "Yes."

"Me too," he says, his voice mostly down to grunts.

And then it comes for me. Just knowing that he's on the edge is enough to push me over. The orgasm to end all orgasms arrives to overwhelm me.

Ian's hands are on either side of my face now, holding my head still, his nose just an inch from mine. He looks like he's about to cry, the way his brows come together and down, the way his mouth presses together as he grunts, sweat pouring down his face to land on mine.

I gasp in sweet release. "Ian!" I sound like I'm crying. "Ian! Ian!"

He pumps into me, grunting and growling as I call out his name and various syllables that make no sense.

We stare at each other the entire time we ride the waves. Neither of us can breathe very well, pressuring our lungs until they're ready to burst and then gasping once or twice. Swept up in the emotions and feelings, we stare and we stare and we stare. In this moment, nothing else in the entire world matters or ever will be this good again. It's a bittersweet thing like no other.

"I love you," he gasps out, still pushing into me, using what feels like the last bits of his strength.

"I love you too," I say right back. Overwhelmed by the emotion taking over, I start to cry. And I'm not talking a delicate, sweet, attractive cry either. I start blubbering like a big old baby.

He rains tiny kisses all over my face, still pushing into me. "Don't cry, baby."

"I'm not sad," I mumble, through my tears, "I'm not sad at all, I promise." It's kind of a lie, but he deserves to be lied to this time. I don't want his heart to break as badly as mine will when I leave.

"Promise," he says, still kissing me, slowing down his strokes.

"Promise."

"Do you want me to stop?" he asks, pausing in his kissing.

"No." I shake my head. "Never stop."

He smiles. "I'm afraid my dick has other ideas."

I feel it kind of slide out of me right after he says that. It makes me giggle.

"Poor guy." Ian looks down at his crotch. "You wore him out."

"He wore me out, not the other way around." I suddenly feel all shy, now that I realize once more that we're in Ian's parents' house and we just had crazy sex. We even did it *sideways*, for God's sake.

Ian props himself up on his side and looks at me, using a finger to trace the outline of my nipple. "You have fabulous breasts, you know that?"

"I bought and paid for them myself," I say, not ashamed one bit that I've enhanced what God gave me.

"I'll bet you look amazing in a bathing suit."

I grin. "I like to think I do."

"I'd like to see that." He sounds wistful.

"Not in this weather you won't." I don't care what kind of sweet talk he uses, I'm not putting a bathing suit on in Baker City during the winter.

"Is it warm in Florida right now?" he asks.

"Yeah, pretty warm. It never gets that cold. But I wouldn't say it's bathing suit weather all year. Just most of the year."

"I googled ranching in Florida," he says, like he's not speaking right to my heart. "Did you know it's one of the bigger cattle ranching states in the United States?"

I frown at him, wondering if he's messing with me right now. "Are you serious?"

"Yeah." He props himself up higher and rests his hand on my belly. "Not that far from where you live, actually."

"Really?" I frown as I think about that. "I guess I have seen some cows by the side of the road. But it's mostly on my way up north."

"Where? New York?"

I laugh. "No. Orlando. To go to Universal Studios or whatever."

"I've never been there. Is it fun?"

"Loads. I'll take you sometime."

"How about now?" he asks, his expression dead serious.

I look at him closely, trying to detect a trick. "Now?"

"Yeah. Let's go." He nudges me on the arm. "Let's go to Universal."

I reach up and fluff his matted hair. "You're silly."

He takes my hand from his hair and kisses my fingers. "No. I'm serious." He carefully places my hand down on my stomach, keeping his over it.

"Why aren't you laughing?" I ask.

"Because I'm serious. If I laughed it would ruin the effect."

I drag myself out from under him and sit up. "You seriously want to come to Florida and go to Universal with me?"

"Yes."

"And you googled ranching out there?"

"Yes."

"Why?" My heart is pumping out a thousand beats a minute. I can't breathe very well, but I'm trying to fake like I can. I don't want him to know that the very idea that he might want to be with me on a more permanent basis sends me into an apoplectic fit.

He doesn't answer me for a long time. Then he rolls over onto his back and stares at the ceiling. "I love you, Candice."

My insides go all funny hearing that. I was kind of hoping that he wasn't really listening to my big declaration during our love making, actually. It's one thing to be all goo-goo over a guy, but it's a whole other thing for him to know I'm all goo-goo over him.

Andie says I don't do flings. For once, I'm agreeing with her on that, at least where Ian is concerned. Ian is definitely not fling material, and now I've gone and fallen for him. Like, *totally* fallen. Did we really declare our love for each other as we came? How lame is that? I sigh. Not that lame when you're in the middle of it, apparently.

I nudge him with my foot. "I love you too, but . . ."

He turns his head to look at me. He seems so sad. "But what?"

I shrug. "But . . . everyone will say we're nuts."

He shrugs too. "Who cares what everyone will say? They're not the ones who decide whether we're happy or not."

I can't stop smiling. "This can't be happening."

He sits up and then stands next to the bed, holding out his hands. "It sure as hell can be happening."

CHAPTER FORTY-ONE

I'm standing next to Ian naked at the edge of the bed. He's staring down into my eyes, holding me close.

"Why not just be spontaneous?" he asks, as if it's the easiest thing in the world to run away with someone you hardly know, from a top-left state to a bottom-right one.

"I don't know. Because it's irresponsible?" My argument sounds weak to my own ears.

"Screw being responsible. I've been responsible my whole life, and look where it's gotten me."

"In a great life with a great family?"

"Lonely. Wishing I were somewhere else living a life with someone I'm not related to by birth."

"But . . . you're country and I'm city." I want to believe this thing between us could work, but it feels like I should try and talk us both out of it. That's what Andie would want me to do. She's going to be so pissed. It makes me feel sick inside.

"I'm not completely country, and you're not completely city either. Don't try and tell me you are."

I shrug. I might have argued this point with him a few days ago when I was slipping and sliding all over the ice, but today, I can't.

He's totally right. I am a cow momma after all. And I did buy a gun and shoot a lion with it. None of that would ever happen in Florida.

He points at my face. "You're trying to come up with arguments, and you can't."

"No, I'm just thinking that I did like the cow stuff, and the boots are really cute here." I don't mention the gun because then he'll give me crap about shooting him again.

"See? And you like chickens."

I scrunch up my face. "I'm not sure about chicken butts, though."

He frowns. "Chicken butts? Who said anything about chicken butts?"

"The egg thing . . ." I say, waiting for him to catch on.

"Listen, if you don't like chicken butts, we don't have to have 'em. I just thought you'd like fresh eggs."

"We? What do you mean *we*?"

He gives me a wonky smile. "You didn't think I was talking about just taking a vacation out to Orlando, did you?"

I'm suddenly having a hard time breathing. I have to back away from him to find the oxygen I need to survive.

"What's the matter?" he asks, his arms frozen out in front of him as I put some distance between us.

"I just . . . I just . . . I just need to breathe." My face is suddenly cold and sweaty while my ears are on fire. "I think I'm about to spontaneously combust."

He chuckles. "That's just nerves."

My gaze darts around the room, searching out my missing clothing items. I need to get dressed. I need to get out of here. I need to *think*, and I can't do that with Ian so close, so cute, so in lust with me.

I'm sure that's what this is. Lust. He's overcome by lust and has tricked himself into believing he loves me. The pain that thought does to my chest is awful. I have to hold my heart to make it stop. Maybe it really is love.

But, *ack*! Guys don't *do* this kind of thing. This is *my* thing, falling for someone completely inappropriate. I totally lied before. I'm not a flinger. I don't do flings *at all*. I only fall in love. That's me. That's who I am. But I've never had someone do it back to me. No wonder all those guys ran away from me. Talk about pressure. Talk about scary shit!

"Tell you what," Ian says, putting his pants on and then his shirt, like he doesn't have a care in the world. "I'll let you think on it, and in the meantime, we can go to the bar and talk to Ginny."

"Yes," I say, pointing at him. "That is an *excellent* idea. Let's fix Andie's life." Before I destroy my own, I need to make sure hers is solid. That's the least I can do before I turn their entire household upside down.

I realize then that this is only going to end badly for the MacKenzies. Either I take Ian away, and we fall even more madly in love and they hardly ever see him again, or I leave him here brokenhearted and even more bitter than ever.

Holy shit. What have I done?

CHAPTER FORTY-TWO

I manage to do my hair and makeup and look vaguely presentable before getting into the truck with Ian and Mack. For some reason, we got saddled with Mack's butt for our mission, but I made Ian promise he wouldn't say a word to his brother about what our plans are. I'll just have to talk to Ginny in the bathroom or something. The last thing I need is Mack reporting back to Andie on all my escapades. What she doesn't know won't hurt her, and I plan to keep it that way.

"So, how's fatherhood treating you?" Ian asks Mack as we head down the long road to the highway.

"Love it," Mack says without hesitation. "Could do without the sleep deprivation, but otherwise, it's perfect. Andie's a great mom. Sarah's a real lucky girl to have her."

"Ma says Andie's got the baby blues."

"Yeah, a bit, but she's working it out. You know how it goes."

I turn around to look at Mack. "How does he know how it goes?"

Mack shrugs. "Happens in the animal world too sometimes."

I nod. This makes complete sense to me. I spent a little time before my nap with my first love, Google, and I learned quite a bit about the hormone tornado wreaking havoc on Andie's body. It made me want to draw her a hot bath, but when I called her to discuss it, she declined my offer.

"If you two want to go out some night, Candice and I could come over and watch her for you," Ian says.

My heart spasms in my chest. How cute would that be? Ian and me, pretending to be parents for a little while.

My face goes white again. Parents? Ian and me? Oh my god, oh my god, oh my god.

"What's wrong with you?" Ian asks. "You feeling okay? You look kind of pale."

"Me?" My eyes bulge out. Is he reading minds now too? "Nothing at all. Not one thing."

He chuckles, shaking his head. "Liar."

"How's the trip going so far, Candice?" Mack asks me. "Andie feels bad that she hasn't had more time to spend with you."

"Oh, it's been great. Ian's been keeping me occupied." I want to die when the words come out of my mouth. More like his dick has been keeping me occupied. Holy crap. We totally did it in his parents' house *and* their barn.

Ian glances at me, but keeps his mouth shut, thankfully.

"So I heard," Mack says.

I'm speechless. Thank goodness Ian isn't suffering the same problem.

"What's that supposed to mean?" he asks, looking in his rearview mirror at Mack.

"Nothing. Just that I heard you all went to town a couple times together." He laughs. "Heard she shot you at the range too."

"She did." Ian nods. "In cold blood, I might add."

I sigh, already tired of this conversation. "I didn't shoot him—Karma did. And I've never been called cold-blooded in my entire life, so don't start now."

He pats me on the leg and then runs his hand up to squeeze my thigh very close to places he shouldn't be touching in public. "I'm sorry, babe. You're right. You're not cold-blooded."

I lift his hand off me and give him the look. "Hands off the merchandise." The last thing I need is Mack reporting back to Andie about Ian and me feeling each other up. I'll never hear the end of that for sure.

Ian glances at me, confused, but then goes back to his driving. We're not far from the highway, and this is the part that has the most holes in the road, so he needs to concentrate. I have a mission to accomplish tonight, and I can't do that in a ditch on the side of the road.

"So what's the plan tonight?" Mack asks.

"Plan?" I'm all innocence. "What plan?"

"Just three people out for a drink, that's all," Ian says.

"You can ease up on the bullpucky," Mack says. "Mom told me everything."

I roll my eyes and snort out my disgust. "Can't anyone keep a secret in this family?"

Ian's smiling way too hard. "Nope. Hey, Mack . . . did Candice tell you that she and I are running away to Orlando?"

Mack leans over into the front seat and stares at me. "Why, no she didn't, as a matter of fact." He nudges me on the shoulder. "Do tell, Candice."

My jaw is stuck open. The only sounds that will come out are ones of frustration and surprise.

"Yeah. I proposed the idea earlier today, and she's all for it," Ian says.

The words pop out of me before I can stop them. "I am not."

"You aren't?" Ian looks at me with concern in his eyes. "Are you serious?"

"No. Yes. No." I take a deep breath and let it out. "I don't know what I am. Confused is probably the best word." I stare out the side window so I don't have to look at his impossibly gorgeous face.

Mack chuckles. "Well, I think it's a good idea, if anyone cares about my opinion." He sits back in his seat.

I'm shocked. I have to turn around and look in the back to see if he's just messing with me. "Are you serious?" He sure is doing a good imitation of someone who is, with that cowboy hat on and those cold blue eyes of his. He's definitely not smiling.

"Why not?" He shrugs. "I married my wife after knowing her only a few hours. I definitely believe in going for it. When you know, you just know."

Ian pats me on the leg. "See? Told ya."

I turn around and slump down in my seat a little. This is all moving so fast for me. I can't believe the MacKenzies would just let Ian go like that, without a word against it. His parents will be furious for sure. A big brother can afford to be casual about it, but his mother, she's going to be mad. She'll probably want to run me over with her little truck.

Mack is talking again, jerking me out of my thoughts. "Mom was just saying yesterday how she wished you'd find someone to go on an adventure with. She says that's what you need. You're just withering away in Baker."

"She said that?" Ian shakes his head. "Damn. Even my own family is ready to throw me out."

"You've got to admit," Mack says, "you've pretty much been a pain in the keister for the last few years."

"Yeah, well . . . I'm done with that." Ian frowns. "Just going to remedy one little misunderstanding tonight, and then I'll be moving on." He looks over at me. "Onward and upward."

I try to smile, but inside I'm dying. What if I'm just a big disappointment to him? What if he walks into my salon and laughs at my work, my life, my friends? It's so different from what he's used to. Is it really possible for city and country to live in harmony together?

"Yeah, I'm really looking forward to getting to know Candice's world," he says.

Oomph. I guess we're going to find out. I try not to let that thought send me into a blind panic.

CHAPTER FORTY-THREE

The bar is lame. It's dark, it smells like stale beer, and it's full of fat guys wearing flannel shirts. Someone burps as I walk in, and I catch a whiff of salami.

"Aw, come on, Dave," Ian says, stepping in between the offender and me. He waves his hand in front of his face as he grimaces.

"Hey, Ian, what's up, man?" The burper holds up a hand, but he can't keep it still. Eventually, he gives up on getting a high five from Ian and lets it drop to his leg with a slap.

"Already wasted at six o'clock? Man, you're toast." Ian walks over and pats him on the back, hard. "How about a cup of coffee, dude? You up for it?"

"Yeah, thass a good idea, I think." The guy is nodding, his eyes glassy.

I walk away before I accidentally see anymore. If that guy barfs, I will totally lose it, and I haven't even gotten ten feet inside the door yet.

"So, we're here to see Ginny, is that it?" Mack asks me.

I look over my shoulder at Ian. He's holding his friend Dave up while the bartender pours him a coffee. I guess Mack is my new wingman.

"Yeah. I need to just chat with her for a second, and then we can leave."

Mack points. "You'll find her in that back room over there. That's where all the dartboards are. Watch out for the boards, though. Make sure you stay on the opposite end of the room from 'em."

He winks when he catches me about to unleash on him, so instead of yelling at him for insulting my intelligence, I say, "Thanks," and leave him at the bar ordering beers.

I see Tate Montgomery across the room and wave at him. He looks as if he's going to stand and come over, but I break eye contact and walk away. I don't want Ian getting another black eye on my behalf. He's already going to look like a hell-raiser when he shows up in Florida with that shiner he's sporting.

It's then that I realize I'm seriously considering his offer to come home with me. I must be crazy. I shake my head to get it off that train of thought. I need to focus on the mission at hand. *Andie now, Ian later.*

I go through an archway and spot Ginny at the far end of the room. She's in the middle of a couple guys and two other girls, one of them being Hannah. My eyes narrow as I take in the scene. Hannah wanted Ian and me to believe she was innocent in the scheme of things, but seeing her here tonight makes me doubt that.

I walk over, ignoring all the eyes that are on me. When I'm halfway to my destination, Hannah notices me and bumps Ginny on the arm. All the people in their little group turn to watch me arrive.

My heart starts hammering in my chest. *Easy now, Candice. You have a gun. You're a badass. Lions fear you. Don't let her intimidate you.* I lift my chin and stick out my boobs a little. No one, and I mean *no one* is going to talk shit about my best friend after tonight. My superpowers are on full alert. Just let Ginny try anything.

"Hello," I say as I step up in front of her. I hate to admit it, but her hair looks amazing, and her boots are adorable. I have no idea how she's walking in the snow with them, though. The soles are black and not inch-thick astronaut rubber like mine.

"Hello. Candice, right?" She looks over my shoulder. "Where's Ian?"

"Never mind where Ian is. I'm here to discuss Andie."

She smiles, pursing her lips a little before she responds. "Is that so?"

"Yes, it is so. Listen . . ."—I gesture at Hannah—"I hear through the grapevine that you've been spreading rumors about my friend Andie MacKenzie."

"Not me." She's so smug I want to slap her, but I resist.

"Hannah says you've been telling people Andie broke you and Ian up."

"That true, Hannah?" She asks without even looking at her friend.

"Nope." Hannah takes a drink of her beer. "I didn't say that."

"You're a liar," I say, pointing at her over Ginny's shoulder. "I'll deal with you later." I turn my attention back to Ginny. "But for now, I'm here for you."

"Oh, I'm flattered." Ginny puts her hand on her heart and bats her eyelashes.

I narrow my eyes at her. "So when you were being all friendly in the hospital, you were just bullshitting me, huh?"

"You're so intelligent." She tilts her head and speaks in a saccharine-sweet tone. "Did you go to college?"

"As a matter of fact, I did. UF. Graduated summa cum laude. Did you?"

"Yes." She sticks her chin out. "In La Grande."

"Community college," Hannah says, leaning toward us to clarify.

Ginny loses her uppity expression in an instant. "Shut up, Hannah."

"You shut up, Ginny." Hannah glares at her friend and takes another sip of her beer.

Ginny's smile is tight. "Anyway, we have nothing to say about your friend Andie, so you can move along." She gestures to the targets at the other side of the room, three feathered darts sticking out of the top of her fingers. "We're in the middle of a tournament here."

I snatch the darts out of her hand and throw all three of them at her board together. One sticks in the edge and the rest hit the wall sideways and fall to the floor.

"Hey!"

"That's your turn," says a guy on the other team. "You got . . ."—he looks at the target—"a whole lotta nothin'." His entire team snickers.

She pushes my shoulder. "You messed up my score!"

I push her back. "You messed up my best friend's *life*!"

Ginny looks like she's about to combust. Her face is bright red, and her eyes are nearly falling out of her head. "You touch me again, and we are *so* going to fight."

"You say one more word about Andie or Ian, and you're damn straight we're going to fight." I bob my head a little so she knows I'm serious.

Her mouth twists up into something seriously ugly. "Andie MacKenzie is a no-good slut who not only ruined my wedding to Ian and my entire life, but Hannah's life too."

I drop my purse on the ground behind me and push up my sleeves. "All right, that's it. I warned you."

Hannah looks worried, but Ginny doesn't. She looks strangely excited by the prospect of me whooping her butt.

The guys back away and start laughing, nudging each other in anticipation. You'd think we were about to jump in a tub of Jell-O the way they're leering at us. *Idiots.*

I'm so busy making sure the material of my blouse is up high enough on my elbows that it won't get ruined that I'm not prepared for Ginny's first move. She blindsides me with a bitch slap to the face, whipping my head sideways.

I recover a split-second later and leap on her without thinking, going for her hair. I know that's the easiest way to get a girl like her on her knees. I'm a fucking ninja when it comes to this shit.

She screams. "Ow! That's my hair, you bitch!"

I yank for all I'm worth, bringing her to her knees with the pain. "If you want to keep it, you'll promise to leave Andie alone."

"Screw Andie! And screw you too, you lunatic!"

I pull harder. "What was that?"

She has her hands up, trying to undo my grip, but there's no way. I'm using my all-steel kung-fu grip. An earthquake couldn't get me off her, even though she's killing me messing with my stitches the way she is.

"Ow, quit!" She gives up on trying to get me to let go and instead punches my thighs and my calves repeatedly.

The crowd is going wild, cheering us on. God, Baker City is full of complete imbeciles. I'm never going to live here. I don't care how cute Ian is. It makes me all the more dedicated to fixing things for Andie. She's stuck here. She doesn't have a choice, but there's no reason why she should have to suffer bitches like this one giving her grief.

I hold tight, blocking out the pain of Ginny's assault. If I let her up, she's bound to kill me or pop one of my boobs at least, and I don't want to have to go through that surgery again for sure. It took forever before I could hold up a dryer again after my implants went in.

"Candice, what the hell?" It's Ian and he's standing off to my right.

"Just stay back, Ian. I've got this under control." I'm grunting with the effort of absorbing Ginny's punches. She has some really bony knuckles.

"What's wrong with you people?!" Mack yells, addressing Hannah and the other spectators. He puts two beers down on the nearest high-top table.

"Ginny, get up." He comes around behind her and lifts her to her feet.

Ian takes me from behind, but I'm not letting go of the wench's hair for anything. This is my only leverage to get what I came here for.

"Let go, bitch!" Ginny screeches.

"Not 'til you promise to stop making up lies about my friend!"

"I'm not telling any lies about that whore!"

"Now, wait a second," Mack says.

That's when I let go of Ginny's hair. This is about as good a confession as I think I'm going to get, but it's good enough for me. Now Mack knows what's going on, and soon everyone else will too.

I let Ian pull me back and put some distance between us and her. My stitches are on fire, but I don't feel any blood escaping, so I consider that a win.

"What'd you call my wife?" Mack is standing at his full height now, and it's pretty impressive.

Ginny stands and tries to right her messed-up hair. It looks like a family of rats had a party in it, so it's pretty much hopeless. That makes me happy.

"You heard me," Ginny spits out. "Whore." And then she really does spit, right at Mack's feet.

I move to go after her again, but Ian grabs me from behind. "Easy there, killer. Let her have her say."

"Have her say? She's lying about Andie, your sister-in-law."

"She's just hurt," he says in a really calm voice.

Ginny turns a murderous gaze in his direction. "Fuck you, Ian. You ruined *everything*."

"Me? *I* ruined everything?" He laughs, but it's pretty bitter sounding.

It seems like everyone in the entire bar has come into the dart room to witness the spectacle. I try to fix my sleeves so they're more presentable and move to stand next to Ian instead of in front of him. He takes me by the hand and makes sure that everyone sees it by lifting our entwined arms and kissing me on the back of my fingers.

"Yes, *you*," Ginny says. "We had a plan, okay? A life we were living together, and you walked away from all of it. From ten years of living our lives together, Ian. Of making plans for our future."

Mack lets out a long hiss of air. "Your plans, not his."

She whips her head around to look at Ian's defender. "Shut up, Mack. What do you know? You never had the time of day for your little brother. Didn't then and you still don't now."

"Hey, that's out of line," Ian says, taking a step toward her.

Mack shakes his head. "Maybe you're right, Ginny, but that doesn't make what you did okay."

"Hey, don't listen to her," Ian says. He's talking to his brother at first, but then he lifts his gaze to the room, scanning all the faces of the people listening in and watching. "None of you listen to her, you hear? She's full of anger and jealousy. Everything coming out of her mouth is a damn lie."

"Is not!" she screams. She points at Ian. "You walked out on me!"

"You cheated on me!" he yells back. "With my brother of all people!"

She sneers. "He asked for it. He basically begged me for it."

Mack looks at her with a shocked expression. "Are you serious?" He looks at Ian. "You can't possibly believe her."

"Of course I don't believe her." Ian is disgusted. "God, how ridiculous can you be, Ginny? Jesus, why didn't I ever see that before?" Ian backs up, like he can't stand to be too close to her. He drags me with him, shaking his head.

She's crying but furious. "You loved me, Ian. You still do. I know you do! That's why you're always out drinking and carrying on. You miss me. You miss *us*." She takes a step toward him with her hand held out.

"Don't touch me!" he yells, throwing an arm out in front of him in a defensive gesture. "Don't even come near me."

"Ian!"

"No!" He drops my hand and holds both his palms out toward her. "Stay away. Seriously, Ginny. You're disturbed or something. There's nothing left between us. Never really was to begin with."

The world kind of slows down at that point. The sounds of the crowd, of the music playing in the background, of my heart beating . . . it all just melds together and becomes one big block of white noise. I watch in slow motion as Ginny makes her next move.

Her eyes flick left and right, taking in the mocking expressions, the shocked disbelief, the giggles coming from out in the crowd. And then in a flash of movement, she snatches several darts from a guy standing near her and starts throwing them at us, letting out a primal scream that I know I'll hear in my nightmares for the next ten years at least.

CHAPTER FORTY-FOUR

"You're starting to become a regular in this place," says Nurse Ratched number two, the same one that was around for my stitches.

I wince as she pulls the tetanus shot needle out of my arm. "Yeah. I just love coming over here. The Jell-O is amazing."

She laughs. "You think the Jell-O is good, you should try the pudding."

"Seriously?" I ask, really paying attention now.

She winks at me. "No, not seriously. It's awful. Stay away from the pudding."

I'm too shocked at her niceness to respond, and she leaves before I recover.

Ian comes walking around the corner of the curtain, holding his upper arm. "How're you doing?" he asks, stopping in front of me.

I'm sitting on one of the rolling beds in the ER of the hospital, so I have to look up to see his eyes. They're bloodshot, and his shiner, courtesy of Tate Montgomery, stands out in stark relief against his pale skin. I feel terrible that he looks so awful. This is all my fault.

"I'm fine," I say. "How are *you* doing is the question?"

Ian leans down until our foreheads are touching. "If you tell me I can come to Florida with you, I'm going to feel great. Perfect."

I reach up and wrap my one good arm around his neck. "You can come to Florida with me any time you want."

He kisses me for a few seconds, and I soak up that love as much as I can. After being darted, I'm seriously grateful for any pleasure I can get in my life.

A doctor walks around the edge of the curtain and sees us both there. "So this is the happy couple," he says, looking at my chart. "Looks like you dodged a bullet tonight."

"More like a few darts," Ian says. "Although I did get grazed by a bullet the other day . . ."

I jump into the conversation. "Everything's going to be okay, I hope?" I'm trying to simultaneously change the subject away from the shooting incident and ignore the pain in my arm. I thought a cougar scratch was bad, but it turns out a two-inch dart hole is pretty awful too.

"Yep. Didn't hit any major arteries, we got you all cleaned out, and the tetanus shot should keep you safe there. I'm just going to prescribe some antibiotics to ward off infection. Who knows where those darts were before they made it into your arm."

"And my back," Ian says.

The doctor nods. "And your back. Right." He marks something on my chart. "I'll be giving you both the same advice." He looks up and smiles. "Avoid taking the pills without food, and stay away from bars where they play darts."

"Gotcha," Ian says, shaking his hand. "Thanks, Doc."

"You bet. Take it easy." He leaves us in the cubicle behind the curtain.

"So you sure you want me hanging around with you in Florida?" he asks.

"It's not whether I want you hanging around; it's whether you'll want to hang around with me."

He reaches up and brushes hair out of my eyes. "How can you say that? You know I love hanging out with you."

"But why?"

"Because. You're smart, you're funny, you're beautiful . . ."

"That's true. I am those things." I smile, too full of happiness to do anything else.

"And you're practically an Internet MD."

"I'm glad you appreciate my medical knowledge."

"Hey, you totally called it. Tetanus shot and antibiotics."

"Yeah, well that was an easy one. Did I tell you I diagnosed one of my clients with postpartum congestive heart failure once?"

"No." He leans down to kiss me tenderly. "But I can't wait to hear all about your medical interventions."

I look down at the floor, my heart overwhelmed with fear.

"Come on, babe. Tell me what's bothering you. Is it because I'm moving too fast?"

I shake my head and lift my eyes to look at him. I need him to know I'm telling the truth. "I'm actually okay with how fast you move. Maybe because I saw it happen with Andie, or learned about it after, whatever . . . I mean, love at first sight happens, right?"

"We're proof it does." He kisses me once and then goes back to listening.

"I'm just worried that you won't like my life back home. That you won't like my business or my partner or my friends."

"I'm sure if they're a part of your life, I'll love them. How could I not?"

I grimace a little. "They're not like your friends out here."

"Good. I need a change," he says. "Besides, you know I didn't go to school here. I'm used to big-city life."

"Eugene is big-city life?" I know from Andie that's where his college is, but I never googled the place to learn anything about it.

"Big enough." He takes me by the hand and goes down on one knee.

"What are you doing?" I ask, panic taking me over.

"Just trying to see you better," he says. "Babe, I just want you to be comfortable. If this is too much, too soon, I'll try to understand."

I run my hands through his impossibly thick hair and lean over to kiss him on the forehead. I love the smell of him, even after he's been in a dirty bar, stuck with darts, and then greased up with hospital cleanser.

"No, it's going to be fine," I reassure him and myself as best I can. "You can just come to Florida with me, and you'll meet my friends and see my salon and we'll go from there. Maybe you'll stay a little while, and maybe you'll just come back home to Baker City and we can be friends."

My heart nearly breaks just thinking that, but I have to give him that out, that escape hatch. I have to know he'll walk away if he isn't happy, because the last thing I'd want is a guy pretending to love me when he doesn't.

"When can we leave?" he asks.

I laugh. "After I spend some time with my goddaughter and cow baby. I have my ticket to leave in about a week."

"Fine. A week it is." He stands and holds out his hand for me to join him. "Ready to go back home?"

"Yep." *Home.* I never thought I would consider Baker City my home, but tonight I can definitely see it as a home away from home, especially with Ian in it.

I step out of the ER and into the cold, but I've never felt warmer in my life, even when snowflakes cover my hair and shoulders.

CHAPTER FORTY-FIVE

My last week in Baker City flies by. I rarely see Ian, what with all the cows dropping babies in the snow, little Candy demanding to be fed all the time, and Andie finally getting some sleep and wanting visitors. Sarah has barely started looking around at things, and it's time for me to go. I'm just a tiny bit stressed to think she hasn't adequately imprinted on me.

I'm also ten times more nervous about Ian meeting my life back in Florida than I was when he first mentioned it. Now it's Andie trying to give me advice and pep talks, a total role reversal.

"You'll be fine, he'll be fine. Believe me, he's very open-minded." As I pack my bag, Andie watches, nursing Sarah like it's second nature. She's so good at being a mom. I'm no longer jealous of her—just looking forward to the day that I can try and emulate her super mommy skills.

"But what about Jorge and Sunil and all my people?" I only have one employee, technically, and that's Sunil. Jorge is my partner, and all the others are independent contractors who rent space from me in the salon. They've all been there for years and years, so long that it's like they're my family. If they don't like Ian, I don't know how it could possibly work between us.

Andie rolls her eyes. "Jorge is gorgeous, Sunil is a doll, and your people are amazing. Trust me, Ian will fit right in."

"He's a cowboy," I say, laughing at the idea of him fitting into a group of gays, immigrants, and fashionistas.

"You'll see." Andie moves Sarah to her other breast. "Love conquers all."

"You really think he loves me?" I sit down on the side of the bed and look at Andie, trying to do the human lie detector on her. Her pupils appear to be staying the same size, and her eye contact is pretty good. I think she's telling the truth.

"Of course I do. I wouldn't be encouraging this if I didn't." She grimaces in pain as Sarah latches on. "I don't want to see either of you get hurt," she says, "but you can't risk nothing and get everything."

"I want to have everything. Like you have." I reach out and squeeze her arm.

"Thanks to you," she says, lifting an eyebrow.

I smile. "I didn't do anything."

"Please," she scoffs. "The day after you took Ginny out, I had two invitations to Tupperware parties, and a girl I've only spoken to twice started arranging a baby shower for me."

"Hey, that's on Maeve. She's the one who started introducing you around."

"But you're the one who showed the whole town that Ginny is a liar."

"Ginny is a liar in jail," I add, happy that she got what was coming to her. That stupid wench made me get a horrible knot in my arm muscle that's probably permanent. I still can't hold up a flat iron for longer than five minutes without my hand going numb.

"That's what you get for committing assault and battery," Andie says. "I talked to the prosecutor. She's probably just going to get a slap on the wrist."

"Better than nothing," I say. "My goal was to get the truth out there, and that's what we did."

"You're my superhero," Andie says warmly, her eyes going moist.

"No crying," I say, pointing at my face. "You'll make my mascara leak all over the place."

"You really have to leave today?" Andie asks in her whiny voice.

"Yes, I really do. Jorge is threatening to move to Fiji if I don't come back to work tomorrow."

"Did you tell them that you're bringing Ian with you yet?"

I grimace. "No."

Andie shakes her head. "Good luck with that."

She knows Jorge well, so there's a lot of meaning in that sentence of hers. "Thanks. I think."

Ian sticks his head in the doorway. "You ready to go yet? We need to scoot if we're going to make that flight."

I nod. "Ready." I zip up my bag and take one last look around the room to make sure I didn't forget anything. The place is empty, but full of memories I hate to leave behind.

Ian comes in and takes my case, and I'm struck by how different everything is now, just two weeks after I arrived. My first day here I didn't want him touching my things or coming near me. He was the bad guy making my best friend miserable. Now I want nothing *but* him touching me, and he was never really Andie's problem. He's been one of her biggest supporters besides Mack. I feel like I've not just gained a little goddaughter in my life, but a whole other family too. I can't remember a time in my life when I was happier. It scares the ever-loving shit out of me.

"Promise you'll call as soon as you arrive. I want to hear everything," Andie says, hugging me as best she can with one arm. Sarah keeps sucking away like nothing's going on.

"I promise." I kiss the baby's fuzzy head. "Don't forget me while I'm gone." Inhaling her heavenly sent, I smile when her tiny hairs tickle my nose.

"She can't forget you. I show her your picture every day. And if you send me videos, I'll play them for her daily." Andie grabs me in another hug. "I don't want to let you go." She's crying again. She still does that a lot.

I pat her on the back. "I'll be fine. And I'm going to visit again soon."

Neither of us speaks about the possibility that Ian and I might not make it out in Florida and that this would make visits to Baker very uncomfortable. We've decided to cross that bridge when and if we ever come to it.

"I'm leaving!" Ian shouts from downstairs.

Andie laughs, wiping her tears away. "He sure is anxious to get to Florida."

"I know," I say, wiping some dust from my eyes. Stupid polluted snowflakes. "I hope he's not too disappointed when his balls start sweating as soon as he gets off the plane."

Andie's laughter is like a balm for my aching heart. I hate leaving this place. I've been living in a fantasy world where Ian loves me, and we have crazy awesome sex every night that just keeps getting better and better, and nothing can stand in the way of our love-at-first-sight romance. I'm afraid the real world will come crashing down on our heads in Florida, and all I'll have left are the memories of Ian. Just like Ginny has. Crazy Ginny who throws darts at people in bars.

"Call me. Don't forget," Andie reminds me as I walk down the stairs.

"I won't forget," I say.

I'm almost to the car when I'm struck by the overwhelming urge to go out to the barn one last time. I've been practically living out there all week, and Candy and I already said our good-byes earlier this morning, but I have to see her just one more time.

"Come on, babe, we have to go!" Ian shouts from the car.

"I'll be right back!" I shout as I run through the snow to the barn. I don't even slip, my body completely adapted to the icy surfaces now.

"Hi, Candy girl," I say to the baby as I stare over the stall door. She's already bigger, even more so than she was yesterday. "I'm going to miss you."

She looks up at me and moos. My heart breaks into about ten pieces. I wish the airline would let me take her with me. I so would have paid to put her in a Great Dane doggie crate, but they said they couldn't transport livestock. Buttheads.

A man's voice comes from deeper in the barn, headed in my direction. "We'll look after her for ya."

I smile, looking over at him. "Thanks, Angus. I appreciate it. I'm really going to miss her."

"She'll miss you too, I expect. No cow on this ranch has ever had so much attention, I can tell you that."

I know his words are meant to soothe me, but now I'm worried. "What if she gets lonely? What if she's afraid to be alone?"

Angus smiles and points to the corner of the stall where the straw is deepest. "Don't think you're gonna have to worry about that so much."

I squint so I can see better. "What is that?" I ask, noticing a movement in the shadows.

"Baby goat. Brought her in yesterday. She's a buddy for Candy, so she doesn't get too stressed."

I throw my arms around Angus and nearly cry with relief, ignoring the pain in my arm. "You are so nice! Thank you so much!"

He pats me awkwardly on the back. "You're welcome. Thanks for helping Ian out so much."

I pull away to look at him.

"Maeve and I are very grateful to you for showing him around out there in Florida. I know he's been wanting to go pretty bad for a while."

"To Florida?"

"To anywhere but here." Angus looks at the ground. "My boy's been lost for a long time. Seems like maybe he's found again, but I guess we'll see."

"Yes. I guess we will," I say softly. "Whatever happens, I want you to know that I really care about him a lot."

He pats me on the shoulder. "I know you do. So does Maeve. Just be honest with each other, and you'll be fine."

I nod, accepting his sage advice. "See you again soon, I hope!" I try to stay cheery, even though I want to cry. Leaving this place is a lot harder than I ever thought it would be. I don't know what I'd do if Ian were staying behind.

Now I think I know what Andie was going through when she came out here to tell Mack good-bye. Once you're in with these MacKenzies, it's pretty much impossible to feel good without them again. No wonder Ginny went ballistic on us. I can almost forgive her for putting holes in me and Ian. Almost.

"Have a safe flight. I have to go see to the chickens," Angus says.

"I thought chicken butts were Maeve's domain."

Angus frowns. "Well, I suppose. But I've got to put a new brooding box together. Seems likes she's got some chicks coming in by mail."

I don't even want to get clarification on that statement. "Okay, well, bye. Thanks for your hospitality."

"You bet. Any time." Angus waves to me as he walks off, and I make my way back to the truck. Ian has the engine running and the heater blasting.

I get inside and put on my seatbelt, hunching over the vent to warm my hands up.

"You ready to get this party started?" Ian asks, his face alight with excitement.

"You know I am."

"Kiss for luck," he says, leaning in toward me.

I lean over and lock lips with him, taking the kiss deeper until my toes are tingling.

"Mmm," he says, sitting back straight and shifting the truck into drive.

"That a good one?" I ask.

"Hell yeah, that was a good one. All your kisses are good ones."

I smile all the way to the airport in Boise, Idaho.

CHAPTER FORTY-SIX

Text message alerts start beeping as soon as the plane lands and I turn on my phone. Jorge has sent me four messages in the last half hour.

R u here yet?
We need u now.
I'm serious, c, come to the salon asap.
R u ignoring me?

"Is there something wrong?" Ian asks me from the seat to my left.

My boobs bounce uncomfortably as we taxi up to the gate. Why do they always have such bumpy airports around here?

I text Jorge back and tell him to keep his pants on. We're at least a half hour from the big reveal. The entire salon is freaking out about me bringing a man back with me, a cowboy no less. They made me ask Ian to wear his cowboy hat. I have to admit, it still gives me the chills to see him standing there in ass-hugging jeans and a black hat.

I sigh. "You never know with Jorge. He could be serious—he could be having a dramatic moment."

"A dramatic moment?"

I try to smile. "My partner is prone to drama. He's very . . . high energy."

"Sounds like my kind of guy."

"Heh-heh . . . well, he's not . . . exactly."

Ian frowns. "I don't get it."

I decide to just put it out there and see what happens. "Jorge is gay."

Ian sits there doing nothing.

I lift my eyebrows at him.

"Am I supposed to say something now?" he asks.

"I kind of expected you to, yes."

He looks like he's thinking hard. "Okay, how about if I saaaay . . . good for him? Does that work?"

I nudge him, some of my stress leaving my chest. At least I know he's not homophobic. "That works. But I'm warning you . . . he's not just a little gay; he's *very* gay."

"I wasn't aware that there were levels of gayness. What level is he?"

I know he's messing with me, but I play along anyway. "He's a level eleven out of ten."

Ian smiles. "I can't wait to meet him."

"Why?"

"Because I'm gay too."

My heart stops for a split second until I see his expression. I laugh out of relief. "You're ridiculous."

"No, you're ridiculous. You're so worried about everything. I can't wait to meet Jorge because Jorge is your partner. He's been with you for over ten years, most of the hours of the day. If I'm going to convince you to fall in love with me, he'll know how to make that happen. I'm counting on him to save my love life."

I cuddle his arm and rest my head on his thick shoulder. "I am in love with you, silly."

"You might love me a little, but I need you to love me all the way."

I have no response for that. I know all of him, but he only knows a piece of me, the vacation Candice. Will he still want to be with me when he knows the real me, the every-other-week-of-the-year Candice? That still remains to be seen.

I'm not doing it on purpose, but a piece of my heart is holding itself back, waiting to see if it's worth the risk to totally let go and hand itself over to Ian for the taking. It's been crushed too many times to believe that two-way love really exists.

The plane finally stops bumping along, and we're able to get off and find our luggage in the baggage claim. My car is covered in dust from local construction, but it starts up without a problem and gets us on the highway in no time.

"I like your car," Ian says. "I've always wanted a sports car like this. And it's black too, my favorite."

Last year I splurged and bought myself a midlife crisis car, even though I'm still at least fifteen years away from that event, hopefully. "Do you want to drive it?" I ask.

"Later. When I get the lay of the land a little. Besides," he reaches over and rubs my thigh, "I kind of like watching you shift those gears."

A flash of Hannah Banana comes to mind and I smile. That poor misguided girl. She ended up with no friends by the time we departed. Ginny cut her out, and so did all those other girls who are now buddying up to Andie. She's going to have to leave town to find someone who will give her the time of day.

"Hey, what was that secret you had on Hannah?" I ask, as the showdown in the diner memory surfaces and dances around in my head.

"What?"

"Remember when we were in the diner and you threatened to tell her secret? Something about the Fourth of July? Was it about Boog?"

"Nah. It was about Tate Montgomery. Boog is Hannah's half-brother, and he gives her tons of shit, so she didn't want him knowing about Tate. She doesn't want anyone knowing about him. I guess he's her super-secret love crush or whatever. She told me about it when she was wasted at a picnic."

I'm frowning, trying to work that out in my mind. "I thought she was hot for Mack."

"She was, but after Andie came to town, she abandoned that fantasy. Apparently, one night she and Tate shared a kiss or some such nonsense."

"Aw, poor girl. Tate seems like a nice guy."

"Tate's all right. He needs to keep his hands off my girl, though."

I smile. I'm Ian's girl. It's official. It thrills me and panics me in equal measure.

I spend the rest of the drive pointing out exits or places of interest, things I want him to see before he leaves. He bought a round-trip ticket so there wouldn't be any pressure on us, or so he claims. I'm not sure that it's working, but whatever makes him happy. The closer we get to the salon, the more nervous I become.

When I pull into my parking space, I have to stop and do some deep breathing before I can get out. Ian's standing behind the car when I finally emerge.

"You look like you're about to drop," he says, taking me into a warm embrace. He kisses my head as I wrap my arms around him and hold tight. "Just relax, okay? Everything's going to be fine."

"It is?"

"Yes. Finer than fine. Now come on." He pushes me off him and holds my hand. "Show me to your salon. I want to see your whole life, starting now."

"Okay." I walk down the sidewalk in the heels I changed into once we were off the plane, loving the feeling of solid ground that doesn't slip under my feet. I'm so much more graceful in Florida than I am in Oregon. "So this is the street that my salon is on. Some evenings the town has big events, and this place is packed."

"It's nice. Is that a trolley?"

"Yes, but not on tracks. It's just a glorified shuttle."

"I like it."

So far, so good. I smile nervously. "And up there you can see my salon. See the awning?"

"Yep. Looks pretty nice from here."

I let go of Ian so I can text Jorge: *the eagle has landed.*

CHAPTER FORTY-SEVEN

We're still ten feet from the front door when it flies open, and Jorge comes running out on tippy-toes.

"Oh my god, she's here! She's back! And she brought a beau hunk with her!"

Jorge has convinced someone to shave a side part into his hair for him. The rest of his hair is greased down and slicked into place, the top part still poofy, and a couple curlicues are stuck along the edges of his face for effect. He's looks like Prince, but the Prince you'd see in an Alice in Wonderland book. He's also wearing his favorite red skinny jeans paired with a hot pink top that he's tied at the bottom.

I speak in a low voice. "See? Level eleven."

Ian whispers back. "Nah, I think he's more a nine, if you ask me."

I giggle as Jorge approaches, unable to hold in my happiness at seeing my friend and partner. He really is a special person. "Incoming!" I say in a singsong voice, letting go of Ian and opening my arms for the embrace I'm about to be tackled with.

Jorge reaches me and wraps his long, skinny arms around me and squeezes while he squeals. "Ooooooh, giiiirl, I have missed you soooo much. Don't you ever, ever, ever, ever, ever go away for that long again." He separates himself for a few seconds to look at Ian before going back to hugging me again. "Or just take me with you next time," he whispers in my ear. "Holy hot cowboy, Candice!"

I know Ian can hear him, but he's pretending like he doesn't. He's just standing there, waiting to be introduced, wearing that cowboy hat, a T-shirt, and jeans. He's getting appreciative stares from pretty much anyone walking by, man or woman. For the first time since I met Ian, I'm feeling jealous. What if he falls in love with someone else while he's out here?

Jorge lets me go and stands up straight to face Ian. He rests his hands on his butt and bends this way and that, getting a good luck at my cowboy lover.

"So you are the one man who finally made the cut."

"Jorge, shush," I say, worried about what Ian will think. I didn't tell Ian that I've never brought a man back to the salon before. This place has always been my safe zone, my home away from home. No man has ever made the cut before Ian—Jorge is right about that.

"I guess I am," Ian says, holding out a hand for a shake. "Nice to meet you. You must be Jorge."

Jorge slaps Ian's hand away and opens his arms. "Hugs. We only do hugs around here."

Ian nods. "If you say so." He steps in and gives Jorge a hug, which I fully expect to be awkward at best. But he surprises both me and Jorge by grabbing Jorge in a bear hug and lifting him up off the ground for a second before putting him back down and letting him go.

Jorge lets out a girly scream as soon as his feet leave the ground. His facial expression is classic, and I hate that I don't have my camera ready. He's in shock, and believe me when I say it takes a *lot* to shock Jorge.

"Oh my . . . now *that* is what I call a hug." Jorge fans his face, and it's not just an act. He's sweating.

"Okay, hormones, relax," I say. "Let's go inside where it's air conditioned."

"You use air conditioning in the winter?" Ian asks, following Jorge inside.

"Yes. It gets so humid, the walls will mold if we don't. Plus we have the dryers going and all the irons. It gets warm in here even in winter."

Ian nods his head all the while he's walking around inside the foyer area. The granite fountain is burbling water into the small koi pond in the floor, and the marble tiles make my heels click as I walk over to the reception area. The essential oils we diffuse into the air usually have an immediate calming effect on me, but today they're not working. I feel like I'm walking the gauntlet with Ian. Will he hate it here? Will he hate my friends? So far things are looking good, but there are a couple more potential roadblocks in the way.

As we approach the front desk, I hold my hand out toward the small, dark-skinned man sitting behind it. "Ian, this is Sunil. Sunil, this is Ian."

"The cowboy. We've heard all about you." Sunil stands and offers a well-manicured hand. "Nice to meet you, sir."

"You can call me Ian if that's all right with you," he says, shaking Sunil's hand.

"Of course, Ian. And you may call me Sunny if you like. All my friends do."

Ian beams.

I'm sweating right along with Jorge. Two down, several to go, but if the appreciative gaze on Jorge's face and the smile on Sunil's is any indication, I'm nearly home free.

I walk into the main area of the salon, gesturing around the room. All the chairs are full, but everyone stops working to say hi or wave. I know they'll all be accosting us later to get all the details from me. For now they have clients to tend to.

"These are the stations Jorge and I rent out to several colorists and stylists. The shampoo stations are over there. In the back we have massage and waxing rooms, manicures, and other spa treatments."

"Wow, seems like you have it all here." Ian nods as his gaze sweeps the room. He smiles and waves back at people greeting him.

"We try." I'm proud and scared. I know we have a nice place, but how much can a cowboy who castrates bulls for a living appreciate a spa salon?

Jorge is standing on Ian's other side. "Take your hat off for me, Ian, baby."

Ian takes his hat off without question and stands there ready for inspection, as unfazed as I've ever seen him. It's like he's actually enjoying himself being the center of attention, the alien who's landed on foreign ground.

Jorge runs his fingers through Ian's hair. "Oh my goodness. So thick and healthy!"

"I'm cutting it later," I say, winking at Ian.

"Lucky girl," Jorge says, staring at some of Ian's ends more closely. "Not a split end in sight. What kind of product do you use?"

"Shampoo. From the grocery store."

Jorge looks at me behind Ian's back, his eyebrows formed into the letter S across his forehead. "Is he pulling my leg?"

"Nope. He's kind of a purist I guess you could say."

Jorge has his finger on his lip and he's shaking his head, back to inspecting Ian's hair. "What I could do with a man like you. Mmm. Mmm. Mmm."

I laugh. "Is Mildred here?"

Jorge rolls his eyes and shakes his head, like a really unpleasant thought is inside it and he wants to get it out. "She's in the back. Getting her *talons* done."

I look up at Ian. "Are you ready?"

For the first time in the trip, Ian looks a little concerned.

"I don't know. Am I?"

I take him by the arm and lead him toward the back. "This is the last person I want you to meet. She's been coming in here every week, three times a week, since Jorge and I opened our doors. She's our most regular regular."

"Your most regular regular?"

"Yes. And she hates everyone."

"Everyone? Even you?"

"Even me. Even Jorge. Even Sunny. She doesn't have a nice bone in her body."

"So what you're saying is be prepared to be hated."

"Essentially, yes." I lower my voice and speak closer to his ear. "Don't tell Jorge that I said this, but deep down inside her is a nice person fighting to get out. But she's not shy about telling you exactly what she thinks, so I'm kind of curious what she's going to say when she sees you."

"Is she older?" he whispers

"Yes. In her eighties by now, although she won't tell us the actual number."

"I'm a little scared, I'll be honest. Grandma Lettie whopped me with a broomstick once, and I never forgot it."

"I remember her from the wedding last year. Trust me . . . she's an angel compared to Mildred."

We stop just outside the entrance to the manicure area. "You ready?" I ask, nervous. I've never told anyone this, not even Jorge, but I kind of view Mildred as the grandmother I never had. She's got a sharp tongue and zero grace when it comes to interacting with people, but she's told me some things over the years that have really helped me, the first thing being that I should take Jorge on as a partner. She recognized early on that he had the energy level and the know-how to make things happen for us. She saw a compatibility between Jorge and me that most people would have missed. She pretends to hate him, but I know otherwise. I let Jorge get his panties in a twist over her because it makes everyone happy. Jorge loves nothing more than drama.

"I guess I'm as ready as I'll ever be," Ian says, wiggling his hat on his head a little, effectively drawing it down closer to his eyes. It makes him look sexier, and I decide right then and there that if Mildred can hate this guy, she has no soul. That's all there is to it.

"Follow me," I say, walking into the back room.

Mildred isn't alone. Our manicurist is there, and another client is waiting for her polish to dry, reading a magazine as she passes the time, her eyelids threatening to fall closed. I have on more than one occasion left people to nap when I knew they didn't have pressing appointments after their session with us. It always seemed silly to me to create a relaxing environment and then hurry people out of it.

"Well, well, well, if it isn't the gallivanting Sally back to grace us with her presence," Mildred says, looking up at me through her Coke-bottle-thick glasses.

"Hello, Mildred. How have you been? I've missed you." I kiss my hand and wave it at her. She's not much for physical touching, but she suffers through my air-kisses.

"Same as always. Not dead yet, but one foot in the grave." She shifts her gaze to Ian. "And what, pray tell, is this?" She gestures with a bony finger in Ian's direction.

I put my hand on Ian's arm and smile. "This is Ian. I brought him back with me from Oregon."

"What for?" Mildred squints up at him, staring at his hat. "You gonna marry him?"

My jaw drops open and my face burns red. "Uh . . ." Ian and I haven't talked marriage. Yes, we've discussed him living out here, but that was it. I'm so embarrassed right now, it's not even funny. I wish I could turn back time and bring Ian in here on a day that Mildred wasn't going to be around.

Ian walks over and takes a seat in the chair next to Mildred. "Maybe. If I can convince her it's a good idea."

Mildred snorts. "Good luck with that." She turns her attention to the manicurist. "Hey! Watch it there, girl. I have sensitive cuticles, you know." She looks over at Ian. "It's so hard to find good help these days. The incompetence is everywhere."

Ian leans over and looks at Mildred's toes. "They look pretty good to me." He points at the heel of her foot that's the current work in progress. "What do you call that?"

Mildred leans over and looks at her feet. "What do I call what?"

"What she's doing to your foot there. Looks like she's got a cheese grater in her hand."

Mildred cackles. "Sure does, doesn't it? Never thought of it that way."

Ian looks worried. "You sure you want her cheese-gratin' your feet?"

"Feels good. Leaves 'em baby smooth. You should try it. Bet you'll like it."

Ian shakes his head. "No, ma'am. I like my feet where they belong. In my boots."

Mildred waves at Jorge who's hiding behind me at the entrance. "Hey, twinkle toes! Why don't you come on in here and do his feet? Bet he could use a little cheese gratin'!"

Jorge's mouth drops open, and he stares at me.

I shrug, completely at a loss.

"You think I should?" Ian asks Mildred. "I don't know. Looks a little dangerous. She's got a sharp thing on you now. Better watch it." Ian points to the cuticle nippers that are working on Mildred's big toe. She's prone to hangnails.

"You're telling me that a big strong cowboy like you is afraid to have his feet done? Come on, don't be such a big puss."

Ian laughs. "A big puss? Did you just call me a big puss?"

Mildred shrugs and picks up her magazine. "I call it like I see it."

Ian sits back in his chair and takes off his hat, resting his booted feet on the edge of the foot tub. "Can't let someone besmirch my good name like that and get away with it."

"Besmirch. That's a quarter word." Mildred's acting like she's not paying him any attention, but I know better. She's just as enthralled with him as Jorge and I are, in her own bratty old-lady way. My heart is melting into a puddle of goo as I watch him work to break down her walls. No one has ever gotten this much conversation out of the woman. And I know her well enough to see that she finds him charming. It's pretty impossible not to.

He tilts his head to face her. "Will you hold my hand during the cheese-grater part?" he asks her.

She cackles. "Get your girlfriend to hold your hand. I'm spoken for."

Ian looks at me. "Will you hold my hand?" he asks.

I come over and stand next to him. "Sure, babe. I'll hold your hand."

He looks over my shoulder at Jorge and winks before focusing on me again. "How about marrying me. Will you do that too?"

CHAPTER FORTY-EIGHT

I'm standing there, holding his hand, confused as I watch him reach into his pocket and dig around.

"What?" I'm sure I don't understand what he's saying.

Is this another tease on Mildred that I'm just not getting?

He pulls a black box out of his pocket and flips the top open with one finger. "You heard me. I asked you if you'll hold my hand during the cheese-grater part and if you'll marry me."

A diamond ring is sparkling up at me from a bed of black velvet. My heart stops beating.

"Oh my god!" Jorge yells in a voice more suited to a game show win. *"He is proposing to her right here in the salon!"* Jorge starts jumping up and down like a human pogo stick. *"Sunny! Get your sweet buns in here!"*

I'm too stunned to reply. My mouth hangs open, but no words will come out. The most beautiful man in the entire world, the one who accepted all my friends and my crankiest client-slash-grandma with open arms . . . literally with open arms . . . wants to be with me forever. Am I in a coma, having a coma dream? Did that cougar really tear me apart, and all of this has been a fantasy cooked up in my drugged-out mind? Am I really still in an Oregonian hospital being poked and prodded by Nurse Ratched?

"Well? Are you going to answer him or not?" Mildred says, as cranky as ever. "We don't have all day."

I look over at her, tears in my eyes. "Should I say yes?"

"Do you love him?"

I nod. "Yes. A lot."

"Is he good to you?"

I nod again. "The best."

"Does he give you orgasms?"

I bark out a laugh. "Yes."

She shrugs and goes back to her magazine. "I'd say yes if it were me, but it's not me he's asking."

Ian points at Mildred with his thumb. "Mildred would say yes."

"If you don't say yes, I'm quitting," Jorge says.

"You can't quit; you own this place," I say, tears running down my face.

"I'll sell out. I swear to God, I will."

Ian holds his hat against his chest and gives me a nervous smile. "Babe, I can't promise you that I'll always be perfect, but I'll do my straight best to try, and I'll make it my life's goal to always make sure you're happy. All you've got to do is marry me, and I'll do the rest."

I can't think of a single reason to say no anymore.

"Yes. I'll marry you." My heart starts beating in a mad rush, and my face flushes pink. I cannot believe I just got engaged!

Ian takes the ring out of the box and puts it on my finger.

"It fits perfectly," I say in a tiny girl voice, turning my finger left and right so the light will catch it and make it sparkle more.

"Of course it does. Andie helped me pick it out." He grins, his face lighting up with love and light. I've never seen anything so amazing in my entire life.

I can't stop crying when all my friends surround me and hug me from all angles. Ian waits his turn, but when he finally gets a chance, he wraps his strong arms around me and buries his face in my neck, lifting me up off the ground.

"Love you, City," he says.

"Love you too, Country," I say back.

"Get a room," Mildred says.

When I peek over Ian's shoulder at her, I see that she's smiling.

CHAPTER FORTY-NINE

The breeze coming off the ocean is as mild and humidity-free as I've ever known it to be. My simple white sundress picks up and floats around my knees as I settle my bouquet at my waist.

"You ready?" Angus asks, holding out an elbow for me.

"As ready as I'll ever be," I say, putting my hand through his arm.

"I feel pretty lucky, being the one to walk you down the aisle." We take it slow since Angus's knees aren't the best these days.

I smile, feeling very shy. "Since my dad passed, I really wasn't sure what to do."

He pats my hand. "I'm your father-in-law now. You can call me dad if you want. Angus if you prefer. I'm just proud that I can have two daughters now when all I ever thought I'd have is sons."

We walk out of the hotel's small banquet room and make our way across a small area of the pool to reach the boardwalk that will take us down to the beach where our wedding party is waiting.

"Thank you for helping Ian get started out here," I say as we walk across the pool area.

"We've always told him when he was ready, we wanted to be investors. He's got a good head on his shoulders and the work ethic to be proud of. He'll make the ranch work."

"I can't believe I'm going to have chickens." I laugh at the whole idea. Angus just finished building the coop for us yesterday. I nearly cried at how cute the tiny little shutters were that he put on the windows.

"You can always make Ian collect the eggs," Angus says, knowing of my extreme chicken-butt paranoia.

"No, I'll do it. People have to sacrifice when it comes to being married. I'm just going to have to deal."

"That's-a girl," he says, smiling and patting me again. "We'll make a rancher out of you yet."

As we begin our walk down the boardwalk, I can see my future husband waiting for me. He's standing at the end, in the sand, next to a priest we hired for a couple hours, wearing a tux and his black cowboy hat. Andie is on the priest's other side, holding a bouquet and standing next to Jorge. They're both in pink. Kelly couldn't make it because she's about to give birth, but she sent me a picture of herself in a pink dress, and I have it tucked into my flowers. I take a peek at it now to remind me that she's here in spirit.

Mack is Ian's best man, and Boog is beside him, looking extremely uncomfortable in a tux, his beard hanging down the front of it.

It's quite a motley crew we have, but I wouldn't want it any other way, and neither would Ian, thank God. I finally found a man who wants me exactly as I am and loves me back as much as I love him.

When I reach the end of the boardwalk, I step onto the sand, thankfully only needing to go a couple of feet before I'm on Ian's arm. Heels and sand don't go very well together, but there's no way in hell I was going to wear flip-flops on my big day.

"I've been asked to keep this ceremony short and sweet," says the priest smiling at everyone, "and the very best way I know how to do that is to ask the couple to write their own vows, which Candice and Ian have happily done. Ian, would you like to start?"

"Happy to." Ian winks at me, but I can tell he's as nervous as I am. His hands shake as he pulls out the paper to read what he's written. The paper trembles.

"Candice." He looks at me and smiles. His lips quiver. "The most beautiful girl I ever met. I knew she was the one for me the day that she shot me in the leg."

Almost everyone laughs. A few of the less-in-the-know guests gasp. I have to bite my cheek to keep from smiling. He is so going to pay for that one tonight.

"And then when she tackled me to the ground and stuffed my face full of snow, I knew she was a fighter, so that made her even more my kind of girl."

I shake my head at him and look over at his mother. She's shaking her head too but smiling through tears at the same time.

"When she threw herself in front of a mountain lion and saved my life, I knew I'd be much better off with her around, what with all of life's dangers that could come upon me as I grow older. I knew then that she's brave and courageous, just the kind of woman you want to have your back when life comes at you."

Several guests are nodding. Others are looking around, probably trying to decide if he's making all this up.

"When she brought Candy the calf back to life and cared for her in the tenderest of ways, I knew that she'd be a good mother to our kids. That's really important to me since I consider myself a family man and plan to have about ten children."

I'm crying now, imagining having Ian's babies. They're going to be amazing people, I know this. I'm not sure about ten of them, though. We're going to have to negotiate that point.

"And when she got in a bar fight with a girl who was trash-talking her friend and took a dart in the arm for me, I knew she was loyal and a great companion. That's the kind of lady you want at your side when you grow old and eventually incontinent."

I can't hear the guests anymore. All I can hear are Ian's words. I'm so in love with this man—it should be impossible to love someone this much. But I'm not changing his diapers, no way.

"Last and not least, when she took me home and introduced me to her wonderful family, I knew that she trusted me with her heart. And I just want to say today, in front of all these witnesses, that I'm going to work every day of our lives together to keep earning and deserving that trust, because I know how valuable that quality is in a relationship."

He nods his head once at me, wipes the sweat off his brow and mouth with a handkerchief, and then says, "Your turn, City." He stuffs his paper into his pocket without bothering to fold it up.

I reach into the front of my dress and pull my vows out of my bra.

Ian's eyes sparkle and the guests laugh as I open the paper up. It's a little sweaty, and some of the ink has smeared. Good thing I've read through it about a hundred times already.

I clear my throat to get the frog out of it, ignoring the tears that are now drying salt tracks down my face.

"If you had told me six months ago that I'd be marrying a cowboy, living on a cattle ranch, and putting my hand on chicken butts, I'd've told you that you must be thinking about my friend Andie." I look over my shoulder at her, and she blows me a kiss while crying.

"But here I am, marrying a cowboy and living on a ranch, and God help me, touching chicken butts every morning."

Ian laughs silently and moves closer.

I tap him with my flowers to make him keep his distance.

"Some people in my life have called me crazy. Maybe even a little silly. They question my need to google things and research medical conditions. Ian is the one person in the world who just accepts those things as part of who I am." I pause and look out at the crowd. "Google is your friend, people. I'm serious. It's not a *person*, it's a collective group of people who want to help each other, and that's a good thing."

I go back to my paper. "The thing about Ian is that until I met him, I didn't know what I wanted in my life. I thought my life was full and perfect. But when I met him and suddenly had him in my face, like literally pushing snow in my face, I didn't know what I'd been missing. Now I do know. There was this person that wasn't in my life who needed to be. Someone who would love me no matter what, even when my boobs deflate and my butt sags and I have stretch marks like Andie does all over my belly."

Ian frowns and shakes his head, forcing me to tap him with my flowers again.

Andie clears her throat, but I ignore her.

"Anyway, what I'm saying is, is that I've found true happiness, and I'm not going to screw it up. I'll honor you, sometimes obey you, do your hair and nails, your laundry on all the odd days of the month, and I'll cook too if you want me to, although I have to confess that the spaghetti I made you was the first time I ever cooked anything, so you might want to invest in some cookbooks or some lessons for me before you take me up on that part of my offer."

"I think you should promise to obey me all the time," Ian whispers.

"Only in the bedroom," I whisper back.

"Works for me," he says, grinning from ear to ear.

I clear my throat to finish. "And last but not least, I promise to be the best rancher's wife that I can be, since I know that's where your heart is, and that's what you really want to do with your life."

I look over and nod at the priest. "Tag. You're it."

The priest gestures to Mack. "The rings?"

Mack hands them over.

"Ian and Candice will now exchange rings, symbols of eternal love binding them together forever."

The simple gold band slides onto my hand with ease. This time, I helped pick it out. Ian was surprised it was so simple, but I explained that I wanted something I could wear when I was messing around with chicken butts and baby cows too. My diamond will sometimes need to come off as the situation demands, but my band will be a forever-and-always thing.

Ian's gold ring looks beautiful against his tanned skin. Just six months in the sun and he looks like a native. All those hours of putting up barbed wire has made him a real Florida rancher. I'm thrilled we found some land not too far away from my salon. I can live with a commute so long as Ian's waiting for me at one end of it, and Jorge is waiting at the other. I look over at my friends and see all of them wiping tears away.

"You may kiss your bride, Ian." The priest takes a step back, and I don't realize why until I'm suddenly dipped down nearly to the sand.

"Kiss me, City."

"Gladly, Country." I grab onto his neck and kiss him for all I'm worth. When he finally stands me back up again, I'm out of breath.

The priest throws his arms out. "Ladies and Gentlemen, I present to you Mr. and Mrs. Ian and Candice MacKenzie!"

Ian takes my hand and holds it up above us. "We shine, not burn!" he yells out into the crowd.

"Luceo non oro!" yells all his family back.

My husband picks me up and carries me across the sand to the boardwalk. As he walks me to the reception room, he grins down at me, his cowboy hat shading me from the hot Florida sun.

"You happy, City?" he asks, his eyes glowing green.

"Happier than I've ever been in my entire life. What about you?"

"Couldn't possibly be happier. You make me want to be the best version of me." He puts me down and brushes some hair out of my face, standing chest to chest with me. "How am I doing so far?"

"Shining, not burning, babe."

"Excellent." He lowers his head and kisses me again, and I forget where we are and what we're doing. I can only think and feel how much I love this cowboy of mine.

AUTHOR'S NOTE

If you enjoyed this book, please take a moment to leave a review on the site where you bought this book, Goodreads, or any book blogs you participate in, and tell your friends! I love interacting with my readers, so if you feel like shooting the breeze or talking about books or your family or pets, please visit me. You can find me at . . .

www.ElleCasey.com,
www.Facebook.com/ellecaseytheauthor, and
www.Twitter.com/ellecasey.

Want to get an email when my next book is released?
Sign up here: http://bit.ly/ellecaseynews

ABOUT THE AUTHOR

Elle Casey, a former attorney and teacher, is a New York Times and USA Today bestselling American author who lives in Southern France with her husband, three kids, and a number of furry friends. She has written books in several genres and publishes an average of one full-length novel per month.